The Rabbit Skinners

John Eidswick

This is a work of fiction. Names, characters, organizations, places, events, and incidents are either products of the author's imagination or used with fictional embellishment. Any resemblance to actual persons, living or dead, or to actual events, is purely coincidental.

For Hiroko and Seiji, sneezers extraordinaire

Contents

Chapter One

June, 2018

Whenever Strait thinks back on the last day he was a whole man, it is the memory of seething heat that hits him strongest. Suffocating, unforgiving heat. And the screams of a child.

On that day, heat was pressing through the steel walls of the surveillance van and into the flesh of the FBI agents inside. Sweat had soaked James Strait's short brown hair to his scalp and was dribbling down his neck and the inside of his flak jacket. Another record high in Colorado Springs, and the air outside was blazing, but the bureau had only equipped the vehicle with one tiny wall-mounted electric fan.

Strait reached up and twisted the fan forward so it blew directly on the woman in front of him. Amelia Garcia nodded her thanks, keeping her eyes riveted to the three closed-circuit monitors in front of her.

From his place on the narrow bench, he stretched out his legs as best he could. Strait was a very large man and the van was small. His space on the bench was constricted by the Kevlar helmet and gas mask beside him he hoped he wouldn't need to put on. He fingered the Glock pistol in the holster strapped to his thigh to confirm again the safety was switched off. A reflexive, needless habit. He knew the weapon was ready to go, as was the MP5 submachine gun at his side.

Strait bent forward with his elbows on his thighs and edged himself closer to Amelia. She sat studying the images on the monitors with a degree of attention that to him seemed superhuman, given nothing interesting had happened on them the entire week of the assignment. Her dark hair was tied back in a short ponytail whose curls peeked out of the back of her helmet. A fine sheen of sweat on her neck.

The screens showed images from cameras pointed at the grounds of the target house. The cult members were living in a spacious home for an upper-class family, two floors and a wide, grassy clearing with tall elms and oaks growing on three sides. Surrounding the entire property was an eight-foot stone wall topped with razor wire. The light from the early morning sun slanted from the east and stretched the shadows of the trees into immense, jagged creatures.

Agents from the local field office had managed to attach the small cameras onto tree branches where they overhung the walls, providing views of the east side, where the front door was, and the north side, with a big iron gate leading to a driveway that curved into the two-car garage.

The agents couldn't get a camera on the far more important west face of the house, where there was only a treeless wall and a door, probably guarded from the inside, that they believed led to the basement. Infrared footage gathered from drones indicated that what the FBI was hunting for was not stored on any of the upper floors, but underground.

Strait put his hand on Garcia's shoulder and gave it a gentle squeeze. They had been going out for about three months and sleeping together for two. He leaned in and gave her a quick kiss on the neck. He saw the corners of her mouth go up slightly.

To Strait, Amelia had it all. Intelligence, beauty, a biting sense of humor. She was one of the few people on the planet who could make him laugh out loud. The only one able to introduce him to good books he hadn't already read. She also had that devotion to athleticism few people appreciated, especially in women, but that Strait deeply respected and found powerfully attractive.

Encountering Amelia, any agent holding the view that federal police work was best done by the male half of the species soon either changed his mind or experienced searing pangs of inadequacy.

All of these qualities were enough for Strait to fall for Amelia, but there was also her quick-witted, playful, vaguely obscene banter on Friday nights while they took in hamburgers and beer at Murphys and the cooing, teasing, almost-remorseful way she looked up at him in bed a few hours later and said, *What else you got?*

Strait kissed her neck again.

"I saw that," said Graham Footer.

"Go back to sleep," said Strait.

"If you two would like to shag, don't mind me."

Special Agent Graham Footer, the third member of the team, was sprawled on a wooden folding chair toward the back of the van. He had tilted the chair on two legs so his head was against the wall and his legs were spread to either side.

Footer, thin, pale and freckled, short red hair standing on end, was an immigrant from the U.K. whose single goal in life since adolescence had been, mysteriously, to leave the land of his birth and obtain a position at the Federal Bureau of Investigation. The attacks on 9/11 in 2001 had intensified his desire and he managed the move on a student visa in 2002 and succeeded, only eight years later, in obtaining dual citizenship and entry into the FBI Academy in Quantico, where he'd been Strait's roommate. He was top of their class at anything that required an excellent brain but little brawn, from calculus to computer science to laboratory forensics.

Strait had personally requested Graham and Amelia to be members of his team because, along with being his friends, they were the most skilled, dependable agents he knew. His team was assigned closest to the cult house, only a block away, and so would be the first to move through the gate if things went to shit. Strait wanted only the best backing him up if he had to face something like that, even though he knew if it all really fell apart, they were probably already dead.

The Barton cult was a threat beyond anything the government had previously seen. Usually, the approach to dealing with a holed-up, well-armed anti-government group was to surround the suspects, cut off supplies of electricity and food, and wait them out. For years, if necessary. The FBI had learned hard lessons from the disasters at Ruby Ridge and Waco.

But with Aemon Barton's group of apocalyptic fanatics, they had to throw out all the rules. The Barton cult was Homeland Security's worst nightmare come true, because they'd succeeded in doing what the top brass thought couldn't be done. The Bartons had produced a very large amount of high-quality VX, the most toxic nerve agent on Earth. They'd also managed to store the unstable chemical in barrels and move it from the production site in Arkansas to this house in a densely populated area of Colorado Springs.

According to credible intel from a defector, stored in the house was enough nerve agent to wipe out the city. If the cult released even a little of it, the winds could carry the stuff to the crowded areas only blocks away and to the city center, killing thousands of people.

Containment was impossible. And time was running out.

It seemed the only action they could take was a sudden, all-out assault on the house. Count on the advantage of surprise to overwhelm any attempt to release the poison. A large force of soldiers from the nearby army base, along with a crowd of officers from every federal law enforcement agency, were on stand-by in town in case it went down that way. Hypothetically, if the assault were pulled off smoothly, the VX could be secured without casualties. Hypothetically. But everyone knew the chance of something going catastrophically wrong was too high for comfort. Waco had been a disaster, and that group hadn't possessed weapons of mass destruction.

In a desperate move to explore other options, Homeland Security had decided to put off an all-out attack for a week and quickly assembled four surveillance teams to stealthily observe the cult to find any information that might lead to a safer solution. Strait, a rising star at the Richmond field office and a decorated infantryman with a tour of Afghanistan under his belt, was put in charge of the four teams.

So Strait, Garcia, and Footer had spent their waking hours of the last week together in this hot van and tried to make the best of what was turning out to be a big waste of time.

Graham sat up and dropped the chair back to its four legs. He wiped sweat from his face and leaned forward and peered at the monitors. "No change?" Strait gave Garcia one more small peck on the neck and leaned back on the bench. "Nothing."

"A whole week without a single serviceable nugget of intelligence, James. Except that I've learned the Americans in this sweltering van smell like my grandfather's urine. Isn't it time for this excruciating detail to end?"

James sighed. "I think so too. I'm going to recommend to Gelder that we set a night for a full-on raid. We don't seem to have a choice."

A crackle in Strait's earphone. The rough voice of Karl Greyson, the leader of Team Three, came into his ear. "We got movement. Rabbit on the run."

"Right on time," said Amelia, pointing to the center monitor.

On the screen, a girl came out the front door wheeling her bicycle. "Rabbit" was the identifier they'd given her. Twelve years of age, the oldest of the three daughters of cult leader Aemon Barton. She was also believed to be one of his wives. Her real name was Laurel Barton. Her long brown hair fluttered in the breeze as she walked. Despite the heat wave, she was dressed in a long-sleeved pale blue blouse buttoned high in the throat and a long skirt of matching color. Except for the pink backpack she had strapped on, the outfit was strangely conservative. But in public she forewent the much more old-fashioned bonnet and prairie dress the leader made all the female members of the cult wear indoors.

She crossed the grounds to the big iron gate. She paused there, scanning the street. Then she used a key to open the gate, carefully pulling together the heavy sections and locking them behind her after she pushed her bicycle through. She replaced the key somewhere inside her dress. After another long and careful look up and down the street, she mounted her bicycle and rode off.

Rabbit was the only cult member who had left the house during the seven days since they'd set up surveillance. She usually started off by looping around the neighboring blocks a couple of times on her bicycle. At first, they thought she was doing this for no special reason, a kid just messing around, but then they realized she was systematically checking the neighborhood for police. So far, she seemed not to have spotted the disguised stake-out van with the "Janus Plumbing" sign on the side.

After her check, she would ride down the hill into town, to the grocery store or other places for errands, always following a route that brought her in range of Greyson's stand-by team about a mile away. The girl was the lifeline to the suspects in the house, bringing them food and other things they needed.

"Like usual, track but don't intercept."

"Whatever you say, boss." Petulance in Greyson's tone. He had pushed hard at the last two briefings to override Strait's directive and intercept the girl. He wanted to take her into custody and use her as a bargaining chip to force the others to surrender. Also, he argued, they could learn more from the girl about what was going on inside the house. Strait knew Greyson didn't like him, some personal grudge, although it wasn't clear why. He was one of those ruthless guys with lots of ambition and little talent, and probably was jealous of Strait, who'd been better than him in every way at the academy.

Whatever Greyson's motives, Strait was dead set against apprehending the girl. Everything he understood about the Barton cult told him the fanatical members wouldn't surrender if the FBI captured the leader's daughter. They would see the action as the start of the invasion of their sovereign land by the evil American government, a sign from God that their long-awaited Final War had begun. Taking the girl would probably make them release the VX.

Yes, he thought, at tonight's briefing. He'd tell Gelder and the others upstairs it was time to set the date. He wanted to make sure every agency had their members in place and synched perfectly, do some rehearsals. Maybe they could execute in three days. If all went according to plan, he'd be winging it back to Virginia by Friday and he and Amelia would be laughing over hamburgers and beer on Saturday night.

A different voice came into his headset. "Team One? This is Anderson."

Jimmy Anderson. That young guy on Greyson's team. He sounded nervous.

"What's up, Anderson?"

"We got a problem, sir."

"What?"

"Agent Greyson picked up the girl."

James sat up. "You're kidding."

"No, sir."

"Why the fuck did he do that?"

"I'm not sure, sir."

"Put that asshole on the line."

"Agent Greyson?"

"Yes!"

"He's out in the parking lot, sir. He's got the girl down on the sidewalk, in cuffs."

"What?"

"Sorry, sir, but there's more."

Garcia and Footer were both listening on their headsets, worried looks on their faces.

"What happened, Anderson?"

"The girl. She had a device."

"A device?"

"It looked like one of those alarm things kids have. Makes a buzzing sound if the kid presses a button? But this was something more. She started thumbing the button on this like crazy the second Greyson jumped her, sir…"

"Fuck."

"Yes, sir."

At that moment, on the monitors, Strait saw black smoke rising from the house.

Chapter Two

Strait brought the van to a skidding halt in front of the iron gate. Garcia in the passenger seat, Footer in the rear. He backed up. "Hold on!" he shouted. In the three minutes since he'd seen the smoke, Strait had told the other teams about the fire in the house and ordered the emergency evacuation of the neighborhood and a full and immediate assault on the cult's house. All available agents were to hit the compound, ASAP, in gas masks.

Strait positioned the van and bashed his foot on the pedal. The van lurched forward and slammed into the gate. There was an explosive sound as the iron lock burst and the halves of the gate shot open. Something punched the windshield and Strait's view was disrupted by a spiderweb crack across the plastic. He thought it was shrapnel from the broken gate but then came another punch, and another, and two holes appeared on the windshield and Strait felt a hot peppering from shattered plastic on his cheeks.

"Down!" he yelled, and he and Garcia dropped on top of each other to the space between the seats just as staccato blasts hit the windshield and the air filled with shards and powdered debris. Strait sat up halfway with his head tilted, stretched out his leg to push the accelerator and reached up and grabbed the steering wheel and started driving the van blind in what he hoped was the direction of the trees nearest the house.

He could feel the tires slipping on the lawn and he turned the steering wheel to the left to direct the front of the van away from the house. Now came the sound of shots hitting, *clank clank clank,* against the side.

The van hit a tree and stopped. Strait looked out the front. They were facing into a stand of trees with the back of the van directed at the house. The windshield was mostly gone, just a few jagged bits sticking out from the edges of the frame. “Anyone hit?” Strait shouted. Garcia had wormed out from under him and was halfway into the back of the van. She looked up at him and shook her head. She had some blood coming from her nose but seemed okay. No response from Graham.

Strait grabbed the radio mic. “All teams, we’re under heavy fire. Repeat, we’re under heavy fire…”

An explosion lifted the van from underneath. He dropped the mic. He and Garcia shoved themselves through the opening where the windshield had been and rolled over the hood. Strait’s head was jerked upwards when the gas mask caught on the bumper as he fell. He tore off the mask and threw it to the ground and risked a look around the side of the van. Just one guy out there, about twenty feet away, carrying an AK and wearing an actual grenade belt.

He whispered to Garcia, “set up a distraction in those trees.”

Garcia looked around with her mouth hanging open. Her eyes were glazed. She seemed confused about where she was. Along with the blood from her nose, she had some coming from one side of her mouth. She picked up a rock. She held up the other hand toward Strait and counted off with her fingers, *one, two, three,* and threw the rock. The moment it hit the trees, gunfire blasted and Strait angled himself past the side of the van and dropped low and shot the man in the head.

Before the body hit the ground, Strait was sprinting toward the house. Heavy black smoke was now pumping out from the east side of the building, about forty feet away. Strait didn’t understand what the smoke meant, why there would be a fire. All he could think was that the sudden outbreak of smoke after Rabbit had warned them meant that things were melting down and the inhabitants had gone into war mode.

As he reached the house, the windows on the first floor began to explode outwards in abrupt showers of sparkling glass. Dense smoke immediately started pouring through the frames where the windows had been and he could hear a child's voice screaming, *Papa! Papa, help!*

A man became visible in the smoke from the window frame closest to Strait, a hammer still raised in his hand from smashing out the glass. He was thin and frail, in overalls too large for him and he had short, grey hair and a wrinkled neck and the sight of Strait standing so close caused him to raise his hands over his head, still holding the hammer, and in a split-second of impulse that Strait could never take back he raised his MP5 and blew the man's head off.

Hysterical shrieking erupted from inside the house as Strait sprinted to the wall and rounded the building. The smoke pouring through the windows was rising and banking toward the south like a mammoth grey-black eel. People on the second floor were knocking out more windows and shards of glass were falling all around him. He charged clear on over to the west face of the house where he found an open door and no smoke.

Four men came out the door firing pistols. James felt a hot sting in his thigh. He dropped his machine gun as he fell to his stomach and pulled from his jacket the Glock and pumped off eight shots in three seconds. Six of the shots hit exactly as he intended, and he saw the heads of three of the men burst into clouds of red. The seventh shot missed the fourth man entirely and the eighth caught him in the shoulder. The man toppled sideways and rolled in the dirt and made to get up while popping off a shot at the same moment Strait shot him in the chest. The bullet hit Strait again in the leg, in almost the same spot. He tried to stand and gasped at the roar of pain in his thigh. He fell flat on his face. He dropped his gun and was blinded by the tears that flooded his eyes. *Jesus.*

He swiped at his face savagely with his sleeve, snatched the Glock from the grass and pointed it at the door. Then he shoved the gun into its holster and picked up the MP5. Using his free arm for support, he forced himself up onto his uninjured leg and hopped to the door. Screams were coming from somewhere in the house. He braced himself and jumped through the doorway into a small out-room which gave way to an open staircase.

He tumbled down the stairs, blind, smacking against hard surfaces, injuries lighting up all over his body. When he came to a stop, he lay with his right cheek on a floor, lit from above with yellow light. He could see blood from his head pooling on cold concrete.

He moved the fingers of his right hand and found he was still gripping the machine gun. His left hand was squashed under his ribcage. He unfolded it and knew some of the fingers were broken.

He bit back a scream as he pushed himself up with his left hand, crouched on one leg and collapsed against the wall. He was facing a metal door that suddenly opened. A man charged out, pistol pointed at his face and Strait shot him twice in the chest.

He fired off a few more rounds into the room and yelled, "FBI! We're coming in. You're outnumbered. Throw down your weapons and lie on the floor if you want to live."

No sound came from inside. Strait took a deep breath and hopped around the man's body and into the room. He zig-zagged, firing in the air. He made for a pillar-like object and propped himself up on it. It was a huge metal pipe, wider than his own body. It reached almost to the ceiling ten feet above him, then bent into another, equally large pipe running perpendicular that ran across the ceiling and led to a huge metal box affixed to the wall. Strait leaned against the pipe and peeked around it. He froze.

The canisters that filled the room were six feet tall and lined up in rows at least ten deep and ten wide. They were connected to each other with a network of electrical wires and flexible aluminum pipes that all wended around and met at to a central container, which looked to have been jury-rigged out of a boiler from an old steam engine train. The boiler in turn had emerging from its side a broader pipe that fed into the wide one Strait was leaning against. His gaze followed again the length of the man-width pipe to where it bent flush to the ceiling and continued to the large metal box, along whose lower surface he could discern a rigging of wires. With a jolt, Strait realized what he was looking at. The canisters that contained the VX agent were rigged to feed their contents into a central conveyance, likely rendered from oil to an aerosol dust, which then led to a giant fan, where the VX would be blown into the air. On a breezy day like today the aerosol would blow southwards to descend leisurely in a massive toxic cloud over much of Colorado Springs.

Strait glanced around. He seemed to be alone in the room. He could see only one door, the one he'd entered through. Maybe he could just stand here, propped up against the pipe, gun pointed at the entrance, and drive off any cult members who tried to come inside to set this thing off. Wait for the cavalry to arrive.

Trouble was, he was at an angle that made it hard to aim at the doorway. Anyone coming in could easily swing to the right and hide behind the canisters, which Strait absolutely did not want to risk shooting at. He shuddered to think how he'd been firing into the air as he entered the room.

He needed to get into a better position. He saw, leaning

against the nearest wall, a few lengths of aluminum pipe. He hopped the few steps to the wall and leaned against it. He could use one of the pipes as a cane, but only if he could grip it. His left hand was useless. Most of the fingers were pointing at odd angles. He had no choice but not hold his gun and hope someone didn't come charging in while he got himself across the room.

He let his MR5 hang by its shoulderstrap and picked up a piece of the pipe. It was about seven feet long. He grasped the pipe and hobbled painfully across the room. He searched for something big and durable he could crouch behind.

Then he saw the girl.

She sat cross-legged on the floor at the edge of the canisters, concealed in the shadows. She wasn't more than nine years old. She was thin and very white with pale blue eyes that stared up at him. Her tangled, straw-colored hair and her pink prairie dress were spattered with blood.

In her hands was a metal box. A transmitter with a flip switch and wires coming out of it reaching to a relay mount with more wires that spread out to all the canisters.

"Wo, there. It's okay, little girl," said Strait, and he felt stupid for saying it, because clearly nothing was okay. "I'm not going to hurt you. What's your name?"

The girl tensed and her lips pressed together more tightly and she placed her finger on the switch. "Stay away," she said. Fire in her eyes.

"Okay, okay, I'll stay away. I'm not going to hurt you. Please, please, please, little girl. Don't do that. It's very dangerous."

"You're a devil," the girl responded. Her voice was quavering.

Strait tried to smile. "Me? I'm really not. I'm just trying to make sure no one gets hurt."

Tears dripped down her cheeks. "You're here to kill us. You killed my papa."

"No."

"Liar! I saw you! My papa was just hammering out the windows for us to get away and you *killed* him!"

Strait cleared his throat. "I didn't come here to hurt anyone. And I know you don't want to hurt anyone."

"He couldn't hurt anyone and you killed him! Coward!"

"Please listen. You pull that switch and all that poison in those cans will kill thousands of people."

From outside, sirens could be heard.

"Devils," she said miserably.

"I can see why you think that. I wish you'd tell me your name."

"I don't tell my name to a devil."

"I swear, I'm not here to hurt you. If you release that gas now, you'll kill your own family too. And yourself."

"We all got masks. We're ready for when the Devil comes."

"Your family is getting arrested now. So they won't be able to put on their gas masks. There's a fire up there too. Why is there a fire?"

"Sister Laurel buzzed in the alarm, so it's time for war. Some didn't want it. Some did. Papa didn't want it. He was trying to stop it. They got in a fight and knocked over the candles."

"Candles?"

"Altar candles."

The sirens grew louder.

Where are Amelia and Graham? Where are my assault teams? But then he realized the last thing he wanted was anyone else barreling down the steps. This girl was on a tripwire. It wouldn't take much for her to pull that switch. He couldn't have anyone coming in here. It was up to him, and him alone, to talk this girl down, fast.

"Little girl, please..."

Then he saw the child's eyes go wide and her head turn just as someone shouted from behind, "James!"

Chapter Three

Six Months later

Strait looked over his hospital room one last time. His packed suitcase stood at the wall. His gym bag was on the floor at his feet next to the bed. Although he wasn't scheduled for discharge for another hour, he gripped the handle of the bag like he was ready to walk out of the hospital that second.

On the wall over his head was a panel of antiquated medical gear intended for use in case of an emergency. None of the menagerie of buttons, knobs, masks, and tubes was used anymore. It was just a strange decoration comprised of survivals from another era, left intact because it would cost extra money to remove them. An ancient defibrillator unit, the black paint on its paddles worn grey from use, rested in a cubby on the wall. A thing that at one time inspired awe by bringing life back to the dying, now a piece of junk. A few decades before, this section of the hospital was a cardiac care unit but had been renovated into a long-term care facility dedicated to the rehabilitation of damaged arms and legs.

Strait reflexively touched his right thigh. After so many months of agony caused by pulverized bones and the aftereffects of multiple surgeries, it was strange not to feel intense pain in this part of his body.

A knock on the open door. A man stood there looking down at him. He was tall and lean, with a wrinkled face and grey hair parted neatly on the side. Glasses with lenses set in a thin metal frame. Even if he weren't wearing the white uniform, Strait would have pegged him for a doctor. There were old doctors and young ones, but they all seemed to be poured from the same mold. This one was hazily familiar, but he couldn't remember where he'd seen him before.

"Good morning, James," the man said. "Can I come in?"

James.

"Sure."

The old doctor came forward smiling, eyes obscure behind the glint of his glasses. Strait stared at his outstretched hand for a moment before shaking it.

"I understand you're checking out today."

"Yes, sir. In about an hour, I'll be a free man."

"Leg all healed?"

"Pretty much."

"No pain?"

"A twinge now and then, but I can walk again. I can run a little too."

"You're heading back to your hometown?"

"I'm catching an Amtrak train this afternoon to Pine River."

"Such a peaceful name for a town."

"It's small. I haven't been back in a long time, but it's a good place to rest up. Excuse me, doctor, but do I know you? Dr. Shelby's my doctor and he said goodbye yesterday."

The doctor drummed his fingers on his clipboard a few times. "You don't remember me."

"Not exactly, sir."

"I'm Kent Swept. I was your physician for that month you were on C-unit."

"Oh." C-unit. The psychiatric ward. Patients had called it Crazy Unit, or just Cunt for short. "Yeah, now I think I remember you. You came by a couple of times."

"You were pretty fogged up back then."

"Yes, sir."

"You don't need to call me sir. I came over to see how you're feeling. It's going to be a big adjustment for you out there."

"Truth be told, sir, I can't wait to go."

"I understand. But you'll be going out to very different circumstances to what you had before."

Strait stared directly at the wall, focused on a spot there.

"In truth, Dr. Shelby asked me to drop by and discuss your disability case."

At the sound of the word *disability*, Strait winced.

"I'm concerned about the changes you're facing." The doctor flicked through the pages on his clipboard. "Let's see, Strait, James. Bachelors degree from Oregon State in biology. Straights As. Oregon was a long way from home, wasn't it?"

"Yes, sir."

"You had to pay out-of-state tuition?"

"No, sir. I spent a year there first to get residency."

"Then you joined the military?"

"Yes sir. Army Infantry. Afghanistan."

"Only one tour. A lot of guys do more."

Strait didn't respond.

"Says here you were recommended for entry to the Green Berets. Not many soldiers have that kind of ability. But you turned it down. Why?"

"Same reason I did only one tour. Knew a scam when I saw one."

"Yet during that tour you earned two awards for distinguished service."

"I guess."

"You guess. Then on to the FBI. At the academy and afterwards, your performance continued to be extraordinary. You broke records in firearms skills, hand-to-hand combat, fitness, running endurance, martial arts, the list goes on and on. Then, in case these achievements weren't enough, you single-handedly stopped a major terrorist attack. And they stuck your face on the cover of *Newsweek* magazine. Pretty much if someone wanted to find a real-life American hero, you were the model for it."

"I don't know anything about that, doctor."

"For a man with the physical capabilities you had, the prospect of being disabled must be depressing. Your leg isn't the problem, is it, son?" Doctor Swept tapped on his right ear. "It's your ear?"

Strait nodded.

"How many vertigo attacks have you had?"

"Five."

"How long do the attacks usually last?"

Strait inhaled deeply. "The worst one so far was ten hours. After they stop, I can't walk for about ten more hours because the room keeps rocking even after it stops spinning."

"Unfortunately, that's normal. And tinnitus in your right ear?"

"It never stops. But I can hear."

"But you have some hearing loss? How bad so far?"

"About fifty percent, they said. But my left ear is fine."

"You saw, um…" Swept again scanned his clipboard. "…Dr. Rogers at the ENT clinic upstairs?"

Strait nodded. "She said Meniere's Disease."

"Which tests did they do? I don't see much here."

"They checked my hearing."

"But no other diagnostics?"

"They did some test where they put these big goggles on me

and tipped me back and forth?"

"That's pretty rudimentary. Anything else?"

"No. But Doctor Rogers was confident about it being Meniere's."

"I'm no expert. But it couldn't hurt at some point to go to another ENT for a full balance and inner ear work-up. An MRI is a good idea also to rule out tumors."

Strait coiled his fingers around the strap of his gym bag. "Rogers said there wasn't much could be done. Said there's no cure."

"He's right. It's irreversible," the doctor said.

"She."

"She. Right." He again consulted his clipboard. "Permanent hearing loss in one ear is typical with Meniere's. In forty percent of patients, it extends to both ears. And your lawyer, Mr. Schaeffer? He asserts that your Meniere's Disease was caused by a gun or explosion. What do you think of that?"

"I don't know. It was pretty crazy in there, lots of gunfire. There was a grenade too, hit the van we were in. It was as bad as anything I saw in Afghanistan. The day I came in here, I was already having this loud ringing in my ear. About two weeks later I had the first vertigo attack."

"For a disability claim, Meniere's is tough to prove. Your assertion that you got it as an injury in the line of duty will be controversial."

"That was Bernard Shaeffer's idea. I don't even want to leave the FBI, but Shaeffer says I won't be able to work again, so I should look into other sources of income. Namely, disability payments from the government."

That fucking lawyer. The one his ASOC recommended

who'd badgered him daily until he agreed to let him submit those documents, trying to sell him on the dream of never having to work again. Like that was a good thing. "This sickness is your golden ticket, boy! Most folks would take the money and run!" were the words the wheezing little man used, and he was completely bewildered that Strait was disgusted by the very thought of it.

They wanted him out.

"I need to be straightforward with you, son," said Dr. Swept. "As I'm sure you know, for the patient, Meniere's is a complete nightmare. A Meniere's patient goes through periods of normality where he seems completely functional, and then, *bam!* out of the blue, a vertigo attack knocks him out of commission for days. The patient usually doesn't seem outwardly sick. He's not in a wheelchair. He's not missing arms, legs, eyes. The general public doesn't understand what people like you go through and some even think the Meniere's patient is faking to avoid work. Patients tend to become socially isolated because no one appreciates what they're going through. On top of that, with every attack, they lose more of their hearing."

"I know all this, doctor."

"My point is that while the government should rubberstamp claims of disability for Meniere's disease, in the present political climate, getting approved for any kind of disability is tough. Just this year alone, I've personally gone to bat for something like twenty disability claims, and only five were approved. About half the patients who were rejected are now homeless, wandering the streets and unable to work. I've got one guy out there who's so out of it, he can't even feed himself. I could measure out my professional life in failed disability claims. Just knowing this makes me question my choice of profession, I can tell you."

"Maybe you should change your profession."

Dr. Swept cast his gaze wistfully toward the window on the other side of the room. "Oh, James, I've considered it, believe me. But realistically, by the time I started seriously questioning the road I'd put myself on, I was too old to start on a different one. It was, if you will, my *destiny*. My *fate*. Do you believe in fate, Mr. Strait?"

"No."

"A disability claim with Meniere's disease has a very low success rate. Doctors end up bickering like children over whether it's Meniere's or some other vestibular disorder. No one knows for sure. This claim that it was caused by the raid is certain to make some pencil-pusher at Social Security say, 'wait, we don't even know what causes this disease, so how can this guy say it was caused by the raid?'"

"My lawyer's the one saying that, not me. But I don't think it's a coincidence that the tinnitus and vertigo started so quickly after the raid."

"You'd be surprised at how obtuse people can be when deciding who gets government money and who doesn't, son. Listen, I have an idea to help your case. Meniere's patients are usually very depressed. If we add depression as a complicating symptom of your vertigo attacks…"

"I'm not depressed."

"…you stand a much better chance of getting awarded full disability payments."

"I'm not depressed."

"Really? You look unhappy."

"Is that strange? I've been stuck in this hospital for six months. The woman I was dating was killed." At this Strait's voice caught in his throat and he paused. When he went on, his voice came out gravelly. “They’re saying my career with the FBI is finished. It’s all I really wanted to do. I’m not depressed, doctor. I’m pissed.”

“Son…”

Don’t call me son.

“…it would be unfair to sugarcoat things. I’ll just say it straight out. You’ll never work as an agent of the FBI again. Your condition is disabling and it’s going to get worse.”

“I want to fix this and go back to my job.”

“Your work ethic is admirable.”

“Fuck my work ethic. This has nothing to do with my work ethic.”

“Listen, son…”

“And you’re not my fucking father, so stop calling me son.”

“Please calm down.”

“I want to go back to the FBI!”

Strait found he was gripping the top bar of the guardrail on his hospital bed so hard his fingers were shaking. He closed his eyes and took a few long, slow breaths. He gradually loosened his grip on the metal bar and looked back at Dr. Swept.

“I want my life back.”

The doctor fiddled with the pen attached to his clipboard.

“Son, who doesn’t?”

Chapter Four

The Amtrak trip to Pine River took two days. Strait had reserved a room, and the FBI paid a month's rental for it, at a hotel called *The Blue Rabbit*, an historic downtown fixture that had existed long before Strait had left town a dozen years before. The Blue Rabbit, a couple of blocks from the train station, was also the name of the restaurant and pub on the ground floor.

Strait was too large to sleep comfortably in the upright seat of the Amtrack train. His long legs were trapped bent in the space between his seat and the back of the one in front of him. While others slept, he listened to music on his ancient iPod. He had everything ever recorded by Crosby, Stills, Nash, and Young on there, and of course everything by Neil Young himself, and countless songs from artists of the same era, the mid-to-late sixties to the very early seventies. A narrow, precious historical window. It wasn't the golden age of contemporary American music. It was the *only* age. It was the music his father had listened to.

As the trip progressed, he grew steadily more exhausted. He tried to politely thwart the attempts at small talk by the bubbly old lady seated next to him who repeatedly offered him salted peanuts from a plastic bag in her purse and jabbered about her grandchildren. Along with the salted peanuts, he ate pretzels and cheese crackers and overpriced, mayonnaise-oozing sandwiches from the snack bar.

At the time the train crossed the northwestern corner of New Mexico and entered the state of Arizona, Strait noticed the tinnitus hiss in his right ear getting louder. The train trundled across a section of the Navajo Nation, the largest Native American reservation in the country. From the window, it seemed a land of bus-sized orange-pink stones strewn randomly by some giant personage upon an unpopulated sand-whipped flatland that gave way to rising, jagged terrain, where scrubby bushes pushed through the crevices with ridges so jagged that the rocky soil comprising them appeared to have been melted, tossed up, and flash-frozen in mid-air. Tiny human habitations appeared sometimes along the train tracks, patches of tenuous structures that flew past before Strait could get a clear look at them.

As they wended their way through the state, the scenery started to look more familiar. A glimpse of Lake Mary brought back a memory of the time his father had taken the family on a weekend fishing trip and his brother Ricky had fallen into the lake and nearly drowned. Strait's fear of losing his big brother in the cold blue-green water was a torture that flashed back to him powerfully even now although he and Ricky—now Richard, a tax attorney in Florida—hardly ever spoke.

The train passed close to the segment of the highway where the police had found his Aunt Sally. Drunk as usual, she'd driven wildly northwards through the state after running away again from her abusive husband and had spun into a ditch, snapped her spine into two, and died. Somewhere much farther south along this stretch he and some high school buddies had driven all the way down to Phoenix and shot up a bunch of cactuses with hunting rifles borrowed without parental consent and had actually outrun a police car that tried to pull them over.

The scenery changed to mountainous pine forest. A storm had passed through and the cool, moist mountain air heavy with pine moved into the train. Strait was caught by surprise at the surge of emotion he felt, a mingling of melancholy and joy.

Evening fell and the landscape disappeared into darkness.

A couple of hours later, the train, with a screech of iron and a clank of bumping cars, pulled to a stop at Pine River Station. Strait was becoming dizzy. He knew the length of time without sleep was dangerous and the lousy food from the snack bar wasn't helping. When he stood to depart the train, the walkway seemed to sway back and forth. *Fuck,* he thought.

He needed to get to the hotel room fast. A Meniere's attack out here would be a nightmare. He'd collapse to the sidewalk and start gasping and vomiting. People who saw him wouldn't understand. They wouldn't see the world spinning like he did and would think he was drunk. If he tried to tell them he had Meniere's disease and ask them to leave him alone on the pavement until the attack passed—but he couldn't do that because he would need to lie there vomiting on the sidewalk for eight hours. All night. He could get attacked and robbed as he lay helpless. Someone might call an ambulance but being in a hospital wouldn't help him. There was nothing to do for a Meniere's attack except let it pass. All they could do is stick him in a bed for the night, same as a hotel but a hundred times more expensive.

Shit! Panic rising. There. Down the street. A blue neon sign three stories above ground with a blink effect that made a cartoon rabbit hop and rest and hop and rest. The name spelled out in ornate cursive: *The Blue Rabbit.* Strait remembered the entrance to the hotel was around the corner. He heard a buzz of voices from inside the bar as he hobbled past, animated, laughing, and smelled alcohol threaded with cigarette smoke drifting out.

The dizziness was hitting him like a tsunami. He turned the corner, which sent the parked cars and buildings on either side of the street careening leftwards. He stopped and propped himself against the hotel wall and stood rigid, sucking huge breaths of night air deep into his lungs, fighting back nausea and praying for the world to stop moving.

He pushed open the door and entered the lobby. Thank God, no other customers at the reception desk, just a clerk sitting there absorbed in her Smartphone game. He stuttered out his name and managed to pull out his wallet and remove his credit card, struggling not to show how scared and sick he felt. The girl hardly looked up as she ran his card. Strait wanted to cry with gratitude when she assigned him a room on the first floor whose front door was only twenty feet down a hallway.

"There's a patio area on the street side. Just go out the other door in the room," she said as she handed him the key.

He weaved down the hall to the door, somehow got the key in the hole on the first try and threw open the door. He nudged it shut, zig-zagged across the room, grabbed a table from in front of the TV and dragged it to the bedside, tore the vomit bucket and other supplies from his duffel bag and tossed them on the table, and collapsed backwards on the bed.

The ceiling light in its round plastic cover directly over the bed began to move leftwards as though attached to a giant, revolving cylinder. The rotation soon became so rapid it was a blur, like the ceiling was being spun on a fast merry-go-round. Strait moaned. He began to gasp in breaths desperately to stop himself from vomiting. Sweat was flowing freely from his skin, but he was icy cold. His heart was beating so hard his whole body shook with each pulse. The tinnitus in his right ear was an airplane roar. The sickness descended upon him, saturated him like poisonous glue, filled every cell of his body and he needed to vomit. Moving his head to the bucket was almost impossible because the slightest movement made the rotating ceiling also buck and bounce wildly. He threw his arm over his eyes in an attempt to lessen the impact of the spinning. He took a deep breath and flipped on his side with his head toward the bucket.

Everything he'd eaten on the train was hurled somewhere around the bucket. Throwing up eased the nausea slightly but it quickly boiled up again and he vomited more violently, retching so desperately that his stomach cramped. He collapsed again on his back and the movement flipped the spinning room on its side and bounced it up and down and Strait lurched back to the vomit bucket for more painful retching.

The spinning went on and on. Strait sank into a dark region, a place filled with a reek of mayonnaise and boiled ham, where life was crushed to fragmentary heaving gasps. With his eyelids pressed tightly shut and his arm thrown over his face, he sensed rather than saw the spinning, but the need to puke was just as bad and the roaring in his ear was so loud it hurt. At some point, the nausea was reduced such that with steady, deep breaths, he could stop retching. He lay completely immobile, spinning for a very long time.

During this attack, as with the others, Strait saw himself stripped of all superfluity and the world parsed down to its most toxic essences. The rotations of the room transmuted to a single nightmare object: a mammoth circular saw. Its flashing silver serrated blade turning and turning as it descended, in stops and starts, to cut him from his life.

As the blade moved closer, Strait called out the name of the child.

Chapter Five

An immeasurable clot of time passed. He sensed the rotations finally subsiding. He opened his eyes, shut them. Still turning some, but not as bad. He waited thirty more minutes and opened his eyes again and kept them open. He could focus on a single spot without it moving. The spot he was looking at was the bucket. Its blue plastic side and the sheet next to his head were covered with vomit. He sighed. At least this time he hadn't pissed or shat himself.

He hazarded tilting his head slightly forward to look at the wall across the bed. There was a framed painting, blue-tinted cartoonish rabbits at play in a pastoral setting. Very slowly he moved from his side to his back. The round ceiling light directly above his head had stopped moving too and he could make out tiny cracks in the plaster spreading outwards from its perimeter.

Through his exhaustion, he felt weary relief. The worst part was over. Like the aftermath of the marathons he used to run, his whole body was sore. His clothes were soaked in sweat, even the legs of his jeans. He turned cautiously to look at the electric alarm clock on the night table. Its neon face read eight fifteen. He'd collapsed around midnight the previous night, so the vertigo attack had lasted a full eight hours.

The worst had passed but it wasn't over yet. He knew from experience that for several more hours, although the room stopped spinning, if he tried to move at all, the room would pitch and wobble, like he was a ship in a turbulent storm. Walking was possible only if he shuffled cautiously in the manner of a very old man.

He needed to get to the toilet. And clean up this mess. And take a shower.

With great care not to move his head too quickly, he sat up.

Shaky. But possible. Bracing himself with one hand on the bedframe and the other on the tabletop, he gradually brought himself up to a standing position. *Yes. Success.* The thought hit him that only a year before, he would have derived the same sense of accomplishment from watching a group of agent trainees at Quantico sag with exhaustion while he, ten years their elder, beat them on a 20-mile training run.

He entered the bathroom and used the toilet. He had to sit down to urinate. His shirt was covered with vomit. At a snail's pace, he undressed and took a shower. He brushed his teeth, wobbling the whole room with each stroke of the toothbrush. After drying himself with one of the hotel's thick white towels, the room teetering when he rubbed his head to dry his hair, he hobbled out of the bathroom and to his duffle bag, got out some clean clothes and put them on so slowly it took him twenty minutes to dress.

Worn out completely, he sat down on the only chair in the room.

He was startled by a knock on the door.

"Hello?" a voice called. He heard a key in the lock and the door opened. A woman was standing at the doorway. She pushed a cart with cleaning supplies. She smiled at him. "Housekeeping. Sorry, but there wasn't a no-disturb sign on the door. Is now okay?"

She was in her twenties and wore jeans and a t-shirt. Her long straight brown hair was tied back in a ponytail. "This'll only take me…oh!" He followed her gaze and felt a spasm of shame. She was staring at the vomit bucket.

"Sorry," he muttered.

"No worries, hon, I got it." He gestured to stop her but the movement jarred the room and made it rock up and down, so he just gripped the arms of the chair with both hands and said nothing. She carried the bucket into the bathroom. He heard the toilet flushing, followed by water running in the bathtub. A minute later she came out with the bucket, now clean. She peered at him. "So it's all true."

"What?"

"That you got hurt. In the raid on that cult."

He turned his head slowly to face her. "Do I know you?"

"You don't remember me."

"Uh…"

"It's okay. I looked way different then. My hair was darker and I had bangs like this?" With the flat of her hand, she gestured down her forehead, from her hairline to her eyes. She looked at him hopefully.

"Sorry."

"Plus I was only twelve. Maybe this'll jog your memory." The woman flipped up the apron and pointed at her neck. Slanting from the base of her throat down to the upper seam of her t-shirt and proceeding into the valley separating her substantial breasts was a jagged scar. Strait looked from the scar to her face.

"Jenny?"

She frowned. "Julie."

"You were my sister's friend, right? You lived down the street from us."

"I lived next door to you. You *do* remember where I got this scar, right?

"That dog."

Her T-shirt was tight and low-cut and showed a toothy cartoon horse with the words "The Horse's Mouth Honky Tonk Bar and Grill." Her breasts were stretching the horse's open mouth, making it smile. He forced himself to look at her face.

"That's right. You saved my life."

"You're exaggerating."

With well-practiced movements, Julie removed the sheets, tossed them into her cart, and put on new ones. She moved over to the curtains along the opposite wall and pulled them open. "That dog would've bit through my throat if you didn't pull him off me."

She drew open the sliding glass door and pulled the mosquito screen closed. A delicious breeze of clean, cool air came into the room.

He looked at Julie, struggling to bring her back into focus. Julie Stepford. That was her name. She'd been a member of his sister's crowd of friends, a flock of giggling pre-teens at least five years younger than him, who'd been scarcely a blip on the map of his seventeen-year-old vision. Strange to see her suddenly all grown up.

"You used to go around with that backpack that had a Care Bears thing hanging from it, right?"

She raised her arms in a hallelujah gesture. "He remembers! All the girls in the neighborhood back then had a big crush on you. You probably didn't even notice. We were all so proud of you when you made it into the FBI and did all those great things."

"Great things?"

"You know what I mean. You stopped those terrorists."

"I didn't do that by myself."

"The TV made it out like you did. Man, you were on the cover of *Newsweek.*"

"I was part of a team."

"You were the leader of the team, right? People in Pine River were sad when you didn't come back to visit."

"I'm surprised anyone noticed."

"Everyone was like, he just disappeared. Doesn't he like us

anymore? Shit like that. You didn't even leave a way for anyone to contact you. How long's it been since the last time you were here?"

"Twelve years."

"I guess I can't really blame you. Especially a guy like you. You were always too much of a superman for this town."

"What are you talking about?"

"Hello? Earth to James. High school football team quarterback and regional teen weight-lifting champion two years in a row? Six and a half feet tall, 260 pounds, none of it fat? But somehow still a really sweet guy and editor of the school paper? The one that every girl was crazy in love with? Am I mixing you up with another James Strait?"

"'You must be."

"Someone like you was just destined for things way bigger than the shit passes for life in this goddamned town. We all wanted something good to come your way after what happened with your mom and dad."

She sat down on the chair next to the opened door. "We didn't even know you were in the FBI. Then one day, it was all over the TV, that big news about the nerve gas cult and there you were, on CNN. Then, on the cover of *Newsweek*. Big headline, American Hero!"

"I'm not a hero."

"Fuck you ain't. I bought five copies of that *Newsweek* and I read that article, like, a hundred times. It talked about your whole history, how you were in Afghanistan, and how now you had to leave the FBI on account of you got this…Manners Disease, and…"

"Meniere's Disease."

"…you were moving back to Pine River. A lot of people gonna be glad to see you home again."

Home? More like no place else to go.

"The article said you get dizzy attacks and there ain't no cure." She looked over at his vomit bucket on the table and her eyes welled up. "I wanted to cry."

"I'm okay."

"Really?"

"It's only a problem when I have an attack. Puts me out of action for a day or two. Like when you get the flu. No big deal. The rest of the time, I'm fine. I just came back to Pine River for a little R and R. Then I'll head back up to Virginia."

"Whatever, it's great to have you back."

"How about you? What've you been up to since you were the little girl next door?"

"Grew up. Like you can see. Started off at Birchcrest Community College, studied to be a dental assistant, but then I met a guy. Got married, the guy shipped off to Iraq. Didn't come back."

"Sorry."

"It was the IED killed him, not you. Then I went back to the community college to finish my dental certificate, but I met another guy. Married him. Got this job at the hotel to support us both while he spent all his time at the bar."

"That sucks."

"Sucked worse to find out he was also fucking every girl he could get drunk enough to convince. I divorced him."

"So now…"

"Then I decided absolutely to finish at the community college and get a better job. I signed up for classes. But…"

"You met a guy?"

"How'd you guess? And got married. A year ago. Seems like it's my fate to not get a dental certificate."

"Your newest husband hasn't died or cheated on you yet?"

"Not yet. He's basically a good guy."

"What does he do?"

"Duane just got hired on as an officer at the police department. Like your father was."

"So…a happy ending for Julie?"

She looked at him fixedly for a long time without responding, a small smile on her face. She wrapped up the sheets and placed them in her cart, picked up her cleaning supplies and went to the door.

"You know what? We need to get you out to our house for dinner. We can catch up on twelve years of missed time. What do you say? Friday night okay? About six? That's when I get off my shift."

"Sounds good."

"It's a date. I'll come by your room."

"Um, what is today?"

"Tuesday. By the way, I'm a shift manager at this hotel, so anything else you need, you let me know. Anything." She gave that sidelong, smiling look again, then shut the door, leaving him alone.

Chapter Six

After Julie left, Strait continued to sit in the chair for another hour. The breeze from the opened sliding glass door flushed out the reek of his vomit enough for him to notice the sour odor impregnated by generations of smokers into the ancient carpet. Smoking wasn't now permitted in this room but it obviously had been for decades before.

Strait closed his eyes. The flush of a toilet somewhere upstairs brought a burbling gush of water inside one of the walls. He opened his eyes and found his vision still didn't bounce and shake. Maybe he could take a short walk. He stood and made his way to the front door, then turned back and walked shakily the length of the room to the sliding glass door.

He slid open the mosquito screen and stepped outside. He was standing in a small patio area with a wrought iron table painted white and two metal chairs beside it. The patio was surrounded by a knee-high ornamental wooden picket fence with a swinging gate looking out on a tranquil side street and the city park.

Pine River Park hadn't changed. Five acres of grassy hills and beautiful shade trees. Visible in the distance was the playground, with swing sets and a slide and a climbing tower strung with thick blue webbing. Strait could make out the frantic movements and squeals of laughter of children at play. He'd spent countless hours there himself as a child romping around, playing tag and kick the can and having acorn fights. As a teenager, after his mother had succumbed in her long, lonely battle with cancer, he'd spent plenty of late nights in the park at illegal beer parties.

He was actually here. *Home.*

A short walk, he thought. One time around the block, slow

and easy. He opened the wooden gate and stepped down the four steps to the sidewalk. He walked past two other cozy patios, identical to his own, then reached the street corner. As he passed the entrance to the hotel, he looked in through the window to see if Julie was there but the front desk was unattended. He continued to the end of the building and the next corner and turned right again. This was the street he'd walked the night he'd arrived. He'd hardly noticed anything then, in the dark, in crisis.

Now he took in the street and his childhood rushed back to him. His father had taken him down here more times than he could count, mostly to Jolly's Ice Cream shop, which, Strait observed sadly, had changed into a chain outlet for an international cellular phone company. When Strait was a boy, the brick wall had a huge, colorful clown face on it, white-gloved hand extended with a triple-scoop ice cream cone. The face was now painted over with a uniform grey-white. Despite the shop's blasphemy of destroying one of his childhood icons, Strait made a mental note to go there and get a new smartphone.

To the left, on the corner, he was relieved to see Boscht's Newstand was still there. Its rotating wire sidewalk racks still brimming with sundry candies, postcards, and cigarette lighters. But friendly old Mr. Boscht, who his father shot the shit with every morning when he bought a newspaper on his way to the police station, was no longer at the counter. In his place was a short-haired young woman in black clothes, a barbed-wire tattoo encircling her arm, glowering at the handful of customers lined up in front.

To the right of the cell phone place, there had been a gift shop with the big Hallmarks sign that the kids avoided because the proprietor, a woman whose face was magnificently ridged and striated from a lifetime of bitterness, hated children. The gift shop was now an alternative music store called Smashed Records and had a red anarchy symbol on the front door.

Strait made his way down the street until he came across a shop that exuded the wonderful smells of rich coffee, fried eggs, hash browns, and sausages. A collapsible wooden sign on the sidewalk next to the door: the Potbelly Café. A hand-painted potbelly stove with an old-fashioned metal coffee pot with steam rising from its spout and a stack of pancakes next to it. A pat of butter was melting on top, yellow streams seeping down the stack through a luscious expanse of syrup.

He went in. And instantly fell in love with the place.

It was a cozy room with a seating area that ran along three walls. The kitchen and the seating area were separated only by a waist-high U-shaped brick wall that served as a counter for putting out dishes to be picked up by a cheerful teenaged waitress in a pink shirt and blue jeans and a white apron. Over the speaker system, a Crosby, Stills, Nash & Young song was playing: *Almost Cut My Hair*.

The waitress was serving a plate of sausages, fried eggs, and hash browns to a short, fat, balding man in overalls sitting at a table along the right wall.

"There you go, Gus. Get you anything else?"

"Just a warm-up on the coffee, Darlin'," responded the man called Gus. He had a leering smile and thick black eyebrows that arched sharply to meet at the bridge of his red nose. "Though the way you move in them jeans is warming me up pretty good as is."

The girl scooted back to the counter to fetch a coffee pot, her brown pony-tail bouncing. When she saw Strait at the door, she called out, "sit anywhere, hon."

There were fifteen tables in the place. Three had customers at them. Strait sat at one near the door, two tables down from Gus. He looked around. Apart from Gus, he liked everything he saw.

Strait held the opinion that there was no place better for making one's heart feel warm than a family-owned café. Especially one with the advanced cultural taste to have a classic rock station playing. The song changed to *Apeman* by the Kinks and Strait was in heaven.

The tables were cut from thick planks of roughly hewn wood. The backless chairs were actual tree stumps. The small wooden rack holding the menu appeared to be handmade. In one corner was a genuine antique pot belly stove with a chimney pipe connected to the ceiling. It looked functional. The iron panel was flipped open so you could see some ashes inside, presumably from last winter, when the device was used to heat the place. Probably they'd fire the thing up in a month or so, when the first snow fell.

In the kitchen area, another woman was cooking at a big grill. Smoke blew up from the flat, heated metal and billowed around her brown hair. She was slightly older than the waitress, mid-to-late twenties, and had a similar look about her, brown ponytail, sharp nose, keen eyes, thin face, but was a few inches taller.

The bell on the front door jingled and a man in ragged jeans and a filthy coat came in. His greasy black hair fell in snarls over his shoulders. Strait could smell him from where he sat, odors of accumulated grime and sweat and urine and stale alcohol.

The sight of him brought back a sad memory about the town.

A substantial section of the state of Arizona, comprising much of the northeast corner, was taken up by the Navajo and Hopi reservations. Only a short hike to the north from Pine River was the southern Navajo Nation border. The reservation was stricken by poverty and high unemployment. Alcoholism, which first had spread like wildfire upon the introduction of drink by white people when they settled the region, remained such a problem on the rez that alcohol was still illegal there. Weekends, when the paychecks or welfare checks came in, dozens of Navajo made the trip across the border to drink in Pine River bars. The highway leading back to the reservation was dotted with white crosses erected alongside it, tragic evidence of the consequences of leaving the rez to binge-drink and trying afterwards to drive home.

Many weekend drinkers merely slept it off where they collapsed. Saturday night and Sunday morning, the downtown area was notoriously sprinkled with bodies of those who'd passed out from drinking. Many of the town's homeless were also Native Americans.

The man's gaze flicked around the room, passing over Strait without focusing on him. His face had been horribly wounded. Starting three inches from the top of the left eye, at a space near the hairline over his temple, and slicing straight over the eye socket and extending crosswise down through his nose to the right corner of his mouth, was a deep scar. The eye was gone. He wore no eyepatch.

He edged up diffidently to the cooking area. The woman said to him, "Hey, Randy. What's the word?"

"Living the dream, Carol." The man named Randy tittered shyly into his hand. Despite his terrible injury, something endearing about the way he did it. Childlike.

"So, where's my weather report?"

The man held up a finger, like he was testing the air. His face darkened. "Oh, Carol. This is bad. The wind. It's blowing from the east since yesterday evening, stronger and stronger. The birds. They got an edge to their calls, a tension. The worst tension I ever heard. Tension swelling up to violence. The pond fish in the city park.

They're sheltering so deep you can't even see them. Violence. Powerful, hateful things, in the air. The spirit tells it to me like that and I can feel it. Violence. Coming our way."

Carol looked long and hard at Randy. "I think that's the worst report you ever gave me."

"It's what the spirit tells me, Carol."

"Sounds like things will get pretty bad around here."

"Yes. But the spirit says too that a hero is on the way."

"A hero'd be nice. What about the weather side of all this dark stuff?"

"The air feels heavier, thicker. Growing humidity. A low pressure system creeping in. The trees are crackling dry. A big storm on the way. Lots of lightning. We'll get hit on Saturday, Sunday at the latest. Bad things coming. Stay inside. Lock your doors."

The woman took a bagel from the display cabinet, split it neatly with a knife and laid on one side a thick slice of tomato and on the other spread a generous amount of cream cheese. She wrapped it and put it in a paper bag and took out from the cooler next to the cash register a large bottle of orange juice and put it into the bag. She folded the bag shut and held it out to Randy.

He took the offering, eyes downcast.

"You take care now, Randy. Usually your reports have a happier feel to them, but you're still the best weatherman in town."

Randy moved sheepishly back toward the door. He was about to go out when his one eye fell on Strait again. This time the homeless man stood petrified, his one eye agape, for at least ten seconds. Then he abruptly walked out.

The fat man called out, "you know, Carol, you keep feeding them, they just gonna keep coming back."

"Now, Gus, he gives me the weather report."

"Can I talk crazy and get a free bagel too?"

"His predictions are better than the ones on the TV. And a damn sight more interesting."

"Feed a rabid dog, the rabid dog's gonna come back and bite you someday. Just sayin'."

Carol folded her arms. "He's a human being, Gus. He needs our support."

Gus scoffed. "From where I sit, the only support you're giving him is for a bad habit." Gus made a motion with his hand, lifting an invisible bottle to his lips.

"I'm just giving him a little food."

"You give him food, he can spend the money he does have on wine instead of food. What he needs is a job. An honest day's work."

"And who's going to hire him around here? You, Gus? You want to take him on at your auto shop?"

"Nah. I don't let white guilt guide my hiring practices."

"I don't give him food out of white guilt. I give it to him out of common Christian decency. That man's gone through hell and if I can make his life a little better with a bagel, then I'm good with that."

"How do you know he's gone through hell?"

A shadow of anxiety flitted on Carol's face. "Well…he's been in prison, for one."

"Oh, that's right. What did he do time for again?"

Carol looked at her feet. "It was a long time ago, something to do with attacking his mother when he was a teenager."

"Attacking his mother, how nice. I can see why you'd want to reward such an upstanding citizen with free food."

"If the way I treat people bothers you, Mr. Bear, you're free to get your breakfast somewhere else."

"But then I'd miss the chance of getting you riled up, Darlin'." Gus ran his eyes over the young waitress as she emerged from the back and made her way to Strait's table. "'Besides," he added. "The eggs are better here."

"What can I get you?" the waitress asked Strait, struggling to hide her annoyance.

Strait looked at his menu. He said in a lowered voice, "I'll have exactly the same as that guy over there. But I promise not to be a loudmouthed shithead when I eat it."

The girl smiled. "You want some coffee with that?"

"Yes, please."

"Cream?"

"Black."

"You want the eggs same as he's got'em?"

"How's he got'em?"

"Sunny-side."

"Would've thought scrambled."

The girl smiled bigger.

"Someone ought to scramble him."

"Thank you," she mouthed. She read back his order, walked over and gave the order slip to the cook and said, "Can I go on break, Carol?"

Carol nodded and the younger woman disappeared through a back door, already pulling out her smartphone before the door shut behind her.

Next to the potbelly stove was a set of shelves with some books and newspapers. Strait picked out the top paper, which was that morning's issue of the Pine River *Sun*. A screaming headline on the front page:

POLICE CHIEF: RIVERBANK BLOOD BELONGED TO MISSING GIRL

Pine River Police Department Chief August Kladspell stated at a press conference today that, although DNA testing was not possible due to degradation from rainfall, blood found at a gory scene on a secluded bank of Pine River was almost certainly that of Jophia Williams, the southside youngster who disappeared while riding her bicycle home from school in May of this year. Police have found no trace of her in the ensuing six months. While Kladspell was not willing to state explicitly that the child had been murdered, he implied evidence found at the scene, including a bloody school uniform, suggests strongly that she was. Responding to queries from the Sun regarding claims of some activists that the police were not doing enough to find Williams, the Pine River police department issued a statement that it will "continue to do everything humanly possible" to locate the missing girl.

"Don't remember seeing you here before."

Strait looked up from the newspaper and realized the man called Gus was talking to him. The single, bushy eyebrow extending over both of his piggy eyes was bunched up in expectation.

"I grew up here. I went away for a while and just moved back."

"Got kin here?"

"Not anymore. My parents died. My brother and sister moved away."

"I'll be damned!" It was Carol in the kitchen who said it. She was staring at Strait with a look of wonder. "It's you."

"Me?"

"I knew you looked familiar when you came in. James Strait, in the flesh." She came out from behind the counter and went over to him.

"Who?" demanded Gus.

"Gus, you're looking at a genuine American hero." Carol came up close to Strait and said, "stand up."

"Stand…?"

"Just do it."

Uncertainly, Strait stood. She was a tall woman, but he towered over her. She reached up and spread her arms and wrapped them over his shoulders and gave him a hug. "Thank you," she said.

"You're welcome?"

The other customers in the restaurants, a mother and two kids at one table, and an old couple at another, were staring.

"Carol, will you tell me what the hell is going on?"

"Gus, this is the guy who stopped those terrorists. The ones with the poison gas? He saved thousands of people's lives."

"That so?"

"He was on the cover of *Newsweek*. You didn't see that?"

"Nah. I don't read that shit."

"An American hero."

"I didn't do anything," said Strait.

"Hell you didn't. Hey, you remember me? Carol German? I go by Carol Baker now, but it was Carol German back in the day. We went to the same high school, but I graduated about the time you were a freshman."

"Sorry."

"So, you're military?" said Gus.

"Army infantry. But the thing she's talking about, I was in the FBI."

A shadow passed over Gus's face.

Shouts came from outside. Regular, rhythmic. A man's voice, followed by a crowd in unison:

What do we want?
Justice!
When do you we want it?
Now!

Gus groaned. "Oh, Christ in a henhouse. It ain't even nine o'clock and they's already out there?"

Through the window Strait saw a small crowd of people marching on the street past the restaurant. Most of the marchers were black. One man carried a sign that said, BLACK LIVES MATTER!

"Thug lives matter, 'smore like it," muttered Gus.

"Gus, keep it to yourself," said Carol.

Among the marchers was a young African American girl of about ten, walking with her mother. She happened to see Strait through the window and her eyes widened. She yanked on her mother's arm and pointed at him. Then she waved at him. Strait didn't understand, but he waved back.

"Another group of people be better off finding gainful employment," said Gus.

"Gus, have a heart. A little girl is missing and they're angry."

"A girl with a father that hates America. Which should tell you everything you need to know, Carol."

"You don't know what you're talking about."

"What's going on?" Strait asked.

"It's there in your newspaper," said Carol. "Little girl's missing. Murdered, they're saying."

"Probably murdered by her father," said Gus. "But *they* say it's the whites."

"Gus."

"Jus' sayin'." He rose and slapped a ten-dollar bill on the table. "Keep the change, Carol. Love, you, babe."

He ambled over to Strait and tossed a business card on the table. "Case you need your car repaired."

"I don't have a car."

"Case you want to buy a car, then. I'll give a discount to an American hero." Gus walked out the door.

Strait looked at the card. *Bear Brothers Auto*. "There went a colorful individual."

"Yeah. Only one color he likes, though."

"He always act that way?"

"He don't mean anything by it. He's basically a sweet guy underneath all that. He gives me a deal on car repairs."

Strait took the last sip of his coffee and stood. The room teetered. He grabbed his chair and stood still, his heart pounding. *Not another attack.*

"Hey, you okay?" asked Carol.

"I'm fine." He placed a 20-dollar bill on the table and left the café as quickly as he could.

Chapter Seven

Strait walked unsteadily around the block. The sidewalk juddered as though shaken by a mild earthquake. If he walked slowly and carefully, he could still progress without too much trouble. But why was he suddenly dizzier than he was earlier in the morning?

He continued south, in the direction of the train station. On the next block, the area became rougher. The only place of business was a seedy-looking bar across the street called *The Hole*. The building on his side of the street had the look of an abandoned factory, three stories, with stained red-brick walls covered with graffiti and windows latticed with iron bars, most of the panes shattered. The sidewalk was strewn with litter and broken glass. Urine stink, cigarette butts. The street met another running perpendicular, and across it was a chain-link fence through which Strait could see two sets of rusty railroad tracks.

Three men sat cross-legged on the sidewalk. They were in a doorway of the abandoned building, passing a bottle in a paper bag. They all had the same look as the one-eyed man who gave Carol the weather report. Stringy black hair, sallow skin, ratty clothes. They studied him as he approached. One held out a hand and said, “Spare some change, bro?”

Strait shook his head and walked past them and turned right at the corner. The walls of the abandoned building extended over the city block. After that, another building, grey concrete, barred windows, and a metal door with a sign over it that said The Window Mission for Homeless Men. Next to the door was a metal box and a notice: ABSOLUTELY NO DRUGS OR ALCOHOL ALLOWED. NO ENTRY AFTER 10:00pm.

Strait continued on. He tried to match this area of downtown with his memories of Pine River and at first he couldn't remember it at all. Then it came to him. A dozen years before, the abandoned building he'd passed had been an import-export warehouse, with linkages to the Southern Pacific Railroad. Part of the place had been a lumber yard, or a lumber storage area. He remembered the name. Magic Industries. And he was pretty sure the homeless shelter he'd passed had been a porn theater.

He turned right at the next corner. Two blocks later, he recognized the cozy porch outside his room. Strait opened the wooden gate and flopped down on one of the chairs. Exhausted.

The side street running alongside the hotel on this side was quiet. Only a couple of cars. One motorcycle. Across the street, Pine River Park. From down the street came the sound of people shouting. A procession appeared, moving toward him, the same marchers he'd seen earlier passing the café. The crowd of about four dozen had not grown in the time since he'd seen them walk by the restaurant. A few held signs: JUSTICE FOR JOPHIA! and BLACK LIVES MATTER! As the marchers passed, he recognized the mother and child he'd seen earlier through the window of the café. The girl saw him and her eyes lit up. She waved and said, "Hey, mister."

"Hey back at you."

"I saw you in the coffee shop. I'm Eliza."

"Nice to meet you, Eliza. I'm James."

"Pleased to make your acquaintance."

The girl's mother tugged at her arm. "Ellie, don't bother that man."

"You that cop," the girl said.

"Me?"

"Ellie." said the mother.

"That superhero cop everyone's talking about. I saw your

picture on *Newsweek*."

"You seem a little young to be reading *Newsweek*."

"I read everything. Did you really kill Osama bin Laden?"

He laughed. "No. Where'd you hear that?"

"Kid at school said it. But you stopped those terrorists, right?"

"Ellie."

"It wasn't just me."

"Ellie."

"Anyways, they're all saying you're a supercop."

"People say funny things."

"Can you help me find my friend?"

"Your friend?"

"My best friend. Jophia. Don't you know? That's why we're marching here."

He suddenly felt uncomfortable. He squirmed in the chair, then went rigid, as the movement jostled the world and sent the first warning punch of dizziness. This missing child, this Jophia Williams, he realized, wasn't simply missing. She was dead. And this girl Eliza was asking him to somehow find her and bring her back.

She stood staring up at him with her face full of expectation. He cleared his throat.

"I don't think I can do that."

The girl's mother gave him an apologetic glance then tugged more urgently at her daughter's arm. "Eliza, leave this man be."

"What do you mean, you can't do that?"

"I can't."

"Let's go. Now."

"But Mama, he can help us."

"I'm sorry," said Strait.

"*Now*, Eliza."

"But he can *find* her, Mama. Why don't you do something, Mister?"

Strait shrugged his shoulders.

The girl was twisting in her mother's grip, trying to pull free. Her face had changed. It was like a reservoir of pent-up anger had burst through.

"Why doesn't somebody find her? Why don't you help?"

"I really want to, but there's nothing I can do…"

"Liar!"

Her mother yanked the girl into the lumbering flow of the crowd.

He noticed then that among the people moving past in the procession, some others were also staring back at him. Most black, a few white. The feeling their looks expressed wasn't the mortification of grief over a dead girl. Instead, it was the same look of accusation the girl called Eliza had shown him. The one that responded, when he said there was nothing he could do, *liar!*

Chapter Eight

When Strait arose the next morning, the world was more stable. Hardly any wobbling at all. He took a shower, dried off, and stood naked in front of the full-length mirror in the living room.

His muscles had gone to waste and his stamina had withered. He'd once been able to easily bench-press 300 pounds. Now he doubted he could do 200 and if he tried, he'd worry about the strain of the lift upsetting the fragile balance in his inner ear.

The thought made him furious.

I'm not going to let this stupid ear problem destroy my life.

On impulse, he lie on the floor and tried some push-ups. Used to be he could do a hundred without breaking a sweat. Now, he did only ten and he could already feel his muscles protesting and his heart beating faster. Worse, the tinnitus became louder.

Can't I do anything anymore? Fuck.

He stood and turned on the radio and spooled around until he found a classic rock station. Bob Seger, *Roll Me Away*. He opened the closet door. His suitcase and gym bag were still in there, unpacked. He dragged them into the room. From his suitcase he took out the few clothes he had and placed them in the drawers of an old wooden dresser. He also removed the three books he had brought. He used to have more but these three were special and went with him wherever he traveled. They were *essential*, as Dad would have put it: well-worn copies of *Blue Highways*, by William Least Heat Moon, *Desert Solitaire,* by Edward Abbey, and *Catch 22,* by Joseph Heller. All three taken from his father's big book collection.

Of all the things Strait and his brother and sister had inherited when their father died—the big furnished house, the two cars, his hunting rifles, his golf clubs, his antique Les Paul guitar—Strait had only taken these three books. His siblings were happy to split the rest between them. They sold it all off as quickly as possible and left town with the cash. Strait had scarcely communicated with them since.

He unstrapped his laptop computer from the suitcase and placed it on the table next to the TV. He removed his gun cleaning kit and his Glock. He'd stowed it in the Yaqui holster his classmates had given him when he graduated from the academy, The gun was not much dirtier than when the hospital had stored it for him. He mentally added ammo to his list of things to buy. He took it out and held it in his right hand. He aimed the gun at the painting on the wall, sighted one of the blue rabbits, lowered the gun. Feeling his fingers around the familiar grip was like hugging an old friend.

It was the same gun he'd used in the raid on the Barton cult. It was strange the agency hadn't confiscated it when he was put on medical leave. They hadn't taken away his official FBI identification card either. Some suit-and-tie upstairs had probably botched the paperwork.

A knock at the door. Strait put the gun in a drawer of the dresser and looked through the peephole. A tall black woman was in the hallway, looking fretfully to her left and right. It was the mother of the girl who'd screamed at him last night. Strait threw on some clothes and opened the door.

"Hello."

"Hello, Mr. Strait. I'm Katherine Nabors. I'm the mother of the girl who talked to you on the street yesterday morning?"

"Oh, yes."

"I'm very sorry to trouble you. May I come in?"

"Sure." He gestured for her to enter. "We'll have to sit outside on the patio. There's only one chair in here." He led her outside, and they sat at the white iron-mesh table.

"I apologize for dropping by unexpectedly. But I assumed this was where you were staying and I was on my way to work and decided it was best to come. The receptionist wasn't at the front desk, so I decided to knock on your door. There were some things I wanted to say to you."

"Oh?"

"First, I'm very sorry for my daughter's rudeness. She's only nine and high-spirited. But that doesn't excuse the way she behaved."

"It didn't bother me. Probably be better if more nine-year-olds had the guts to speak their mind about something more important than video games. You want anything to drink? Coffee?"

"No, thank you."

She looked out on the street and the park beyond. "This is a refreshing little spot."

"I like it too."

"Pine River's your hometown, isn't it?"

"How did you know?"

"The *Newsweek* article."

He gestured toward the north. "Went to school at Belmont Elementary. And my father was a cop here."

"I know. I've heard a lot about your father. Folks say he was a good man. They say he was always decent to everyone, even the people he'd arrest. It makes it especially sad what happened to him."

"He knew the risks. Are you from Pine River too?"

"Yes. I too was born here. And I'm guessing we're about the same age. But I doubt our paths ever crossed, seeing as how I went to Regent Elementary." She pointed in the opposite direction, toward the other side of the railroad tracks. "Don't think there were any white kids at our school. How long has it been since you've been back to your hometown?"

"Twelve years."

She laughed. "Mr. Strait, I believe you must not like this town very much."

Her laughter was unexpectedly bright. She had one of those smiles that involved the whole face, bright white teeth showing, dimples all the way up the cheeks, eyes crinkling around the edges. With her straightened hair parted on the side and falling over her shoulders, she reminded Strait of Michelle Obama.

"I like the town okay. I just had to get away. I was eighteen. I wanted to see the world."

"I sure can understand that. Uh huh. But you never came back? Not even for a visit?"

Strait turned her question over in his mind.

"I don't mean to pry."

"No problem. It's just that the strongest attachment I had here was my family. Especially my dad. But I have no family left. My parents are dead and my brother and sister moved away."

In the silence that followed, Strait looked at Katherine Nabors from the corner of his eye. She was tall and straight-backed in the chair and seemed dignified. She was dressed in pink slacks and a sweater with intertwining black and white curlicues. She wore small earrings, simple studs with tiny blue stones, and a wedding ring.

Strait tried to guess her profession and thought some kind of office worker. A secretary or a receptionist, something that required someone highly efficient, with good organization skills, who looked pleasant for the public too.

"You sure you don't want some coffee?"

"No, thanks. Like I said, I came here to apologize for my daughter's behavior, and…"

"I want some coffee."

They went inside and continued to talk. The coffee machine provided by the hotel was old and stained, and the coffee itself, which came in a pre-stuffed ring of fibrous material, looked prehistoric.

"You should be proud of your daughter," said Strait, pressing the start button. "Looks to me like she's smart. Does she take after you?"

"Eliza inherited her father's intelligence, not mine, thank heavens."

"Your husband's a smart guy?"

"He's a professor. Cultural anthropology. He's an expert on cultural perceptions of class, race, and gender and how the forms of their trajectories in history interact with the economic conditions of a country. Way above my head."

"I don't even know what you just said. Did your daughter get her fearlessness from you then?"

"Like me, Ellie speaks her mind. I guess she's pretty brave, but these days her sleep is haunted. Since Jophia disappeared, she has bad dreams every night."

"We can go on back outside until the coffee's ready."

"By the way, Mr. Strait," Katherine said after they sat outside again. "I'd like to invite you over to my house for dinner."

"Oh, you don't need…"

"I insist. My motive is partly selfish, because I want my daughter to apologize to you in person."

"But it's really not necessary."

"Saturday night then?" As she said it, her eyes leveled and

her gaze sharpened in a way that made him realize she wouldn't take no for an answer.

"Saturday night? Um, it'll be an honor."

"Good. I'll pick you up at six o'clock. I'll be having some friends over, and I think they will want to meet you."

"Oh?"

"Don't worry. No one will make a fuss. Especially given how shy you are." In the set of her lips the trace of a smirk.

"Shy?"

"Shy. Nearly seven feet tall, built like a bull, and you're the most soft-spoken, reticent, polite man I've ever met."

"I'm not reticent."

"You're one of those people who's obviously reticent to other people but who isn't aware himself of how reticent he really is."

"Should I bring something to the party? Food?"

"Just yourself. Although by the looks of you I think I'll need to fix you a double helping. You might be reticent but you sure don't eat reticent. How tall are you?"

"I don't remember."

"Like I said. Reticent. I'm sorry. I'm being too personal."

"No problem."

"You sure?"

"It's pretty hard to offend me."

"One more thing, Mr. Strait. I have a favor to ask of you."

"You can call me James. What favor?"

"The same thing my daughter asked for. I want to respectfully enquire whether you would consider looking into this matter for us?"

"This matter…?"

"The matter of Jophia Williams. My daughter's best friend. The missing girl."

"Mrs. Nabors…"

"Katherine."

"Katherine. A missing child is a job for the local police."

She folded her arms. "James, can I tell you that the local police are not the least bit interested in finding her?"

"Why do you think that?"

"The local police haven't done, excuse my language, jack shit, about finding her. That poor girl disappeared on her way home from school. Jophia's older sister Bernie tried to file a report with the police that same night but was turned away."

"Sometimes they're required to wait…."

"And the next day, she was turned away again. She was told, in a very condescending manner, 'Now, you just calm yourself, Bernie. Settle on down. She'll turn up soon, you'll see.' It took two days for them to even take down on paper the report that she was missing. Two days! While that nine-year-old could have been wandering around in the woods by herself. With the bears and the snakes. That was six months ago. And between then and now? They didn't do one single thing to find her."

"They did nothing? Are you sure?"

"Well, just to make it *look* like they weren't ignoring the case, they spent a couple of hours checking for witnesses along the route Jophia rode her bicycle. They questioned some people and checked some video cameras along the way, but found nothing. Oh, and they took Jophia's father into custody and harassed him at the police station for about sixteen hours. They still think he had something to do with it."

"I take it you disagree."

"I know Marvin Williams personally. The man wouldn't hurt a fly. He also has an alibi. He was with my husband fishing up at Deadeye Creek during the time she went missing."

"Well, that's strange…"

"So after six whole months passed without any progress in finding Jophia, some hiker found her school dress all cut up and a lot of blood by the riverbank."

"Pine River?"

"Yes, way out past Fishtail Road. But they didn't find Jophia. Then the cops waited another whole day to send out police to check the scene. Since then, they've done absolutely nothing. Chief of police Kladspell held a press conference, but that's all. He's hinted that she's dead. So in their way of thinking, they don't need to exert themselves too much in finding her."

"Are you sure that's what they really think? Usually, when a murder occurs…"

"*If* a murder occurs. A lot of folks don't think she was murdered."

"Okay, when a child is missing and *might* have been murdered, the police work even harder. When my father was a cop, the department was too small to have specialists. No missing persons department, no homicide department. So it could be they aren't well-versed here in Pine River in how to work a missing persons case. Another possibility is that they're deliberately misleading the public about the status of their investigation as a strategy for catching a criminal."

"I understand all that. I watch TV. But I swear, James, if you knew the people involved in this, you'd know that's not what's really happening."

"What do you mean?"

Katherine looked off into the distance, her mouth set tightly against letting out words she didn't want to say, words that caused her pain.

James said, "For what it's worth, last night I got on line and read up on the news coverage available about her case. I'm sorry to say this, but as someone with knowledge of how criminal investigations work, it doesn't seem from what I've read that the police are doing a bad job."

"And I'm sorry to say this to *you*, James, but that department is full of racists. There, I said it."

"Why do you think that?"

She looked away. "I have my reasons."

"Um, okay. Let's just say for argument's sake that the department is full of racists."

"It is. And they aren't looking for Jophia like they should because of that. So to investigate her disappearance, we need someone who isn't a racist. You're not a racist, are you?"

Strait rubbed his temples. "Of course not. But the FBI doesn't have jurisdiction in this case. I'm not allowed to interfere with a local police matter. If a criminal hasn't crossed a state line while committing a crime, the crime isn't federal, so the FBI can't touch it. Second, I hate to say this, but statistically, if not found within 48 hours, child kidnap victims stand almost no chance of being discovered alive. Add the fact that a large amount of blood was found at the scene and the probability falls even lower. Third, even if my first two points weren't enough to prevent me from helping you, I've got a serious health problem. I'm on medical leave from my FBI position, so I'm technically not even an active agent, which makes my participation even more questionable, legally speaking. Bottom line, I can't help you. And I think you should let the police handle this thing."

The gaze she aimed at him was ice-cold.

"Thing?" she said.

"Um…"

"Thing?"

"Poor choice of word."

"We're not talking about a *thing*, James. We're talking about a flesh-and-blood human child, a little girl with a name. Jophia Williams."

"I'm not saying she's a thing."

"My daughter's best friend."

"I know how you feel…"

"You don't know shit about how I feel. Do you think I came here looking for some white savior to fix us black folk 'cause we can't help ourselves?"

"Um, no?"

"Good, because we don't need any white saviors."

"I wasn't thinking anything like that."

"You don't think of yourself as a white savior?"

"I don't even know what you're talking about. I'm not a savior in any color."

"Damned good to hear, we don't need that shit. The black community can take care of itself, thank you very much."

Strait sat for a few seconds swimming in confusion.

"I approached you," she continued, "because you've been trained with special skills, and presumably you have the conscience to use them to help your fellow human beings. Unlike the goddamned police we have in Pine River. You say you read all the news stories from that local garbage newspaper. Did you read the editor of that paper is a friend of the police chief? They go to the same church. You learned exactly *zero* about Jophia's disappearance except what Chief Kladspell wants you to know."

"I guess…"

"Read my lips, James. The police department is *not* investigating this case. *Deliberately.*"

"But why wouldn't they investigate it?"

She stared at him like he was the stupidest person in the world.

"Because she's black, James."

Strait squirmed.

"I can see you doubt me."

"It's not that I…"

"You doubt me."

"I don't know what to say."

"Look, go talk to Jessie over at the Rainbow Church. Pastor Jessie Brightwater. She'll tell you everything you need to know about this case and that chief of police. Will you at least do that?"

"Katherine, I already said I can't help. It's a problem of jurisdiction."

"It's an FBI matter if a crime was committed that involved crossing into another state, right?"

"Yes, but…"

"The state border is only a few miles that way." She pointed toward the only section of the landscape that didn't have mountains. "Pine River flows that way. If Kladspell is right and, God forbid, Jophia's really dead, her body probably floated across the state line into New Mexico."

"Katherine…"

"You don't believe me at all, do you?"

"I'm not saying that."

"You're thinking it."

"I already told you, I have a health problem. Sometimes I can't even walk."

"You're pissing me off, James. You can't even admit you don't believe me."

"I don't know what to believe. I need more information."

"Then get more information. You can't even come out straight and say you don't believe me to my face. This conversation is making me frustrated. You offered me some coffee earlier. May I get some now?" She folded her arms viciously across her chest. "*Please?*"

Strait got up and went inside, relieved to be doing something other than participate in the conversation. He found two mismatched cups in the cabinet that seemed somewhat clean and poured out the coffee. He stole glances at Katherine through the sliding glass door, part of him hoping she would decide to storm off, another hoping she'd stay.

He brought the coffee out.

"You want any cream or sugar?"

"No. I'll have mine *black*."

He set a cup in front of her. She sniffed at it. She glanced up him with unbelieving eyes. "What is this shit?"

"Coffee?"

"Guess it'll have to do. Maybe you need a new coffee maker. Single men can't take care of themselves. Some kind of problem with their chemicals. Are you planning to move out of this horrible hotel room?"

"The FBI paid a month's rent, room service included. Although after trying it once yesterday, I had some Chinese food delivered instead."

"You have a sickness that makes it so you can't move around?"

He nodded.

"But you moved just now to fetch me this bad coffee."

"The dizziness comes and goes. Yesterday it would've been much harder to get you this coffee. And two days ago, I couldn't get out of bed."

"What's the name of this sickness?"

"Meniere's Disease."

"Ah." She leaned back in her chair.

"You've heard of it?"

"Of course I've heard of it. I'm a nurse."

"You're a nurse?"

"An RN. I work at the county hospital."

"You don't happen to specialize in ear disorders, do you?"

"No, I specialize in children. I'm a pediatric nurse. I'm afraid I don't know much about Meniere's. Other than it's a real bitch." She sipped her coffee, winced, put the cup down. She leaned up close to him and spoke more softly than before. "But I do know someone who can help you."

Chapter Nine

The next morning, after eating a bagel he picked up at the Pot Belly Cafe, Strait set out on foot to visit the Pine River chief of police. Under his arm, he carried the newspaper he'd borrowed from the cafe with the big headline on the missing girl.

After Katherine had left his room yesterday, he'd spent the day taking care of errands. He'd bought a new smartphone at the phone place next door and found a bank and opened a local account. He had some savings to rely on, along with medical leave pay from the FBI, so he was safe financially for the time being. He located a nearby Walmart too, where he'd bought a bunch of supplies not provided by the hotel. He also purchased several boxes of ammunition for his Glock and got information from a salesman of a shooting range just outside of town. He figured he'd get out there after taking care of the next big thing on his list: buying a car.

While he'd taken care of errands, he'd run Katherine's claims about the police over in his mind and decided she must be wrong. Sure, every department had some racist cops. Just like in every pocket of society. And it seemed too that since the election racism had become a more visible and ominous presence in American life. But that didn't change basic social and legal forces in the twenty-first century that prevented wholesale police neglect in investigating a missing child.

He'd been around law enforcement enough to know the idea that a police agency would dodge an investigation of a missing child made no sense. Even if the police department had changed into a hive a racists since his father's time, the consequences of such neglect, when exposed, would be horrendous. Public outrage. Lawsuits. Governmental defunding. Prison sentences. If Katherine wanted to find racism, she should look at the media coverage of the girl's disappearance, not the police behavior in response to it. The shameful practice of news media providing more coverage of white victims of crime over black ones was well-documented. Strait had looked up some online articles about the Jophia Williams case in the Phoenix and Tucson newspapers. They mostly regurgitated the shallow, unengaged stories published in the Pine River *Sun*. He found no story in the national news. If Jophia Williams were a white girl, especially a cute, princess-like white girl, such as JonBenet Ramsey, CNN would roll out nonstop "breaking news" about it.

Strait interpreted Katherine's claims as a combination of misplaced anger and justifiable racial paranoia. Plus misunderstanding of the intentions of the police, given their strategic silence about the investigation. Strait liked Katherine. Even though he knew she was wrong, he decided it would be worth talking face-to-face with chief of police Kladspell to get his side of the picture firsthand and help her understand the situation better. Since his father had been a decorated officer of the department, and Strait himself was also in law enforcement, he had a good chance of getting a straight word from the chief.

Strait had talked to Julie at the reception desk on his way out and told her about his intention to visit the police department and she said the old building had been torn down years before. Now a brand new one had been erected about a mile away, on Lumber Road. She gave him directions.

"You might see my husband Duane down there. He's got red hair and freckles and kind of a flat, shovelly face?"

"Shovelly face?"

"You know, long and flat? Like a shovel?"

"Okay."

"You feeling better now?"

"Lots better, thanks."

"Then you can still come to dinner tomorrow? You didn't forget, did you?"

"Of course not. What should I bring?"

"Nothing but your big, handsome self."

Strait smiled. "I'll bring you a new pair of glasses."

"I can see just fine. Come down here to the lobby at six o'clock."

It was a beautiful Autumn day. Only a few puffs of cloud drifting in a blue sky, not cold, not hot. Lumber Road had two lanes, one leading into town, the other leading out. On both sides, stands of pine trees were punctuated by the odd office or store or church. After a mile of walking, he came to the new police department.

He was shocked at the size of it. When his father was a cop, the building that contained the police department was on the northeast side of town, not far from the old Magic Lumber sawmill. That small building had been a blemished wood-and-concrete eyesore with noisy plumbing and a leaky roof. The new department was easily twice as large, housed in a clean, modern, two-story edifice with blinding white walls and broad gleaming windows. From the outside, it seemed far too big and fancy for Pine River.

The glass front doors opened automatically at his approach. A scrawny, balding man in uniform sat at a reception desk, squinting through glasses with thick black frames at a TV on the desk with a football game on. Strait could smell the reek of cigarette smoke on him even from ten feet away. The man had a plastic bag of beef jerky in his hand and was working away at a piece in his mouth, his bony jaws rolling under his skin.

“Can I do you for?” he asked Strait without looking away from the TV.

“I’m here to see Chief Kladspell.”

“Got an appointment?”

“Not exactly.”

“Then you ain’t seeing him.”

Strait said “Who’s playing?”

“Cowboys and ‘skins.”

“Cowboys winning, I hope.”

“Fuck, yes. They was tied up, then McFadden took a fumble off Jackson and brought it up 16-9. Just a minute to go.”

From the TV, a rise in the roar of the crowd, and the announcer was saying, “and Jackson gets the pass from Cousin for the TD, tying the game up 16-16 with 44 seconds remaining!”

“Shit!” the man roared. He pounded the desk with his fists, knocking the jerky bag open and flinging out chunks of dried meat.

The announcer continued, “now getting ready, and it’s Baily squaring off for the kick, and…he scores! Field goal to Baily and the Cowboys win 19 to 16!”

The receptionist jumped up whooping and threw his hands in the air and high-fived Strait. Beef jerky sailed everywhere.

The man flopped back down in his chair grinning and shaking his head with amazement. “What a game!” he said.

“Too bad I missed it,” said Strait. He removed from his pocket a small black leather case, flipped it open and showed the man his FBI special agent shield. The receptionist raised his eyebrows.

“Officer, the reason I came to see Chief Kladspell concerns a matter of law enforcement. Can you at least get him on the phone and tell him I’m here?”

The receptionist stared at the I.D., his jaws doing double-time on the wad of jerky. "Hold on."

He put the phone receiver to his ear and pressed a button. He spoke with his mouth muffled by his hand. He hung up and gestured behind him. "Down that hall. Last door on the left."

The corridor was covered with plush brown carpet that smelled new. The walls had photographs sheathed in glass, affixed at regular intervals, of mountainside settings, a hunter with rifle raised at deer amongst the trees, a bear in a river flinging out a fish with its paw, two long-antlered bucks in combat.

He came to a door with a brass plaque:

August Kladspell
Chief of Police

He knocked. "Come!" he heard from within.

The chief of the Pine River police department sat behind a desk that seemed far too big and expensive for the kind of job he held. The well-shined reddish-brown wood looked like real mahogany. The office was also surprisingly large, with fine wood paneling punctuated here and there with the mounted heads of animals. The room had the feel of an office designed for a president of a successful company rather than for the police chief in a small town.

August Kladspell was at least a decade older than Strait and wore his age badly. He was fat enough that the buttons of the blue shirt on his uniform were about to burst open. His ponderous jaws and cheekbones were well-coated with fat that loosened about his neck and jowls into a doughy, sand-colored mass. His hair was clipped into a buzz cut. His pale blue eyes were small and pushed back so far into his head they seemed like two subterranean animals peering out from their holes.

Strait studied the man's appearance and pegged him as one of those men who'd aspired to a career in the military but couldn't make the cut because of some physical or mental inadequacy. Such wannabe-but-never-can-be soldiers often gravitated to law enforcement as a consolation prize.

Strait put out his hand. "Chief Kladspell. James Strait. Good to meet you."

The latter seemed to debate whether to return the gesture, then reached out his own hand. As Strait expected, Kladspell tried to show his authority with a powerful grip that might have been impressive when he was twenty years younger. Now Strait only was impressed by the queasy feeling he had at the contact of his palm with the man's plump, pulpy fingers, which reminded him of those red bite-sized sausages his mother used to pack in his school lunch.

Kladspell gestured for Strait to sit on the chair in front of his desk. He appraised him, buried eyes glinting.

"So Merle says you're FBI," he said.

Strait tried to place Kladspell's drawl. Arkansas? Tennessee?

"Yes, sir."

"So, what did I do to prompt a visit from the feds on this otherwise fine morning?"

"More like a social call."

"Long drive from Phoenix for a social call."

"I'm not from the field office. I came from Quantico."

"All the way from Virginia? Now I'm downright flattered."

"Actually, this is a kind of homecoming for me. I grew up here in Pine River."

"You don't say."

“Yes, sir. Haven’t been back in twelve years. I don’t remember you being here then.”

“If I’d been around, there’d be no reason we’d come into contact, would there? Unless you got arrested.”

“No, sir. But my father was a deputy here. Under Chief Tanner?”

Kladspell’s eyes widened. “Strait…say, you ain’t Ben Strait’s boy?”

“Yes, sir, that’s me.”

The chief broke into a toothy grin. “I’ll be darned! Ben Strait’s boy! Your father’s a legend around here, son. His picture’s on display upstairs.”

“I was at the ceremony where that picture was unveiled. In the old building.”

“They moved the whole section over. You want to go up and see it?”

“Not really.”

“I understand. Hard to lose a loved one to an act of violence.”

“Yes, sir. Pretty nice building you have now.”

“Yep. Praise the Lord for Homeland Security money. The feds ain’t all bad.”

“They give you extra funding?”

“Something about the president’s strategy of keeping the homeland safe by beefing up security in small towns not far from Mexico. They even bought us some of them high-tech observation drones. It’s a lot of bullhockey from where I sit, but I ain’t going to complain about the perks that come with it.”

“This building is a lot bigger. Did you increase the number of officers? It seems like the place is empty.”

“No big increase. We still have only twelve officers plus two dispatchers. Six on day, six on night. Two detectives, me and Merle."

"Merle's a detective?"

"Yep. Although between you and me, he don't do much detecting. Gosh!" Kladspell clapped his hands together. "Ben Strait's own son! I hear tell your father was a fine officer, though I never met him in the flesh."

"When did you move here, Chief Kladspell?"

"Fifteen years ago."

"You're to be congratulated," Strait said, absently taking the newspaper from under his arm and unfolding it so the headline was visible on his lap. "To come to a small community like this and become chief of police."

"Oh, it wasn't anything, son. I was promoted to the position two years ago, and I was an officer with this department for all the years before that. Add another ten years when I worked in another department in Tennessee." He pointed at the newspaper. A photo of himself under the big headline about the blood belonging to Jophia.

"See you been reading about our latest soap opera."

"Sounds like your job's been complicated lately."

"You can say that again."

"I overheard folks at the café downtown talking about this missing girl."

"And what were they saying?"

"Some people think the department has given the girl up for dead."

"Wrong."

"… and isn't doing much to find her, in the case that she's still alive,"

"Wrong."

"or to find her killer, in the case that she's been killed."

"Wrong. We've worked like dogs to find that girl. We've questioned all the people we could up and down Sower Road, where she was riding. We've checked security cameras all the way from the industrial district to that auto shop way out on the southside. We've searched the river too, as far as was practical. Those people are just full of bullhockey."

Bullhockey?

Strait said, "I'm not saying I believe any of this. I'm just telling you, as a fellow lawman, what I heard."

"Sometimes stopping crime is easier than stopping crazy ideas. A girl disappears this long? You know as well as I do, chance of her being alive is about the same as Pilate's chance of getting into heaven. Am I right?"

"You are right."

"But that don't mean we ain't exploring every possible lead to find her."

"I thought so. But you can't reveal what you're doing, otherwise her abductor could be tipped off."

The chief nodded. "Excepting we ain't got no leads whatever."

"Really?"

"Nothing solid. But that don't mean we ain't figured things out." The chief leaned back in his chair and stretched. His stomach pressured his shirt buttons nearly past their safety limits. "Between you and me, for all the noise the blacks are making about this being racism, we already know who done this, and it's one of theirs."

"You have a suspect?"

"'Suspect'? Son, we got the perpetrator dead to rights. That girl's father killed her. He was the first and only one on our radar from the start."

Kladspell's calling him "son" was starting to grate on Strait's nerves.

"Why do you think it's the father?"

"You know who he is, don't you?"

"No."

"He's none other than Marvin Elijah Williams."

"Marvin…"

"The Chicago Six?"

It came back to Strait. Back in the eighties. They'd spent a week in his domestic terrorism class at the academy studying the case. They had called themselves the Moorish Revolutionary Army. It was one of the many splinter black liberation sects that viewed even radical groups like the Black Panthers as too tame and considered the non-violence of Martin Luther King as Uncle Tom betrayal. After the victories of the Civil Rights movements of the sixties and seventies, these on-the-fringe-of-the-fringe extremist groups had managed to smolder on for years without being completely extinguished. When its leader, who called himself Sheik Ali al Africa, died in 1998, he was replaced by his much more charismatic and ambitious son, Azziz al Africa, who exploited the newborn worldwide web to spread fiery rhetoric about the dream of a Black Islamic state founded in the west. At one point, Azziz held sway over the minds and finances of about 5,000 followers, mostly from big city poor black neighborhoods in the U.S. In 2001, the group tried to raise its visibility by pursuing more literally its stated goal of violently overthrowing the United States government. In all, they'd carried out half a dozen bombings, mostly amateurish attempts that did little damage and killed no one. They were substantially more destructive in what would prove to be their last attack, the bombing of the federal tax offices in Chicago. Six employees died. In the end, most of the MRA leadership was imprisoned or dead and by the year 2002, the group had disappeared.

"I remember the group and the trial, but I don't remember a Marvin Elijah Williams."

"He wasn't one of the actual Chicago Six. He was a defendant in one of the other, less famous trials that came after. He wasn't indicted for killing anyone himself, but he did help out on one of the bombings by driving two of the perpetrators to a store to buy parts for making bombs. At the trial, this boy claimed he didn't know they was making bombs. He was convicted and sentenced to twenty years in federal prison. Served only fifteen, supposedly for being a model prisoner. When he got out, he thought he'd settle in a quiet place, out of the public eye. His father used to live out here and Mr. Williams inherited the old man's cabin up there in the woods on the southside. Now we're stuck with him."

"His politics the same?"

"At his parole hearing, he said he gave all that MRA stuff up, took our Lord Jesus into his heart, loves white people now. If you believe that, I got some twin towers in New York City to sell you cheap."

"If he was in prison, how does he have a nine-year-old daughter?"

"Conjugal visits. Can you imagine? A crime like that and he still gets to have his jollies. He's got an older daughter too, but she was bred before he was sent up."

"Okay, whatever he believes, why do you now suspect him of kidnapping his daughter?"

"Not *kidnapping* his daughter. *Killing* his daughter. Because on top of his being an America-hating, white people-hating, Jesus

Christ-hating terrorist, Marvin Elijah Williams is a psycho. A real whack job. He sits out there in his cabin talking to himself. Anyone with white skin knows to steer clear of that place."

"His wife?"

"She's even crazier than him. So crazy she got carted off to the state hospital in Phoenix couple of years back. And there she sits to this day."

"He has custody of the daughter?"

"He's got custody of *two* daughters. Although the older one is eighteen now, I think. She's basically took on the role of the younger girl's mother. She's the one that takes care of both the old man and the child. That nutcase can't take care of himself."

"If you think he killed his daughter, why haven't you arrested him?"

"We brought him in. Questioned him here all day. He's got an alibi. A professor at the university said they were fishing together when the girl went missing."

"So you think the professor is lying?"

"I'm saying it wouldn't be the first time their kind lied to protect a friend from justice. Now those protesters out there are saying that I'm a racist and we're not doing our job, but that's just wrong. My own daughter is married to a black man and he's as much a part of my family as my daughter. A good, honest man. I worship quite happily together with black folks at our church. I find it profoundly insulting to be called a racist when I'm just doing my job."

Strait gazed at the bookshelves behind Kladspell. A whole shelf was devoted to Bibles and scripture-related books.

"Those protesters must make your job awfully hard."

"You can say that again."

“No other conceivable suspects?”

“Not unless you count space aliens come down and grabbed her as conceivable. Nah, we got our man. But we can’t arrest him because he has that fake alibi. We’re working on that, though.” The smile on the chief’s face was smug.

“Have you considered the idea the girl is still alive?”

“Sure we have. But you know how these things go. We found her school uniform on the riverbank all tore up and lots of blood.”

“But no body.”

“As sure as I’m sitting here, her father threw that girl’s corpse in the river or buried it somewhere in those woods. We’ll never find it.”

“Besides the dress, did you find anything else?”

“Just a teddy bear. With its head missing.”

“Tests of the blood found at the crime scene?”

“Tried. A big storm hit and the blood was too watered down by rainfall to get a decent sample.”

“What about the blood on the dress?”

The chief made a show of looking embarrassed. “It was pretty much washed off when we found it.”

Strait sat in silent turmoil for a few seconds over what the chief was telling him.

“I’m surprised you couldn’t get any viable blood. How about tests of the fabric? Analysis of the slice pattern? Could you determine the kind of instrument was used to cut the dress? How about stray hairs or bits of skin? Sometimes…”

“Wo, there, Virginia!” interrupted Kladspell. His face had reddened dramatically as Strait spoke. “Who’s investigating this thing? You or me?”

“Sorry, Chief. You are, of course. I don’t mean to step on any toes."

"That's good, because we've got the situation well in hand, believe you me."

"Good to know."

The chief looked at his watch. "James, I need to get going. Got some officers I need to whip some Christian sense into."

"I understand," said Strait, rising from his chair.

Kladspell stood and shook Strait's hand, his sausage fingers squirming away again against Strait's skin. He walked Strait back to the front door of the building. Merle was no longer at the receptionist desk. Instead there was a sign that said *Back in 15 minutes*.

"James, I'll let you get back to your vacation now. How long you figuring this homecoming trip of yours will last? You heading back to Quantico soon?"

"I haven't decided."

The chief laughed. A throaty, insincere laugh.

"I recommend you don't worry about these local dramas. They ain't none of your concern." The chief held Strait's gaze for several seconds. Something unspoken conveyed. A shaded threat: *Back off. Or else.*

"Thanks, Chief Kladspell."

Outside, Strait began to walk back to the hotel. He was hardly feeling dizzy at all.

He stopped on a street corner. Cars were shooting along in both directions. The traffic in the lane closest to him was fastest, the cars picking up speed as they prepared to split off to the highway onramp heading away from town, where they'd hit the interstate and escape to cities far away. It was the same street Strait himself had taken on a Greyhound bus to Phoenix on the first leg of his journey to Camp Pendleton and the training that would take him first to

Afghanistan, then to a university in Oregon, and finally to the FBI training camp at Quantico, Virginia.

The cars in the other lane were coming out of the high velocity they'd held on the highway, pressing brakes sharply as they cruised down into the tranquil downtown area with its low speed limits and narrowing roads. Strait looked up the street one way, then down the road to the other, considering. He started walking again, playing the experiences of the last couple days through his head.

They're all saying you're a supercop...Can you help me find my friend?

The local police haven't done, excuse my language, jack shit, about finding her.

That department is full of racists.

Wouldn't be the first time their kind lied to protect their own from the forces of justice.

Don't worry about these local dramas. They ain't none of your concern.

I want to help, but there's nothing I can do.

Liar!

When he returned to his hotel room, he called Katherine.

"Hello?"

"Katherine? This is James Strait."

"Reticent boy! What's going on?"

"Can you meet me a little earlier than Saturday? Say, today?"

"Why?"

"You know the place by the river where the chief thinks Jophia was killed?"

"Yes."

"I want you to take me there."

Chapter Ten

"James, I can't take you to the river today. I need to work late. Why do you suddenly want to go over there?"

He considered telling Katherine about his encounter with Kladspell, his hinted-at racism, his implied threat, but some vague twinge of reckoning, a nudge of intuition, told him not to.

"I just thought more about what you said and figure it can't hurt to take a look."

"Well, I can't take you, but I'm sure Pastor Jessie will be happy to. She's the one I told you about. Let me call her." A short time later, she called back to say the pastor had agreed to drive him and asked that Strait meet her at the church after lunch.

Katherine gave him directions to the church, which turned out to be only a few blocks from the hotel. A benefit of a small town. Everything was within walking distance.

Strait had a couple of hours. He went to a drug store and bought some zip-lock bags, surgical gloves, and rubbing alcohol.

A couple hours later, Strait stood outside the Dove Unitarian Church. It was a plain one-story building painted a serene sky blue, surrounded by a calm expanse of grass edged with a flower bed. No spire topped with a cross. The only things that marked the building as a church were a painting rendered in childish hand on the side of the building of a dove in flight and a modest marquee next to the front door with moveable plastic letters: SUNDAY MORNING CHAPEL 8:00, CHILDREN'S HOUR 9:30.

He entered. A short hallway was immediately inside the door. On the wall on one side was a bulletin board. On the other was a poster announcing a street demonstration, a photo of a crowd of people marching holding a BLACK LIVES MATTER! banner.

Strait continued into the building to the main room where services were conducted. The chapel was very different from the one of his youth at Pine River Catholic Church. No stained glass, no baptismal font, no candles. No raised dais draped with linen. The simple cross formed from two tree branches attached to the far wall had no anguished Christ nailed to it.

Strait was mildly allergic to religion. His mother had held a fervent belief in the Catholic Jesus that she engaged with church attendance on the canonical milestones of the birth, death, and resurrection of the Savior and without fail on every Sunday. She had pulled the family along to her church on the north side of town, its three-spired building a flamboyant monument to Christ. On things religious, Strait's father had been indifferent. He centered his spirituality on reading adventure books, playing his old Les Paul, hunting deer, and scrupulously enforcing the law. He gave in to occasional church attendance to satisfy his wife and did not oppose her making a captive audience of their children. Except for the yearly Easter egg hunt and the pranks they played on befuddled Sister Agnes, Strait and his brother and sister hated church even more than school. If his church had been more like this warm, quiet place, he wondered if he would have felt better about religion.

Dove Church was pew-free. Instead of the rectilinear hard-backed benches Strait was familiar with, a few dozen folding chairs were set up in no particular order. Closer to the front was a carpeted area with bean bag chairs and bolsters and a single folding chair set up in front of them. *Children's Hour.*

"Hello?" called Strait. His voice echoed softly in the empty room.

"In back!" called a female voice. Strait crossed the room to the doorway on the other side where the voice came from. A spacious kitchen was there. A woman was standing in front of an industrial-sized aluminum sink with her hands in a large bowl of dough.

"James?"

"That's me. James Strait."

"Jessie Brightwater. Nice to meet you. I'd shake your hand, but…"

"It's okay. Nice to meet you."

Pastor Jessie Brightwater looked to be in her late twenties. She had long, frizzy, oat-colored hair that she wore tied back, and she had on blue jeans and a shirt of similar color to her hair that looked like it'd been woven from hemp. She took him in with intelligent hazel eyes. "Katherine wasn't kidding."

"Pardon?"

"She said you were a giant."

"Oh."

"How tall are you? Six six? Six seven?"

"Depends on the time of day."

She looked embarrassed. "Sorry. I shouldn't have mentioned your height. You must get tired of hearing stuff like that."

"It's okay."

Pastor Brightwater rinsed her hands. She pulled off a sheet of clear food wrap from a box on a wire shelf above and covered the metal bowl.

"Katherine says that despite your being an FBI agent, you're not evil. Is that true?"

"I'd like to think so."

"And you want to see the site at the river."

"Yes."

"Why?"

"I'm provoked by mysteries. They give me insomnia. So I want to check out a couple of things."

"So you can sleep better."

"Yes."

"Okay. I'll drive you. But first you have to give me a hand with the watering."

She took him through the chapel area to another door that led to the back yard. It was a cozy space, a garden on one side and a playground on the other. She led him to a hose.

"Use this. Don't get the water on the leaves, just the roots. And don't over-water. I'll be back in five minutes." Pastor Jessie went inside.

Strait brought the end of the hose over to the edge of the garden. The rectangular space ran the length of the yard and was divided into two parts, one for flowers, the other for vegetables. It had been a long time since he'd taken care of a garden, but he'd loved the one his family had when he was a boy. He placed the end of the hose at ground level and ran the water gently to minimize erosion. He moved it every minute or so until the whole garden was watered enough.

"You do that almost as well as the kids do," said the pastor. She stood at the door.

"Thank you?"

She'd taken off the apron and put on a thick blue sweater over her hemp-shirt and untied her hair so it flowed freely over her shoulders.

"I meant that as a compliment. Children have a natural feel for gardening, which we citified adults tend to lose."

"You'd do better to plant these flowers along the edges of the vegetable patch to cut down on bugs. And throw in some bean plants throughout. They're nitrogen fixers."

She smiled. "I underestimated you on the garden thing. Shall we go to the river?"

"Mind if I take along this spade?"

"Help yourself."

They went out through the back gate to the street, where a Nissan van with the church name on its side, and another painted dove in flight, was parked.

"You strike me as someone who would bicycle to work," Strait commented.

"You read me right. My bike is in the back of the church. But we have this van for church business."

"Does this count as church business?"

"It sure does."

She drove from the downtown area and turned on to the main artery going through, Lumber Road, the same one Strait had walked going to the police station.

"So Katie said you're staying at that old hotel downtown?"

"Yeah. The Blue Rabbit."

"I've heard that place is pretty run down. How is it?"

"Pretty run down."

"Well, if you need help finding…what are you looking at?" said Jessie.

"Oh, nothing." Strait turned his gaze from the rearview mirror, where he'd noticed a black motorcycle behind them. He was pretty sure it was the same one he'd seen parked on the street outside his hotel room. He glanced through the mirror again and watched as the motorcycle moved in and out of traffic, keeping enough distance between them to look like it wasn't following them, but not disappearing either. Jessie took an off-ramp about 5 miles out of town and turned down a dirt road which led into the forest. The motorcycle disappeared. Probably his imagination.

"I've never talked to a pastor before," he said.

"Don't worry. We're pretty harmless. Especially the Unitarian ones."

"I grew up Catholic. But now I'm pretty lapsed."

"Are you an atheist?"

"I don't know. I guess after the stuff I saw in Afghanistan, I'm not inclined to believe in a loving God who's interested in our welfare."

"Not surprising. There's so many horrors in the world, it just makes me want to sag sometimes. I've certainly had my doubts too."

"You don't sound like much of a cheerleader for God."

"We Unitarians believe that humans have a responsibility to God, or whatever an individual wants to call it, to live a conscientious life to better our lot here on Earth. And to better the Earth itself. About the last thing I would try to do is 'convert' someone. I'm not really a cheerleader for anything. A better word is probably 'facilitator.' A facilitator for propelling people toward the goal of doing their best to make this world a better place, and if they find inspiration in the teachings of Christ to enable that process, all the better."

They passed some side roads that were barely more than trailheads. Jessie spied a landmark invisible to Strait and slowed down. She began to make a left turn onto a side road but braked suddenly. The way was blocked by a sign:

NO ENTRY! VIOLATORS PUNISHABLE WITH UP TO 5 YEARS IN PRISON AND A FINE OF UP TO $100,000. BY ORDER OF THE PINE RIVER POLICE DEPARTMENT.

"Shit," she said.

"The pastor said a bad word."

"Shit yes the pastor said a bad word. They blocked the road."

"Because there's a crime scene?"

"It was open before. They're trying to stop protesters from getting in."

"Protesters?"

"Last Saturday, we had a demonstration up here. Two hundred people. We even had a reporter come all the way from Tucson. And the chief didn't want the negative publicity so now he's keeping everyone out."

"We can just step around the sign."

"But it says five years in prison."

"It says up to." He opened the van door. "Besides, there's no one here to catch us."

"I wouldn't put anything past that snake." But she still got out and followed Strait up to the sign. They stepped into the trees on one side and moved around the sign and onto the trail. It was just broad enough for a car to drive on. He took care to walk on her right side, so he could hear her through the ear that wasn't half-deaf. In spots, the branches of trees spanned the trail and cut off the sunlight from the cloudless sky. As they walked, it felt strangely like a relaxing hike in the woods instead of a visit to a murder scene.

About fifteen minutes in, Strait perceived the gurgling, rushing sound of water in motion. The Pine River. Something was wrong with the distinctive sound. It was flattened and dull, like he was hearing it through a wad of cotton. He realized, with a drop in his spirits, he couldn't hear it well because of the damage in his right ear.

They came to a clearing. Some of the pines and elms and oaks had been cleared to make a pleasant resting point for hikers.

"This is the place. They found her school uniform right over there." Where Jessie pointed, Strait could see a path cut from the clearing and glints of moving silver. The Pine River.

"When she disappeared, was she carrying a school bag? Or anything else?"

"I think she was. But they didn't find any bag. And they didn't find her bicycle."

Strait walked to the riverbank. The river was wide and fast and deep. The green reflections of trees from the far bank were flung upon the skein of blue from the sky, their stretched limbs wobbling frantically as though waving for help, then dissolving into the swirls and rips on the surface only to reassemble themselves to be smashed to bits again by the indifferent swells of water that followed.

It was easy to see how a body could be swallowed up forever in this river.

"Where exactly was her dress found?"

Jessie moved closer to him. "Over there." She gestured to a flat area a little farther down along the water.

Strait walked over. "Between these two thickets?"

Jessie nodded. With an edge in her voice, she said, "I saw the footage on TV. Right where you're standing, that's where the girl's dress was found. It was all muddy and slit up the middle. And a Teddy bear with its head gone. Sorry, but I really hate this place. Do you mind if I wait for you back there?" She gestured up the path they'd come from.

"No problem. I'll be done soon."

After she had gone, he used the video camera on his smartphone to record a pan of the entire area. He crouched and examined the ground closely. He saw nothing out of the ordinary. He held his face close to the ground, searching for any hint of blood. He saw footprints everywhere, like hundreds of people had danced through this place. Footprints atop other footprints. Any footprints left by the perpetrator would have been destroyed by all the protesters who'd been here.

Strait went to the trees on the edge of the clearing to his right. He got down on his hands and knees and crawled through the grass and studied the ground. But even here, the grass had been crushed flat by dozens of feet. The crime scene had been ruined by countless invaders. Had Kladspell allowed the demonstration to occur here to destroy evidence? Surely he must have known about the protest in advance. If he'd approved people coming here before, why then did he now forbid them to come?

Strait stood upright again and the ground pivoted and trembled. He froze and stayed very still, heart booming in his chest. *Tilting his head up and down. Disrupts the inner ear fluid.* Keeping his head rigidly erect, he moved to the side of the path, where a few young trees grew. He examined their bark but found no splashed blood left by a flailing victim or a swinging axe or club. A divot was lopped out of one of the larger trees, but it looked years old.

Strait checked the stand of trees on the other side of the path and but found nothing there either. No evidence that anything out of the ordinary had happened. He unzipped his backpack and removed the spade. He returned to the small trees and knelt next to them, careful to keep his head upright. It was hard to dig like this, because the only way to see what he was doing was by forcing his eyes downward while keeping his head upright. With some trial and error, he managed to make a hole about a foot deep. He put on the medical gloves and picked up some of the dirt and brought it close to his face.

It was slightly moist. No visible blood. He pressed it to his nose and sniffed, but no blood smell.

He tried again in three other places, including a patch next to a tree bounded in the shade of several others, where the soil was very moist. But he could tell by sniffing at it that no blood was there either. Strange.

Strait knew the chief's claim that no viable blood samples could be drawn from the site because of the rain was probably bullshit. Kladspell was either fantastically incompetent or he was lying.

Closer to the bank, Strait noticed a small cloud of flies circulating around a football-sized stone. He took a ziplock bag from his pack and held it open in his left hand. He placed his right hand into the cloud of flies. A few lighted on his skin. He peered at them closely. The insects moving jerkily over his hand had a blue, metallic sheen. Blowflies. The first insects to start feeding on dead bodies.

He placed his hand into the sandwich bag, shook off the flies, and closed it. With a pin, he poked a few holes in the plastic. He put the sandwich bag inside his backpack. With the toe of his boot, he flipped over the stone. The oval space underneath was wet. He knelt and studied it as best he could without tilting his head. The moisture could be water, but the blowflies hovering over it signaled blood. He jabbed the spade into the ground. He pulled up a mound and dug again. The third shovelful turned up a few writhing maggots. He dug another half a foot before finding what he was looking for.

Blood. Thick, red liquid fudged up with mud exuding a brassy odor. And seething with maggots. He took out two more sandwich bags. He separated out a sampling of the maggots and placed it in one and put a spadeful of bloody dirt in the other. He dug around the hole, widening it, into an area that held no blood.

A noise came from behind. He turned quickly and caught a glint of light that disappeared, returned, disappeared again, from up the hill opposite the clearing. He tried to ignore the surge of dizziness that came with the sudden movement of his head. "Jessie?" he called. In response, he heard the sound of boots hitting hard and fast on what sounded like a wooden surface.

The shallow slope of the hill led toward a summit mostly obscured by trees. When he got to the top, Strait was surprised to find a small house. It seemed abandoned. A wrap-around porch with a wooden railing on two sides, one facing the clearing below. The exterior of the house was neglected. The white paint had gone grey and was peppered with dirt flung up by past storms. The windows were covered with locked storm shutters. Strait climbed the few steps to the porch and tried the front door. Locked. The porch was filthy with branches and dirt. But there, impressed in the dirt on the wood, were fresh boot tracks. Someone had been up here, watching him. The glint of light he'd seen was a phenomenon familiar to him from his time in Afghanistan. Binoculars.

He crouched. The tracks showed where the man had come up the stairs and onto the porch and where he'd turned and run away. The edges of the tracks heading off the porch were less defined, blurred by the haste of retreat. The boots were much smaller than his own, smaller even than the average man.

"Find something?" Strait spun around to see Jessie standing next to the railing. When his head stopped moving, the world continued onwards and he grabbed the railing to stop himself from falling down.

She said, "I didn't mean to startle you. Hey, you okay?"

Strait sat down on the steps.

"Oh, my God. Katie said you had that sickness that makes you dizzy." Jessie's hand on his shoulder felt as weightless as a butterfly. "What can I do to help?"

"I'm…okay," Strait said, staring straight ahead, trying to will the dizziness away. The wobbling settled some. He said, "Were you up on this porch?"

"Me? No. I was down there on the trail waiting for you. But I heard you call my name."

"You know who owns this house?"

"No. I think it's one of those summer rental cabins. There's a lot of them up here. Why?"

"I thought I saw someone. And there are boot tracks." He showed her.

"I don't know. Lots of hikers come through here. What?"

"Did you hear that just now?"

"You mean that chainsaw sound?"

"Yeah."

"Logging country."

"Where does this trail lead?"

"I think it just swings back to the main road. The hiking trail from this spot is actually on the other side of the road we came in on. Because there's no bridge here to cross the river."

"I wonder who owns this house."

"Maybe there's a mailbox with the owner's name on it?"

They walked the length of the porch and checked around back but found no mailbox. Strait took pictures of the footprints before they left.

"Why'd you take pictures?"

"No special reason. Just cop's training. Take pictures of everything."

As they walked out, she said, "so, if you don't mind me asking, does this medical problem of yours prevent you from socializing?"

"Socializing?"

"Like, you know, going out and having fun?"

"Fun?"

"What I mean is, are you up for going out with me sometime?"

Strait stared at her. "Are you asking me out on a date?"

"Is…that okay?"

This wasn't something he'd anticipated. He chewed over the possibility. He decided he liked how it felt.

"Does that smile mean you think it's a completely ludicrous idea posed by a crazy woman? Or does it mean yes?" She leaned toward him and looked up into his face. "Jesus. Are you blushing?"

His gaze wandered off into the treetops. "It's not a completely ludicrous idea," he said. "But are you allowed to date? I mean, you're a…"

She punched him on the arm. "Yes. Unitarian pastors are allowed to date," she said. "We're not Catholics, for God's sake."

They made their way back to her car and drove back to town.

"Since it's not completely ludicrous, how about dinner with me tonight?" she asked.

"Um, Yeah, sure. Oh, wait. No. I can't. I'm going to an old friend's house for dinner."

"How about tomorrow?"

"I can't tomorrow either."

"Old friend's house for dinner again?"

"No, a new friend's house for dinner. Actually, it's Katherine."

Jessie smacked her own forehead. "Oh, wow."

"What?"

"I totally forgot. *I'm* going to that party at Katie's too. Hey."

"Yes?"

"Why don't we go together?"

"Sounds good. But I think Katherine's driving me there."

"We can meet at the party then."

"It's a date."

"But let's get together some other time too. Maybe a hike? Or picnic in the park? If you can find time in your busy social schedule."

"How about Sunday?"

"I work on Sunday."

"Right, of course. But only in the morning, right?"

"I have morning services. Then I hit the Meadows Park to work the soup kitchen for the homeless all afternoon."

"You go out to that park? You're brave." The Meadows was a notorious hangout for drug-dealers.

"After the soup kitchen, I come back and do an evening service."

"Monday?"

"Monday, I need to go out of town on a business trip."

"Pastors go on business trips?"

"It's a social justice conference up in Boston. Co-sponsored by the church. Goes on for five days. I'm actually part of a round-table on organizing grassroots food and shelter services for the homeless. I plan to start a program in Pine River for homeless kids."

"Are there homeless kids in Pine River?"

"You'd be surprised."

"Yeah, whatever, homeless children. What about our *date?*"

Strait said it in a fake-whiny voice.

She considered. “I know! How about if you come to the service in the morning, then after the kids’ service we grab a bite to eat somewhere? After that, I’ll head over the Meadows to feed the homeless folks. You can even join me, if you want.”

“You may not believe this, but I’ve never been to a homeless soup kitchen on a date.”

“Something to scratch off your bucket list. Speaking of homelessness, Katherine says you’re staying at the Blue Rabbit. Are you going to move out of that horrible place?”

“Eventually. The FBI has paid for that room for a month, so I might as well stay there.” Strait sighed. “They’re trying to give me a disability settlement so I don’t have to worry about working anymore.”

“You think you’ll get it?”

“No idea.”

“I get the feeling you don’t really want it.”

“I want to go back to active duty.”

She nodded. “Do you want me to drop you off at the hotel?”

“Actually, any chance you can drop me off at the police station?”

“Really? Why do you want to go there? Another date with an old friend?”

“’Friend’ isn’t the word I’d use for him.”

After Jessie let him off and drove away, Strait entered the police station. No one was at the reception desk. Just a sign saying “back in fifteen minutes.” Strait walked down the corridor to the chief’s office. Strait rapped on the door.

“What is it now, Merle?” came Kladspell’s irritated voice. Strait walked in.

The chief gaped up at him from his desk. "How'd you get in here?"

"Special trick I learned at the Bureau. It's called 'walking up to the door and opening it.'"

"Why did you come back?"

Strait opened his backpack and removed the sandwich bags containing blood and tossed them on Kladspell's desk. Blood, flies. Writhing maggots.

"What the heck are these?"

"Samples I dug up at the crime scene by the river."

Chief Kladspell's mouth hung open.

"I went out there just out of curiosity. I noticed these flies buzzing around one place and…"

"I told you to stay out of this."

"Yes, but…"

"But?" Kladspell's eraser-tip eyes were bulging. "I told you to keep away from this."

"I was going to, but I happened to go to the river and found these flies buzzing around, so I dug a small hole and…"

"You *happened* to go to the river? Out of all the places you could go, you just accidentally ended up at the exact spot I told you to stay away from?"

"Sorry, Chief. I was curious, that's all."

"I put up a sign over there yesterday telling people to keep out."

Strait looked sheepish. "Well, yeah, I kind of, stepped around the sign. But the good news is, I found some blood and insect samples. From these, you can probably determine at least if the blood really did come from the girl, plus calculate the time of death. If you're lucky, some of this blood might even belong to the…"

Rage brought Kladspell halfway out of his chair.

"Get that shit off my desk."

"Huh?"

"I told you we got everything under control in this investigation. I don't need this shit."

"Chief Kladspell, this is standard evidence that all investigators use to…"

"You telling me how to do my job?"

"Of course not. I'm just trying to help."

"Like heck you're trying to help. What is with you feds? You come in here, act like you know everything, start taking over. This ain't your case, it ain't your jurisdiction, and I don't need your goddamned help."

"Are you crazy?"

"For the last time, you take that shit off my desk and you get the hell out of here. I'm going to call up the FBI field office in Phoenix today and tell them you're interfering with a local case that's out of your jurisdiction. If you weren't Ben Strait's boy, I'd put you in jail."

Strait snatched up the zip-lock bags and put them in his backpack.

"Next time I catch you looking into this case in any way, I'll have you arrested for obstruction. Do you understand me, Strait?"

Strait made for the door. Kladspell hammered his fist on the desk. "Don't you walk away from me, boy!"

Strait left the office and proceeded down the hallway. The chief bellowed at his back, "I'll lock you up, you son of a bitch!"

Strait marched through the lobby and past the still-unmanned front desk. He shoved the glass door open with both hands and walked out. The sun was going down and the sky at the western horizon was thickening to molten orange. He started walking to the hotel. Kladspell's response burned at his thoughts so fiercely he could barely form a coherent thought.

What the fuck is wrong with that guy?

Had Strait wounded his pride? Was he territorial? Was he hiding something? Or was he just an empty-headed asshole to the core of his disgusting sausage-fingered self?

By the time Strait was halfway back to the hotel, a single truth came into focus. The police in charge of the investigation of the disappearance of Jophia Williams were incompetent or worse. That left only one lawman in town who could do the investigation correctly, and it wasn't someone on the payroll of the Pine River police department.

All at once, Strait's spirits lifted. All his reluctance about looking into the case melted away. The choice was made for him. What difference did it make if he lost his career over this? He'd probably lost it anyway.

He thought about Kladspell's threat to put him in jail and felt strangely free.

Chapter Eleven

On the way back, Strait came across the town post office. He went in and bought a twelve by sixteen coldpack envelope. At first, the clerk at the counter wasn't sure they had any coldpacks in stock, but after some searching, she and the manager managed to find one. He took the coldpack to an unoccupied prep table. The envelope was a pouch lined with insulating gel that kept contents cold. He inserted the zip-lock bags with blood and insect samples and addressed the envelope to Graham Footer at the FBI Forensics Science Research laboratory section in Quantico. He sent it by certified, expedited mail with overnight delivery.

Graham would be surprised to hear from him. In the six months since the raid, he'd scarcely spoken to his old friend. The few times he had, they'd restricted their interaction to light banter. They never spoke of the raid and never talked about the hospital, even though they were on the same floor for about a month. They never talked about the hellish meeting they were forced to attend two days after the raid, each of them in a wheelchair. They never talked about the lies Gelder made them tell the cameras.

Graham Footer was one of the few living people who knew the truth about the raid. He knew about Amelia, how Strait had told her to create a distraction to cover him and how he'd left her to die. He often thought of her, and dreamed of her, blood starting from her lips and a dazed look in her eyes, and was always assaulted by a blast of shame, his heart jumping with panic and despair at what he'd done. A mistake he could never forgive himself for. Just like the other mistakes with the old man at the window and the girl in the basement. Mistakes that would burn him for the rest of his life. Mistakes he never spoke about with anyone.

He knew he could never allow himself to be close enough to any human being such that he could trust them sufficiently to confide that he'd made these mistakes.

He wondered if he should cancel his date with Pastor Jessie.

After leaving the post office, he headed toward a liquor store he'd seen the day before a few blocks away. He needed to get something to take to Julie's house. He'd never been much of a drinker. Now, as he scanned the beer section, he felt like he was in a foreign country. The microbrew revolution had really taken off since he'd last bought beer. The amount of space given over to the omnipresent national brands Budweiser, Sawdust, and Coors in past years was now taken up by a dozen local beers he'd never heard of. He had no idea what to buy. He finally went with a six-pack of Pine River Brown Ale, which at least had packaging that looked promising, a pleasant watercolor image of snow-covered Mt. Humphreys rising over the logo. He also picked up a bottle of red wine for Katherine's party tomorrow.

A man with long black hair at the end of the aisle was scanning the wine bottles next to the check-out counter. Strait recognized him. It was Randy, the one-eyed guy from the Potbelly Café who Carol paid a bagel for his "weather report."

The Native American was scanning the nasty high-alcohol brands popular with winos. Strait watched as he chose a bottle and carried it to the woman at the cash register. He pulled out a handful of coins from his stained pants and spilled them on the counter. He spotted Strait and his lips spread into a half-toothed smile.

"Hero!"

"What?"

"Our American hero! The one can fix all this shit."

"Fix what?"

"This *shit*. You are the *chief*."

Something taunting in the way he said it.

"Fix what?" Strait repeated.

"All. This. *Shit*. Chief, you got the sun in your fingers and blackness in your soul."

Strait forced himself to smile, although he felt inexplicably angry.

The clerk counted Randy's coins and put the wine in a paper bag. He picked up the bag and headed for the door. Suddenly, he spun around.

"Special agent Strait!" he called. "I'm serious! You're the one who needs to fix this shit."

"Thanks for sharing."

Despite the man's demented appearance, there was something disturbingly lucid about the way he then spoke.

"You been thinking every day why you came back to this town, haven't you? You been sitting in that hotel room at night. Rolling it around in your head. Brooding about it. This town. You used to hate it, didn't you? You got no human connection left here. No human connection left *anywhere*. Your friends are gone. Your family's gone. You hate it here. But you still came back, didn't you? Why'd you do that, Chief?"

"Drink that bottle and you'll feel better," Strait answered.

Randy jabbed his finger at him. "I'll tell you why. You did it because it's your *destiny*."

"That's enough."

"It's your *destiny* to fix this town. And fix *you*."

"Get away from me, you crazy fuck!" Strait shouted.

Randy smiled at him and left the store. Strait paid for the beer and wine, his mind boiling.

Where the fuck did that come from? Why did this nut job bother you so much? He's crazy. Who cares what he says?

Back in his room, he sat on the bed, still fuming. He forced himself to look at the pictures of the footprints at the locked-up rental cabin by the river. He had captured three sets, from the mystery guy with binoculars who was watching him, from his own boots, and from Jessie's shoes. Binoculars Man left two kinds of footprints, stable from when he'd walked onto the porch, and blurred and elongated from when he'd sprinted down the trail toward the road. Judging by the size of both, Binoculars Man was not much larger than Jessie. Jessie's footprints, however, were not nearly as dark as the man's because she was lighter. The man was as short as Jessie, but made a much deeper impression in the dirt. A short, bulky man.

Strait thought about the buzzing sound he'd heard, which Jessie had thought was made by a chainsaw. Strait hadn't said anything to her then, but he knew the sound hadn't come from a chainsaw. It came from a motorcycle. The one the man used to escape.

After taking a hot shower and dressing, he turned on the TV news. Another mass shooting. The shooter was a white supremacist who'd armed himself heavily and gone to a peaceful street demonstration against police brutality in Purdue, Indiana. He'd fired on the marchers with a semi-automatic rifle, killing seven.

There were days it seemed the country was falling apart.

He turned off the TV in disgust. He forced himself to think about other things. He considered his skyrocketing social life. Dinner plans with Julie and her husband tonight. Dinner with Katherine and her friends tomorrow night. A date with Pastor Jessie on Sunday. A real social butterfly.

At six o'clock he went to the front counter. He found Julie smiling big at him.

"You're looking a lot better," she said. She led him to her car. She was wearing jeans and a T-shirt with a profile of a bucking bronco under the words *Pine River Rodeo 2002*. "I want to apologize in advance for my husband in case he says anything to piss you off."

"Nothing pisses me off."

She smirked. "Yeah, right. Tell that to the dog you killed for attacking me."

"I didn't kill it."

"If it didn't escape under that fence, you would've killed it. Anyhow, my husband is a little sensitive about stuff now. He made it through the academy on the second try and finally got hired on at the police department but he really wanted to go career military."

"But he couldn't?"

"He got injured."

"Sorry to hear that."

"He lost a toe. That's all. But it was enough. He's embarrassed about it. Losing a career over a toe. It's not even his big toe. Plus, you know, he tells people he lost it when his vehicle hit a roadside bomb. But, just between you and me? That ain't true. He lost it because of his own stupid mistake."

"What did he do?"

"He was drunk and shot himself in the foot." She burst into a reedy smoker's laugh. "Can you believe that?"

"I've heard worse."

"He's got a giant chip on his shoulder. And he really fucking hates the government. If he starts dissing the FBI, don't take it personal."

Strait nodded. He knew the type. Gung ho military guys who

loved the life and wouldn't accept being forced out of their military career even if they lost a leg or an arm. To lose your career over a toe lost because you were playing with your gun…shameful. Unthinkable. The kind of mistake you never forgive yourself for.

Julie's car was a two-door Ford Mercury Cougar that only needed to age a few more days to become an antique. But it was so poorly maintained that it wouldn't have brought a vintage price. The car was a faded rust-orange color that gave it a diseased feel. The passenger side door had a deep dent in it and the handle was gone. To let him in, Julie needed to climb over from the driver's side and use a pair of pliers to open it from the inside.

"Sorry about the shit ride," she said. "But a hotel clerk plus cop's salaries don't get you much."

"Nothing shit about it. Reminds me of the car I had when I was seventeen."

Julie laughed. "I remember that piece of junk. The tailpipe would drag on the asphalt and wake everyone up when you came home late."

"That was a beautiful car. A classic. My dad drove it when it was new twenty years before."

"That piece of shit might actually be this piece of shit we're in right now. Got it from the Bear Brothers for only fifty bucks. God knows how many people had it before."

"Bear Brothers. Hey, I met one of them at the Pot Belly, I think."

"Which one?"

"Name's Gus."

She made a face. "Gus Bear's a sleeze. There's three brothers in all. They buy old cars and fix'em up and sell'em. Sometimes people even donate their old cars to avoid the state disposal charge."

She pulled a pack of cigarettes from her purse. “Mind if I smoke?”

“They’re your lungs.”

She hit the car cigarette lighter and with one hand pulled a cigarette from the pack and put it in her mouth and lit it. She opened the window halfway and blew smoke outside.

With a painful squeak emitted from somewhere in the steering mechanism, Julie pulled onto Lumber Road. She headed the opposite direction as the police department, toward the west.

“Gus Bear’s a real asshole. People call him little bear, on account of he’s so short. Not to his face, of course. Karl Bear, he’s middle bear. He’s a real weirdo. He runs the office at their shop. Always dresses in a suit with a bowtie? Big bear is a sweetie-pie, like a giant teddy bear. His name’s Lennon. He’s the one who gave me a deal on this car.”

“You actually paid fifty dollars for this clunker?”

She jabbed her cigarette toward him. “Don’t insult the driver’s car. Your fate is in her hands.”

“I love this car. It’s a thing of superior beauty and craftsmanship. Which reminds me, I want to buy a car.”

“The Bear Brothers always got something for sale in their yard. But talk to Lennon. Gus and Karl aren’t crooks, but Lennon’ll give you the best deal. Actually, scratch that. They like me a lot, and if I ask them to treat you nice, you’ll get a better price. Let me call them first. But…can you drive? I mean, with your…?” With her finger, she made a twirling motion around her ear.

“I can always tell in advance when an attack is coming. I won’t drive if I feel any symptoms.”

“Okay. I’ll call them tomorrow morning. Then maybe you can hook up with them after? You got their number?”

“Gus gave me a card.”

"Word."

Julie turned onto a side street. They were in a part of town he'd hardly seen while growing up. The southwest side was the domain of low-income white folks who didn't quite descend the social ladder far enough to live among the even lower-income white population who lived farther south in the settlements in the foothills.

As though reading his mind, Julie said, "Yep, I'm officially trailer trash. But I don't live in a trailer."

Strait hated that term, trailer trash. While in Afghanistan, Strait had entrusted his life to many soldiers from similar places and knew the designation was a slander. The people living here were among the hardest-working, most decent people he'd ever known, not very different from the people in the upper middle-class neighborhood where he and Julie had grown up except that most of them worked more hours for less money.

They passed homes with yards of patchy yellow grass cluttered with broken toys and tireless cars propped up on bricks. A two-story structure with naked children in front chasing each other with a hose. Another with a shirtless man asleep on a lawn chair, his belly and chest completely covered with tattoos. One house was scarcely more than a sheetboard shack, but had fresh paint, a lovingly tended flowerbed, and an American flag on a pole.

After a few more turns down side streets in the cluster of residential blocks, Julie pulled into the driveway of a house. "Home, sweet, home," she said. Strait got out of the car and the quiet was ruptured by an uproar of barking dogs from behind a tall slat fence surrounding the back yard. A man inside the house bellowed, "Shut the fuck up!" To which the dogs barked even louder. They started slamming themselves at the fence and clawing desperately at the wood.

"Sorry about the pit bulls," said Julie. "They're actually very sweet." She opened the front door. "Come in!"

The living room had faux-wood paneling on the walls and a shag carpet caked with dog fur. Julie's husband was propped backwise on a recliner facing a wide-screen plasma TV, a can of beer in his hand. A football game was on. Julie said, "James, this is my husband, Duane Dumphey. Duane, this is my old friend James Strait."

Her husband glanced at him for half a second and turned back to the TV. "Hey, Bruh. Sit down and have a beer. Check out the game."

The only other place to sit was a ratty sofa with coarse tan upholstering. When Strait sat on it, Duane flipped open the lid of a portable cooler he had next to this chair. It was full of ice and canned beer. All of it was Sawdust, the cheap, popular, tasteless brand that Strait had heard had become even more popular than Bud. Several empty cans lay next to the cooler. Duane pulled out another can of Sawdust and tossed it to Strait.

"Thanks."

"James brought some beer too," said Julie.

"Bring it on over and stick it in the cooler."

Julie's husband was much shorter than Strait, but nearly as broad. Strait wondered if he was even shorter than Julie. He was wearing a Denver Broncos T-shirt and his arms were pale and freckled. He was brawny but well-padded, without visible sinews or veins pushing through the thick layers of fat on his arms. He was muscular like one of those guys who spends hours a day lifting at the gym and drinks lots of beer afterwards. Clusters of pimples lay in the fatty curvature of his outer biceps. His face was shovel-shaped and heavily freckled and his short-cropped hair was fiery red.

Julie brought the six-pack of Pine River brown ale and started placing the bottles into the ice. Brad grabbed one of the bottles out and stared at it. He gave Strait an incredulous look. For a second, Strait thought he was going to say something like, "kind of pussy drinks this shit?" But he shoved the bottle into the ice and turned his attention back to the TV.

"Who's playing?" said Strait.

"Broncos and Cardinals."

"Nice TV."

"Yeah. Rent-to-own's the shit."

"Guess you're rooting for Arizona?"

"Fuck Arizona! Peyton Manning, all the way!" Duane made a fist and pumped it up and down.

"But Manning retired, didn't he?"

Duane eyed James suspiciously. "What difference does that make?"

Julie said, "Honey? Can you get the barbecue going?"

"But we're watching the game!"

"You said you'd take care of the barbecue." Julie tried to weave a cheerful lilt into her voice.

"Yeah, yeah," Duane said, his voice slurring. "But don't I get a day to rest? I've been working, like, four days straight."

"But, Sweetie, I told you we had a guest today."

Duane heaved a dramatic sigh and pulled himself out of his chair. He made his way unsteadily to the sliding glass door leading to the back yard. Five pit bulls charged up out of nowhere and began jostling each other to get inside. The dogs noticed Strait and exploded into a storm of bloodthirsty barks, shoving each other aside in a bid to be the first to get through and kill him.

"Shut up, you fucking animals!" Duane pulled the door open

just far enough to slip out. He kicked one of the dogs out of the way and slammed the door shut before any could get in. Immediately the dogs crowded around and started leaping on him playfully as he cursed them. They followed him to the other side of the house.

"He'll put them in the shed," said Julie. "James, I'm totally sorry. I was so hoping he wouldn't be an asshole."

"Him? I met five worse assholes before I had breakfast this morning."

"You're such a sweetheart."

More bellowed curses could be heard outside, followed by the slam of a metal shed door. Duane reappeared, pulling a wheeled barbecue grill. Strait noticed he walked with a limp.

"I better get the meat," Julie said. She ran to the kitchen and came out a few seconds later holding a plastic grocery store bag. "I'll take it to him," said Strait. He took the bag from her before she could respond and snatched up a couple cans of Sawdust from the cooler. He opened the sliding glass door to the yard and walked out. "Hey, Duane, how about we do this thing together?"

"Don't need your help."

"I know you don't."

"I can do it by myself."

"Course you can. But I've been stuck in the hospital for so long, it'd be therapeutic for me to do something like this again."

"What were you in the hospital for?"

"Julie didn't tell you?"

"No."

"I heard it was on the news."

"Oh, yeah, that." Duane scoffed. "You're some kind of military hero."

Strait scoffed too. "Yeah, right, *hero*. I don't know what idiot put that out there. But I was in the hospital because I got my leg half-shot off. And the inside of my ear was damaged by an explosion, so I get dizzy spells. They fixed the leg, but can't fix the ear."

"That sucks."

"Shit happens."

"You're FBI, right?"

He started to make his way to a shed on the other side of the yard. Strait followed him.

"Yeah. Or was. Looks like they're forcing me out."

"Got to fucking hurt," he said.

"Like a motherfucker, Dude. But I'm not going to just roll over and let it happen. I'm going to get my job back."

Something in Duane's face, a sinking of the features, a shine in his eyes. He ignored the pandemonium of the dogs as they heard the men approach the shed. At the side of the metal structure were a bag of charcoal and can of lighter fluid. Duane handed the charcoal to James and took up a can of lighter fluid himself. They walked back to the barbecue grill.

"How about you lay the charcoal and I'll light her up?" said Duane.

"That'll work." It was a fifty-pound bag of charcoal, but most of it had been used. A barbecue couple. "Should I use all of it?"

"Yeah, just use her up. I got another bag in the shed."

While Strait was building a pyramid of charcoal in the grill, he reflected that what he'd said about the therapeutic value of doing a thing like starting up a barbecue was really true. The simple, mundane act brought a flood of good feelings, like he'd lived in a foreign country for a long time and had now returned home.

Duane shot a stream of lighter fluid from the can and doused the charcoal. The smell of the fluid came up thick and strong and brought back to Strait a life he'd left behind in this town, a life of Saturday football games on the tube and Sunday barbecues in the backyard, corn on the cob and potato salad and the neighbors dropping by because they were drawn by the smell of smoke rising from sizzling meat.

When the fire was going strong, Strait took the two cans of Sawdust where he'd set them on the ground and handed one to Duane.

"So you're a cop?" he said.

+++

Two hours, some good barbecue, and several beers later, they were seated on plastic chairs in the yard, laughing like old friends.

"Gotta say it, James," said Duane. "When Julie talked about you, I hacked you all wrong, Bruh. I thought you were some stuck-up New York fed, but you're a homeboy." He slapped James's leg.

Julie laughed. "I told you he was a good guy. Everyone's says he's a fucking hero and shit, but he still acts just like a regular guy."

"I'm not a hero."

"See? He's humble."

"Really. I didn't do anything."

"That *Newsweek* article says different."

Duane gulped down beer and said, "Guess I'm the only one in this town ain't read that article yet. I didn't know anything about you. Why didn't you tell me before, Jules?"

"I didn't even know he was in town until two days ago, and I hardly ever see you. You're always at the bar and when you get home, I'm already asleep."

Duane nudged Strait with his elbow. “Women! Can’t live with’em, can’t fuck without’em!”

Strait gazed at the stars.

They’d spent much of their time talking about Julie and James’s childhood. He tried to get Duane to talk about his new job at the police department, but with little luck. Strait had also responded laconically to questions about the FBI battle with the cult and his subsequent time in the hospital, his shot-up leg and his upcoming disability proceedings. Duane seemed transfixed as Strait described the horrors of Meniere’s disease. Strongly affected, he exhaled heavily after Strait was finished.

“Sometimes it’s the smallest things that make the biggest fucking problems,” he said.

Duane kept drinking, heavier and faster than Julie and James. He was tilting back and forth unsteadily in his yard chair. Early on, after Strait had finished two beers, he had experienced an ominous shudder of the ground, so he stopped drinking. He was still nursing the mostly-full third can of beer he’d opened an hour before.

He said, “So, been hearing about this missing girl.”

“Missing girl?”

“You know, that girl that went missing a few months ago? The one they’re protesting about. Some people are saying she’s still alive.”

“Oh, that black chick. Yeah, people are full of shit.”

“Oh?”

Duane sneered. “Only ones sayin’ she’s alive is the blacks! They’re sayin’ she’s alive and Chief Kladspell’s covering it up. What bullshit.”

“So you think she’s dead?”

“Of course she’s dead. And I know who done her, too. Her

terrorist father. All the guys at the station think so."

"I heard he has an alibi."

"Yeah, a friend covering for him. But that don't mean shit. Except now we can't touch him, because the guy giving the alibi is some big shot dude at the university. Well, excuse me, *professor*, but some of the boys at the station still believe in justice, and they're…" Duane's voice trailed off and he glanced at Strait warily.

"What?"

"It's not me, understand? But some of the guys are pissed off we can't bust that motherfucker."

Strait smiled. "So some are thinking of giving her father some sideways justice?"

"You didn't hear that from me."

"Nah. Understandable. You guys did all that work to catch the bad guys, and then the fucking law stops you from doing your job. You all have obviously done all you could to investigate her disappearance. It sucks. I mean, like, how many guys did you have down there processing the crime scene at the river? Must've been three or four of you at least. Overtime too, right?"

"Oh. Yeah. Sure. Only two of us, though."

"Two CSIs?"

"What?"

"You know. CSIs. Crime scene investigators. With those white whole-body spacesuit things?"

"Oh, like that TV show."

"Right. Except you know the TV show is full of shit."

"Um, yeah, sure, of course. Me and my partner was the ones who answered the first call."

"Who called it in?"

"Some guy. A hiker."

"Did you guys get to interview him?"

"No, he called it in anonymous from a payphone. And hung up."

"Too bad. So just two uniformed plus how many CSIs?"

Duane looked puzzled. "We don't have none of them guys. Just us two. There was lots of blood."

"You saw the blood?"

"Oh, yeah, Bruh. It was *sick*. I took some pictures with my smartphone."

"Your smartphone?"

Duane chuckled. "Yeah. Want to see?" He removed the phone from his coat pocket, flipped through some photos, and handed the phone to Strait. They depicted the same spot Strait had visited, but this time, the center part of the area he'd explored was red. The blood was pooled in one place and not splashed around. He scrolled through more pictures that were taken from different angles.

He handed the phone back and took a sip of his beer. "I thought I read in the paper the rain washed away all the blood."

"Yeah, a couple minutes after we got there, a big storm hit. Just slammed us to shit. Big hailstones, whole nine yards. We had to run to our car and hightail it out of there. When we came back the next morning, the blood was all washed away."

Strait sat silently staring at the beer can in his hand.

"But the chief said there wasn't no need to take any blood anyway," continued Duane. "Plain as day what happened. Her father, that white-hating Muslim terrorist, chimped out and killed her. Dress all knifed up, the same one her sister said she was wearing when she went missing. Had the name of the school on it. And a headless fucking teddy bear that her sister said was hers."

"Why her father?"

"His character. He's got a violent temper. They got him on a domestic couple years back. Put his wife in a mental hospital, I heard. Not to mention he was in prison for bombing a building, for fuck's sake. He's the only one could've done it."

Strait nodded thoughtfully.

"Why are you so interested in that nigger girl anyway?"

"Honey," cautioned Julie. "Don't use words like that."

"Why not? James a Bruh."

"But he might get the wrong idea."

Duane held his hand to his heart. "Excuse me for my political incorrectness! Why are you so interested in that sweet little African American girl-child?"

Strait shrugged. "Just curious."

The phone rang inside. "That's probably my mom," said Julie, and she went into the house.

For a time they sat in silence. Duane finished a beer, made a show of crushing the can with one hand, and opened another one. He belched and slapped James on the knee. "You're like the smartest fucking bro in the world."

"I am?"

"You got out of this shit-ass town, didn't you? All the way up to the FBI! What did you do there?"

"I was assigned to SWAT, which is a part-time gig. And they let me teach a domestic terrorism class at the academy over the summer. Other than that, I worked as a regular agent at the field office."

"Was it a good job?"

"I want it back."

"You boys getting along okay?" Julie, standing at the doorway.

"Blood brother lawmen talking shop," said Strait.

"That was my mom. She remembers you and says welcome back to town."

A powerful jolt shook Strait. He grabbed the arms of his chair.

"Hey, what's wrong?" Julie said.

"I'd better go." said Strait, rising. His heart jumped as the patio shook violently. The roar in his ear leaped in volume. "I need to go back to the hotel."

"Oh, no," said Julie. "You're having an attack?"

"The first symptoms. It's better I get into my bed with the lights off and try to stop the attack from starting. Or be ready when it hits."

"You want to lie down here? You can use our bed."

"Not a good idea. You saw what it's like when I have an attack. I throw up on everything."

"Oh, that's okay." She pointed at Duane. "So does he."

"I really need go back to the hotel now. Sorry."

"Can you get out to the car okay?"

Strait stood carefully and took a few steps. Difficult but possible.

Duane rose too and lunged at Strait and gave him a bear hug, which for a few seconds catapulted his world into a seesawing frenzy.

"I love you, brother," said Duane, exhaling a thick beery reek on his neck. Strait held his breath and willed himself to slap Duane hard on the back a couple of times, a bro-backslap, although even a momentary touch of this man made him sick.

Chapter Twelve

They rode back to town in Julie's car with the windows wide open. Cool evening air blew on Strait's face. The impending attack dissipated. Julie wanted to walk him to his room, but he told her truthfully that he could make it by himself. By the time he got to his room, he was feeling like he'd dodged a bullet.

In front of his doorway, he found a paper bag with a note, written in flowing cursive: *Drink this instead of that garbage you have now. -Katherine.* Inside the paper bag was a plastic one: five pounds of imported Columbian coffee. And a separate container of coffee filters. Strait smelled the coffee through the bag. Heaven.

He turned on his computer and plugged in the LAN cable. Small town hotel, no wifi. He dialed into a VPN server he'd set up under a fake name through University of Amsterdam computer department. From there, he linked to a website in Germany and signed into another VPN server he'd set up there under a different fake name. He then used that VPN to connect to a server in Costa Rica, from which he signed into a Skype account.

Easy privacy chain to break if someone at the agency were very motivated, but it was the best he could do without using the FBI's own security architecture. Strait put on some headphones and adjusted the microphone over his mouth. The signal purred a few times and an answering machine picked up.

"You have reached the magnificent abode of Graham Footer. If you're a friend, leave a message after the tone. If you are not, and this in particular refers to telephone sales people, bugger off."

The line beeped and Strait said, "Graham?"

The phone clicked. "James?"

"Yes."

"It's splendid to hear your voice. I was thinking of calling you to see how you've been faring since you moved to…Costa Rica?"

"I'm not really in Costa Rica. I'm in Pine River."

"What's with the cloak-and-dagger, James?"

"Maybe not needed, but I've got a situation down here. A nine-year-old African American girl went missing. There's talk in town that the police are racist and not doing a proper investigation. After talking to the police chief and one of his officers, I'm starting to believe it's true."

"Aren't you supposed to be resting?"

"I am, but this thing kind of fell in my lap." Strait told him the whole story, from his turbulent arrival in Pine River to Eliza's asking him to help find Jophia Williams to Chief Kladspell's threatening to throw him in jail to Duane showing him pictures of the crime scene on his phone. He was careful to say nothing about sending Graham the blood samples.

"Wow. Quite an active a couple of days."

"You can say that again."

"Your Mr. Kladspell seems the paragon of incompetence."

"Either that or he's hiding something."

"To be sure, James, this is all very upsetting. But you're not on active duty, are you?"

"I guess not."

"Of course you're not. You're on medical leave. On top of that, this case is out of FBI jurisdiction."

"I know. But…"

"You're supposed to be convalescing."

"I know all that, but…"

"So why on Earth are you investigating this case?"

“I still can’t get it out of my head that Kladspell refused to look at the samples I brought him. What kind of cop does something like that?”

“A stupid one.”

“And what kind of cop would take photos of a crime scene on his personal smartphone and show the pictures to a stranger at a party?”

“Another stupid one.”

“So…”

“You could pave the world with stupid cops and missing girls, but that doesn’t mean you need to get involved with them.”

“You know, Graham, all that’s needed is for the DNA in the blood I found to be matched with the girl’s DNA for us to say confidently that she was murdered.”

“Just from a statistical point of view, you could say that now.”

“Much more confidently. Confidently enough for me not to worry that the girl is still alive out there.”

“But…”

“And as one who works in forensics, wouldn’t it interest you to know the results of analyses of the blood and the maggots and flies from the crime scene?”

“Moderately, but…”

“Excellent! Because, guess what? I mailed you samples of both.”

“What?”

“Expedited cold-pack. They’ll be on your desk in the morning.”

“Um, James?”

“Yes?”

"Have you heard nothing I've said? I'm always thrilled to receive maggots from you, but we're not permitted to do this. Even if we were, I have a backlog of samples I still need to analyze before I could even get to yours."

"Can't you just slip it through?"

"'Slip it through'? Do you hear yourself talking? Every analysis is logged and tracked. Reports are written and filed in the offices from whence the investigations are conducted. We have a *system.*"

"Are you sure there isn't a way? For an old friend?"

"I could get fired."

"Not if you're careful."

"It would take me a month."

"No way to expedite it?"

"What would be the point?"

"The point would be to determine whether or not the blood actually came from the girl."

"It probably did."

"But there's a whole community here who thinks the girl is still alive. This would put their doubts to rest."

"Do you even have the girl's DNA profile to compare this with?"

"A loose end I need to tie up. I'm planning to visit her father to get something. Maybe I can send you some hair?"

"James, this is dubious in so many ways. And as I said, I have a backlog of other samples I need to…"

"I'm guessing those other samples are from victims who are already dead."

"Ah!"

"What do you mean, ah?"

"I mean, ah! As in, ah! I suddenly understand the real reason behind your interest in this case."

"You don't."

"You feel guilty."

"I don't."

"You do."

"This has nothing to do with…"

"That girl was also nine years old…"

"No connection."

"You're attempting to compensate."

"Bullshit."

"For the girl. And for Amelia."

"Bullshit, Graham."

"None of that was your fault, James."

"It has nothing to do with that! There's a principle at hand here."

"Which is?"

"If the girl is still alive, someone might still be able to save her."

"And you're the designated hero, is that it?"

"Please, Graham. You know I don't think that."

"This little girl wasn't thrown in your path by fate. You have a choice here."

"I know."

"You just feel guilty."

"You're wrong."

Silence on the other end of the line.

"And her best friend begged me to search for her."

Silence.

"She's just a kid, Graham. Like you said, nine years old."

Silence.

"How old is your daughter?"

"Oh, fuck a duck, alright! It's only my career on the line, so why not?"

"Graham Footer, you're a God."

"Yes, yes."

"They should make you King. And replace that other schmuck on the throne now. That…what's his name?"

"Elizabeth."

"That's the one."

"She's a queen, not a king."

"That's what I mean."

"James, it's been lovely as always. I'll be in touch."

"Seriously, I owe you big for this."

"I think we both know the truth is that I owe *you*. We all do. Which is one reason I'm going ahead with this."

"Whatever. Let me know what you find out."

"I shall. And James?"

"Yes?"

"Stay safe."

Chapter Thirteen

The dream always started with Amelia. In the van peppered with bullets. Particles of pulverized glass suspended and twinkling in the air. Strait kicks out remains of the windshield and he and Amelia dive out and roll over the hood. A bone-shuddering explosion lifts the van. It's not the explosion that melts him but the look on Amelia's face. That glazed-over, confused look. Like she doesn't understand where she is.

In the dream he knows the reason for that look, but at the time it really happened, he didn't—or did he? That a bullet had snapped into her body through a gap in her vest. But the pain hadn't quite burned in yet. All she felt were those weird, intangible sensations you sometimes get in the first seconds—the freezing, clammy skin, the nebulous awareness of unbalance—after your guts have been torn to bits.

She was dying. And he left her.

Then he's in the cold basement of the compound, his leg spouting blood. He's propped up with the metal pole. The child glaring up at him. Her finger on the device that will release the poison. His finger on the trigger of the gun pointing at her.

Please don't, little girl. I just want to help you.

Liar!

He jolted awake up in a sweat, heart pounding, nauseous, the room quaking, the girl's accusing face welded into his mind's eye.

He got out of bed and padded across the carpet to the bathroom. He showered and dressed, his ear hissing like a snake. After his shower, he headed out for the Pot Belly Café. Carol wasn't behind the counter. The younger waitress was there. She served him coffee and took his order.

The café was almost deserted. Only one other person in the place, an old lady in a wheelchair on the other side of the room, sipping delicately from a cup of tea and gnawing on a toasted bagel.

As he waited for his food, he ran all he knew about the disappearance of Jophia Williams through his mind. How had she been kidnapped? What kind of person would have taken her and why? According to what Katherine had told him, Jophia almost certainly hadn't been kidnapped by a family member, because no family members were involved in her life outside of her father and older sister. She insisted that Marvin Williams had no motivation to hurt his daughter and wasn't capable of doing so anyway. She said that Williams "couldn't hurt a fly" and swore her husband was with him the day Jophia vanished. Kladspell and Duane painted a completely different picture of Marvin Williams. According to them, Jophia's father was a dangerous, terroristic psycho. Who was right? Next on Strait's list of things to do was pay Marvin Williams a visit.

In a way, he hoped it somehow still turned out to be a family abduction. Because statistically, the other prominent possibility was far worse. Stranger abductions of children almost always were done by pedophiles.

Jophia vanished on May twenty-seventh, sometime between 1:30 and 2:30. According to Katherine, she always rode her bicycle to and from school on Sower Road. Sower cut through the industrial zone on the other side of the railroad tracks before traversing a region mostly empty except for forest, then continued up into the southern foothills where she lived. Three men standing outside a biker bar in the industrial zone said they'd seen her riding her bicycle that day at about 1:50. The men's alibis checked out.

Her bicycle hadn't been found, suggesting that the kidnapper had taken it, which implied he had driven a vehicle large enough to throw the bicycle in quickly. Maybe a pick-up truck with an open bed. Or a van. Another possibility was the perpetrator had hidden in the trees and jumped out at her while she passed. And hidden the bicycle in the forest. Maybe hidden her body there too.

Had the police searched the forest? He hadn't had a chance to ask Kladspell, and it seemed unlikely he'd get a chance to ask him now.

The strangest aspect of the case was that no trace at all had been found of the girl for six whole months. Then, all of a sudden, the gory scene at the river had been discovered. The anonymous hiker had phoned it in at about 4:00, and Duane and his partner had arrived at about 5:30, when it was already getting dark and a storm was about to hit. *Took you long enough, you racist alcoholic shit.* Duane wasn't carrying so much as a rudimentary forensics kit and possessed no knowledge of how to use one even if he had.

"You look deep in thought."

"Huh?"

The waitress was standing there with a tray of food.

"Just daydreaming," he said. He moved his arms from the table so she could set her food down.

"I like thoughtful guys." She smiled at him and walked away.

Strait jabbed a fork into his eggs and took a bite and continued to think. So the lazy officers returned after the storm and stuffed the dress and headless teddy bear in plastic bags, almost certainly without bothering to wear gloves. If in the off chance DNA or hair could be found on the clothes that signaled who the criminal was, his lawyer could now easily get a judge to throw out the evidence.

He took a bite of egg and sipped at his coffee. *Okay, screw the evidence*. Go back to motive. Whatever the perp wanted to do to the girl, he'd taken his sweet time about it. Six months.

"Morning, soldier."

Strait looked across to find Gus Bear seated at his usual place. Little Bear.

"I didn't notice you come in."

"I was in the toilet taking a dump." said Gus. "Part of my morning routine. Taking a dump at the Pot Belly."

"I see."

"You look like you're thinking so hard smoke's set to come out your ears."

"I was wondering what to get a friend for her birthday."

"Must be a hard friend to buy for."

"You could say that."

"Hey, your friend Julie called me up. Said you want a car."

"I do."

"I got one in now, runs fine. Why don't you and me go to the shop after breakfast and give her a look? If you like her, we can take a dip over at the bank, and she'll be all yours before lunchtime."

"Sounds great."

Gus's vehicle was a tow truck. A suitably nasty one for a guy engaged in the low end of auto dealings. A grinding boat of rust. The yellow paint on the heavily dented body was pocked and scratched and Gus drove with the tow-chain hanging so low it swung perilously when he made turns. The passenger door squeaked painfully when Strait opened it and needed to be slammed hard to get it closed all the way. The thick cushions on the seats were so soft they threatened to swallow Strait alive. They were covered with polyethylene that was scarred with cigarette burns. It was clear from the heaps of drink cups and cheeseburger wrappers in the space between the seats and the back of the cab that Gus enjoyed eating his lunches sitting in the driver's seat and flinging the wrappers over his shoulder into the back.

Little Bear drove south on Sower Road while indulging in a rant against all manner of thorns in his side, ranging from the dog shit he'd nearly stepped on that morning to his goddamned runny eggs at the café to the evil federal government, which to his mind had enabled creeping Shariah law for eight years and was only now beginning to repair that damage. He finally noticed Strait's silence.

"Hey, big man. You listening to me?"

"Isn't this the same road that Jophia Williams was riding on when she disappeared?"

Gus gaped around like he was just realizing they were on a road.

"Yeah, probably. 'Cause we used to see that little black girl bicycling by our shop almost every day on the way up the hill."

Strait turned to look at Gus. "Your shop is on Sower Road?"

"Sure. That's where we're headed." Gus gestured through the windshield. "Up there about a mile."

"You knew the girl?"

"I wouldn't go so far's to say I *knew* the girl, but she come by the shop a lot. Sweet kid. Real friendly. My brother Keith sometimes gave her a cup of water. Why?"

Strait stared at him.

"Woe there, FBI! You caught me!" Gus Bear grinned and made a show of putting his hands up, then quickly put them back on the steering wheel.

Strait didn't smile.

"Seriously, soldier. I had nothing to do with that. My brothers neither."

Strait continued to stare at him.

Gus stuttered, "We weren't even there. At least me and Lennon. We went up to our mother's house. Keith was running the shop that day. And the police came by and checked the surveillance camera out front." Gus started to look openly scared. "You don't really think we had anything to do with this, do you?"

"No."

"Jesus." Gus put a hand to his heart. "Had me damn near to pissing my pants. With all due respect, because I know you're one of the rare good ones, I live in fear of what the damned government's going to pull on me next. First, they took my house and gave it to my ex-wife, then they hit me with a shitload of back taxes. But I'd never hurt a child, I got two girls of my own. Just the idea of it is too…"

"I don't think you did it."

"Good."

"Do you visit your mother a lot?"

"She's old. Needs help around the house. I go up there most days, and Lennon too. We rotate."

"How about Keith?"

"He don't go up there much. He gets carsick from the drive. He does help out at the farmer's market, though."

"You sell at the farmer's market? I thought you did cars."

"You know everyone out here's got a big garden. We pool together our extras to sell. There's a regular one our way. They run it out of the parking lot at that animal processing place. You know it?"

"Vaguely. My father took me up there once or twice after we went hunting."

"How about your mother? You see her much?"

"My mom died when I was a teenager. Cancer."

"Sorry to hear that."

They drove in silence. Strait took in the industrial region. Gritty metal buildings. Rust and smokestacks. Trash blowing around on the street, machine parts on the sidewalk. Painted signs faded so much from smoke and age you could barely read them. Pine River Recycling. Farge's Bottles. R & L Tool and Dye. Magic Aluminum. A bar called Cruds with about a dozen Harleys parked out front. A message stenciled in red on the front wall: NO CLUB COLORS INSIDE.

Six blocks later they emerged onto a stretch of two-lane road with pristine pine forest on either side. They drove for another couple of minutes without seeing any other vehicles. *This is probably where she was taken. Somewhere along this strip.*

The road began to slope upwards and the auto shop appeared on the right side. It was the only building visible in either direction. It seemed to have been carved out of the forest. It was marked by a roadside plank sign mounted across two wooden poles: BEAR BROTHERS AUTO SHOP. It was a single-floor building with an office entrance on the left and an open bay on the right large enough to fit two cars. One vehicle was raised on a hydraulic lift and a man was standing under it with a big wrench. He nodded at Gus as they drove in.

Gus steered the tow truck around to the back of the building, where an unpaved space had been cleared of trees. About ten cars were parked there. Gus pulled in and he and Strait got out and walked around front. The repair area was strewn with oily auto parts. The walls were covered with posters of half-naked women and hunting shots of armed men showing animals they'd killed. Gus said to the man standing under the car, "Lennon. This guy's thinking of buying that station wagon."

The man called Lennon was a giant. Despite the cool autumn temperature, he wore only a plain, oil-splotched white t-shirt. His head was shaved. He was so tall he needed to bend to avoid hitting his head on the lifted car. He was at least three inches taller than Strait, which moved him close to seven feet. His t-shirt molded his huge shoulders and thickly muscled chest and stomach so with each movement you could see every crevice and bulge rolling under the fabric.

"Good to meet you." Lennon had a soft voice and gentle smile that was out of sync with his Herculean build. "Sorry for not shaking your hand, but..." he held his hands up to show how oily they were.

Strait nodded and Gus said, "Keith, my other brother, is in the shop office. I'll introduce you." He opened the door leading from the garage to the other room and gestured Strait through.

Strait was startled by how orderly the office was. Unlike the chaos and filth next door, this room was antiseptically clean. The polished wooden desk was tidy. A receipt pad and appointment book were arranged neatly on the surface, along with several sharpened pencils. Next to them was a well-worn copy of the Holy Bible. No computer. No posters on the walls of lively girls or dead deer. Seated stiffly behind the desk was a man in a neatly pressed suit with a red bowtie.

"This here's my brother, Keith. Keith, this is James Strait. He's interested in that Country Squire."

Keith Bear had short brown hair marbled with grey, parted meticulously on the side. The lips that formed his small mouth were so thin they were nearly invisible. His chin jugged forward substantially and had upon its protruding tip a deep cleft like a miniature set of buttocks. He studied Strait without offering a greeting, his eyes obscured by the glint of his glasses.

"Strait here used to be with the FBI."

"Is that so?"

Gus laughed. "He scared the bejesus out of me on the way up here when he pointed out that little black girl went missing on the same road our shop is on. I told him you were the only one at the shop that day 'cause me and Lennon was up at Mama's."

Keith stared up at Strait with a look of unsettling intensity. "You don't think I had anything to do with that, do you, Mr. Strait?"

"No."

"Because I didn't."

"I understand."

"That little girl was nothing but a ray of sunshine to me. A real child of God. Why anyone would want to hurt her surpasses my reckoning."

"Did she come by here often?"

"I saw her ride past almost every day. While I was standing here in this very spot, tending to the shop finances. I would always see her at the same time, three-fifteen p.m., or maybe three-sixteen or three-seventeen, right through that window. While she made her way up that hill yonder, pumping away on her bicycle. On three occasions, she came in to request water, and once she requested to use our facilities to relieve herself. Poor, poor girl."

"Did you see her on the day she disappeared?"

"I did not."

"Any opinions about what happened to her?"

Keith Bear seemed to be struggling with some interior turbulence. He scrunched up his face and ran his fingers over his scalp. "Most likely it was some goddamned pervert. That road out there branches a little farther on to the state highway and continues onwards to Phoenix. It would be a simple matter for some goddamned pervert to discover a girl by herself afoot on the road, snatch her up, and disappear. This country is crawling with such goddamned perverts. That is my thinking on the matter." Keith nodded as though in agreement with himself.

"Why did she ride her bicycle on the road? Isn't there a school bus to take her home?"

Gus said, "there's one for kids who go to Southside Elementary, which is the one she's supposed to go to. But her father wanted to mix his child with those others at that fancy new school east of town."

"You mean the Montessori school?"

"I don't know what they call it. A lot of folks think it was her father that done her."

"You know her father?"

"I sold him a car once. I treat him respectful to his face, but most folks think he's crazy."

"If it was her father, wouldn't he have to grab her somewhere down the hill from here? I mean, before she passed here. Keith didn't see her that day."

Keith cleared his throat. "It's also possible she rode past when I was out back inventorying. Or perhaps while I was relieving myself in the toilet."

"What about the car you have for sale?"

"It's an '82 Ford station wagon. The price is 300 dollars."

"I want to see it."

Keith gestured with his buttocks-chin toward the back door. Gus led them out to the lot. The station wagon was at the end of the row of other old cars and trucks. Gus flipped out a batch of keys from his pocket and opened the driver's door. "1982 Four-door Ford

Country Squire. A real classic."

The car was sided with brown-red paneling in a field of tan. The dashboard was beige and the steering wheel was inset with a rectangle of faux dark brown wood. It had an old-style AM-FM radio and a pull-out knob for the headlights.

"It looks like it's about to exhale its last breath," said Strait.

"I'll allow she's been around the block once or twice. She's got over 150,000 miles on her. But I personally like this car because she's got a story."

"A story?"

"It was a family car. The Brysons. A mom, a dad, two kids, a boy and a girl. We actually sold this car to them about three years ago. Good folks. About two months back, they were coming home from a little league game. All happy. The boy's team won. And they were crossing an intersection over there on Pine and Walnut when this drunk driver come out of nowhere, ran the red light, and slammed into them. Mrs. Bryson, she was killed instantly, and the other three died of their injuries within twenty-four hours." Gus gestured to the passenger side. "We tried to clean it up, but a good cosmetic would end up making the car cost a few thousand, easy. Hardly worth it."

On the right side was a rough patchwork job, where the destroyed door had been replaced by an unpainted one, and a side panel of a different color than the rest of the body had been installed. The area around the paneling was still dented and scratched.

"That's a terrible story."

"Yeah. But the trick is that this car? We ended up hauling it over here and I figured we'd sell it for scrap because it was *destroyed.* The whole car flipped over and hit a light post. Its back end and most of the frame underneath were bashed up practically beyond saving. But Lennon? That big boy noticed that we just happened to have the same kind of frame in the pile out back. And he got it into his head that night he'd save the car."

"Save it? Like…a patient?"

"Lennon's a little funny up here." Gus tapped himself on the forehead.

Funny compared to Keith? Strait thought.

"So Lennon stayed up all night working on the car. He cleaned it up and set the whole thing right just from the throwaways we had lying around. At exactly the time the sun rose, he took it out for a test drive up the hill. Chugged and coughed a little, but otherwise she ran fine again."

"A resurrection."

After completing the paperwork at the bank, Strait drove his new station wagon back to the hotel.

Chapter Fourteen

Strait parked the car on the side street just outside the patio entrance of his hotel room. He went in and showered and dressed. At 5:30, a knock came at his door. Strait opened it and Katherine was there in the hallway, a big smile on her face. She wore a light blue nurse's uniform.

"Look at our shy hero! You were half dead last time I saw you. Now you look only about twenty percent dead."

"You really are a nurse."

"Did you get that coffee I left for you?"

"Yes. Thanks. I had some this morning."

"It was better than the hotel crap, wasn't it?"

"Much better. Is wine okay?"

"Okay for what?"

"For the party tonight?"

She chuckled. "I thought you meant to drink in the morning instead of coffee. Sure, Honey, wine is fine."

The sun was close to the horizon and Pine River park was falling into shadows. Chill wind was picking up and clouds edged with purple-black were rafting across the sky and leaves were dropping steadily from the trees. The sun slanted light that caught the leaves as they fell and sparked off them, creating the look of fireflies dropping dead.

As they crossed the parking lot, Katherine hunched against the cold holding the collar of her uniform closed. Strait pointed out the car he'd bought that day. An expression of disgust appeared on Katherine's face. "We'll take mine," she said. Her car was a shiny new red Nissan. As they buckled in, she said, "My husband and I share this car, but he usually lets me drive it because he likes to ride his bicycle to work."

"You said he's a professor, right?"

"Yes. At the university. He's an expert on our species, but he still can't cook worth a damn."

"There was no university when I lived here."

"Northern Arizona University put in a satellite branch. I guess it was built after you left town to do all that hero stuff. My husband's looking forward to meeting you. They all are."

"They?"

She had been driving northwest toward an area not far from where he had grown up. An upper middle class, family-friendly residential area. Strait continually glanced around at the surrounding terrain, a habit he'd picked up in Afghanistan, and he noticed a black motorcycle behind them.

"Is something wrong?" asked Katherine.

"No. So, who's coming to your party?"

"Lots of folks. They're coming to meet you, James."

"Meet me?"

"Relax. No one will make you not be reticent."

Strait took a furtive look out the sideview mirror. The motorcycle was gone.

"So, I talked to Pastor Jessie. She told me that you and she went to the river. And that you had visited Chief Kladspell."

"I visited him twice."

Strait told her about how his find of blood samples at the river had led to his return to Kladspell's office and how the chief had responded.

"That man is a horror," said Katherine.

"His handling of the case is a horror, I can say that for sure. I don't know if it's because of incompetence or something else."

"He's hiding something, sure as day."

"Maybe. Will the girl's father be there tonight?"

"Jophia's father?"

"Yes. Kladspell didn't have a high opinion of him."

"A more misunderstood soul, you will not find. No, Marvin will not be there tonight. He refuses to come to town anymore."

"Because…?"

"Because he's unfairly denigrated by almost everyone. So, you said you found some blood samples at the river but Chief Kladspell won't accept them. What will you do with them?"

"I sent them to a friend to have a look at what's in them. Just between you and me, I'm not supposed to do that. And I need to tell you that it's very likely the only thing he'll find is that the DNA from the blood matches Jophia's DNA. Which will make it virtually certain she's dead."

Katherine didn't respond.

"One reason I wanted to talk to her father is to find out if he might have anything that has her DNA on it. Maybe hair, maybe something else. I guess if he doesn't come to town, I need to go to him."

"You don't want to go out there alone. I'm off tomorrow, so I can take you."

"You don't need to do that."

"Yes, I do," she responded with that stubborn set to her voice that Strait had already learned meant she wouldn't take no for an answer.

"Okay."

"Marvin's scared of strangers. If he sees you coming, he'll probably run into the forest. And his older daughter's downright dangerous with a shotgun and won't be shy about using it on a big, white stranger. It will help if I'm there."

"Okay, thanks."

"By the way, Pastor Jessie will be at the party."

"I know." His heart did a little trill at the sound of her name.

"I'm given to understand," said Katherine, "that she and you are now an item."

Strait stiffened. "An item? We had one conversation."

"But there's chemistry, am I correct?"

"Chemistry?"

"Chemistry. Of the organic kind? Between you and Jessie. Oh! By the way, I hope you're not allergic to rabbits."

The home of Katherine Nabors was a medium-sized two-story Tudor with a modest front yard of manicured grass and tidy flower boxes under the windows. The door of the two-car garage opened automatically as they drove in and Katherine parked and they climbed out. The front door of the house was open. The burble of many voices seeped into the evening air.

Katherine led the way into the entrance hallway, Glass-covered photographs, all black and white, hung in metal frames on both walls. They were shot with remarkable artistry and the subject matter of every one was Katherine and her daughter Eliza. One depicted Katherine pushing the girl very high on a park swing, the image of Ellie blurred subtly in its motion as she shrieked with laughter, while at the same instant the photographer had captured the expression of anxiety on the mother's face as she looked up at the nearly airborne child. Another picture showed mother and daughter smiling brightly at the camera, faces pressed together, seemed to capture joy in its essence.

"Who's the photographer?" Strait asked.

"That would be me," said a man who appeared at the other

end of the hallway.

"This is my husband, Francis. Francis, this is James Strait."

"Nice to meet you, James." They shook hands.

Francis Nabors was a tall, dignified man in his forties with a scrupulously trimmed beard. He wore glasses with thin, dark plastic frames and a three-piece tweed suit.

"These pictures are great."

Katherine smiled up at her husband. "They would be better if he'd vary his subject matter a little."

"But my whole universe is in those two faces," said Francis. "Welcome to our home, James. Or should I call you Jim?"

"Either way's okay. But most folks call me James."

"I recognize you from the magazine cover. Please come in and meet the others. And help yourself to some food and drink."

The living room was spacious enough to accommodate the twenty or so guests who were seated on the three long, beige sofas or milling about a banquet-sized food table at the far wall in twos and threes, wine glasses or beer bottles and plates of food in hand. Lively conversations were in flow. The people looked to be similar in age, mostly thirties and forties, but their clothes represented huge differences in economic class. Some were dressed in suits and ties or formal dresses, others in casual department store clothes, and some wore what seemed like the stuff homeless people would pick up for a quarter at a thrift store. Most of the guests were black.

A few people cast glances at Strait and their eyes widened in recognition. An elderly, cadaverously thin Asian man rose from a sofa and approached. He adjusted his wire spectacles with a bony hand and peered up at Strait.

"Hello?" he said.

Strait reached down and shook the old man's small hand.

“It is nice to meet you.” The man had a strong Japanese accent.

“Nice to meet you too, Mr….?”

Katherine put in. “This is Dr. Junichiro Watanabe. He’s chief of staff at the hospital ENT unit. He is a specialist in Meniere’s disease.”

Only a few white side-creeping hairs clung to the man’s head. The clothes he wore, crisp blue jeans and a long-sleeved button-up shirt with wide blue and white stripes running horizontally, had such a vibrancy of color and stiffness of texture that Strait thought he must have bought them at Walmart and thrown them on in the car on his way to the party. The man was sufficiently short that the top of his head was at about the same level as Strait’s ribcage.

A young Asian woman came up and stood next to the old man. “He’s more than a specialist,” she said. Her words had no hint of Japanese accent. “He wrote the book on Meniere’s disease. Or the best one, anyway.”

“And you are…?” Strait asked.

“I’m Rina Watanabe,” she responded as she shook his hand. “I’m also a doctor. And I’m his granddaughter.”

Rina Watanabe was taller than her grandfather. She seemed to be in her mid-twenties, slender in a well-exercised kind of way. She had a seriousness of bearing that seemed old for someone so young.

Katherine said, “she works on my unit. The best children’s doctor in the state. She’s the reason I got to know Dr. Watanabe, senior.”

“She’s attempting to deflect attention from her being the best nurse at the hospital,” Rina said.

A girl flew up out of nowhere, pigtails bouncing. She was

wearing a T-shirt with the little Mexican boy from *Coco*.

"James!"

"I think you've already met my daughter, Eliza."

Strait beamed down at the girl and she smiled back up at him and pranced a little on her toes.

"Sorry I called you a liar."

"It's okay."

The elderly Dr. Watanabe had not stopped staring fixedly up at Strait.

"Damn," he said. "You *big*."

"Let's not make James feel conspicuous, doctor," said Katherine.

"You a goddamned *giant*. How tall are you?"

"I'm not sure."

The old doctor spoke in a commanding voice. "You come into my office Monday morning. Seven o'clock sharp. We do tests on your ear. And measure how tall too."

"Um…"

"No um. You got somewhere to be, tall man?"

"Um…"

"You got job? No? Good, decided. Nurse Katherine here bring you." With that, the aged doctor walked spryly off toward the sofas, his granddaughter at his side.

Strait stared at the doctor and Eliza yanked his hand.

"You aren't a liar. You're helping find my friend now."

"Mr. Strait is doing what he can, Eliza," said Katherine. "But he can't make any promises."

Eliza saw something by the front door and she brightened. She waved her hand at three other girls about the same age who had just entered the house with their parents. Without another word, she sprinted over to them and the other girls broke away from their own adults and were soon deep in chatter.

"Oh, look who else is at the door. Your new girlfriend." said Katherine.

"Katherine."

"Chemistry."

Pastor Jessie was at the door, scanning the room. Her eyes lighted on James and she smiled. Katherine lowered her voice. "James and Jessie sittin' in a tree…"

"Kathy!" said Pastor Jessie as she walked up to them. She hugged Katherine. "Thanks so much for inviting me and look at this banquet! You ever consider quitting that nursing job and going into catering instead?"

"No, I haven't. Especially since I paid a caterer to set all that up and didn't make even one dish."

The two woman laughed while Strait stood there. Then Katherine said, "I better see how they're doing in the kitchen." And vanished.

Jessie was wearing blue jeans and a blue sweater. She wore no make-up. She glanced at Strait, a little nervous, a little shy, a little excited. She wore her frizzy hair untied so it fell fluffed up and chaotic over her shoulders. Strait thought maybe in his entire life he'd never seen a woman more attractive.

"Hello, James."

"Evening, Pastor."

"You look nice."

"You do too."

People kept showing up at the front door. There were now about thirty guests. Jessie and James maneuvered through to the food table. On one end were over a dozen appetizers, including tiny cocktail wieners wrapped in browned dough, grilled mushrooms stuffed with a kind of pate made with ham, cream cheese and garlic, mashed potatoes swimming with butter, baked clams in orange sauce, crispy zucchini wedges with streams of miso sauce, and spicy chicken wings. On the other end was a cornucopia of entrees, including honey glazed chicken, roasted peppers, some kind of spicy Chinese beef dish, grilled salmon. Strait wanted to dive headfirst in it all with his mouth wide open.

"You hungry?" asked Jessie.

"I am now."

Strait got a plate and utensils and followed the pastor in piling up his dish with samplings of almost every choice. Then, seemingly by magic, a small hand materialized out of thin air and its fingers, as warty, weathered, and strong as the talons of an eagle, grabbed him by the wrist. He felt his hand twisted away from the gravy he was on the verge of pouring onto his mashed potatoes.

Dr. Watanabe senior was glaring up at him. "No salt!" he said.

Strait was dumbstruck.

"With Meniere's, you cannot eat salt. All this here," Watanabe stroked the flattened shape of his hand like a blade over the food table while still restraining Strait's wrist with his other in a grip that seemed supernaturally strong for a man his age and size, "filled with salt."

"What?" said Strait.

"Salt!" Watanabe started pointing at each dish down the line, saying with each jab of his finger, "Salt! salt! salt! salt! salt! salt!"

Watanabe released his wrist and Strait started reflexively to dish the gravy again on his potatoes and Watanabe grabbed his food and threw it, plate and all, in the nearby trash can.

"What the fuck?" said Strait.

"What the fuck is right!" said Watanabe. He shook a finger up at Strait's baffled face. "What the fuck you think you doing? Don't they tell you at hospital? You have serious problem. Fluid in ear don't drain out right. You eat salt, that stops fluid draining out, make problem worse. Problem get worse, you get dizzy. Get dizzy, lose hearing, go deaf!"

Strait hovered in indecision. Everyone in the room was staring at them. Then Jessie gently placed her hand on his arm.

Strait felt deeply sad as they assembled a plate of food for him out of the marginal bits on the table that had no salt. Mostly, it came down to unseasoned vegetables. He and Jessie obtained glasses of wine and noticed Katherine standing behind one of the sofas and waving at them. She was pointing at an open space she'd saved for them.

James and Jessie sat and put their plates on the coffee table in front of them. Katherine's husband called to the children, "girls, it's time for you to go upstairs and let the adults talk." The girls pranced out of the room.

Katherine announced, "Everyone, I want to introduce our guest of honor. Mr. James Strait." The room burst into applause.

Strait forced himself to smile. He leaned over and whispered in Jessie's ear. "What the hell is going on?"

"Please go with it," she whispered back.

The applause continued and Strait felt like shrinking right through the cushions of the sofa. There was nothing more uncomfortable for him than being the object of attention. When the clapping finally died away, Eliza's father said in a loud voice, "so, Mr. Strait. Not to put any pressure on you, you understand. But as everyone here knows, my wife has asked if you might be so kind as to use your skills and resources to help find little Jophia Williams. Even though saying yes poses some complications for you, you've still kindly taken some steps to look into the matter. Is that a fair summary?"

Strait took a gulp of his wine. "There isn't much to say. I've talked to the chief of police about the investigation, but he wasn't what you would call cooperative. He believes that Jophia was…"

He glanced nervously toward where the girls had gone.

"They're upstairs playing. They can't hear you," Eliza's father said.

"…he thinks the girl—Jophia—was murdered and her body was dumped in the river and will never be found. He wasn't happy about me trying to help out with the case."

Katherine said, "perhaps he would be happier about it if Jophia were white?"

"I don't know about the racism thing, to be honest. My sense from talking to him is that Chief Kladspell is out of his element. I doubt he's ever investigated a murder before. He doesn't know the first thing about forensics. He's also proud and defensive about his position and feels threatened when someone like me pops up and finds something he missed. It was hard to pin down anything seriously racist about him."

"Yo, there, Mr. Strait?" The creaky voice came from a black woman with snarled hair standing near the food table. She wore a ratty-looking purple flowered skirt and an old *Ghostbusters* t-shirt. She had the kind of face people get when they don't stop scowling for decades. "You need to know that chief is a racist motherfucker."

"Zelda, hold your comments till later," said Katherine in a much sharper tone that Strait had previously heard her use.

Zelda put her fists on her hips. "Katherine Nabors, you know they ain't one word to say about that man 'less you first say what a racist shit he be."

Katherine cleared her throat. "My apologies, James. But Zelda has a point. You need to know that many of the African Americans in this town have been directly impacted by the racist behavior of this chief and his deputies."

Strait felt Jessie squeeze his hand. She looked intently into his face and nodded as if to say, "it's true."

"Can you give me any examples?" he asked.

"Many. That time the hardware store on Duffy Street was broken into and Kladspell had his officers go down to the south side and harass every young black man they could find. They were throwing them up against walls and searching them without any cause except they were black and male. And when they found anything at all, even just a knife or one joint, whatever, on a kid, they'd haul him into jail and charge him to the max. No evidence at all that the burglar was black. Another time, they had some labor trouble at Magic Lumber. A small sit-down protest, only about forty men. I think it was to get longer lunch breaks. The protesters were mixed race, some black, some Latino, some white, some Native American. They camped out on the mill floor and refused to budge. The police swooped in and arrested them all in front of the TV cameras. Once they got them to the jail and out of the view of the cameras, they locked up the blacks and natives and Latinos but let the whites go. There are many other examples. But here's something much worse. People of color around here know too well there are some parts of town where they better not walk around alone at night."

"Why not?"

"James, imagine you're a black man. You finish up your job

at a bar downtown at 2:00 in the morning and start on your hour-long walk home, necessary because you can't afford a car. You hit that empty stretch of road out past the railroad station leading out to the south side. Suddenly headlights break the darkness and a truck roars up with five hooded men carrying baseball bats. They jump out, yelling nigger this and nigger that and beat you so bad you don't even get out of the hospital for a month. You lose your job and can't walk without pain and what little money you had or will ever have is gone because you didn't have health insurance."

If five guys with baseball bats jumped me, they'd be the ones in the hospital, thought Strait, but he said, "did that really happen?"

"Yes. To Mr. Jimmy Hoist. A decent man, married, father of two, his life ruined."

"That's horrible. But what's the connection to the police?"

"One of the attackers told Jimmy he wouldn't get help from the Pine River police because, I quote, 'we *are* the police.' And one of them even handcuffed him while they beat him."

"Sorry, but anyone can buy handcuffs."

"True, but on top of that, the police department hardly investigated the incident at all."

"Really?"

"Oh, they made a show of rousting some frat boys and searching their rooms, but no arrests were made. Three years later, the case remains open but inactive. And that's just one of a dozen incidents. Granted, it was worse than most. But other assaults have happened, same kind of thing. Bunch of white guys jumping a black man walking alone at night. Sometimes with baseball bats, sometimes with boots and fists, always with hoods or Halloween masks. A lot of folks think it's The New Confederation that's doing it. And some of the members are local police."

Strait winced. The New Confederation was a white supremacist group that had become unnervingly popular in the last year. Originally a moribund offshoot of the old White Citizens Councils in the south, the group had been re-envisioned and had spread like wildfire across every state since the election.

"Whoever's doing it," continued Katherine, "Kladspell and his gang don't make a serious effort to find who it is. Good chance there are policemen under at least some of those masks."

"But no evidence."

"Not yet."

"How about going to the news?"

"We've tried that. Over and over. The Phoenix papers ran a couple of stories about Jimmy Hoist, but the other incidents weren't as severe and were considered too local."

"How about the local paper?"

"The local paper doesn't do shit. The editor is a friend of Kladspell's, but even if he wasn't, there are no competent journalists over there."

Strait sat thinking about all he'd been told. He said, "Well, Kladspell didn't say anything unambiguously racist to me. But he did say he was offended at being called racist. He said his daughter married a black man."

Zelda scoffed loudly. "That just means his daughter's rebelling against his racism and he can't do shit about it."

"Look, let me be completely clear here. I'm not supposed to be involved in this investigation. I could get into big trouble not only with Kladspell but with the FBI. The only thing that's making me willing to look into the case at all is the chance that Jophia is still alive. If I see compelling evidence that she's not, then I can't do any more."

"We understand, Mr. Strait," said Katherine's husband. "But she *could* still be alive, right?"

"It's not impossible."

Jessie prompted him. "You checked the crime scene yourself, right?"

"Yes, and I managed to obtain some samples. I'm…looking into them now."

"What kind of samples?" Zelda asked.

"I dug up some blood. I'm having it checked in a lab."

Sounds of surprise ran through the room.

"What are you checking the blood for?" Zelda demanded.

"I'm checking the phenotype and DNA profile. I'm going to visit Jophia's home tomorrow and try to get something from her father with her DNA on it. If I find a match, then, sorry to say it, but this becomes a murder case, and I won't have anything to do with that."

"How long will it take to get the results?" asked Katherine.

"I'm not sure, but it can take weeks. In the meantime, I'll try to find out what happened to the girl in ways that don't cross the chief of police and don't get me in trouble with my own boss in Virginia. But you all need to accept that it's very likely the blood will turn out to be Jophia's."

"What if the DNA doesn't match?" asked Katherine.

"I'll cross that bridge when I come to it. But it at least will suggest that Jophia is still out there somewhere. But it also might mean that someone tried to hurt Jophia on the riverbank and got injured and bled while it happened. It's pretty common. With a violent crime, the criminal leaves some of his own blood too. DNA from that kind of blood might lead to an arrest, but it doesn't mean the girl is still alive."

An oppressive silence hung in the room.

Katherine poured Strait a glass of wine.

Old Dr. Watanabe said something in Japanese to his granddaughter. She leaned toward Strait and said, “He says that’s your last glass of wine tonight.”

Strait stared at the two doctors in disbelief.

Francis Nabors said, “Mr. Strait, we certainly appreciate your efforts. Before you came, we all conferred about this whole situation. As long as Jophia is not found, we’ll never stop believing she is alive out there somewhere and we’ll never stop trying to find her. But we don’t have any resources ourselves. We’ve voluntarily searched that whole forest out on Sower road, and the riverbank too, a lot farther than the police did. We’re at our wit’s end. Frankly, if you don’t find her, no one will. And if you don’t stop the monsters who took her, no one will. And they’ll still be out there, maybe grabbing other children and doing God knows what. So we appreciate anything at all you can do to help, given your considerable skills.”

“I can say that after the chief of police threatened to put me in jail if I didn’t stop looking into this case, I was pissed off enough to defy him and send off the samples I found to a friend to have them analyzed.” Strait stabbed at the salad on his plate with a fork. “But to go any further really will put my liberty at stake. Interfering with a criminal investigation is a serious charge.”

“Of course, we understand the risk you’re taking even doing what you’ve done so far, Mr. Strait. If by some chance there is a way for you to still help to hunt down these criminals without putting yourself in danger, whatever it is, we’d be very generous in our appreciation.”

“I understand how you feel, but…”

“We are prepared to pay you. To help find Jophia and the

criminals responsible, we've collected a sum of money to pay you…"

"I really can't accept…"

"We understand how you feel. But we ask you to please consider our offer carefully before answering."

"This isn't about how I feel. It's a legal issue."

"Please, James," said Katherine.

Strait looked around the room and saw many earnest people staring at him. Entreating him. Desperation in their eyes. He wanted to shout at them all, *What do you expect from me? It isn't my duty to risk jail over some dead nine-year-old girl!*

A dead nine-year-old girl.

Strait closed his eyes.

He took a deep breath and exhaled slowly. He opened his eyes and found Eliza standing in front of him. Her friends were standing behind her. She was looking up hopefully at him. In her hands was a rabbit.

"Eliza, we told you to stay in your room," said Francis.

"But Papa, I just wanted to show James my rabbit." She leaned forward and stretched her arms out farther to offer him the rabbit. "James, this is Peter. He's my rabbit."

Strait took the rabbit and held it to his chest and stroked it. He put the animal on the coffee table and held out his arms to Eliza and she stepped up and put her head on his chest. He folded his arms around her.

"Okay," he said, as much to himself as to the people in the room. "I'm going to give it my best shot to find Jophia. And to find the person who took her, regardless of the results of the blood analysis. But I do this alone and I do it my way. Please don't offer me money because I can't accept it. I won't say a word to any of you about what I find until I decide it's worth telling. And everyone in this room needs to promise not to tell anyone what I'm doing. Is that clear?"

Eliza moved to her mother and sat on her lap, smiling at Strait.

Francis said, "Mr. Strait, I don't know how we can possibly express our gratitude…"

Strait nodded, feeling like he'd just thrown his life away.

"Okay, everyone," announced Katherine. "Enjoy the party. There's plenty of food left."

Strait reached to have some more of his salad but found the rabbit was already eating it.

Chapter Fifteen

Although the crackle of a seething fire in the ceiling could be heard and the room was filling with black smoke and the heat was so intense outside it seemed the marrow of his bones was boiling, the basement of the cult compound was freezing. Strait's fingers were turning to ice where they touched the metal pole he used to keep himself upright. His leg was pulsing with pain and gushing blood on the floor and the blood was turning to red ice.

The VX canisters were not in rows as expected but in concentric rings of increasing circumference, thousands of them, and he was in the exact center. Bullseye. Ground zero. The surfaces of the canisters were gleaming silver and he could see himself in their surfaces, features elongated across the curving surfaces, a line of unfamiliar, deformed men who all carried his name.

Also in the dead-center was the girl. Seated on the floor, tears streaming down her cheeks, her finger on the button of the device that would release the poison.

"Please, little girl, don't press that button! I want to help you!"

"Liar!"

"What's your name, little girl?"

The girl looked up at him, bewildered.

"You know my name, James."

He was so startled to see Eliza sitting there that something in his head became unanchored and the room began to turn, faster and faster. Nausea bubbled up in his stomach. He tried to take deep breaths, but the room was filled with smoke and every breath burned.

He opened his eyes and he was now outside, gunfire pinging

and cracking on the body of the van and Amelia struggling to scramble out through the smashed windowshield. They both tumbled out. An explosion shook the earth and lifted the van and threw it down.

Strait shouted at Amelia to distract the shooter in the clearing. She seemed confused about where she was and her face was ribboned with blood. Strait glanced at the man in the clearing and back at her and all the hope in his life was sucked away because it was no longer Amelia standing there but Pastor Jessie.

He woke gasping in the dark hotel room, confused about where he was.

It was only four-thirty and the sun wasn't up yet, but he knew he wouldn't go back to sleep. He made some coffee and turned on CNN. The news these days seemed to be from a country descending into chaos. Mass shootings, domestic terrorism, police brutality, tribal hate. All skyrocketing. If the inheritors of the Earth were decided on this day, they would not be the peacemakers or the meek, but instead the dishonest and the cruel.

Decent people. They seemed to be disappearing from the species. People like Jessie. Like Katherine. After saying goodbye to the guests the previous evening, with an extra-long goodbye to Jessie, Katherine had driven Strait back to his hotel room. He'd asked her in the parking lot to give him directions to the house of Marvin Williams. Father of Jophia. Former black militant and convicted terrorist bomber. He wanted to talk to him face to face.

"I said I'd take you up there," she answered.

"You don't need to do that."

"Actually, James, I do." She said it with one of her smoldering looks that indicated she would not permit disagreement. "I'll pick you up at 9:00."

Strait grew sick of the news and turned the TV off. He took a shower and got dressed. He used the time he had left before Katherine would arrive to clean and oil his gun. Afterwards, he took out one of the five boxes of ammo he'd bought at the Walmart. Each box held a hundred 9mm parabellums. The "official" bullet of NATO forces. The bullet sixty percent of police used. His Glock held a 17-round magazine. He filled the magazine to capacity and snapped it into the weapon. He attached the Yaqui holster to his belt and put the gun into it. He put on his coat.

Strait was not one of those men who needed a gun to fill out an incomplete or damaged manhood, but having the gun in his holster again after all those months in the hospital undeniably felt good. Like a missing limb was finally restored. He also wasn't one of those pro-gun nuts who got off on the power weaponry provided mere mortals and spent their lives immersed with other gun-nuts in arcane talk about gun technology or fairytale conspiracy theories about the evil government coming to steal all the guns from law-abiding citizens. Strait was as knowledgeable and skilled at weapons as anyone he knew, and he had profound respect for guns and for the responsibility required in using them. He carried this knowledge, skill, and respect silently, like his father had taught him to.

Strait was waiting on the curb when Katherine pulled up in her Nissan. A chill wind had mounted from the north and the sky was threatening rain. Another ten degree drop and it would be cold enough to snow. As she drove him around the block and headed south toward the railroad crossing, she talked about Jophia's father, Marvin Williams.

"Even with me there, James, he might not talk to you. That poor man's been put through everything and more."

"'Poor man'? But he was part of a terrorist group, right?

Convicted of conspiring to bomb a building?"

"He swears he didn't know the real reason those men were buying that stuff."

"And you believe him?"

"Yes."

"You seem so certain."

"If you heard him talk about it, you'd believe him too. They told him they were buying supplies for a building project at their church. Marvin says if he'd known, he never would have driven them."

"Of course he'd *say* that. That 'church' he was a member of advocated the violent overthrow of the U.S. government. You're not saying he didn't know that, are you?"

"But that's not why he joined the church. If you know the man like I know him, you'd understand. He was attracted to the passion of it, the idea of African Americans taking power for themselves, freeing themselves. The violent talk at the church was only a small part of the overall message, and I think Marvin just conveniently ignored that part. He was idealistic."

"He was stupid."

"And he was only eighteen years old. When you were eighteen, how smart were you?"

"I was pretty stupid. But I was smart enough not to get involved in a violent organization that killed innocents while promoting its cause."

"What did you do instead?"

"I joined the army."

Katherine burst out laughing, then her face grew serious.

"You know what Marvin did to get convicted? He drove a car to a hardware store. That's it. Nothing else. He gave a couple of church acquaintances a lift. So they could buy some random hardware stuff that could have been used for a hundred things other than bombing. And they told him—and even testified so at their trial—they were going to use that stuff for repairs on the electrical system at the church. For giving them that one, ten-minute ride, Marvin was sentenced to twenty years in a maximum security prison. Marvin is a small man physically. Not a fighter. He was brutalized there. Beyond anything you can imagine. It messed with his mind. Despite all of this, he managed to pull himself together enough to start a family. He's been an excellent father to his two kids, even after that poor, mentally ill wife of his was institutionalized. He's struggled to make a decent life for himself and his daughters. But now, the same garbage is happening again. The police are trying to railroad him."

"Chief Kladspell said he's got an alibi for the day Jophia disappeared."

"That's true."

"But he thinks the alibi is phony."

"He's dead wrong. My husband was with him. But alibi or not, Marvin Williams isn't capable of hurting any child, much less his own daughter. His kids are everything to him."

They crossed the tracks and drove through the grim industrial area that Gus had passed through with Strait the previous day.

"This is the way Jophia would have ridden her bicycle?"

"Yes. Her school is east of the hotel where you're staying, maybe ten minutes on foot."

"The day she disappeared, teachers saw her leave?"

"Yes, along with several kids, including Eliza."

"I wouldn't want my nine-year-old girl riding her bicycle in this area."

"It's not as bad as it looks. And the guys working down here, and even the bikers at the bar we just passed, it's a point of honor for them not to hurt kids. Any guy who tried to mess with her would be the one who'd have something to fear because the men around here would hurt him. Still, no way Marvin could drive her home, because he can't afford a car. Welcome to poverty, Mr. Strait."

"I thought private schools were expensive."

"Not this one. It's funded in part as a magnet school for the district, but it gets extra private funding. Actually, your organic chemistry woman Jessie does some fund-raising for it at her church. It's a damn good school, which is why we drive Eliza all the way down there every day even though we could send her more easily to the one in our neighborhood."

"Strange there's no school bus going out this way."

"Not enough kids to ride it."

They passed out of the factory area to the open, empty road. Pine forest rose on either side, green foliage darkening to black under the threatening clouds.

"Now we're heading toward two of Pine River's most exciting enclaves of poverty, one for blacks and one for whites. You remember this area?"

"Not very well."

"Originally, this was going to be a development." She gestured toward the right. "About six or seven years ago, this land was owned by the family of one of the original white settlers. They decided to sell it. Two big companies, an electronics firm and a soft drink corporation, were going to buy it and build factories. The tech firm planned a big training program for new employees, so you could get a good job there with only a high school education. There was talk of some planned housing development over that way, you know those new kind of sustainable communities, where they leave something like fifty percent green space? Those projects would have turned a lot of people's lives around who live out this way, both black and white."

"What happened?"

"Magic happened."

"Magic?"

"Magic Industries, Inc. I know you've heard of it. Magic Lumber? That's their local business. But they have tentacles everywhere. And they foresaw money in the forest around here. So, in a back-alley deal, they stopped the other companies from getting a foothold by buying all the land at a higher price."

"That's business."

"Maybe. But the whole population out here was really counting on the jobs those industries would bring. With Magic, the jobs will be fewer, the salaries will be lower, and the conditions will be worse. That company is notorious for terrible treatment of its workers. Accusations of racism too."

"Magic doesn't seem to have done anything with the land yet."

"Not yet. But, trust me, the day will come when they cut down all these trees and replace them with something bad."

Bear Brothers Auto Shop appeared on the right. The garage doors were open and the car Lennon had been working on was still hoisted on the pneumatic lift. But Lennon was nowhere to be seen. When they passed to the other side of the building, Strait glimpsed Gus in his overalls in the back lot carrying an engine part.

Strait pointed. "I know that guy."

"Who?"

"The one in overalls, at that auto mechanic shop. Gus Bear."

She made a face.

"You don't like him?"

"I've heard he's a very unpleasant man. How do you know him?"

"He sits at a table near mine when I have breakfast at the Pot Belly Café downtown. He makes small talk. And he sold me a car yesterday. The one I showed you last night."

"Figures."

"You don't seem to like my new car."

"No one in their right mind would like your new car. It's an eyesore."

"It's got an interesting history." He told her the story of the accident that killed the previous owners and how the car had been resurrected by Lennon.

"I remember that accident. Okay, then, I suppose I approve of the purchase of this eyesore."

"Do I need your approval, Mom?"

She laughed. That bright, pure laugh. "No. But men like you have a habit of not knowing how to take care of themselves."

"Men like me?"

"Large, shy men."

"What a shallow stereotype."

"Which you've demonstrated repeatedly to represent quite well."

"I'm deeply offended."

She laughed louder. "No, you're not."

Strait smiled. "How have I demonstrated this?"

"Bad coffee. Bad car. Bad eating habits. No brains about when a woman likes you."

She slowed and peered at the wall of forest to the right and soon found the cut in the trees she was looking for. She turned into it and they were on a rutted, unmaintained access road.

"Jophia rode her bicycle home on this bumpy road?" asked Strait.

"Sometimes in the rain and the snow. Welcome to poverty, James."

After driving a few minutes, Katherine turned onto a side path that was even more poorly maintained. He glimpsed through gaps in the trees shanty-like structures, ramshackle barns, patchwork gardens. A stone water-well. A hand-painted sign nailed to a post: RABBITS 3 DOLLARS PETS OR MEAT. A metal mailbox that had been peppered with gunshot on one side. He saw people here and there, all black, carrying farm tools, one carrying a hunting rifle. Katherine had to stop once and back up into the trees to let pass a half-functioning Chevy four-door from another epoch, crammed with seven people.

They drove up a hill that was curiously barren of trees and which flattened out to a tranquil flatland. The car was stopped by a reef of tree stumps. Beyond it, he could see a dilapidated shack with one side collapsing inwards.

"This is where we get out," said Katherine. "We still need to walk some from here. And there's another hill to go up. One reason I hate coming out here."

"He really lives out in the middle of nowhere. It must have taken Jophia more than an hour to ride her bicycle this far."

"Yes. And she could have walked down in ten minutes and caught the bus to the county school, but she chose the Montessori one instead. It was her idea to go there, but her father supported her. Such a bright girl, full of promise."

They left the car and moved around the tree stumps and

walked past the broken slat-board shack. It was hard to tell if it had been a habitation for humans or horses.

Katherine was breathing hard from the exertion of climbing the hill. "Do you remember this area?" she said between breaths. "One of the oldest enclaves of black folks in this part of Arizona. Population steadily declining."

"I kind of remember." Strait said, but the truth was when he was growing up people from his neighborhood had stayed away from this area. Some boys at his high school bragged one time about how they'd driven out here at night and used a baseball bat to smash up mailboxes, but Strait himself had never been here.

"Most of the people inherited their land and the houses on them from ancestors going back a hundred, hundred and fifty years. That's how Marvin got this land. It was owned by his father, who died not long before he got out of prison."

Strait didn't feel the exertion as much as Katherine and he walked the last fifty yards faster, putting some distance between them. He was the first to reach the clearing, which still was sloped enough to make it a poor place to put the house in front of him.

Marvin William's house had that unique feel of a building designed by someone with no background in the conventions of architecture but nonetheless was very skilled at crafting things with his hands. It was constructed atop a stone foundation that endeavored to compensate for the slope of the land by stacking large rocks, probably within a wooden frame which had long since fallen away, in such a way the upper layer was flat and the bottom sloped along with the hill. The gaps between the stones were then filled with concrete. The house had an odd design, a hodgepodge of add-ons formed from different kinds of wood at different periods extending from the original rectangular structure. The blue paint on the planks that made up its long southern exterior wall was faded nearly to white, and the shutters on two long windows could open outwards to catch the sun. The only entrance door he could see was in a strange place, on the short side of the house facing west. Firewood was stacked up beside the door, split logs stacked and partially covered with a sheet of dark green plastic. Next to the woodpile was a block of stacked rabbit hutches, about ten of them, all empty. The door was covered with tiny hand-painted blue, green, and yellow flowers, now very faded, and there was a small window on its upper half, covered with a dingy-looking lace curtain. Touches of decoration from a woman no longer present.

Strait approached the house and a man's voice came from behind. "Don't you fucking move."

Strait felt pushed against the back of his head the unmistakable shape of the business end of a double-barrel shotgun.

Strait spun around, cracked the shotgun aside and threw a vicious kick into the man's kneecap. He snatched the gun away and whipped it around and snapped it into the man's nose. The man dropped to the ground screaming. Strait shucked the shotgun and aimed it at his face.

The man was on his back, eyes wide, one hand on his knee, the other waving frantically at Strait. "Okay, okay, okay," he said. Blood was splashed from his nose across one side of his face. Strait had nine and a half pounds of pressure on the ten-pound trigger. He held for a few seconds, inhaled, blew it out. He decreased the pressure. How could he shoot a man so stupid he hadn't even pumped the shotgun before aiming?

Katherine had come up from behind and was standing with her mouth wide open.

Strait asked, "Is this Jophia's father?"

“Yes!” Katherine sounded like she was gagging.

“He tried to kill me.”

“Marvin! Are you out of your mind?”

The man on the ground was shorter than Katherine and thin and wrinkled as a tree root. He had a scraggly beard spotted with grey and bloodshot eyes. The scrawny arms poking from his t-shirt were scrofulous and sore-ridden. The shirt had a picture of Sponge Bob on it.

“Don’t shoot me!” he begged. “Katherine…this…stranger was at my door! What was I supposed to do?”

Katherine bent and slapped at Marvin’s head. “How about saying hello, how can I help you, like a normal person? You don’t shoot someone for knocking on your door!”

“Why didn’t you call and tell me you were coming?”

“I did! But you never answer your phone.”

“I have the ringer off.”

“This man’s here to help you, you fool.”

“Help me?”

Strait lowered the gun. “To help you find your daughter.”

He moved the gun to his left hand and put it at his side, barrel downwards, and reached his right hand out to Marvin. The man stared up dubiously at the offered hand.

“You really here to help?”

“Yes. But don’t point any more guns at me.”

Marvin let Strait help him up.

“You all come on inside.”

The three walked up the porch steps, Marvin limping. He was about to open the door for them when someone else did it from the inside. A woman stood there. She looked like a much younger, healthier version of the man. Same flat nose, same scraggly hair and wiry build, same manic rage in the eyes.

"What the hell is going on, Papa?" Then she saw Katherine and her face softened.

"Katherine? What you doing here?"

Katherine pointed toward Strait. "I'm with him."

"Just a misunderstanding, Bernie," Marvin said.

The woman fixed Strait with a furious look. "You a cop?"

Katherine said, "Bernadette, calm down. He's here to help us."

"After all the shit that's gone down around here, don't be telling me to calm down."

"Don't act uncivilized to our guests, Bernie," said Marvin.

Strait suppressed the urge to point out that Marvin had threatened his guest with a shotgun only a minute before.

"We'll offer this man a cup of tea and hear what he has to say."

Bernadette gestured with a jab of her finger for them to enter.

Fifteen minutes later, they were seated in the living room of Marvin's house. Furniture worn down with use, but everything was clean and tidy. Against the wall was an antique cabinet with wood-framed glass panes inscribed with roses in which could be seen neatly stacked dishes. Well-cared-for possessions. A bookcase formed from bricks and fiberboard. Strait scanned the titles and saw books about philosophy, history, civil rights. Marvin was settled on a recliner, the brown fake leather faded and cracking in places, his injured leg straight out on the footrest. An ice pack was tied to his knee with a towel, and he was pressing a second ice pack to his nose. Bernadette had brought them tea, although the way she shoved the cup at Strait, sloshing it, and the way she now glowered at him from her place standing at the doorway across from him made Strait wonder if he could drink it without risk of poisoning.

Marvin's expression wasn't any better. "Okay, you in my house. Talk. Who are you?"

"Sir, my name is James Strait. I'm with the FBI…"

Marvin's eyes bulged. "Get the fuck back *out* of my house." He started to rise. "Get me a gun, Bernie. I'm going to shoot this motherfucker."

Katherine snapped at him like he was a disobedient child. "Marvin, sit back down. You aren't going to shoot anybody. You don't even know how to use a gun. No wonder everyone thinks you're crazy. Just *listen* to the man."

"Mr. Williams, some very decent people, Katherine here, and her daughter and husband, and Pastor Jessie, asked me to help, so I'm here. I think something strange is happening in this town regarding your daughter's disappearance."

Marvin said, "Strange don't begin to cover it. We're dealing with a racist conspiracy goes all the way up to the fucking governor's mansion."

"Oh?"

"Listen. I've been living in this house for five years, and not one month has gone by without my getting harassed. I can't trust nobody. No one white anyway."

He eyed Strait, waiting for him to disagree, ready to fight him if he did. "They all been trying for years to make me suffer, put me back in prison. Drove my poor wife right over the edge. Then the latest thing, my girl goes missing. On a road she's ridden her bike on a thousand times, in an area she knows like the back of her hand. And that girl's *smart*. I don't mean book smart, but she's that too. I mean street smart. With all the shit they pull on us, she knows not to talk to strangers and she knows how to handle herself. Whoever took her wasn't no stranger. It was some authority figure, like a police. You know they took me in and interrogated me all day? With no lawyer? I says I won't talk without no lawyer, and they keep saying, fuck the lawyer, we have some questions need answering. I said, I have an alibi, check it out. I was with my friend Francis fishing. They say, bullshit, that alibi's fake. Meantime, they ain't doing *nothing* to find her. To find out if someone is out there who's got her locked up somewhere and…" Marvin's voice faltered. His eyes glassed up and he made a choking sound as the words he tried to form were broken up in his throat.

His daughter went to him and put her arm around his shoulder. "Now, Papa, don't you worry, we're going to find her. We're going to find her," she repeated, with more determination in her voice.

Strait said, "I want to help you."

"How?"

"You mention you've been harassed since you moved here. Can you tell me more?"

"Sure I can. I could write a book 10,000 pages long about it. This here was my daddy's house. I moved in after they let me out of prison. You probably know how I ended up there."

"You were a member of the MRA."

"Yes. For the white man, there ain't no scarier words than Moorish Republican Army, right?" He said it in a challenging way, again expecting Strait to argue.

Instead of arguing, Strait said, "I agree with you. The racist white power structure was completely blown away then over the idea of black people actually arming themselves in the service of getting civil rights. It was scary enough that Dr. King had brought massive protests to the streets and won equal access to public services and promoted voting rights, and terrifying that Malcolm X was openly calling for militant action, but the MRA was the one that *really* made the racists piss their beds at night."

Marvin blinked in surprise. "You know more than I thought you would. True, some of the brothers were calling for violence, but I sure wasn't." Marvin had a dazed look in his eyes that Strait at first thought was due to shock from the incident with the shotgun but now he understood it was that jittery stare some people get from being in constant danger for years. The eyes of prey. "I got swept up in the propaganda. I was young and stupid."

"How did you help them?"

"I drove them to a hardware store for some stuff."

"Stuff?"

"Hammers and screwdrivers. Couple rolls of electrical wire and duct tape. A lot of nails, nuts, and bolts. We were building our own sanctuary back then where the most faithful brothers and sisters could live. It was a beautiful thing. And we were all working together on the building. The tools and stuff were supposed to be for that."

"But?"

"The nuts and bolts and nails were used as shrapnel in the bombs. I swore I didn't know. I really didn't. But the judge and jury didn't believe a word of it and I was convicted just like the ones who did the bombing. I spent fifteen years in a maximum security prison."

"Hush, Papa," said Bernadette. "Try to think about something else."

"Bernie's right. You need to look ahead now," said Katherine.

"Look ahead? My wife's in a mental hospital, my youngest daughter's missing and our chief of police is saying I killed her.

Trying to get me back in prison. He'll do it too, you just wait and see. They always find a way."

"Can you tell me more about your daughter?" said Strait.

"What do you want to know?"

"If I can get an idea of the sort of kid she was, her hobbies, interests, personality. Her normal movements during the day, I might be able to get more of a notion about what happened to her. Also, I know it's been a long time, but if you have any possession of hers that might have some of her DNA on it. A toothbrush, maybe. Some of her hair. If not, we might arrange to get a DNA sample from you. That might be enough to know if the blood at the riverbank was hers or someone else's."

Marvin stared at Strait and his eyes clouded over. "Jophia is the smartest kid in her class, but she wears it humble, you know? She wants to become a scientist."

"Jophia is about the most decent kid around," said Bernadette. "You probably think, sure, we're family, of course we'd say that. But it's really true. She always wanted to help people."

Marvin smiled shakily. "Quarters for the homeless folk."

Bernadette nodded. "Back when we used to go to town, if we'd run into a homeless person, she'd be all over Papa, saying, 'Daddy, give me a quarter so I can give it to that man.'"

"Animals too. She loved animals. You see those empty cages outside."

"Yes."

"Rabbit cages. I used to breed them, mostly for meat. Got to do what you got to do, right? But she ordered me to stop, on account of she loved rabbits. So I stopped. My daughter was always bringing home animals, wanting just about anything for a pet. Squirrels and pigeons."

"Don't forget the baby bear," said Bernadette.

Marvin laughed. "Oh, yes, the baby bear. Jophie come running up the patch over there saying, 'Papa, come quick, can I keep it? Can I keep it?' without saying what *it* was. She pulled me by the hand over that ridge and suddenly we're two feet from a baby bear. And the mama bear was only twenty more feet off. Oh, the Lord never saw a man hoist a child into the air and sprint faster for shelter than I did that day."

"Did she ride her bicycle on the same path every day? On that road past the auto shop?"

"Yes."

"Never went another way?"

"No other way to go."

"Do you know the men who own that shop?"

"Oh, sure. Truth be told, those three are almost the only white folks in town that have treated me civilly. I don't have it any more, but I bought a car from them and they knew I didn't have money so they let me buy on credit. No interest. When the car broke down, they gave me big discounts on the repairs."

"So you don't think they had anything to do with Jophia's disappearance?"

Katherine cut in. "I'm given to understand that the police questioned all three brothers and they had good alibis. The police, along with reporters from a Phoenix newspaper, looked at the security camera footage from their shop, and they said there was no sign of the girl or of foul play."

"I thought you didn't trust the police, Katherine."

"Well, not exactly."

Marvin said, "I don't trust the police at all, but I do trust them Bear brothers. They might be a little strange, but they would never hurt my girl," said Marvin. Bernadette nodded in agreement.

"Anyone else you can think of who might have wanted to bother Jophia?"

"There are people who would want to bother *me*. The cops. I think if you want to hunt for who took my Jophia, that's the group you should check out. Anyone with the government too. Them or the confederates."

"The confederates?"

"You know. New Confederation people."

"Oh, right. I heard they were active here too."

"Damn right they've been active here too. Bernadette, where's that paper we found last week?"

Jophia's sister went out of the room and returned with a folded piece of paper. She handed it to Strait. On the cover, it had a symbol, a twisted cross with beams of light coming out of it, which was drawn on the green head of a cartoon frog. The frog's big eyes had a mischievous, sidelong look, and its fat red lips formed a sadistic smile. Under the frog were the words

NORMIES, TAKE THE RED PILL! THE NEW CONFEDERATION IS EXPOSING THE STINKING HYMIE CONTROLLED GOVERNMENT AND ITS NEGRO ARMY! MAKE AMERIKA GREAT AGAIN!

"Jesus," said Strait.

"Jesus got nothing to do with it. Last month, someone threw a rock through that window. Another time, they spray-painted 'Nigger die!' on our shed. We've found human shit and dead animals tossed on our yard. I could go on and on, back through the years, but it's gotten worse lately."

"I don't suppose you've reported this to the police."

"No fucking way. Half the police are confederates

themselves."

"Newspapers?"

"The only thing worse than the cops are the reporters. I go to a newspaper and they write a story making it sound like I imagined it all or I made it up to trick people. Crazy black American ex-con terrorist imagines he's a victim. No sir, I don't trust the police and I don't trust the newspapers."

"Maybe you're selling them short. They can't all be bad."

"James, I can tell you're a decent man. Even though you smashed my nose. But all my life, I've been cheated, lied to, and brutalized by white people. White cops. White reporters. White politicians. I'm finished with trusting any of them. I'm on my own. The second I find Jophia, we're going to pack up and head north, take the whole family to live with my brother up in Baltimore. No justice up there either, but at least there's power in numbers."

"I'm white. How do you feel about that?"

"If Katherine says you're okay, I believe her."

Strait perceived a sound outside. A sound that didn't belong. He turned his head just in time to see a man across the clearing aiming a rifle into the living room.

Strait leapt over the table and landed on top of Marvin as gunfire blew out the window. The chair collapsed backwards and the two men fell to the floor under a shower of splintered glass. Strait rolled off the old man and dropped to his hands and knees and started to maneuver back under the window when another blast of gunfire belted through in an abrupt flash of glass splinters that slapped Strait across the right side of his face like gust of fire. On the left side of the window frame he raised himself onto one knee and pulled his Glock from under his jacket and aimed it at the front door. Katherine and Bernadette were both on the floor, Katherine howling with her face in her hands, Bernadette silent. Marvin hadn't moved from where he'd fallen backwards in the chair.

Strait stepped to the door with gun drawn and threw it open and stepped to one side. No sound. He ran back to the window and at an angle popped off three shots, then leapt back to the door and ran outside.

The sunlight seemed fantastically bright, like he was viewing the world through a gold-yellow filter that burned away all but the most essential features. He dropped into that light and rolled behind the wood pile as a gun cracked and bullets ripped into the logs near his head, sending puffs of wood dust into his eyes. The shots seemed to be coming slantwise from where the trees were thickest. When Strait had caught sight of the shooter through the window, he saw a man in combat fatigues wearing some kind of helmut. The weapon looked like an assault rifle. An AK-47, judging by the sound. What to do?

Strait shouted, "Hey asshole! You picked a really bad day to kill Marvin Williams. Because I'm a cop."

Silence.

"So why don't we make this easy? You throw down your weapon and come out with your hands over your head so when the army of other cops I called arrive in a minute, you'll seem cooperative instead of caught in the act of trying to kill a cop."

Silence.

"Or how about you and me have a little talk? I'm really curious to know why you would come here and start shooting through the window like that. You must be really pissed about something."

Silence.

"Want to talk about it? I want to understand you better."

Through the atmosphere rendered dreamlike by the yellow-gold blanket of sunlight slanting from the west and illuminating the floating specks of wood pulverized by the man's bullets, not the slightest sound could be heard. A gust of wind sent dry leaves hissing across the clearing.

Strait knew the man was still out there because he hadn't heard him move away. He was aiming his weapon at Strait behind the pile of firewood, waiting for him to show himself so he could shoot him dead. He hadn't responded at all. Why?

Because he's confident.

Of course. He knew Strait was bluffing about an approaching army of police because he hadn't had time to call anyone and it would take any police a long time to get up the mountain anyway. He wasn't worried about shooting a cop. His target might have been Marvin, but he planned to kill everyone in the house.

In his mind, he had already won.

In his mind.

Strait wanted to hear precisely where the man was and for that, he needed him to shoot again. What could provoke this guy into shooting at the wood pile without Strait actually coming out? What was his greatest insecurity? There wasn't much to go on, but if he was forced to do a spot profile, he'd say this guy's most sensitive spot was…

"Hey, why the hell aren't you answering me? Are you a…faggot…or something?"

The man instantly shot twice at the lumber pile and Strait cried out in pain, secretly happy because the sound of the gunfire had given him all he needed. He moaned loudly and cursed. With his left hand he jostled the far side of the lumber pile as though collapsing against it, and flailed his left arm above the wood there, then lowered it as gunfire spit at him. Strait leaped to the other side of the woodpile, stood with his gun aimed and fired three shots and dropped to the ground again.

The man screamed. This scream was authentic because he was hit. There was a sound of breaking timber as the shooter lurched into the forest. Strait jumped around the woodpile, weapon raised. He had the fucker. It was just a matter of running him down.

But halfway across the clearing the world shuddered and Strait's vision bent sideways. He fell to one knee. Nausea overcame him and he collapsed on his side, the world in full spin. He closed his eyes and vomited. He groaned and vomited more. With a kind of surreal fascination he realized the abrupt pooling moisture he felt at his groin was his own urine spreading on his pants.

Through the wildly hissing tinnitus, he heard footsteps approaching. The shooter had returned. Strait was completely helpless. He couldn't lift his weapon. Didn't even know where it was. He couldn't see anything through the vertigo to find his gun, to pick it up, to aim it. He couldn't even move his head to look at the man. He wanted to sob. What a pathetic way to die.

Chapter Sixteen

"You're back to looking ninety-nine percent dead." Katherine said, smiling down on him in the bed. She said it in a lighthearted tone, but her voice trembled. Next to her stood Jessie, who looked far more troubled.

"Oh, God, I'm so sorry," she said.

They were in a hospital room. Strait was attached to IVs that dripped anti-vertigo medicine and saline solution. They'd loaded him up with Valium too. The spinning had stopped. He felt drained and sleepy. He was careful to remain motionless. He knew he was in the second phase of the attack, where any attempt to walk or move his head made the room wobble violently. He was hazily aware it was night, probably very late.

"What are you sorry about?" asked Strait. Even the movement of his mouth as he spoke sent seismic waves through his head.

"That I encouraged you to do this. You could have been killed."

Strait forced himself to smile. "Not a chance. I had the drop on that guy the second he appeared."

"You saved our lives today, James," said Katherine.

Jessie pulled up a chair beside the bed and took Strait's hand in hers. She started crying.

"Oh, don't," said Strait. "I'm fine. We're all fine, aren't we? What about Marvin and Bernadette?"

It was Bernadette whose footsteps he'd heard when he collapsed in the clearing. She'd approached him brandishing the shotgun. After she saw he wasn't shot, she coaxed Katherine and Marvin to come out. Katherine had driven back down the hill until she could get a signal on her cell phone, then called Dr. Watanabe at the hospital. The old man had come in an ambulance with his daughter and a couple of techs. The movements involved in loading Strait onto a gurney and into the back of the ambulance and of driving down the bumpy road caused him agony that none of the others had any comprehension of. He vomited and vomited, tears pouring down his face.

More incalculable time had passed in the emergency room. Strait was sedated and pumped full of anti-vert. Over his protestations, he was wheeled on a gurney for a CAT scan of his brain and another of his lungs. The room they put him in was big enough for three people, but he was the only patient. While he waited, Katherine and Jessie had come into the room.

"No one was shot. Marvin was shaken up pretty bad, but Bernadette was just angry. After we got you in the ambulance, she dragged me into the woods to look for that man. That girl's got no fear. She brought the shotgun. She kept saying she was going to kill that man when she found him. There was a trail of blood that went on through the trees about a mile and ended in the road. The guy drove off on a motorcycle, it looks like. We saw the tire tracks."

"Did you call the police?"

"No."

"You need to. This is serious."

"You still don't understand, James. We can't trust the police to help us. It was probably one of them shooting at us."

"That a stretch."

"I'm not calling them."

"If you don't, I will."

Dr. Watanabe appeared in the doorway and approached the bed. He looked down at Strait through his spectacles. "Tall man.

Good news. You don't have brain tumor."

"I already knew that. They didn't need to do those tests."

"Hospital rules for admission if you have dizzy. Katherine-san, Jessie-san, I need time with patient."

Jessie looked into his face, guilt-ridden.

"It's not your fault. Really. I'll see you tomorrow, right?" he said.

"Tomorrow?"

"We have a date. Remember?"

"James, we'll do the date another time. You need to rest."

The doctor nodded. "Tonight, you stay here. Tomorrow, I give you full tests for Meniere's."

"I don't have time," said Strait.

Dr. Watanabe frowned. "Katherine and Jessie. You talk to tall man later. I need to talk to him now, doctor to patient."

Katherine said, "okay. I'd better get back up to Marvin's again. Bernie has gathered a big crowd of folks up there to guard the house. They'll need help with the cooking. James, call me, okay?"

"And call me too," said Jessie.

"Katherine, *you* call the police," said Strait.

"This will not happen."

After they were gone, Strait said to Dr. Watanabe, "you know about the shooting, don't you?"

"I don't know."

"There was a man in the woods up at Marvin's house and…"

"Not my problem."

"But you were up there. You saw the broken window? The bullet holes?"

"I saw broken window, but nothing else. Not my problem. You my problem."

"Just do me a favor, Doc. Check to see if anyone has been admitted to the hospital with a gunshot wound today. This is the only hospital in the area, so if he went anywhere, it was here."

"Okay, I ask. But you stay here tonight. And all day tomorrow. Starting in morning, I give some tests. Take about eight hours."

"Sorry, I can't. Somebody tried to kill me today and I need to find him."

"You just had vertigo attack. You can't walk."

"I should be able to walk by sunrise. Then I'm out of here."

"Tall man, you stay here. Number one is take medical tests. After, shoot people."

"No tests."

"You need help."

"I'm not taking any tests."

Watanabe slapped him.

Strait held his hand to his cheek, stunned. He stared at the old doctor through a room sent rocking by the blow.

"You a big stubborn stupid baby," said Watanabe.

"You hit me!"

"It hurt? Good!" The old man clapped. "Good job, Dr. Watanabe! Listen. You a good, big, tall man, and you do great things for people in town to find that girl for Katherine-san and family. But you got a heavy sick. And if that girl alive? You not going to help her. This sick stop you. Right? But you too *ganko* to do right thing."

Strait gazed up at the old man in a kind of stupor of wonder.

"I can't believe you hit me."

Watanabe softened his tone. "James, I can help you. Meniere's is not a joke. You *need* help. If you don't let me help you, that girl? She dead."

"Okay. I'll take your tests."

"Good. I happily smack sense into your stupid head."

"Doctors hitting patients. Is that the Japanese way?"

Watanabe laughed. "You joking? Japanese people not same as American people. Japanese people follow rules. I hit patient in Japan, I go to jail."

"In America too. An American doctor hits a patient, he goes to jail."

Watanabe smiled. "I see. And you will put me in jail now?"

"No. I'm kind of impressed, actually."

"It is like I say. You American."

***

The next day, Watanabe subjected Strait to a battery of tests of balance and inner ear functioning, most of which he'd never had before. The worst test required him to have the tip of a cold plastic funnel inserted into his ear and the water flushed forcefully inside, a hair-raising experience that brought on a momentary rush of vertigo. In another, he needed to trace the movements of objects on a computer screen with his eyes. Strait completed the tests at about five o'clock. Watanabe sat with him in consultation and informed him that he was satisfied Strait really had Meniere's disease.

"Could it had been caused by the gunfire? Or a grenade? Going off close to my ear?" Strait asked.

"No idea," said Watanabe, scribbling notes in the case file he'd made for Strait.

"No idea?"

"No idea. Nobody know what cause Meniere's. Hypothesis say liquid in inner ear don't drain good because blood flow too weak. Another hypothesis say it's herpes virus. Another say injury jawbone.

Gunshot problem? I don't know."

"But you must have an opinion."

The doctor ignored him.

"Um, speaking of gunfire, were you able to check if anyone came to the hospital with a gunshot injury?"

"No one came."

"You checked?"

"I checked. No one came. Maybe you no shoot someone."

"Oh, I shot him, alright."

"Maybe wound not bad enough for hospital." Watanabe finished writing. He handed a prescription to Strait. "This is Dimenhydrinate. Motion sickness medicine. You can chew, so it work fast. Take this at low dose each day as you need. Take at higher dose if you get dizzy."

"Will that stop the dizziness?"

"Worth try. Also, this is more special, I give you this." From a black satchel on the floor he pulled out a paper box. Kanji characters were printed on the front. Inside were about a hundred thin, yellow and white cylindrical packets. "I bring this from Japan. No find in America." He poured Strait a cup full of water and said, "drink this."

"I'm not thirsty."

"Not just water. With medicine." He shook a packet up at him. He ripped one end off and gestured for Strait to pour the contents into his mouth.

"What is it?"

"Called *seireitou.* A kind of Chinese medicine. Good for Meniere's. Take every day, three times. If you get dizzy, take double."

After a moment's hesitation, Strait poured the powder into

his mouth and swallowed it with the water. It tasted mildly sweet and bitter at the same time.

The doctor then produced from his satchel a much larger tube, made of what looked like thick foil. This also had kanji characters written on its side. "I give you a box of these. Emergency time, drink this. It is liquid, very thick. Almost glue. You cut off one end and hold your nose and swallow all at one time."

"What does it do?"

"It suck every drop of water from your body. Very powerful. Taste like shit."

"Is this stuff legal?"

"Don't know."

Strait filled the prescription at the hospital pharmacy. The doctor insisted on giving him the two medicines from his satchel for free.

Chapter Seventeen

Jessie had asked him to call her when he was done so she could drive him home, but he felt like walking. The clouds of yesterday had disappeared and the late afternoon sky was blue. That absolutely pure blue you got in Pine River at the edge of winter. When he entered his hotel room, he opened the curtains and the sliding glass door to let the fresh air in. A second later, he heard a knock at the door. Outside, he found Julie. Her eyes were red from crying.

"Can I come in?"

"Sure."

She was wearing tight jeans and the same honky-tonk bar t-shirt she was wearing when he'd first seen her in this room after returning to town. *The Horse's Mouth.*

"Duane and me had a fight," she said.

"Should I ask what about?"

"His drinking, as usual. And you."

"Me?"

"He's jealous of you."

"Me?"

"He thinks I'm attracted to you."

"That's crazy."

"He gets so angry sometimes when we argue. He doesn't hit me, but he throws shit. Chairs, bottles." She started crying. "I'm scared. Can you hold me?"

"Um…"

She leaned against him and started sobbing into his chest. He put his arms around her shoulders and patted her back. Her sobs gradually subsided. She looked up at him. Her dirty blonde hair was strung messily across her tear-streaked face.

"Do you think he'll hurt me?"

"Do you think he would?"

She nuzzled against him. "All I know is that when I'm with you, I feel safe."

An awkward silence followed. Then Strait felt Julie's hands moving down to his ass.

He jumped back and put his hands on her shoulders and looked into her eyes. As gently as possible, he said, "this is a misunderstanding."

For a moment she seemed paralyzed, frozen in the moment with a look of shock on her face. Then she ran from the room.

He went to the hallway and called after her, but she was already gone.

He shut the door, feeling emptied out, confused. What was he supposed to do?

A knock came at the door. *Shit, not again.*

He was surprised to find Jessie standing in the hall. She ran to him and hugged him tight.

"Thank God you're okay."

"I'm fine."

"I thought you were going to call me."

"Oh, shit. I'm sorry. I…had a lot on my mind. And ended up walking home."

"I tried to call you but you didn't answer. I was so worried."

"I'm okay."

She held out a paper bag. "You hungry? I picked you up some sandwiches from Murphys."

Strait realized he was starving. He'd only eaten a couple of bites from the low-sodium lunch at the hospital.

"I can't say no."

"I'm sorry too."

"About what?"

"That I pushed you to help find Jophia. You almost got killed."

Strait smiled. "I wasn't the one who almost got killed."

Jessie sat on the chair and James sat on the bed.

"Katherine sort of told me, but can you go over what happened yesterday?"

Strait recited all the events at the cabin, from his taking the shotgun from Marvin to the gunman's attempt at killing them, to the ambulance ride to the hospital with Dr. Watanabe.

"Jesus."

"Never a dull moment."

"You're not dizzy now?"

Strait considered it. "Wow, not at all. Usually I'd still be pretty shaky at this point after an attack. The doctor had me take this Chinese medicine stuff. Maybe it's working."

With the fingers of her left hand, Jessie was picking nervously at one of the fingers of her right.

"Who do you think was trying to shoot Marvin?"

"Maybe someone in that group of racists that's been harassing him. The New Confederation."

"Did you get a look at the person?"

"When I jumped up to shoot, I caught a glimpse. He was a small guy. Had on combat fatigues. He had on a motorcycle helmet with a visor, so I couldn't see his face. Bernadette said later the guy escaped on a motorcycle."

"I want you to give up trying to look for Jophia. It's too dangerous."

"No way."

"What if Kladspell tells the FBI? You could lose your job."

"I think I've already lost my job."

"What if he puts you in jail?"

Strait smiled. "He'll have to catch me first."

Jessie pulled over the night table and placed it between the chair and the bed and took the food from the bag. Deli sandwiches on toasted wheat, piled high with sliced turkey, tomatoes, lettuce, onions, pickles, olives and thick slabs of cheese. It was one of the most beautiful things Strait had ever seen.

"I had them keep the sauce and mayo off yours to reduce the salt."

"Thanks. Let's eat."

"Oh, shit, the cheese," she said, as Strait was about to take a bite. "Cheese is full of salt." She snatched the sandwich from him, lifted the top piece of bread, and took out the cheese and gave the sandwich back to him.

Strait was devastated. Cheese was the best part. He took a bite and chewed a mouthful of the sauce-less, cheese-less sandwich.

"How is it?"

"Okay."

"Oh, I forgot." From her bag, Jessie removed a small bottle of red wine. "Ta da! Do you have any cups in this place?"

Strait produced an old plastic tumbler and a stained coffee cup from the kitchen.

"We need to get you into a more livable place." Jessie poured the wine into his coffee cup. "Only one glass, right?"

Strait frowned. "Right."

"Hey, what's that?"

"What?"

"On the floor."

Jessie put down the wine bottle and picked up the folded, yellow piece of paper on the carpet in front of the door. "Looks like someone slipped you a note."

Strait unfolded it. The paper was dirty, splotched with oil. The handwriting was a childish scrawl:

Chief, I got important info about that missing girl. Meet me tom. morning, Pot Belly.

Randy Street

"What does it say?"

Strait the read note aloud.

"Let me see."

He handed her the note and she read it silently. "Randy Street? That homeless guy with one eye? How do you know him?"

"I've run into him a couple of times. You know him?"

"Sure, I know Randy. He comes to our community kitchen."

"What's that?"

"It's a soup kitchen for Pine River homeless people. I told you about, remember? We had it on Sunday at the Meadows, about the time you were getting shot at. But Randy wasn't there. He also comes by the church sometimes. He gives me a weather report in exchange for food."

"He does the same at the café to get free bagels."

"His weather reports are very poetic and almost always more accurate than the TV reports. He's a sweet guy. Had a hard time in prison, I hear."

"Do you know what he was in prison for?"

"I never asked him. I heard rumors he assaulted his mother."

She looked over the note again. “The missing girl is Jophia?”

“I think so.”

“How could he know anything about Jophia?”

“No idea. I do know he sort of confronted me at a liquor store. Told me it was my destiny or something to fix everything that’s wrong in this town.”

“Your destiny, huh?” She smiled coyly. “Maybe it’s true.”

He sipped at his wine. “I don’t believe in destiny, but I agree that something needs fixing around here.”

“So you’ll go meet Randy tomorrow?”

“Yeah.”

“I’d like to go with you, but I’m leaving for that conference tomorrow morning.”

“That sucks.”

“It’s only a week.”

For a while, they ate in silence. Strait stole looks at her. Her frizzy, straw-colored hair fell over her shoulders and down her back. She seemed in some ways like a kid, laughing out loud at the slightest thing. She had one of those smiles that involved her whole face and a laugh that used her whole body. She was far freer than Strait had ever been. Yet she was also disciplined. She followed a daily exercise regimen, jogging and bicycling. She had no meat on her sandwich, a strict vegetarian. Her weekends were devoted to managing that soup kitchen, in addition to her sermons and the children’s hour at the church. During the week, she was engaged in one act after another of community service.

She took another bite of her sandwich, then put the remaining half on the wrapper, took a big sip of wine, leaned in toward him so her pretty face was close to his. She peered into his eyes and said, “Does sex make you dizzy?”

He went into a coughing fit. She patted his back and apologized until he stopped.

"Yes," he said. "A different kind of dizzy."

He leaned in and kissed her.

It wasn't until the sun came up that they got around to finishing the sandwiches and drinking the wine.

Chapter Eighteen

The next morning, Strait kissed Jessie at the doorway and they parted ways. She went to catch a bus that would take her to Sky Harbor Airport in Phoenix, and he headed to the Pot Belly Café to talk to Randy Street. He sat down by the stove. Gus Bear was already at his table, immersed in a newspaper. Strait ordered coffee from the young waitress. It seemed the girl was in charge of the whole restaurant this morning. She was running back and forth between the grill and the customers.

"Where's your sister this morning?" asked Strait after he'd ordered.

"Sister?"

"Yeah, Carol."

"Carol's not my sister."

"Oh, sorry. You look a lot alike."

"No, she's just my boss. She got hurt. She was hiking in the mountains over the weekend and fell off some rocks, cut herself up bad. She's at home recovering."

"Too bad. If you see her, tell her from me to get well soon."

Strait took a newspaper from the rack. The headline was to do with the president and his latest spat with most of the countries in Europe. Strait flipped through the paper. At the bottom of the page six was a small photo of an African American boy under a muted headline:

NEW MEXICO BOY FOUND DEAD IN ARIZONA

The story was as troubling as it was short.

(APA) *The investigation into the disappearance of a ten-year-old Gallup, New Mexico boy who had been missing for several* *months ended tragically Monday when his body was found near the town of Lupton, in Apache County. Peter Letoche vanished while coming home from school on March 17th. Although the cause of death remains unclear, Otto Chee, the longtime Lupton resident who found the child's body, stated that he appeared to have been "killed by a wild animal." The Apache county chief's office will work closely with the Gallup police department to determine what if any crime had occurred and whether federal investigators are needed, stated Gallup serious crimes task force head Leif Steerson. An autopsy is to be performed at the Gallup Medical Examiners Office.*

The waitress brought his order. He picked dismally at the unsalted eggs and potatoes on his plate, considering. He pulled out his phone and found the number for the Gallup police department.

He was about to call it when Randy Street entered the restaurant. He came over and sat in the chair Strait gestured to. Randy wore a threadbare grey coat that was too small for him and a pair of plaid, thrift store trousers that were too large. The man within these sad garments was small in height and morbidly thin. Strings of long, black hair fell over the spaces where his skin, pulled tight over his skull, formed concavities at the temples and beneath his protruding cheekbones. Strait wondered if he had AIDS.

Randy's one black eye studied Strait across the table, unblinking.

"Thanks for your note. Do you want something to eat?"

"Nah, I'm good."

"I don't mind. I can get you something."

"Nah, Chief."

"You keep calling me chief. Any special reason?"

Randy Street's lips formed a subtle smile. Then he leaned far forward and said in a whisper, "they might be watching me."

"Okay," said Strait tentatively. "You said you know something about the girl."

"I know where she is. And I know who got her."

Strait sat up. "Where? Who?"

"I ain't talking till I get promises from you."

"Like what?"

"I need protection, man."

"I'll do my best."

"The other night, I was in the alleyway over there behind the bar next to the homeless shelter? I heard these two dudes talking. They was talking about that missing girl. They said…"

"Howdy, soldier!" Gus Bear pulled up a chair. "Mind if I join you?"

Strait said, "Actually, I…Randy!"

The homeless man had stood abruptly and made for the door.

Without acknowledging Randy's fleeing, Gus said, "How's the car running?"

Strait ran out the door after Randy. He looked up and down the street. No one. He ran toward the train station to the next block and looked left and right, but no Randy. In only a few seconds, the one-eyed man had managed to disappear.

Chapter Nineteen

Strait forced himself at the café to subdue his impulse to beat Gus to a pulp. He left without eating and returned to the hotel, where he found Julie at the front counter. She was fiddling with some receipts on the desk. She avoided eye contact. Her left cheek was swollen and blue-purple. Her left arm was in a sling.

"Jesus, what happened to you?"

"Oh, nothing." She forced a smile.

"Doesn't look like nothing."

"I'm embarrassed. You know they have that robot bull over at the bar?"

"No."

"I got into a contest last night and drank too much and took a couple of hard falls from the bull." She managed to hold his gaze for all of two seconds before glancing away.

"He beat you up, didn't he?"

She laughed nervously. "Of course not! We argued some more when I got home and kissed and made up."

"Oh."

"Listen, James, about what I did last night…"

"I don't know what you're talking about. But you sure you shouldn't be at home in bed?"

"It looks worse than it is. Besides, we need the money."

"Anything I can do?"

She shook her head.

"Stay away from bulls, okay?"

She nodded and went back to fiddling with the receipts.

He had seven furious messages on the voice mail of his hotel room. All of them were from Special Agent Bureau Chief Gelder at the Virginia field office. Each message was a variation of, "what in the goddamned hell do you think you're doing, Strait? Interfering with local law enforcement? Are you crazy? Call me back immediately." *Thanks, Chief Kladspell.*

Strait picked up the phone and dialed the police department in Gallup, New Mexico. When the receptionist answered, he asked for Leif Steerson. He identified himself as a law enforcement officer in Arizona calling about a criminal case.

A few seconds later, a gruff voice came on the line.

"Steerson."

"Officer Steerson. My name is James Strait. I'm with the FBI."

"FBI?" A noticeable lightening of tone in his voice. "My father's FBI and so is my aunt. Would be myself if it weren't for my wife. You with the Albuquerque field office?"

"I'm stationed in Virginia, actually. Or was. I'm calling from Arizona."

"Ah, you must be calling about that boy they found over in Lupton."

"Yes. Sorry for calling when I know you probably have your hands full with that case."

"That and a lot of others. Crystal meth. It was a scourge before, but after that *Breaking Bad*? Every bonehead with a trailer wants to reinvent himself as a new drug kingpin."

"Well, there's a local case here, a missing girl, that has some similarities to what I saw in the paper this morning about this Peter LeToche."

"Oh?"

"Yes. Girl's the same age and went missing not long after your boy. There's evidence she was murdered, but no body. Can I ask if you have any idea how the boy died?"

"Sure. Don't take this as gospel, but between you and me, I'd say there's a fair chance the kid was killed by a mountain lion. I saw the body. He had lacerations at least superficially consistent with a mountain lion attack. Especially around the throat, which is what they go for. I've seen two other attacks in my life, and the injuries look the same."

"Are mountain lion attacks unusual?"

"Sure, rare as getting struck by lightning, but it happens. Plus we've had other attacks like that in recent years. Their habitat is getting disrupted, you know."

"Any idea where the boy has been? He disappeared eight months ago, didn't he?"

"Yeah. Good chance with this one that he ran away from his family and was secretly living with his uncle. It's that kind of family. Lots of domestic problems."

"His uncle lives in Lupton?"

"No. He's got a house out there in Defiance, out in the middle of nowhere. Got a job at the casino. But it wouldn't be hard for a kid to get himself across the border to Lupton. Probably could walk it. Only weird thing is the kid was missing his shirt."

"So, you talked to the uncle?"

"Yeah, a few times. He refuses to admit to having the kid out there living with him, but I think he did. He just didn't want to get in trouble."

"Seems strange that a kid that age could run off by himself and stay with a relative for nine months and not get caught."

"We've got a lot of those kinds of cases around here in the poorer districts. In fact, I'm looking right now at our missing kids wall and we've got five kids up there. All Gallup and vicinity.

Peter's still up there, so we'll need to take him down, but that leaves four. Probably all of them are runaways or family abductions by relatives trying to stop abuse."

"Five missing kids?"

"Yep, all black. Between the ages of four and seven."

"What?"

"Between the ages of four and…."

"No, before."

"All black?"

After a lengthy pause, Strait said. "Officer, you've been a great help. I'm not sure if this needs to go federal, but it's good to have in the data just in case."

"Just for the record, I don't think the disappearances are connected. Seriously, I've been at this station for fourteen years, and that wall is always filled up with pictures."

"You're probably right, but if nothing else, my superiors will go ape-shit if I give them this report and don't include details like that. Would you mind giving me some background on these kids? Sorry for being a pain in the ass."

"Oh, no worries. Got an email address? I can just send over scans now. Won't take but a minute."

"That'd be great."

"Could you do me a favor back?"

"Sure, anything."

"Could you come to my house and convince my wife that FBI agents have a better life than Gallup policemen?"

Strait laughed and said next time he was in Gallup, he'd give it his best shot. He gave officer Steerson his email address. After he hung up, he turned on his computer. By the time his email came up, Steerson had already sent him the files.

He was about to open them when it dawned on him that what he really needed to do was find Randy Street. But he was so exhausted. The medicine, along with lack of sleep and the shocks of the past days had drained him.

Without really wanting to, he lay on his bed. The medicine Watanabe had given him was making him groggy. He started thinking about the best thing to do next. Maybe he could find Randy Street at that homeless shelter next to the railroad tracks. He yawned, then yawned again. He shut his eyes, forced them open, then they fell closed again.

When Strait awoke, the whole day had gone by and it was late evening. He pulled himself out of bed and made a cup of good Columbian coffee. As he sat drinking it on the bed, he reached over and plugged the phone in. It immediately rang. *Fuck. Gelder.* Strait took a deep breath and picked up.

"Hello?"

"James? It's Graham."

"I'm relieved to hear your voice."

"Usually you're irritated to hear it."

"I was expecting someone even more irritating."

"That would be Bureau Chief Gelder?"

"He called you too?"

"Yes. After calling you many times with no luck. He's rather miffed with you, mate. And lucky me, I also received a call from Karl Greyson. You remember him, don't you?"

"The asshole who got us shot and Amelia killed?" Strait cleared his throat. "Hard to forget."

"And the asshole who is now my boss at laboratory science. I should also remind you that he was officially exonerated."

Strait scoffed. "Officially. But he should have been brought up on charges."

"You sound irritated."

Strait sighed. "In the last forty-eight hours, I've been threatened with arrest, shot at, and hospitalized with a vertigo attack."

"Is that all?"

"On the plus side, I slept with a beautiful woman."

"She isn't the one who tried to shoot you, I hope."

"No. She's a pastor at the local church."

"You slept with a pastor?"

"You got a problem with that?"

"Who tried to shoot you?"

"I don't know. A guy in combat fatigues who drives a black motorcycle. I've seen him following me twice." Strait related his visit to Marvin Williams and the attack on the cabin by the man with the AK.

Graham was silent for several beats. He said, "I don't think these kinds of experiences were what your doctor intended when he advised you to rest."

"What did Gelder call you about?"

"It went something like this. The chief of police of your town rang up the special agent in charge in Phoenix, a chap named Matt Grippe, who in turn called Gelder to complain about you. There's some kerfuffle over who's in charge of you. Are you under the supervision of the Quantico administration? The Virginia field office? The Phoenix field office? The regulations aren't clear. But everyone agrees that you've been naughty and must stop. They're worried their golden boy will tarnish his gleaming reputation as a national hero."

Strait sighed.

"It's no coincidence their anxiety is erupting at the same time Congress is voting on an agency budget increase."

"Christ."

"Here's what's happening. I'm being transferred to Pine River for a short time. A special assignment. I'm to personally check up on you and constrain your adventurousness."

Strait groaned. "Seriously?"

"Yes."

"Why you?"

"Because we're friends. And they trust me."

"Graham, I didn't want you tangled up in this."

"Is that why you sent me blood and larvae samples?"

"I'm sorry."

"It's okay. This will give me an excuse to get away from my wife and children. You know how much I detest being around them."

"Wait. Does Gelder know I sent you those samples?"

"He only knows what your lovely chief of police told him. Does Kladspell know you sent me the samples?"

"No. Just that I tossed them on his expensive desk."

"This reminds me of the second reason for my call. I have the test results for you."

James sat up. "Really?"

"Yes, sir."

"That was fast."

"Some strings for you, I pulled," he said, affecting a creepy, English-accented imitation of Yoda.

"I hate it when you talk like that."

"The results came as rather a shock."

"Oh?"

"To review, you asked me to check blood and insect samples from the area Kladspell is calling the scene of a murder."

"Right."

"First off, none of the juicy larvae contained any discernable human DNA. Which leads to the second point. There are a couple of odd things about the larvae and full-grown flies you sent. The crime scene was estimated to have been found by that hiker less than a day after it was produced, correct?"

"Yes. Which means it appeared five or six days ago."

"But the flies were found only a day after the scene was reported, correct?"

"Yes."

"You did a thoroughgoing survey of the area, I expect."

"I did what I could."

"You mentioned in your note that no other flies were in the area?"

"Right."

"You also found no pupae anywhere, even though you found larvae and flies."

"Yes."

"Okay. This information provides us a hypothetical timeline. Blowfly eggs hatch within twelve to twenty-four hours. Larvae then go through three instar stages. The larvae you found were in the final stage, about fifteen millimeters long, which is reached at day five. Another day, they would have turned into pupae and clambered a few centimeters into the neighboring soil. To confirm, you did dig into the soil around the blood?"

"Yes, I dug into the areas where the blood wasn't pooled."

"When again did the hiker call the police about finding the crime scene?"

"Sunday, late afternoon. At five-fifteen, I think."

"And you dug up the larvae on Thursday afternoon. Which makes the crime scene appear sometime in the early morning hours of Saturday. Probably the middle of the night."

"Makes sense. But I could have pieced that together without the damned flies."

"Here's the trick. The adult flies you sent me are not blowflies."

"Really?"

"Yes, sir."

"I thought they looked like blowflies. They're metallic-looking."

"They weren't metallic-looking enough to be blowflies."

"How could you tell they weren't blowflies then?"

"Blowflies are larger. They're blue. The ones you sent are just houseflies."

"Is this important?"

"I wasn't sure if it was or not. But it was strange."

"Don't houseflies also lay eggs in stuff like blood too?"

"Yes. But the larvae *were* blowfly larvae."

"Huh?"

"You heard me correctly."

"How did you know?"

"They look different."

"You can tell just by looking that larvae is from a blowfly instead of a housefly?"

"I paid attention in our forensic entomology class."

"I still don't see why this is important."

"I was puzzled, so I contacted a friend over at the Museum of Natural History who specializes in this stuff. He's one of these guys the police around here consult on time-of-death situations. He's an absolute zealot about flies."

"A fly zealot?"

"Yes. Luckily for us. I left the samples with him in the morning and he called me at home at 11:30pm that same night. Woke me up, his voice brimming with excitement. He'd spent the entire day looking at the larvae and the adults. Not only that, but he conferred with several of his colleagues."

"Wow."

"Do you want to know why he did that?"

"Yes."

"Because, my friend, the larvae feeding on that blood were strange larvae."

"Strange…?"

"He examined the larvae in detail and found that they are not native to your region of America at all. In fact, they are not even from America. He'd never seen larvae like these. That's why he consulted colleagues from far and wide to pin down where these bugs came from. He even did a CT scan of them."

"You're joking."

"No. They have a little machine for doing CT scans on maggots."

"Are you going to tell me what they found out?"

"The maggots are from…drum roll…New Zealand."

Strait spent a long moment in silence, unable to puzzle out this information.

"New Zealand? You mean, the small island country near Australia?"

"Yes. The species is intrinsic to the New Zealand islands. It's called *Calliphora quadrimaculata.* The doctor assured me that finding these here is highly unusual given how far away New Zealand is. However, it's not a complete shock. In these days of international travel, blowflies are real globetrotters, it seems. The airports don't scan for their eggs. What *is* very surprising, however, and relevant in terms of processing this particular crime scene, is that these larvae generally don't thrive in the climate of the area where you found them. They like higher-altitude environments, preferably mountaintops."

Strait considered this. "So, the implication is whoever committed this crime killed the girl up in the mountains, left her there for a few days before carting the body down and dumping it in the river. The body had eggs laid in it. Eggs from a species of blowfly that is, strangely, not from around here. And some of them spilled in the dirt as he did it. Then the rain came and washed most of the blood away, but some got under, or remained under, the rock, as did the maggots that hatched from the eggs?"

"An astute reconstruction, my friend. One that is, however, completely wrong. That is, given the next piece of information." Graham said. "Before I give it to you, I need to confirm that you didn't send me all of this as a practical joke?"

"What are you talking about?"

"The blood didn't come from a human."

"How's that?"

"It's not human blood."

"What do you mean?"

"It's chicken blood."

"No fucking way."

"Actually, it's *bird* blood. I'm conjecturing the type was chickens. Judging by the amount of blood, it came from a whole goddamned gaggle of the feathered beasts. Buckets and bucketsful.

Which reminds me, you didn't happen to find any feathers?"

"No feathers."

"Then the chickens, or whatever bird was used, were slaughtered somewhere else and their blood was drained into containers and carried to the bank of that river and poured there."

Strait said, "Sloshed all over Jophia Williams's dress. In order to…"

"Fake the little girl's murder."

Strait's head was throbbing. "She wasn't killed."

"Not unless she has chicken blood in her veins. Of course, she could have been murdered elsewhere. She could have been killed in the same place at the riverbank but without bleeding. However, the presence of lots of chicken blood in the context of her clothing presents a rather serious complication to these exotic hypotheses. It seems most probable that whoever put this blood by the river was trying to fake her death so as to keep her alive for his own use without worrying about interference from those searching for her."

A chill shot through Strait. *For his own use.*

"Are you a hundred percent sure it was bird blood?"

"Checked the cells myself. Wasn't hard to see. The erythrocytes were completely nucleated, a sure giveaway of a bird species."

Strait cleared his throat. "So, we've got to assume this girl is out there somewhere, alive."

"Yes."

"Graham, you're a genius."

"That's why I have a big G on my cape."

"So, what is the connection between all this stuff and the information about the blowfly larvae?"

Footer chuckled. "Probably no connection at all. But it's

interesting, isn't it?"

"Not really."

"You need to learn to better appreciate the natural world, mate."

"I'll take it under advisement. I could still use your help if I keep looking for this girl. But I don't want you to get in trouble."

"Oh, in for a dollar, in for a pound, as they say."

"I think that's, in for a penny, in for a pound, but whatever. Are you certain you're willing to help? I mean, Gelder is sending you down here specifically to stop me."

"James, in all seriousness, I'm conflicted about helping. But there is a higher principle at stake here."

"Which is?"

"The evidence says the girl is probably still alive."

"You're a good man, Graham."

"By the way, I grew curious about what kind of wanker this chief of police is. So I ran his name through some of the company databases."

"What did you find?"

"Originally from Tennessee. Serious churchgoer. He belongs to a fundamentalist sect that will not permit even watching movies or TV. A very dull man. Doesn't drink, smoke, or swear."

"He'll swear if you push him far enough."

"His father was a soldier in the Army, moved around a lot, but the family settled in Tennessee long enough for the young August Kladspell to attend high school. Upon graduation, the lad tried to join the army himself, but they wouldn't accept him."

"Why?"

"He's blind in one eye. Odd that such a small thing would keep you out of the military, but I guess it affects your binocular vision, which affects your ability to shoot straight. So Kladspell joined the Tennessee PD, which I gather is not particular about lazy eyes, about the time you were in junior high imagining what a girl looked like naked. Do you still wonder about that?"

Strait issued an agitated grunt. "Kladspell?"

"Overall, he comported himself well in the Tennessee department. However, five years in, Kladspell's story does get interesting. One day, out of the blue, he was hit with a brutality charge. It seems he injured a fourteen-year-old Mexican-American boy rather severely with a flashlight, while yelling some unkind comments about our brethren south of the border. But the kid was a golden boy, straight As and so on. Plus he was the son of a prominent Latino politician. Lawsuits were threatened. Push came to shove and the sordid business was hushed up without leaving a stain on Kladspell's official record. But he needed to voluntarily resign."

"Then he moved to Arizona?"

"Yes. And he was hired in at a high rank at the Pine River police department."

"How did he manage that?"

"Nothing here about that. Maybe he had help from the inside. He seems to have performed competently in the Pine River police department enough to rise within a decade to the head position."

"Hard to see how we're talking about the same man."

"Maybe you caught him on a bad day."

"Hey, Graham?"

"Yes, darling?"

"You have your system up now? Can you check out some other names for me?"

"Sure. Whose privacy do you want to invade?"

Strait asked him to look up Julie's husband, Duane Dumphey.

He could hear Footer tapping away on a keyboard. After a pause, he said, “this Dumphey fellow is the husband of your childhood sweetheart?”

“My childhood neighbor.”

“Okay, Dumphey, Duane R., twenty-eight years old. Graduated police academy March of last year, and began active duty at the Pine River department in April. Grew up in Pine River. Doesn’t sound like the brightest bulb on the marquee. He spent a night in jail at age seventeen after he and a group of friends became inebriated and vandalized some mailboxes. No charges were filed, however.”

“You can see that in the database? I thought youth records were deleted if no charges were filed.”

“We have our ways. Also, little Duane was a poor student in high school. He was held back a year and still couldn’t graduate. He finally got his diploma by taking the GED. He joined the army. He signed on for a tour in Afghanistan. A soldier, then a cop.”

“What about his missing toe?”

“Missing toe?”

”He got injured.”

“Hang on.” More tapping on a keyboard.

“Oh, yes, I see. He didn’t completely finish his tour in Afghanistan. He was kicked out on a medical after one year and nine months. He lost the small toe of his right foot. Gunshot wound. Not much of an injury, but the way it influences the overall stability of the foot translated into a discharge. It seems he can’t walk or run very far without developing crippling pain. Wow. He was discharged with only a small fraction of the benefits, it seems.”

“Stuff happens.”

“He must be bitter.”

"He drinks a lot. I have a few more names, please."

"Shoot."

"Gus Bear."

"Bear as in the forest animal?"

"Yes."

The sound of computer keys tapping. "Nothing."

"Nothing? Try a fuzzy search."

"I did that."

"Do you mean, there's no one in any database in the entire country with the name Gus Bear, not even with any close spellings?"

"That's correct."

"How about Lennon Bear?"

Tapping. "There are teddy bears for sale made with a resemblance to John Lennon, but no human beings named Lennon Bear."

"Keith Bear?"

"I have some people with that name, but none living in Pine River."

"They're using fake names."

"So it seems. Who are they?"

"Three brothers who sold me a car. They run an auto repair shop called Bear Brothers Auto. It's on the route where Jophia Williams disappeared."

"The plot thickens. It could be a simple matter of fitting the names to the name of the shop. You know, for advertisement purposes. Their real name might be Ribowinovitz, which doesn't have quite the sales moxy as Bear."

"Can you check who owns Bear Brothers Auto Repair?"

"Hold on. Yes, it's right here. The name on the deed is one Jinny Schwartz. She purchased the place five years ago. She's…let me see…she's sixty-four years old, moved to Pine River from Alabama five years ago too. But, wait, she became married shortly after buying the car repair shop. Her name is Jinny Wilson now."

"But not Bear?"

"Not Bear."

"How about Gus Schwartz?"

"Let's see. There are quite a few of them, and, yes, one lives in Pine River."

"And?"

"And he's eight years old."

"Lennon Schwartz?"

"No one in Pine River by that name."

"Jesus. Who are these guys?"

"Maybe get me a photograph of them and I can do a facial recognition search. Or better yet, some fingerprints…"

"I have another name. Randy Street. Native American. Homeless. I think he's a member of the Hopi tribe."

"Hold on."

"I heard he recently did time in prison. Rumor has it he attacked his mother."

"Hmm…I do have a Randall Street. Yes. Arizona. Inmate. Not Hopi. Navajo. Released April of this year."

More tapping on the computer.

"He's missing an eye?" asked Graham.

"That's the one."

"Hold the presses."

"What?"

"Jackpot."

"What did you find?"

"You said he served time for attacking his mother? This is

false."

"What did he do?"

"Mr. Randall Street served time in the Arizona State Federal Penitentiary for sexual assault. Of a nine-year-old girl."

Chapter Twenty

Strait couldn't sleep. At hearing the news about Randy Street, his first impulse was to hunt the homeless man down and force the information about the girl out of him. But it was after midnight and he didn't know where to search. In the dark in bed he lay in a whirlpool of indecision, and tossed and turned all night. What was the best plan?

He finally fell asleep around five o'clock and when he woke up, he was stunned to find it was already past four in the afternoon. He forced himself to get up, took a shower and dressed, considering what he should do about Randy Street. He fetched the newspaper and opened it when he sat down with a cup of coffee. His blood went cold at the headline.

FATHER ARRESTED IN GIRL'S DISAPPEARANCE

The search for nine-year-old Jophia Williams took a dramatic turn last night as police converged at the secluded southside cabin of the girl's father. Marvin Williams, 47, was taken into custody after a brief stand-off between Pine River police department officers and a group of armed individuals claiming to be protecting the suspect. The police department had initially rejected Williams as a suspect after an investigation demonstrated he had an alibi. But suspicions were reawakened when Francis Nabors, a professor at Northern Arizona University who had claimed he was with Williams on the day of the girl's disappearance, reversed his original statement to the police and admitted he had lied. Nabors, a professor of cultural studies, told police originally that he had been on a fishing trip with Mr. Williams on the day Jophia Williams vanished. Nabors confessed that he'd fabricated the alibi when he was confronted with surveillance camera evidence that showed him working in his office building at the same time he claimed to be with Williams. A former member of the black militant group Moorish Republican Army, Williams served fifteen years in federal prison for conspiracy in the bombing of a law office in Chicago.

Police Chief August Kladspell said the fact that Williams lied suggests an organized attempt was made by community residents to shield Williams from justice. "The southside community out there worships this man and will do anything to protect him," said Kladspell at an evening press conference.

Twenty minutes later, Strait roared up to the police department in his clanky station wagon and saw Kladspell in the parking lot getting into his car. Strait stopped behind him and jumped out.

At the sight of Strait, the chief turned and reached for his sidearm. He had it halfway out when he recognized who it was.

"Wo there, city boy! Don't they teach you in the FBI that moving up fast on a cop can get you shot?"

"We need to talk."

"We don't need to do anything, Strait."

"You arrested Marvin Williams?"

Kladspell laughed. That annoying, self-satisfied chuckle. "Yep. I'm looking forward to throwing that one away."

"All because Francis Nabors lied about his alibi?"

"Good enough for me. Marvin Williams is guilty."

"Did it occur to you that Francis gave him an alibi to protect him from being unfairly accused? You've got no evidence that Marvin did anything."

Kladspell snorted. "Look at you, on first-name basis with a

terrorist and his lying sympathizer. I don't need evidence. I have knowledge. From fifty-three years of experience on this planet and a good sense of what makes people tick. I talk to God every day too, something you might benefit from trying. All three point me directly to Marvin Williams."

"But you don't have a case. No jury will convict him."

"We'll figure that out. Just have to get a confession."

"Okay, Chief, since you know so much, what do you know about Randy Street?"

"Who?"

"Randy Street is a homeless man who arrived in town in April, less than a month before Jophia Williams went missing. He'd just been released from federal prison where he was serving a sentence for sexually molesting a nine-year-old girl."

"Bullhockey."

"That's your response?"

"Strait, we've got three convicted pedophiles in this town. I know exactly where they live. I drive by their houses nearly every day, so they know I'm watching them. We had more of those perverts living here when I became chief, but after experiencing firsthand how seriously I take their presence in this town, they acquired the wisdom that there were other towns more suitable for them to live in. I hope over the next year the other three will arrive at similar wisdom. If we had any child molester named Randy Street, I'd know about it."

"Looks like one slipped past you."

Kladspell smirked. "Okay, Strait, just to go along with your joke. If I was interested in talking to this so-called child molester, this Randy fellow, where would I find him?"

"I don't know. He disappeared."

Kladspell chuckled again. "Well, ain't that convenient? You want me to release your friend Marvin Williams because the real criminal is some phantom named Randy Street who just happened to have vanished into thin air, so I can't even talk to him."

"He's real, chief. Look him up."

"I don't need to, because he's not real. If he was, I'd know about him."

"Are you seriously saying that there's no chance that a convicted child molester, even a homeless drifter, could have slipped past you? Do you know what you sound like?"

"No one slipped through."

"Just like nothing slipped through your investigation of this missing girl? You didn't even bother to analyze the blood from the river."

"I already told you, the blood was too diluted to use."

"For DNA testing? Do you know the first thing about forensics? About processing a crime scene?"

"You'd better shut your mouth, Strait."

"I brought you viable samples from the crime scene to analyze. You threw them back at me."

"You brought me samples of *something* you *claimed* was from the river. Big FBI hero, trying to make me look bad."

"What the fuck are you talking about?"

"It was probably your own blood."

"It was chicken blood."

"What was that?"

"You heard me. I had it analyzed. Someone threw chicken blood on the river bank to make it look like the girl was murdered."

"Okay, Strait, I've had enough. I told you to stay away from this case. You got sixty seconds to get in your car or I put on the bracelets."

Kladspell put one hand on his gun and the other on the handcuffs hanging from his belt.

"Chief Kladspell, please listen to reason. The girl is probably alive. Randy Street is a convicted child molester who could have her in captivity somewhere in those woods. You arrested the wrong man."

"Forty seconds."

"Jesus, if you don't hunt down Randy Street, I'm going to."

"Thirty."

"Asshole."

Strait turned and walked to his car and was in the driver's seat by the time Kladspell reached zero.

Chapter Twenty-one

Strait drove from the police department to the Pot Belly Café. It was approaching dinnertime, but the rush hadn't hit yet and the place was nearly empty. He marched in intending to talk to Carol to see if she could give him some idea of where he could find Randy Street. He saw no one in the kitchen area, so he sat down and looked at the menu. The younger waitress emerged from a back room and approached Strait with the order pad.

"Hi, James. Don't usually see you in the afternoon."

"Carol still at home?"

"No, she's here today. She went upstairs for something. She'll be down in a minute. Can I get you?"

"Cup of decaf."

As Strait watched her walk away, he noticed Gus Bear was sitting in his usual booth along the adjacent wall watching her too. Gus saw him and grinned. "Hey buddy, how's it hanging?"

Is this prick always here?

"Pretty low, tell the truth."

"Ain't the car, is it?"

Carol entered the room from the back. She had a clipboard in one hand and a cane in the other. She froze when she saw Strait, a look of anxiety on her face. She composed herself and continued into the kitchen area, hobbling on the cane.

The waitress arrived with a steaming cup of coffee. He said in a lowered voice, "can you ask Carol to come over here?"

Soon, Carol came over to the table, limping badly.

"You should be sitting down."

"It looks worse than it is."

"What happened?"

"Hiking accident. You wanted to ask me something?"

"I'm looking for Randy Street."

Her face went rigid. "Why?"

"He tried to tell me something important yesterday. But…" Strait shot a look at Gus, who was absorbed in his newspaper. "…we got interrupted."

"I haven't seen him."

"Any idea if he'll be in today?"

"No idea. None at all. As a matter of fact, he told me last time he was leaving town soon. The weather's getting cold. He was going down to Phoenix. Probably he hit the road already."

"Is something wrong?"

"Why?"

"You seem nervous."

"Everything's fine."

She turned and started to hobble away.

"If you see him, tell him I'm looking for him. I'm at the Blue Rabbit."

She nodded without turning around.

Strait saw Gus Bear jiggling his coffee cup in his direction.

"Women, huh?" he said.

Strait took a copy of the Arizona *Republic* from the shelves. He took a sip of his coffee and opened the paper and looked again at the same story he'd seen in his hotel room, about the arrest of Marvin Williams.

"Hey, Buddy?"

I'm not your buddy, Gus. Or whatever your real name is.

"Heard you got a problem with your ear. Makes you dizzy?"

Strait nodded.

"You got this condition because of your FBI work?"

"Probably."

Gus twisted his face into an expression that seemed almost sympathetic. "I have the highest respect for you men in uniform. It breaks my heart to hear about the sacrifice you made."

Strait kept his gaze fixed on Carol, who was busying herself with serving orders. She was doing too much, too frantically. She glanced at him once and looked away.

Gus said, "my father was in the service."

"That so?" Strait said.

"Infantry."

"Oh."

"Died in 'nam when I was six."

"Sorry."

"You and me both lost fathers. To foreigners."

Strait finished the last of his coffee. At the counter, when he paid his bill, he told Carol again, "Let me know if you hear anything from Randy, okay?"

She nodded curtly and turned away.

After leaving the café, he headed toward the train station. His boots crunching on broken bottles, he walked alongside the condemned factory. He turned right at the train tracks and continued along the decaying building until he came to the iron door with the metal box with the sign on it announcing the hours and rules of the homeless shelter. He flipped open the lid and pressed the red buzzer inside. Nothing happened. He pressed it again. After the third try, a gruff voice crackled on the intercom. "Door ain't open 'til eight."

"I'm looking for someone."

"Get lost." A slamming noise came over crackling through the ancient speaker.

Strait pressed the red button again.

"Fuck you want?"

"I'm investigating a crime and a man who sometimes stays here contacted me and said he had some information about it."

"You a cop?"

"FBI."

"Fuck. Hold on."

Strait could hear from deep in the building a door banging open and shut, footsteps banging up, a heavy bolt being thrown. The big metal door creaked open. The man standing there was acne-covered and wearing a frayed Slayer concert T-shirt. His black hair was trimmed close to his skull. On one flabby bicep was a tattoo of a carrot. On the other was a tattoo of Jesus Christ on the cross.

The man said, "I can't tell you shit. We have privacy rules."

"Do your privacy rules hold even in a life and death situation?"

The man eyed him dubiously.

"What sort of life and death situation?"

"The kind where a child is alive now and if she isn't found quickly will die."

The man sighed dramatically. "Follow me."

Strait trailed him into the building. A spring mechanism slammed the door shut and he was in a hallway so dark he could barely make out the walls. He could tell by the uneasy shifting under his feet that the flooring was a jury-rigged succession of unanchored plywood panels thrown over whatever holes or rips were in the original floor. They turned left into another hallway, this one lit at the end with a single lightbulb dangling on a wire.

"My office," the man said, tossing open a door. A blast of light flooded the hallway as they entered.

The room was a mess. Candy bar wrappers and greasy bags

from fast food joints and old pizza boxes were scattered on a floor with carpeting so threadbare the waterspotted wooden floor could be seen in the holes poking through. The room had a desk piled with papers and an antique wooden office chair with a slatted back. A ratty orange sofa was against one wall under a row of posters cautioning against the sharing of needles and unsafe sex. One poster had a close-up rendering of the face of a winsome Jesus in his crown of thorns, spiked to the cross, eyes twisted upward toward a bright star shooting beams of golden light earthward. One small window overlooked a much larger room on the floor below. The second room was lined with folding army surplus cots arranged in rows. Three or four of the cots had men lying in them but most were empty. In front of the room, on the opposite side from the small window, was a raised platform with a podium and a severe wooden cross nailed to the wall behind it.

"We got a few old-timers we let stay here even during the day 'cause they're too old to move around." He shoved up his hand at Strait. "Conrad Shoemeal. You can just call me Con." Strait shook it tentatively. "And your name is...?"

"Strait."

Conrad rubbed a pimple on his cheek. "Good to hear you're straight. Lot of the faggots come in here have AIDS." The man pulled back his hand from Strait's and held it aloft, far from him, and gave it a look of disgust. "You never know what you're going to catch when you touch'em, nowaddamean?"

"Mr. Shoemeal, who runs this place?"

"The Window Mission. As in 'when God closes a door, he opens a…'"

Strait glanced around. "Are there any windows in this place?"

Shoemeal tapped his hand on the small pane separating

himself and the big room filled with cots. "This is the only one. Place used to be a porn theater. Do you fucking believe it? This was where they had the projector. My office was the projectionist booth. They tore out all the seats down there and put in those cots. Where them bums are sleeping is where guys used to jerk off."

"Are you here full-time?"

"More than. I live here. This is my office and my bedroom. Behind that curtain's my bed."

An uproar came from the floor. Two old men were grappling over something, arms flailing. One pulled away and began marching resolutely across the room, his eyes up at the window. He yelled, "Con! Con!"

"Oh, fuck." said Shoemeal. From behind his desk, he produced a thick black metal rod, about the length of his forearm. With a flick of his wrist, the rod doubled its length. He approached the door just as the man threw it open.

He had sharp cheeks, a broad nose, and bronze skin on the way to yellow from liver damage. His hair hung well over his shoulders and a black beard with starbursts of grey grew unevenly from his cheeks and chin. His red eyes were sunken so deeply they seemed to be disappearing into the exorbitant half-moons of fat beneath them. "Yazzie stole my smokes," he yelled.

"Jesus fucking Christ, Emerson."

Shoemeal slid open the window and brandished the black stick. He bellowed down at the man who'd grappled with Emerson. "Yazzie, give him his cigarettes, now. Or I'll come down there and fuck you with this stick."

Yazzie dropped the pack of cigarettes on the floor and stepped away from it like it was a rattlesnake. "He can have'em," he called up. "I only wanted to see what brand they were."

“Thanks, Con,” said Emerson. Shoemeal held up the black stick and brought it down with a fierce whack on the surface of his wooden desk. “Emerson! If you ever come into this office again without knocking, I’ll beat your fucking face in.” Emerson darted from the room.

Shoemeal stared sadly through the small aperture. “Getting so you can’t trust even the old-timers to behave.”

“That’s a Peacekeeper RCB, isn’t it?” Strait had personally trained recruits using several brands of retractable fighting batons. The Peacekeeper International Rapid Containment Baton was the most vicious fighting stick on the market. Its strike tip was an inch wide.

Con’s blubbery lips hung open. “The fuck you know that?”

“I trained with them.”

Con’s eyes widened. “Hey…you’re that guy.”

“What guy?”

“That guy from the cover of *Newsweek*.” Shoemeal smiled like a small boy in wonder. He held out his hand. “Wow. You’re an American hero. Let me shake your hand.”

“I thought we already did that.” Strait reached out his hand, then pulled it back. “Do you really hit them with that stick?”

Shoemeal frowned. “Of course not. We’re Christians here.” He pointed to the tattoo of the writhing-in-agony Jesus on his arm. He recited, “Our sole duty, performed energetically without regard to self-interest, is to help those lost from Christ back on a straight path to righteousness.”

“Then why do you have the stick?”

“To grease the wheel.”

Strait narrowed his eyes at Shoemeal. “Sticks like this are only legally permitted for law enforcement officers.”

"Really? I got it at the army surplus store."

"I'm looking for a homeless man. A Native American with one eye. Goes by the name of Randy Street."

Shoemeal's thoughts bubbled behind his pimply face. "Lot of guys come through here. Maybe I know him. But it's hard to remember."

"Hard to remember a Navajo with one eye?"

"You trying to find Injin Joe for what he done to Tom and Huck?"

When Strait didn't share his smirk, Shoemeal said, "Did I mention how we get our funding here?"

"No."

Shoemeal held out his hand and wiggled his fingers. He whispered, "donations."

"Donations?"

"*You* know, brother. Donations. They keep the heat on, the toilets clean…"

"A donation? Are you fucking kidding me?"

Strait took a step forward. He was easily eight inches taller than Shoemeal. The man's eyes widened and he raised the fighting stick. Strait grabbed the stick with his right hand, twisted it down crosswise, and snapped his right elbow back into Shoemeal's nose. Con fell backwards with a cry. The table he landed on collapsed under his weight. Strait stood over him wielding the baton.

"Listen carefully, Con. A child's life is in danger. Randy Street has information that will help me find her. You want a donation?" He raised the baton. "How about if I donate this stick to your head?"

Shoemeal squealed. "Okay!"

"Okay what?"

"He ain't been here a few days but I know where he hangs out!"

"Where?"

"The Meadows, man. That park on the corner of Jersey and Plymouth. Southwest side. If he ain't there, someone'll know where he is. Just ask'em for Doll Man."

"Doll Man?"

"Everyone calls him Doll Man."

"Why?"

"Dude likes dolls. Them Indian dolls? He makes them. He sells them to tourists."

"If you're lying to me, I'll come back here with something a lot bigger than this stick."

"I swear!"

Strait left Shoemeal on the floor nursing his bloody nose. He took the baton with him.

Chapter Twenty-two

It was well after dark when Strait got to the Meadows. The parking lot was empty. Weeds poked up through cracks in the asphalt. One of the two streetlights was broken, smashed by a lobbed rock, and the other was buzzing and cracking, bursts of energy snapping its dull yellow glow on and off.

He stepped from the car and looked over the decrepit lot and the blackness of the park beyond. He collapsed the baton he'd taken from Shoemeal, making it small enough to fit into his coat pocket. In a holster under his jacket, he carried his Glock. As he moved across the parking lot and out of the flickering street light, broken glass and used hypodermic needles crackled under his boots. He stepped over the curb and into the darkness. He could make out, with the help of the frail, yellow-blue sheet of light cast by the moon and a sprinkling of streetlights on the other side of the park, an open area about an acre wide, spotted with trees around the perimeter. Past the farthest edge of the park, the dim outline of neighborhood houses. He could hear leaves trickling to the ground in the light breeze moving through the trees. It was hard to believe this was the most dangerous park in the town.

But everyone knew that those peaceful-looking houses, known as the Stacks, were bases for all manner of criminality, and everyone knew there was no tranquil meadow in The Meadows. The area was ground-zero for all the big city shit that manifested itself just as horrifically in this small town as it did in Phoenix, maybe even more so because there were fewer police to stop it. No children played in the playground. At one time an attempt was made to create a duck pond in the park, which withered to nothing and left a concrete-lined hole. Strait recalled a dead teen girl was found in the hole back in 1998 or 1999, her body set ablaze.

Strait heard whispering. He squinted and perceived in the gloom, under the stand of trees closest to him, a group of people. As he approached, he saw about a dozen of them seated on the grass or on scraps of cardboard. Their clothes were ragged and filthy. They were passing a couple of bottles around. None of them was Randy Street.

"Hello," said Strait.

"Howdy, officer," said an old bald man with a long beard. He held up a wine bottle. "Want a drink?"

"No, thanks. I'm not a cop."

The man cackled. "Suit yourself, officer." He took a long swig and handed off the bottle to a woman seated next to him. She spoke in a fretful, oddly genteel voice. "Oh, heavens, Mr. Policeman. Are we breaking the law?"

"I'm not a cop."

"Would you like to join us?"

The woman could have been forty or seventy. Her hair was a nest of dirty black and grey snarls that fell unevenly down her shoulders. She wore a very large dress, brightly flowered, that swallowed up her body from neck to foot. She had puffy cheeks and compassionate eyes.

"Thank you," said Strait. "But I can't stay long."

"Oh. That's a shame," she said. "you seem like such a nice young man."

The tribe had gone silent and were watching Strait.

He raised his voice so they could all hear. "Do any of you know a man named Randy Street?"

Some of the people glanced at each other and others kept staring at Strait. No one answered.

"Doll Man?" Looks of recognition flashed on several faces. The mention of Doll Man had provoked especially strong recognition on the woman's face, which she then tried to hide.

"Ma'am, do you know Doll Man?"

"Who?"

"Doll Man. Native American with one eye?"

"Young man, I would like to help you, but I'm afraid I don't know anyone who fits that description."

Three men stepped out of the dark and approached Strait. As if on cue, the old woman with the ratty hair and the others stood and moved away.

The new men were teenagers. Black, lean, cocky. Different in every way from the homeless on the ground. They looked like they'd dressed themselves from a catalogue for gangbangers.

"Yo, what up?" said one of the young men. From his bearing and confidence, and the way the others stood behind him, this one was clearly the leader.

"Who this white boy?" said another.

"Five-O for sure," said the third.

"White boy, what you doing in our park?"

"I'm looking for someone. Goes by Doll Man. Got one eye."

"Cops gots to show their badges."

"I'm not a cop."

"Then ain't no need you be looking for nobody."

"Look, this is important."

The three gangbangers seemed to communicate without speaking. They stepped around him smoothly so no matter which way he faced, two were standing behind him on either side, outside his line of vision.

Before they'd even stopped moving, Strait cracked the palm

of his hand into the leader's face. The kid collapsed and Strait flicked open the combat baton and turned on the other two. One made a half-decided move toward pulling a gun from the back of his pants and Strait grabbed him by the wrist before the gun was halfway up, gave it a vicious twist that made him drop the weapon. He slashed the baton downward and hit him on the back of the thigh. The kid screamed and fell clutching his leg. The third gangbanger, wide-eyed, took a step back.

"Listen to me," said Strait. "I'm trying to find that missing girl. Jophia Williams. You know about her, right? Doll Man told me he has information about where she is. Why are you being such assholes?"

The leader got up, his expression showing injured pride. Some blood was coming from his lip.

"You looking for Jophia? Why didn't you say so?" He brushed off the grass from his pants, the gesture an attempt to hide his fear. "In that case, we'll give you a pass."

Strait picked up the gun the second kid had dropped and looked at it. He suppressed a smile. A .22 caliber pea-shooter. He stuffed it in his pocket and said to the kid, "I'll hold on to this until you're old enough to use it." He turned to the leader. "Doll Man?"

"Here's the straight-up, G. He come around here today about noon. Looked like he was in a real hurry. Hung out with them over there." The boy gestured to the group of homeless people. "Talked to that old lady with the crazy hair. They good friends. Then he be gone."

"Is that normal for him?"

"Nah. He usually here by noon and stay all day and sometimes all night. Never seen him run off like he done today. He's a good dude, too. Gives us all dolls."

"What's up with the dolls?"

"They that special kind, man. That the Indians make. Them Kachina dolls? All like little badass warriors and shit. He makes'em, sells'em to tourists. But he gives us special ones for free."

"That lady over there is his friend? She said she doesn't know him."

"She lying."

The kid made a sign and the three turned and walked away into the dark.

Strait approached the homeless group again. All were there except the woman. "Okay, everyone. Where did she go?"

The people stared off in every direction, toward the sky, the ground, the surrounding gloom, everywhere except Strait.

"She's not in trouble. I'm not here to get Doll Man in trouble either. I'm just looking for a missing child and Doll Man probably knows something that can help me find her."

Silence.

"Can any of you tell me where Doll Man is?"

A few cursory shakes of the head was all Strait got as a response.

Strait fished an old receipt from his pocket and wrote his name, phone number, and hotel room on it. He put it on the grass. "Here's where I'm staying. If you see or hear anything from Doll Man, tell him I still want to talk to him. Or if you have any information about him, contact me. There's a reward."

He stepped back. The tribe behaved like he wasn't there. "Okay, then. You all have a nice evening." Strait walked back to the parking lot, struggling with what he should do next.

Just as he reached the asphalt, the woman stepped out from behind a tree. She held out a plastic trash bag to him. He took it and looked inside. It was hard to see well in the dim streetlight, but the contents appeared to be small, human-shaped figures. Dolls.

"Mister Randy is an artist. A spirit warrior," the woman said. "He's like a son to me. But I'm not his real mother. Like all boys do when they're in danger, they go back to their mothers. That's where Randy went. His mother's house at the reservation."

"How did he get there? He's on foot."

"I don't know. He just told me he was going there. Maybe he's walking all the way. Randy asked me to watch over these dolls until he comes back. But he's not coming back, is he, Mister Policeman?"

"I'm not a policeman."

"But he's not coming back, is he?"

"I don't know."

"When you go to his mother's house, take these dolls to her for safekeeping. They are priceless works of spirit art. I can't keep carrying them around if Randy doesn't come back. And I can't throw them away."

"Do you know exactly where on the reservation she lives?"

"No, I don't. But his mother's name is Etta Street. I haven't seen Etta for many years but we used to be close friends. We went to the same school as girls."

"Ma'am, I don't think I can take these dolls. If Randy doesn't come back, wouldn't you like to keep them?"

She lowered her voice. "Did you see those men?" She gestured into the dark, in the direction the gangbangers had gone.

"Yeah."

"How long do you think these dolls will last with their type in the park?"

Chapter Twenty-three

At sunrise, Strait hit the road out of town going seventy-five miles an hour, which was the top speed he could squeeze out of the old station wagon. He roared onto the interstate and headed in the direction of the Navajo reservation. Before leaving, he'd found the address of the only Etta Street in the region and keyed the location into his smartphone and had the little GPS map open, the phone propped up inside the cup-holder.

Pine trees whipped past the car on both sides of the highway. The old engine ground away, making the body of the car, as well as Strait's bones, rattle. The drift in the steerage made the machine weave unsteadily. The car seemed always on the brink of collapse, but it kept on running. Even with the weaving of the auto and the flash of shooting trees straining his vision, he felt no strong Meniere's symptoms. Just the continuous hiss and whine of tinnitus in his right ear.

The pine trees turned to scrub and cactus as he got closer to the reservation. He turned things over in his mind. He was sure that Jophia's father was innocent and Kladspell had the wrong man in jail. To show his innocence, Strait needed to find out what really happened to the girl. For that, he was sure the key was finding Randy Street. *Please let her still be alive.*

Strait gunned the station wagon down an off-ramp and shot to a place where the road T-boned at a green and white sign with an arrow pointed right and the words above it: "Navajo Nation 4 miles".

Within minutes, he was on the reservation. He saw on the GPS map that Etta lived only about six miles away, in a cipher of a settlement called Small Hat. The Google Earth photos showed a handful of nondescript buildings tossed randomly upon the scrubland etched with cactus and creosote. The land here was thorny bushes and dust, sparsely inhabited. The houses he passed came only once every few minutes, rough old structures separated from each other by expanses of scrub and rock. He drove by a tiny outpost, a hand-painted wooden sign that said INDIAN FRY BREAD ONE DOLLAR, OSTRICH EGGS THREE DOLLARS. A few minutes later, he drove past the sign that announced he was now entering Small Hat, population 74.

The GPS map brought Strait to a flat-roofed house with the exterior painted robin's egg blue. Christmas lights were strung along its rain gutters. He stopped the station wagon in front of the house and the dust it kicked up continued to surge forth so that for a moment Strait's vision was blocked by a roiling tan cloud. He got out and moved through the dust to the front door and knocked. A few seconds later, the door opened and a woman stood squinting up him through thick glasses.

"Yes?" she said.

"Ms. Street?"

"Yes?"

"Etta Street?"

"Yes?"

Randy's mother was very short and very obese. She was garbed in a sunflower-covered tent of a blouse that hung almost to her knees. She wore yellow sneakers. The glasses through which she blinked up at Strait had a fat black frame and lenses so thick they looked like they could be used to discover new galaxies.

"Ms. Street, my name is James Strait."

"What do you want?" She squinted up at him in confusion.

"Do you have a son named Randy Street?"

"Yes, sir. Randy is my son."

"Do you happen to know where I could find your son, Ms. Street?"

"Are you a policeman?"

"No ma'am. I'm an FBI agent."

"Is Randy in trouble again?"

"I'm here because your son contacted me to say he had some important information about a crime. But then he disappeared."

"What's he done?"

"I'm not thinking he's done anything, but I need to know what he wanted to tell me."

"Sorry, mister. I ain't seen my son in a long time. I don't know where he is."

"Does he ever call you? Or do you hear about him through a third party?"

"No, sir."

"Ma'am, I hate to bother you, but this involves an endangered little girl. Do you know anyone who might know where I can find him?"

"You sure you ain't with the police department?"

"I'm not."

Suddenly there was fire in her eyes.

"You're with the police department. Admit it."

With a movement surprisingly swift, she reached behind the door and brought out a double-barrel shotgun, shucked it, and pointed it up at his face.

Strait raised his hands over his head. "Ma'am, I swear I'm not a policeman. Your son left me a note saying he had information on her whereabouts. But I have nothing to do with the police department. I tried to work with them, but they weren't helpful."

The woman hawked deeply in her throat and spit on the

ground.

“Of course they weren’t helpful. They’re a bunch of assholes.”

“I completely agree with you, ma’am. A bunch of assholes.”

She took a deep breath. She lowered the gun. She said, her voice softened, “Mister, my son ain’t no saint. To get himself another drink, he’ll connive a million ways into your wallet. But he’d never hurt anyone. He just don’t have that kind of heart. I suppose you know he went to prison for attacking a little girl, but that was all a lie. He never done no such thing.”

“Please forgive me for saying this, ma’am, but didn’t the girl herself testify against him?”

“She lied.”

“I see.”

“You don’t know that story, do you?”

“No. I’d like to know it, though.”

“Come on in then.”

She led him into the front room of the house. It was a large room, taking up the entire length of the house, sparsely furnished. A fireplace was on one wall. There were only two places to sit, an aged sofa with a tapestry draped over it and an ottoman from another era. A table, made from a cylindrical slice of a tree topped with a polished rectangular slab of wood, separated the chair and sofa. Above the fireplace was a long wooden shelf with what looked like a collection of dolls on it. Above the shelf was an iron gun rack. Mrs. Street placed the shotgun on it.

She pointed to the ottoman. “Sit down. I’ll bring some tea.”

“Thanks, but I don’t need any tea.”

“You do if you want to talk to me.”

He sat on the ottoman and studied the room while she went to the kitchen to make tea. The house was humble in every way, furnished with bargain basement stuff and homemade objects, but very neat and clean. Strait imagined at another time of the day or week, Mrs. Street would have friends come over for tea and cookies and they would chat contentedly for hours, exchanging cooking and firearms tips.

Etta Street returned carrying a tray with a teapot and two cups. She poured one out for him and took another for herself. They sat in silence, sipping.

"Did Randy make those dolls above the fireplace?"

"Yes," she responded sourly.

"I've got some more he made you can add to them." Strait took out the bag the homeless lady had given him. He passed it to Mrs. Street. She looked in the bag and made a face. She tossed it on the floor.

"You don't seem to like Randy's dolls."

"Of course I don't like them. They're Kachina dolls."

"Something wrong with Kachina dolls?"

"Kachina dolls are Hopi."

"You don't like the Hopi?"

"I like the Hopi just fine. We've had our differences over the years, especially with the Big Mountain fight, but we get along okay now. I got plenty of Hopi friends. Randy makes those dolls for the tourists to get extra money. On a good day he makes enough for a goodly amount of wine. But the Hopi Kachina doll is sacred. It's not something you just throw together and sell to the white tourists like you're selling some plastic Disney toy. Especially if you're Navajo. You don't see people selling Jesus Christ on the cross, do you?"

"You've never been to a Catholic church, have you?" he said.

"It's just that here's this Navajo boy, making these Hopi

things for the tourists, and they don't care about how ridiculous that is, how sacrilegious. The whole thing is ugly."

"Can you tell me why Randy ended up prison?" asked Strait.

"Because of Bruno German."

"Who?"

"Bruno German. The president of Magic Industries."

"Magic Industries? The one that bought all the land on the south side of Pine River?"

"I don't know anything about that. But I do know that they destroyed Randy's life. He was a very bright boy in all his marks at school. At Massik High, he was editor of the school paper. He was hoping for a scholarship to go to a good university and study journalism. But he couldn't get one and we didn't have enough money to send him. So he did what a lot of kids on the rez do. He joined the Army. Figured he could do his two years and use the G.I. Bill to go to the university that way. That's how Randy's father done it, but he died before he could graduate."

"How old was Randy when his father died?"

"He was still a baby. So Randy joined the army. It was in March of 2002. Six months later, 9/11 happened and Randy found himself shipped off to war in Iraq. Thank you, George W. Bush. Randy came home two years later with his leg destroyed. He got shot in the thigh."

At the mention of getting shot in the thigh, Strait involuntarily put his hand on his own thigh where he'd been shot.

"Took him months to recover. The V.A. was worthless for him, so I did most of the nursing myself, right here in this house. After Randy came home and learned to walk again, he got a job at Magic Lumber. It was hard work, especially with his bad leg and his being small, but he never complained and he did well. The workers were an even mix of blacks, Latinos, and whites, but almost no Native Americans. And *all* the managers were white. Pretty quick, Randy started getting assigned the worst shifts, experiencing all sorts of abuse because he was a native. Blacks and Latinos had it bad too, but not as bad as Randy. Anyway, he started organizing out there, got a little union together of others, mostly natives, who'd been treated badly. My son was the leader. They made complaints to management, got rejected, made more complaints. They finally hired a lawyer. They had a strong case, because they had actual secret recordings of racist insults against natives by one foreman. If they went to court, Magic was facing serious damages and maybe even prison time for some of the higher-ups. Then, out of the blue, Randy gets this invitation to go out to Bruno German's mansion in Utah. Told him there was a special job for him out there, easy maintenance and grounds work mostly, which would last a month, but with double pay. Implied that Bruno German had learned about how Randy'd been treated, so this was his way of trying to fix things. Randy wanted to say no, but the others pressured him to go ahead and do it because he might be able to influence Mr. German directly."

Mrs. Street sighed deeply. "And God help me, I encouraged him to take it too. So Randy moved to Utah. The place was a real mansion, with tennis courts and about twenty bedrooms and a little forest and a duck pond and everything. Outside of the big crew of servants and groundskeepers, only three people lived here, Mr. and Mrs. German and their daughter, Mary. Princess of a girl, nine years old, spoiled to shit. And she's the one who after two weeks accused Randy of molesting her."

Mrs. Street took out a flowered handkerchief from a bag beside the sofa and dabbed her eyes. "And Randy was put in prison.

God knows he isn't perfect, but everyone who really knows him understands he could never hurt a child."

"I'm surprised a girl that young would lie about something like that. And lie effectively enough to get someone convicted."

"You're naïve, mister. Mary German, the little princess, wanted a pony. Not a toy pony. A real pony. And her father told her, sure, Sweetheart, Daddy will get you a pony. But first, you need to do something for Daddy."

"Are you saying this girl lied about Randy in order to get a pet horse?"

"Yes."

"How do you know this?"

"Grapevine. Workers at the property who overheard stuff and told other people. After they stuck Randy away to rot in that prison, Bruno German's labor problems disappeared. And that evil little bitch really did get her pet pony."

"What happened to the recordings Randy made of the abuse?"

"Someone broke into his trailer and stole them."

"Does he know Bruno German was behind all this?"

"I never told him. Can't prove any of it, so what good would it do? But my son's mind is so broken, I doubt he can connect ideas together rationally anymore. If he understood what they did to him back then, he probably doesn't even remember now. Randy spent ten years locked up with actual sex criminals and other violent felons." Etta moaned. "They cut out his eye!"

She put her face in both hands and started sobbing. After a few seconds, she pulled herself together and wiped her eyes.

"Mrs. Street, have you told the police about any of this stuff about Bruno German?"

"Of course I did. Back during the trial. Newspapers too. They all thought I was crazy."

Strait sat in silence pondering what he'd been told. Etta's story sounded incredible. The part about the nine-year-old Mary German falsely accusing Randy was especially hard to believe. But something deep inside, a strong intuition that had served Strait well all his life in his judgments, nudged him toward thinking the story was true.

"So Randy got out ten months ago, having served only half his sentence. How did he get out so early?"

"Good behavior, they said."

"You haven't seen Randy since he got out?"

"He came around here one time, when he first came back to Pine River. He tried to stay here, but soon enough he was getting drunk, stealing money from my purse and what not. I kicked him out. If he decides to stop drinking and get his life together, I'll be willing to talk with him."

"Mrs. Street, my only goal in talking to Randy is to find out what he knows about this new girl's disappearance. He gave me this note."

He handed her the paper Randy had slipped under his door. She read it and something appeared in her eyes, a shimmer of softness in a world-hardened face. She cleared her throat.

"That's his handwriting, alright."

"The girl might still be alive, Mrs. Street."

For a long time, the woman looked over her son's handwritten note. She seemed to come to a decision.

"Mr. Strait, I can tell you're a decent young man. So I want you now to leave my house."

"Um…"

"And when you get outside, face toward the sun. Walk straight until you see a big boulder, looks like an egg. To the left of that boulder you'll find a trail. Follow it about a mile. You'll come to a rock ridge, about fifty feet high. Go all the way up to the base of the ridge."

Strait stared back at her. He waited for her to say more, but she was looking away, at the dolls over the fireplace or maybe at the gun above them. He stood and put his teacup on the table and walked to the door and opened it. He turned back and said, "thank you."

The boulder she'd indicated was twice as tall as Strait and shaped like a wrinkled, shelled egg rotting from inside. The trail was clear, a well-worn pathway cutting through the sun-baked land, snaking through the scrub and dust. The path sloped steadily upward. Strait walked across the landscape of rocky outcroppings and sagebrush. The sky was cloudless blue and vertiginously huge. The only sound came from the buzz of a distant chainsaw.

The path headed westwards toward a jagged spine of rock, a ridge rising from the slope like a minor mountain the size and shape of a ship. The afternoon sun was making for the opposite side of the ridge and Strait's lengthened shadow bobbled and beat against the craggy terrain behind him.

The path led right up to the foot of the ridge before splitting into two trails that wound along the perimeter. Some distance down the right branch, the face of the hill dissolved into a black space.

A cave.

He hadn't walked ten feet toward it when he saw movement at the entrance and Randy Street emerged. The one-eyed man didn't seem surprised to see Strait there.

"You found me."

"Yep."

"It's like they say. You're a supercop."

"I had a little help from your mother."

"I'm not angry at her."

"No reason you should be."

"You want to kill me?"

"Of course not."

"You're lying. You want to strangle me to death." Randy said the words calmly, without recrimination.

Strait was about to argue the point, but then he realized Randy was right. There was a part of him that was prepared to do exactly as he said. Randy even had his planned method of killing him correct, two big hands around that scrawny sunburned neck.

"You said you know where Jophia is. Did you take her?"

Randy's one eye grew wide. "Is that what you think?"

"I don't know what to think. You served time for molesting a girl the same age. Then you tell me that you know where this girl is. So what would you think if you were me?"

"Oh, James. My man. Supercop. That whole thing, and now this whole thing? That's all the work of the rabbit skinners."

"The what?"

"Rabbit skinners."

"What does that mean?"

"I didn't do nothing to no girl. Not then, not now. But them rabbit skinners? They got to test me. I heard'em talking in the alley. I found the head by the trees. Ripped off. Prove me worthy."

"You went to prison because the girl testified against you. She said herself that you molested her."

"Rabbit skinners made her lie. She was just a kid, couldn't help herself. She was hypnotized, under the power of the rabbit skinners. Know what I'm saying?"

"Where's Jophia?"

Randy grinned. "She's up there, man. She's next to the sun."

Strait's fingers folded into fists. "Can you be more specific?"

"The sun, man. She done went up to the mountaintop. Where the eagles crawl and the snakes fly. She's with the chickens, man. Where the bears play and rabbits pray."

"Are you saying she's dead?"

Still grinning, Randy peered unblinking into Strait's face, eyes glassed over with a kind of manic energy.

"I said, is she dead?"

"She's alive as me."

Strait's voice came out hoarsely. "I'm going to ask one last time. Where exactly is Jophia Williams?"

"I already told you. Next to the sun."

Strait grabbed Randy by the shirt and yanked him forward. He wrapped his fingers of his hand around the man's throat. He squeezed. Randy simply stared up at him. No trace of fear.

"Where the fuck is she, you lunatic? Give me an address!"

"I really was going to tell you," Randy said, his voice straining under the pressure of Strait's fingers. "But you snitched on me, man."

"What are you talking about?"

"I don't tell snitches nothing."

Randy stared fixedly up at Strait, in a long moment of silence that would have been absolute if not for the chainsaw buzz in the distance. Strait realized the noise had gotten louder and was coming from the sky. Strait looked up and saw right above them the octagonal shape of a drone descending, its engine buzzing like a massive housefly. At the same moment came the clatter of many boots on the rocky landscape. Strait looked across the way and saw at least ten uniformed police officers racing forward with their guns drawn.

Julie's husband Duane was in the lead.

He shouted, "Randy Street! You're under arrest. Put your hands over your head."

Strait loosened his grip on Randy. "I didn't know."

"Right."

"They followed me here without my knowledge. Trust me."

Randy grinned. "Trust you?"

"I swear…"

"White cops. All the same. Even white supercops."

"Hands in the air, now!"

"Please, Randy. Tell me where she is."

"Where who is?"

Five, six, seven deputies knocked Randy to the ground and piled on top of him. He disappeared under a mound of uniformed bodies. He didn't make a sound.

Duane walked up to Strait. "Thanks, James," he said in a voice laced with sarcasm. "We couldn't have found him without you."

"You motherfucker."

"Is that any way to talk to a fellow lawman?"

"You tailed me."

"Come on, James. We're all on the same side."

"But Kladspell wouldn't even believe me when I talked about Randy."

"He thought more about it. And he did some research and decided Randy really was the man we should be looking for. But we didn't know where to find him. So Kladspell came up with the idea that since you were already going to find him, why not let you do the tracking for us? We could just follow you. And now, thanks to you, this pervert injin is in our custody. All's well that ends well."

"Duane, I think I was wrong about Randy Street. I'm pretty sure he didn't have anything to do with kidnapping the girl. But I think he knows who the real kidnapper is and where the girl is. He was about to tell me when you all came charging in."

"Bullshit."

"Goddamnit, Duane, he was. Now he'll never tell us."

"Don't worry. We can get whatever we need out of him."

"He'll never tell you anything."

"We'll figure out a way."

"You're going to regret this."

"I don't think so."

Strait stepped up to him. "You beat up your wife."

"And you *fucked* my wife."

"What?"

"I saw you two, you know. I followed her. I saw her go into your room. Then she didn't come back until the middle of the night."

"She was upset because you had a fight with her. I gave her a hug. Nothing more. Then she left. I don't know where she went after that."

"Lying sack of shit."

Strait raised his fists.

"Go ahead, hit me," said Duane. "These guys will gun you down like a dog."

Strait glanced toward the handful of men who were not on the ground restraining Randy. They had their guns drawn and pointed at him.

Strait lowered his fists. "If that girl dies because of this, I'm coming for you, Duane."

He shouldered his way through the police who still had their guns drawn. They looked questioningly as Duane, but he shook his head. Strait walked back down the trail without looking back.

He emerged at Etta's house and saw her standing outside, ringed by four large Pine River cops.

"Etta, I'm sorry. I was tricked." She glared at him.

Disgusted, he walked across the road to where his car was parked, now in the middle of the line of a half a dozen police cars.

"Never!" Etta shouted at him, her face red with fury, and she said some more words Strait couldn't catch.

Strait cupped his hand over his bad ear. "What?" he said.

"Never trust a white man!"

Chapter Twenty-four

Strait had a hard time sleeping. He went out for a walk at midnight to see if that would help get him tired enough to overcome the waves of guilt he felt at getting Randy Street arrested. He thought about calling Jessie at her hotel in New York, or even Katherine, but it was already very late and what would he say to them? That he'd failed? Again? He'd agreed to help the people find this little girl, and so far all he'd done was indirectly get two probably innocent men arrested. And he was no closer to finding Jophia than he was when he'd never heard of her.

When he returned from his walk, he passed the front desk. The teenaged night clerk smiled up at him and asked if he wanted to play hearts with her. He declined.

"You must be quite a guy," she said.

"How's that?"

"Julie quit her job because of you."

"What?"

"Julie's husband thinks you and Julie are…"

"That's bullshit. Nothing happened between us."

"Don't get mad, man. I'm not saying it's, like, your fault. But her old man made her quit. And even if nothing happened, I think she had some kind of, like, thing for you? Just sayin'."

Strait went to his room and tried to sleep. After tossing and turning for hours, he gave up. At first light, he gassed up the car and drove 30 miles out of town to the Pine River County Jail. A surly, short-haired, baggy-eyed woman in a guard uniform sat behind a thick plastic slab with a small hole cut into it. He told her he wanted to visit an inmate by the name of Randy Street. Without looking up at him, she gestured at a sign: VISITING HOURS START AT 5:00.

He returned to the jail at 5:00 to find a long line already formed in front of the plexiglass enclosure where the same baggy-eyed woman roosted. When Strait finally came to the front of the line, she said, "name and I.D."

He pulled out his driver's license and said, "James Strait."

"Not *your* name," she said impatiently. "The name of the inmate you're visiting."

"Sorry. Randy Street. I think he was brought in yesterday."

The woman eyed his I.D., then clacked the keys of her computer. "Nope."

"What do you mean, nope? I was with him when he was arrested."

"Ain't saying he was and ain't saying he wasn't. I'm saying that if he was here, he didn't put your name on the list."

"My name needs to be on a list?"

"Yes. Visitor's list."

"How can I get my name on the list?"

"The inmate needs to put your name on it. Sir, there are people waiting."

"Should I call him and ask?"

"Not my problem, sir. Next."

In the parking lot, Strait looked up the number to contact inmates and tried to call Randy. A recorded voice said calling hours were only in the morning from 9:00 to 11:00.

The next morning, after another nearly sleepless night, he tried to call again. The first five times he tried to call, he got a busy signal. When someone finally answered, the voice was aggressive.

"Yeah?"

"I want to talk to Randy Street."

"Who dis?"

"A friend."

"Friend don't do it, homes. I need a name."

"James Strait."

The man then bellowed to what must have been a large room full of men. "Yo, there a Randy Street here? Tell him he got a phone call. James something. Strait, I think."

Muffled shouts in the background. Then the man came back on. "Dude says you can suck his dick, man." He hung up.

When Strait put down the receiver, he went out to his car and drove back to the reservation to ask Etta Street if she could talk to Randy for him and convince him to put his name on the visitor's list. Or to at least talk to him on the phone.

The front door of the house was open and James felt a wave of dizziness hit him when he saw inside every piece of furniture and every adornment and photograph were gone. In the short expanse of time between her son's arrest and Strait's return, Etta Street had moved out of the house she'd lived in for decades, where she'd given birth to her son, where she'd nursed him back to health from his war wounds. The boarded floor was already accumulating dust. The only belongings that remained were the Kachina dolls on the shelf over the fireplace and the empty iron gun rack bolted to the wall above them.

Chapter Twenty-five

When Strait arrived back at the hotel room, he collapsed on the bed. Completely exhausted. He needed to find Jophia Williams. But how? He'd run out of leads. He considered going to Kladspell again, but it would only result in his arrest. He sat up on his bed and took his medicine. The Chinese powder left a bittersweet aftertaste on his tongue.

He lay back on the bed and stared at the ceiling. Why didn't he just quit? He had every justification. The whereabouts of Jophia Williams was not really his problem, was it? She was almost certainly dead. And maybe the police really had arrested the perpetrator already. Strait couldn't say with absolute certainty that it hadn't been Marvin. Or Randy. He wondered if Marvin had been released, or if the chief was holding both of them.

Strait rolled on his side and closed his eyes. *That's right. Not my problem*. If he dropped the case now, he might still have a shot at rejoining the FBI. The low-salt diet and the medicine had reduced his symptoms by eighty percent. He could function again. He could do the job. If only he'd drop this stupid crusade to find the girl. *Not my problem.*

Strait sat up. *Fuck that.*

He got out of bed and went to the bathroom sink and splashed water on his face.

A knock at the door.

James opened it. In the hallway was Graham Footer.

"James!"

"Graham?"

"You don't look happy to see me."

"I just didn't expect you so soon."

"I told you I was coming." Graham entered, eyed the room dubiously and sat on the only chair.

"You're looking better than the last time I saw you."

"Not surprising, given that was in a hospital and we were both half-dead."

"You're still awfully short, though. And freckly."

"Do I hear a trace of jealousy in your voice?" Footer examined Strait for a few seconds with a look of restrained amusement. "I've been sent here to make sure you aren't doing anything to embarrass the agency by getting involved in the case of this missing girl."

"I know."

"Right. Now that we have that out of the way, where are we with the case of this missing girl?"

"A lot has happened since I last talked to you." Strait filled him in on everything that had passed since their last conversation. His search for Randy Street at the homeless shelter and the park and the fights he got into at both, and his drive to the reservation, his conversation with Randy's shotgun-wielding mom that led to Street's arrest, and his failed attempts afterwards to visit him at the jail.

"Crikey,“ Graham said after Strait was finished. "Let me get this clear in my head. You beat up an employee of a Christian mission and absconded with his military baton. Then you used the baton to beat up three teenagers in a park. Then you almost got yourself shot by a woman and then, within minutes, also almost were gunned down by a troop of police officers because you threatened to punch one of them in the face. All in the space of twenty-four hours."

"It wasn't specifically his face."

"James?"

"What?"

"You're a very violent man."

"Only when people give me a reason to be."

"It makes me hesitate to give you the present I brought."

Graham unzipped his backpack and pulled out a black case. He handed it to Strait.

Strait ran his fingers over the heavy plastic, lingering over the section next to the handle that had JAMES STRAIT embossed into it.

"Jesus. How did you get this?"

"It was still in your locker. Someone stowed it there while you were in the hospital."

"I thought for sure they'd have decommissioned it. Or kept it for ballistics. Or passed it on to someone else."

"That legendary bureau efficiency. They probably forgot about it."

Strait flicked the latches along the side and opened the case. Inside was the MP5 submachine gun he'd been issued as a member of FBI SWAT. The same one he'd used in the raid on the Barton cult.

"And this," said Graham. He held out the triple magazine pouch that Strait used to carry with him on every FBI SWAT raid. The ammunition holder was made of leather and attached to one's belt. Each of the three pockets held a 9mm 120-round magazine. Strait held it. He could tell by the weight that all the magazines were bulleted to capacity.

He removed the machine gun segments and snapped them together. He held the rifle up in front of his face with both hands as though waiting for it to reveal something. He slapped in a magazine and pointed the gun at the TV.

"You okay, James?"

Strait lowered the weapon. "Yeah. I think so. I have mixed feelings, you know? But overall, it's good to have her back."

Graham gazed at him with an expression half grave, half amused. "I brought you that gun against my better judgment, but I have a feeling you'll stay alive longer if you have it."

"Looks like you're not really here to stop me."

"Gelder and Greyson think I am. That's what they ordered me to do. But I'm here in fact to help you. I'd like to be careful to do it while maintaining the appearance of not doing so. I don't want to lose my job."

Footer pulled a folded piece of paper from his wallet and handed it to Strait. On it were strings of numbers, symbols, and letters.

"These will get you into the entire set of databases we have, anonymously, You can search for any information without having to ask me to do it."

"How did you get these?"

"I didn't 'get' them, James. I generated them. Suffice it to say that there are tranches of illicit, password-generating platforms the agency learns of while investigating the dark web, platforms for which, if one fiddles with certain parameters and codes, one can convert oneself from a cop to a customer."

"Thanks." Strait placed the paper in a drawer. "Isn't there any way the agency can take an above-board stand in this? I mean, this Kladspell idiot is genuinely endangering the child. That's got to count for something. How about if you talk to Gelder or Greyson directly about what's going on? Explain we have an extraordinary problem down here. They can't both be complete shitheads."

"I did try to talk to both of them already. And yes, they can. But they also are factually correct in stating the FBI doesn't have jurisdiction in this matter."

"Yet, here are you, willing to help me surreptitiously when you're supposed to actually stop me."

"Higher principle and all that, mate. But let me ask you conversely, do you think there is absolutely no way of talking sense into this Kladspell person?"

"No way. I don't know if it's because he's crazy, stupid, or corrupt, or all three combined, but unless I actually find Jophia, he won't take any action based on what I say. And I think if he sees me again, he'll put me in jail."

"You know, James, Mr. Street is in jail. If you were in jail too, you could probably talk to him. Maybe you should consider that."

"Are you kidding? Obstruction of justice can get you twenty years in this state. I'm not willing to do hard time on the chance I *might* find out if he knows something. If I could get into the jail for just one day, then get right back out a free man, I'd consider it."

Graham sat musing, his thin, pointed nose tilted upwards. He said, "you know, there might be a way to simultaneously have and eat this cake."

Chapter Twenty-six

It was one o'clock in the morning when Duane and his five companions, all police officers, left the Horse's Mouth. They came into the parking lot back-slapping drunk, talking over whose house they should go to for more beer. One said, "let's go to the south side to one of them nigger afterhours and put everyone on the floor. We can threaten to arrest them unless they give us free beer and weed."

"Wait," said another. "Wouldn't that be illegal?"

The men burst into laughter. They abruptly went silent when a very large man stepped out of the shadows and blocked their path.

"Evening, gentlemen," said Strait. He smiled down on Julie's husband. "How's it going, Duane? How's your wife?"

"Who the fuck is this?" asked one of the men. Duane gestured at him to hold back and said to Strait, "The fuck you want?"

"To ask you a question."

"What?"

"Can you help me find my wallet?"

"Get the fuck away from me, Strait."

"I think I left it here in the parking lot." Strait made a show of glancing around at the asphalt and gesturing helplessly.

"Fuck you."

"You guys are cops, right? And I'm a citizen asking for assistance."

The men glanced at each other uncertainly.

Strait bent to look at the pavement and moved close enough to the men to say in a lowered voice, "I bet you faggots together can't take on even one FBI agent."

A deputy kicked Strait in the face. Strait screamed and brought his left hand protectively to his nose and made a defensive motion with his right, which brought a kick from another deputy to his stomach. Strait fell, tried to rise, made a blind flailing motion at the men and they all jumped on him at once, stomping and punching. Duane shouted, "stop!"

They took a step back, breathing hard from the exertion and Duane stepped up and gave Strait a kick to the ribs. On his side, clutching his chest, Strait groaned.

"Let's take him in," said Duane.

"On what charge?" asked one of the men.

"Assaulting a police officer."

They yanked Strait up to a seated position and got his hands behind him locked them together with flexicuffs. Duane used his cell phone to call for a police car. When it came, they hauled Strait to his feet and shoved him into the back seat. As he fell in, no one put his head down and he slammed it into the top of the frame. He cried out in pain.

At the jail, Duane and the others brought him to a bank of folding tables with an ink pad and a thick pad of paper resting in a metal frame. A uniformed woman read his name out loud and asked if it was correct. She looked him in his face and her eyes widened. She said to Duane, "you know who this is?"

"He's a drunk who took a swing at six cops in a parking lot."

"How much have you had to drink, sir?" she asked Strait.

"Nothing. I'm sober."

"Right," Duane sneered.

"Give me a piss test if you don't believe me."

The female officer responded, "we will." Then, turning to Duane, "this guy's a national hero. He was on the cover of *Newsweek*."

"Whatever. Book him."

They locked him in a holding cell with five other men, three white, two black, all sitting on the floor or the benches. A metal toilet with no seat in the corner and a bad smell in the air. He could tell by looking at the other men that none of them was in for anything serious. Probably stuff like public nuisance and shoplifting. Penny-ante drug charges. Strait crouched in a space by the wall and stared ahead. That look he'd learned in the military that gave the appearance of lightly sleeping menace. The others left him alone.

An hour later the guards brought another man to the cell. Native American. He was short and thin and terrified, not a day over sixteen. Hair trimmed awkwardly into a bowl cut, with a perfectly straight fringe crossing the middle of his forehead. After the guard slammed the metal door behind him, his wide eyes darted around the cage at the others. He held his arms stiffly pressed to his sides, his fingers twisted into fists to keep himself from shaking.

"Looks like we got us an injin," said one of the white guys.

The other white men laughed. The two black prisoners kept their heads down. The white guy stood. He was wearing a muscle shirt and had orange hair trimmed close to the scalp. Strait pegged him for one of those guys who was all muscle and no brain, a high school dropout who worked under the sun repairing holes in the street and drinking beer all night while watching YouTube videos of real-life murders and war crimes. He was strong and lean but was already wearing a paunch. His eyes were dull and amused. He stepped up to the native boy.

"Yo, Kimosabe. Got a cigarette?"

The boy shook his head.

"Then what you got? Come in our cell, you got to pay admission."

"I don't have anything."

"What did they arrest you for, Chief? Let me guess…" The white man placed a finger and thumb on either side of his forehead and made a display of straining himself to think. "Um, wait, it's coming to me…I got it! Drinking in public? Am I right?" The other white men laughed. Small smiles appeared on the lips of the black men.

"Chief, give me a cigarette. Or you got to pay your admission another way."

"Leave him alone."

Strait had not altered his thousand-yard stare when they all turned to look at him. The white kid gaped at him. "What did you say?"

"I don't need to say it again."

For a moment the kid was too flustered to respond. He stood red-faced, gawking at the giant who'd interrupted his fun. Strait knew what he was thinking and feeling. He'd encountered many like him in the Army. If the white kid had even a few working brain cells, he'd back down, let it go.

As it turned out, the boy had no working brain cells.

He marched up to Strait. "Stand up, old man."

Strait showed no reaction.

"I said, get up," the boy shouted.

Strait waited. The boy raised his arm over Strait's head and punched downwards. Strait snatched him by the wrist and twisted. The kid cried out and dropped to his knees. Strait stood and twisted harder and the boy screamed again. None of the others in the cell moved.

"I told you to leave him alone," said Strait. He said it quietly, in the mildly scolding tone a parent would use. "Say okay."

The kid only made grunting sounds, trying to withstand the

pain. Strait twisted his arm another inch. “Say it.”

“Okay, okay,” gasped the kid after a few more seconds.

Strait released him. The boy stepped around him, glaring furiously, and went back to the other two white men, who both looked away from him.

“I didn’t want no fucking cigarette anyway.”

***

It took a few more hours for Strait to be processed. They stuck him in an orange jumpsuit with ACD, for Arizona Corrections Division, stenciled on it and put him into a cell. The interior of the jail was larger and cleaner than he thought it would be. The cell was made out of what appeared to be a single piece of some kind of durable synthetic material, like the entire room had been manufactured in a giant mold, with two slab-like pieces that jutted from the side to make beds and another formed into the shape of a sink. The only added parts to the structure were a metal toilet with no seat and a silvery film applied on the surface of the wall to make a mirror. The door had no bars and no window. It was open. Strait was the only inmate in the cell. Katherine had mentioned that the jail was only a few years old, built when the state contracted with a private prison company, Rainbow Futures. Strait had seen a news story in which a state legislator was protesting “unconscionable” delays in the courts that were causing inmates at the jail, who had not yet even been convicted of a crime, to stay there for a year or even longer. The cost of running the place was supposed to be lower than a directly state-funded institution. Strait didn’t know if it was true, but they did seem to save money on staffing. In the cell block they put Strait, he saw only one guard, a flabby, mildewed guy who sat perched in the booth at the entryway reading a magazine. The only view the guard had of the cell block interior were images on four monitors on his booth wall.

A voice over an intercom announced lunch. Strait followed the other prisoners down a hallway and two flights of metal stairs. At each juncture of the staircase was a hallway with another row of cells. Strait was one of the first to reach the bottom of the staircase and enter the lunchroom. The room had about fifteen long folding tables and a set of carts on one wall containing food trays. Strait grabbed a tray and sat down at a table where no one was sitting. He studied the room. As other prisoners came in, they chose tables that were arranged along racial lines. Whites at one table, Latinos at another, Blacks at a third. Across the room, he saw a table with a growing number of Native Americans. A single security camera anchored to the ceiling at one corner observed the room. No guards.

Strait by chance had chosen a table where other whites sat. Or maybe they followed his lead. They nodded to him as they brought their trays and sat around him. He noticed the red-haired kid from the holding cell wasn't there, at least not yet, but he could see the skinny native guy he'd helped, sitting at the native table. No sign of Randy.

Strait ate quietly, taking in the surroundings. Eventually a total of about fifty prisoners entered, far fewer than could fill the tables. The privatization of the prison hadn't brought enough customers, Strait thought. One of the last inmates to come through the staircase doorway was Randy Street. He was so small that the orange jail jumpsuit nearly swallowed him whole. He took a tray from a cart and made his way to the native table. Others there greeted him as he sat down.

Strait stood. As he made his way across the room, he could feel many eyes on him. Conversations stopped in mid-sentence and the noise diminished. As he approached the native table, one of the men stood and blocked his path. He was an immensely large native man, about the same size as Strait, with massively muscled arms emerging from the rolled-up sleeves of his uniform. He said, “you going the wrong way.”

“I want to talk to Doll Man. Randy Street.”

The man didn’t look at where Strait pointed. Randy was studiously ignoring him.

“I’m not trying to cause trouble. Randy told me on the outside he needed to tell me something important. I’m asking you a favor. With respect. Let me talk with him for five minutes.”

The man grinned. “Respect. That’s amusing. Like I say, you in the wrong place. Unless you going to step up, you go back and sit with the other white pussies.”

Strait turned and walked away.

“That’s right, Cherry. Go back to your white friends and eat shit and die.”

Instead of joining the group of white men, Strait took his lunch tray to an empty table. He ate his lunch and considered his options. He wasn’t going to be in here long. If all went well, he’d be sprung pretty soon. He needed to find a way to Randy as fast as possible.

He noticed then that the skinny native from the holding cell, the one Strait had saved from the orange-haired white kid, was talking to the native leader and to Randy Street too. The skinny native was gesturing at Strait. The big one said something firmly to Randy, who reluctantly nodded. The big one waved at Strait to come back over. When Strait got there, the leader said, “you got five minutes.”

Randy Street edged hesitantly over and met Strait along the wall, where they stood silently facing each other.

"What do you want?" said Randy.

"I didn't set you up."

"Right."

"The cops set *me* up."

"Why are you in jail?"

"Because I threw a punch at the police who arrested you. Listen, I talked to your mother and she told me you were innocent of the charge that put you in prison. Is that true?"

"Who cares?"

"Is it true?"

Randy stared at the tiles on the floor.

"She says you're innocent of the kidnapping of Jophia Williams too. Is that true?"

"Why the fuck you bothering me?"

"If you're innocent, I'll work my ass off to get you out of here. The best way for me to do that is to find Jophia Williams. You said you knew where she was."

A smile played on Randy's face. "I already told you. She's on the mountain, under the sun."

"That doesn't mean shit to me."

"It's the truth."

"Give me some clear information I can use and I'll get you out of here. I can help you on the outside too. Get you a place to live."

Randy sneered. He gestured around him. "I already got a place to live."

"A more comfortable place."

"Where could I be more comfortable than around my people?" He gestured toward the other Native Americans, who were all staring at Strait with naked belligerence.

"You don't care if the girl dies?"

Something flickered on Randy's face. He opened his mouth to speak, then closed it.

"Come on, Randy. I can make you a deal today, but that's it. I'll fight like anything to clear your name, but only if you tell me something that leads me to Jophia Williams."

"And if I don't?"

"I'll be the prosecution's lead witness at your trial."

Randy sighed. He leaned closer and gestured for Strait to do the same. He said in a whisper, "You need to go to the why."

"Huh?"

"Go to the why. The big white why. Just outside of town. You want the doll? Look under the grass. Dig, dig, dig."

"Are you fucking with me? The big white why?"

"The big white why is where the animals play."

"Animals?"

"Wild dogs, bears, snakes. Animals hating on animals. They play with chickens. They skin rabbits."

"Time's up." The big native had come up and was now an inch from Strait, nearly pushing him to move away.

The full realization of what had happened settled over Strait like a poisonous fog. Randy Street was either really insane or playing a cruel game with him. Either way, Strait had failed completely in his attempt to get information from him about the whereabouts of Jophia Williams.

He fetched up his tray and sat at the white table. The other whites cast sidelong, threatening looks at him. He picked at the jail food and wondered why.

***

After lunch, there was nothing to do except go back to his

cell. He sat on the slab that passed for his bed and waited. In Afghanistan, he'd learned to sit in silent, motionless contemplation for long periods of time. The contemplation animating his mind on this day was ugly. He'd never felt more like a failure. Maybe it really was time to go on disability and spend the rest of his life sedated on medication. Grow fat and watch endless TV and wait to die.

As the afternoon extended closer to evening, Strait started to wonder if something had gone wrong. Graham's plan called for Strait to be out of here by three o'clock. It was already five.

"Howdy." A man was standing at the doorway. He was bald and had a rust-brown handlebar mustache, veined with grey, with sweeping endpoints that hung partway off his cheeks. Strait recognized him as one of the men who'd been sitting at the white inmate table. On his neck was a swastika tattoo.

In the hallway behind him was a group of other men, at least six of them. One of them was the red-haired kid from the holding cell.

"We was wondering why you was talking to them teepee monkeys today."

"That's my business."

"Afraid it ain't. You living in our unit, it's our business. See, in here, we stick with our own kind. We was ready to welcome you, but then you went off to talk to them injins. So you got some explaining to do if you want to live in peace with us."

Strait yawned. He gestured at the man dismissively. "Don't worry about it."

Handlebar laughed. "Boy, you ain't listening. I'll give you one more chance. See these convicts behind me? We all Aryans, all together."

"This is a jail, not a prison, so they aren't convicts."

"We all done prison time before, smartass. And we don't mix with them mud people down there. So why did you? And if you don't give me an answer, you're going give all of us something else."

Strait stood and faced them. He smiled calmly. "You're the mud people."

"James Strait!" shouted a voice. The men at the door stepped back. A guard moved past them into the cell. "James Strait?"

"I'm James Strait."

"Come with me."

"Keep in touch, losers," Strait smirked at the men as he passed, relishing the impotent fury they radiated at him.

The guard took Strait through a series of locked doors to the other side of the jail. He paused outside one. He removed a pair of handcuffs from his belt.

"Bracelets," he said.

After he handcuffed Strait, he unlocked the door and led him into a carpeted administrative area with offices. Here were several more jail employees, these in formal office wear. Apparently, the jail needed administrative personnel more than it needed guards.

The guard took Strait down a corridor past several unmarked offices and finally knocked on the door of one.

"Come."

Inside was a meeting room with a desk surrounded by chairs. In one chair was Graham Footer. Strait suppressed a laugh when he saw him. Footer was dressed in a bowler hat and glasses with broad black frames he'd purchased at a thrift store in town. He had on a turtleneck sweater, magenta in color.

In another chair was a woman with rinsed blonde hair tied

back, slender and tanned and looking serious and professional in a dark-blue jacket. The lawyer, Strait supposed, who Graham had enlisted. In a chair opposite her was a jowly old man with a pock-marked nose who Strait didn't know. Judging by his uniform, he was a high-ranking person at the jail. Seated next to him was the Pine River chief of police. Kladspell aimed a scathing look at him.

The old man said, "Mr. Strait, I'm Clegg Barnes. I'm warden of this jail."

"Nice to meet you, sir."

Kladspell spoke impatiently to the warden. "Okay, Clegg, you got me down here. You going to tell me what's going on?"

"It was best you hear it in person, August. If I got this information from any other lawyer, I'd be skeptical, but I have a lot of respect for Cindy here and I thought it was best you listen to what she has to say."

"Chief Kladspell," said the woman. "My name is Cindy Lewis. I'm with the Pine River legal defense league."

"I know who you are."

"For Mr. Strait's benefit, because he doesn't know what's happening, we're a group of lawyers serving northern Arizona by providing free legal assistance to those who are victims of bias crimes and police misconduct. Warden, may Mr. Strait sit down?"

The old man gestured toward the open chair between the lawyer and Graham. Cindy said, "Mr. Strait, you look like you've been through a lot. Are you in any pain?"

"I'm okay," he responded and took his seat. Graham glanced over without seeming to know him.

"The man sitting next to you is Mr. Geoffrey Twiller. He's a British tourist visiting Arizona. Chief Kladspell, Mr. Twiller states that at the time Mr. Strait was arrested by your men, he was in the parking lot and witnessed the whole thing. Mr. Twiller says that he saw several of your officers assaulting Mr. Strait."

The chief scoffed. "I can't believe I came out here for this." He flapped his hand at Strait. "This one's been a nuisance since he came to town. Dropping by my office, asking all sorts of questions, interfering with my investigation. Then he turns up drunk at the bar where my officers were relaxing during their time off. He starts mouthing off and takes a swing at one. They try to calm him down, but he just gets worse and he attacks them. You can see how big he is, just picture it. It took six men to restrain him."

"Geoffrey" responded, "that's rather a mischaracterization of the event at hand." Strait marveled at the change Graham made to his voice. "Your men behaved barbarically. They kicked the legs out from under this poor man and stomped on him with their boots when he was defenselessly curled up on the asphalt. It was dreadful to see."

"Well, Mr…what was your name again? Tiller?"

"Twiller."

"Maybe in Britain, violent criminals are restrained with polite language and a cup of tea, but we're in America now and we're more into responses that work."

"There's no cause to become peevish, chief inspector," responded Graham, delicately touching the sides of the turtleneck collar and appearing distressed.

Cindy Lewis said, "Chief Kladspell, you state that Mr. Strait was drunk. But a urine test taken at the jail a short time after he was arrested showed no alcohol in his system."

"Okay, then maybe he turned up sober at the bar and took a swing at my officers. Drunk or sober don't change the reason he got arrested."

Cindy Lewis removed a laptop from her briefcase and opened it. She brought up something on the screen and turned it toward the chief. "Chief, Mr. Twiller had a video camera when he was in the parking lot."

"Hold on there, Cindy," said Warden Barnes. "You didn't tell me there was a video."

She ignored him and started the video. It showed Duane and the other men coming from the bar, shouting loudly. One cop could clearly be heard saying they should go to a "nigger afterhours" and threaten people with arrest in order to extort alcohol and drugs. It showed Strait approaching the group of police and speaking to them, then bending down as though searching for something on the ground. The men, for no apparent reason, then started kicking and punching Strait. Rather than fight the men, Strait seemed to be flailing weakly in a useless attempt to protect himself from the blows he was receiving.

The video continued, showing Duane's one last kick, the wait until the police car arrived, and Strait's getting yanked up and dragged to the car, banging his head on the doorframe.

Both the chief and the warden seemed to be in shock. The warden snatched a look at Kladspell, then turned back to the screen.

"As I described," said Graham. "Barbaric."

When the video ended, the warden closed his eyes and shook his head in disbelief. Kladspell yelled at Graham, "Who gave you the authorization to videotape a police encounter?"

"Authorization?" said Graham. "I was videotaping the exterior of a large American honky-tonk bar. We don't have establishments such as these in my country and I was recording it as a memento to show my friends and family when I returned to Devon. Are you seriously asserting that I am required to obtain 'authorization' to record a gang of police beating up a private citizen? A gang who just happened to voluntarily conduct their assault right in front of my camera? I thought I was visiting America, not Russia."

"I want that video."

"I won't let you have it."

"Well…you better not put it on YouTube."

"I'll put it wherever I desire."

The lawyer cut in. "Chief Kladspell, you claimed that your officers were assaulted by Mr. Strait and forced to defend themselves. This tape unambiguously shows that what you told us was a lie."

"Wrong."

"You lied when you said your officers were attacked…"

"Wrong."

"…by Mr. Strait, when it was they who did the attacking. Mr. Strait, tell us what really happened."

"I was in the parking lot and I lost my wallet."

"Why were you in the parking lot?"

"I came to the bar looking for a friend who sometimes goes there. But she wasn't there. I waited a while, then decided to go home. But when I was walking into my car, I put my hand into my pocket and noticed my wallet was gone. I knew I had it when I left the bar, because I checked as I was walking out, but then it wasn't there. So I figured I must have dropped it somewhere. So I started to look for it, and that's when this group of police officers came out, so I asked them to help me. Instead of helping me, they jumped me."

"Do you know why?"

"I have no idea."

The warden said, "August, I know you run a tight ship over

there, and I'd gladly put my life in your hands if it came to that. But I have to say, seeing this video is a shock. I'm no judge or lawyer, I think Mr. Strait has a strong case against the department for brutality."

Kladspell's face was red and he was trembling. He looked like a stick of dynamite whose lit fuse was about to reach its end.

"I don't want to press charges," said Strait.

"What?" said Cindy.

"It was just a bar fight. They were drunk and stupid. Back in Afghanistan, fights like this were a way to pass the time. Besides, those six losers couldn't make a scratch on me."

Cindy nearly screamed, "Mr. Strait, have you seen your face? It looks like your nose is broken."

Strait smiled. "This? Six guys, and this is the best they could do? If I'd decided to fight back, and I didn't because I'm a nice guy, all of them would've looked a lot worse than me. I don't need to press charges."

"But these policemen attacked you for no reason. I came to the jail today as a first step to represent you."

"Thanks for doing that. But I never asked you to help me. I don't even know you. But there is something you could do. I want a letter of apology. Kladspell here has it out for me. I want a letter from him to protect myself if in the future he tries to conjure up some legal way to mess with me. And I want these bullshit charges against me dropped and to walk free from this moment."

The lawyer seemed flabbergasted but she collected herself enough to say to Kladspell, "okay, if Mr. Strait receives a letter of apology from the six assailants for their vicious, unwarranted assault on him, and another letter officially acknowledging that he did nothing whatsoever to deserve arrest, and the charges against him are dropped and he's set free immediately, he's willing to forego pressing assault charges. Chief Kladspell, is that okay with you?"

Kladspell and Strait had their eyes locked on each other. A silent, vicious conversation was going on between them.

"Okay," Kladspell spat.

"I want the letter today. On Pine River police department letterhead." said Strait.

"Fine," the chief snapped.

Strait held up his handcuffed wrists. "Get these things off me."

Chapter Twenty-seven

Cindy the lawyer drove Footer and Strait back to town. Footer continued to masquerade as fussy, sartorially-challenged British tourist Geoffrey Twiller. In the car, he railed peevishly about the chief for trying to confiscate his video and at Strait for refusing to take legal action.

"Here I am, a visitor to your country drinking up the local atmosphere, minding my own business, and I happened to record this attack on you, Mr. Strait. So on my own time and expense, I contacted a solicitor for you. And what do I obtain for my pains? Nothing."

"Look, man, you did me a solid. I owe you a beer for that."

"A beer?" Graham turned to him and said incredulously, "Is that what you call the canned, frigid, tasteless bilge imbibed in this country?"

"Sounds like you don't like America very much."

"After today, I feel like doing nothing other than washing my hands of the lot of you. Truly an inscrutable people. Please drop me off at the train station, so I can begin my journey home immediately."

After they dropped the angry Brit at the station, Cindy drove Strait to his hotel room. Before he got out of the car, he said, "Listen, I'm sorry if I came off as ungrateful back at the jail. But I have my own ways of doing things. And I'm very grateful for your help. I'd still be in there if it wasn't for you."

Cindy held out her hand and gave his a perfunctory shake. She handed him her business card. "In case you need it in the future."

He was back in his hotel room no longer than ten seconds

when a knock came at the door. Strait let Footer in. Graham tore off the fake glasses and turtleneck sweater and flopped onto the chair with an exaggerated sigh. "Thank Christ I can finally remove this absurd ensemble from my body."

"Why did you dress like that? You looked ludicrous."

"It was a well-considered costume."

"You sounded ridiculous too. Who was that you were trying to do? Quentin Crisp?"

"God, James, don't tell me you're homophobic."

"Of course not. My brother is gay."

Footer raised his eyebrows. "Really? I didn't know that."

"Well, we're not so close. But that has nothing to do with his sexual orientation."

"Okay."

"I just thought your imitation of Quentin Crisp was humorous, that's all."

"I was trying to present a character that looked very different from my real self, so I won't be recognized in the future. And I wanted to act like the kind of person that would unnerve that bigoted chief of yours to the most extreme extent possible."

"On both counts, great job. And thanks much, my friend. But the bad news is that all our effort produced no result."

"You couldn't find Randy Street?"

"I found him, but he just said a lot of gibberish. I think he probably is seriously crazy."

"Do you still think he's innocent?"

"I'm not completely sure what to think. My gut says that his mother's story about him being framed by the CEO of Magic Industries is true."

"If true, it's not surprising if the man has been driven a little dotty. Did you see Marvin Williams in the jail?"

"No. Not in the lunchroom anyway."

"Are you convinced of *his* innocence?"

"Again, I'm not one hundred percent certain, but my gut tells me he had nothing to do with his daughter's disappearance. But I don't fully understand why Katherine's husband lied about being with him at the time of the kidnapping. I tried to call her, but got no answer. And no answering machine. Francis's lie really does shake Marvin's alibi. So many things about this case don't make sense. On top of that, I've got fuck-all about where to look next."

"I hate to say this, but maybe you should stop looking."

Strait shut his eyes.

"I mean, I'm in favor of looking for her if there's a place to look. But there's a point where you have to stop."

"Maybe you're right."

Footer stood. "Mate, you gave it a good shot. You should be commended for that. As for me, I think it's really time to hit that train station. I'll tell Gelder and Greyson that you are doing absolutely nothing to embarrass the Federal Bureau of Investigation. Okay?"

Strait's shoulders sagged. "Okay."

"Are you going to walk with me to the station?"

"Do you mind going by yourself? I feel like being alone."

"I understand. Talk to you soon."

For five minutes after his friend left, Strait sat immobile on the bed, contemplating the zig-zagging patterns in the old institutional carpet. They seemed shattered, chaotic, an ugly design from a previous era.

Why had Francis lied? He took out his smartphone to call Katherine's home number again. No answer. He drove to her house and knocked on the door. No one was home. The lights were off and the car was gone. The house seemed dead.

Chapter Twenty-eight

A moment after Strait returned to his room, there was a tap at the door. Through the peephole, he saw Carol from the Pot Belly. She was glancing anxiously up and down the hall. Her hands were pressed together and her fingers were doing a nervous dance.

Strait opened the door.

"James, I really need to talk to you."

Strait gestured to the chair and she crossed the room and sat down. She was still limping.

"How's the leg?" asked Strait.

"Getting better. Listen, I need to tell you something important while I still have the courage."

"You want a beer?"

"No."

"I want a beer."

Strait took a bottle of local craft beer from the fridge and sat on the bed and opened it. He poured some of the Chinese medicine from the paper envelope into his mouth and washed it down with a swallow of beer.

"You're trying to find Jophia Williams," she said.

"How did you know?"

"Everyone knows. And you tried to talk to Randy Street at his mother's house on the reservation. And now Randy is in jail for her disappearance."

"It's true. But I was only trying to get information from him, not get him arrested. The police followed me without my knowing."

"I lied to you about not seeing Randy. I was the one who drove him to his mother's house."

"I thought so. Did he tell you why he wanted to leave town?"

"No, but it wasn't hard to figure out, knowing what I know about him."

"Why did you lie to me?"

"Because I figured the police wanted to arrest him and I wasn't sure if you had something to do with that."

"I didn't, and they arrested him anyway."

"You need to hear the truth about him, James. And me."

"If you mean that he spent a decade in prison after a little girl accused him of molesting her, I heard all that already from his mother. She says he was innocent."

"Do you believe that?"

"I'm not sure. I think his mother was telling what she believes is the truth. But Randy's a pretty creepy guy."

Strait was surprised to see anger flare on Carol's face. "You don't know shit. Listen. A long time ago, Randy Street was a worker at Magic Lumber."

"I heard all about this already from his mother. She claims Bruno German, the CEO of Magic, set Randy up by getting his daughter to falsely accuse him. All to stop the labor problems he was having."

"Trust me, you don't know everything. Because Etta doesn't know. Magic Lumber is owned by Magic Industries, which has loads of other companies too. Over the years, it's branched into many other areas besides lumber, including import-export and even contracts with Homeland Security. There are lots of subsidiary businesses with names that would never give you a clue of their real owner. For example, they own the private jail in town under the subsidiary Rainbow Futures."

"You mean the jail where Randy is locked up?"

"Yes. You're familiar with it?"

"Passingly."

"Magic also owns Sawmill Brewery. The one that makes Sawdust beer."

"Really? That's the worst beer I've ever tasted. I can't understand why it's so popular."

"Magic also has controlling shares in a pro football team that won the Super Bowl a few years back."

"You know a lot about this company."

"My uncle is the CEO."

"Seriously? Bruno German is your uncle?" Strait had a flash of memory. "Your maiden name was German."

"Right. My father Randolph was Bruno's younger brother."

"Was?"

"He died about ten years ago. I guess about the same time yours did. Bad heart."

"Sorry."

"Dad and Bruno never got along. They were so different. Dad was basically an old hippie, long hair, acoustic guitar. He recited poetry and played acoustic folk songs at the local café on open mic nights. But his brother was, and still is, more like one of the Koch brothers."

"Must have been tough on you when your father passed."

"When he died, I hadn't talked to him for a long time. Several of our branch of the family emigrated to America after World War II. Some even live here in Pine River, but I pretty much have had no contact with them most of my life. But when I was a kid, we still had some family connection. I spent my summers at Uncle Bruno's mansion in Utah. He treated me like a second daughter. His real daughter, my cousin Mary, was about the same age and we were best friends. Uncle Bruno named his company after us, Mary, me, and his wife Gwen."

"Huh?"

"*Magic*. M, G, C. Mary, Gwen, and Carol."

"Oh. That's…nice."

"Nothing about that family was nice. After Randy started organizing the workers at the lumbermill and hired a lawyer to fight against the company with evidence of abuse he'd secretly recorded, my uncle tricked him into going out to the mansion in Utah. And he got my cousin Mary to accuse him of molesting her."

"Randy's mother claims he convinced her to do that by promising to buy her a pony. Sounds like a stretch to me."

"But it's true. Remember, she was my best friend. I knew her very well. In her mind, she was a *princess*. And she always wanted a real pony to ride around the grounds on, you know, like in a fairytale? So my uncle said, I'll get you a pony, princess—but I need you to do something important for me first."

"How did you find out?"

"She told me! All matter-of-factly, because she was getting a new pony. But she told me it was a secret and I couldn't tell anyone."

"That's incredible. I wouldn't think a little girl could do something like that. Even if she wanted the pony, lying convincingly in court…"

"She never actually testified in court. She provided a videotaped affidavit though. She was absolutely convincing. Gave an Academy Award performance. Even at that age, I knew what an awful thing she was doing. She was my best friend until the day she told me, and after that she wasn't even human to me. Looking back on it, I can see more clearly that she lived in an environment where people who were not rich and white were actually considered to be less than human, so in her mind, she probably thought something like, "he didn't molest me, but he's an Indian, so he's doing some other bad thing that he hasn't got caught for, so it's okay."

"Did you tell anyone?"

"I told the important adults in my life. But none of them believed me. They all acted like I was nuts. Because how could a sweet girl like Mary do a terrible thing like that? It wasn't possible. Or maybe some of them were even in on Uncle Bruno's plan. My uncle's branch of the family is like that. Everything comes down to money and protecting their kingdom. When it comes to that, anything goes."

"Did you go to the police? Teachers? The newspapers?"

A black blob seemed to descend from the ceiling and drip over her. "I gave up," she said softly. "It kills me every day that I didn't have the guts to try something else or to go to Mary and somehow make her take back what she said, but I was too weak."

"It wasn't your fault."

"Yes, it was."

"You were only a kid."

"I don't know."

"I do."

"I'll never know."

"So what happened afterwards between you and the rest of your family?"

"I continued to live with my father, but our relationship died. I turned rebellious. I was only ten, but acted like an angry teenager. In high school, I had a lot of problems. Drugs, alcohol, running with a bad crowd. I got pregnant and had an abortion when I was fifteen. That kind of stuff. It wasn't until I met my husband Eugene, when I was seventeen, that I got my life back on track. He was twenty-five and already owned the Pot Belly, which we now run together as partners. Life has been good ever since."

"Haven't seen your husband around here."

"He doesn't work at the café anymore. He's a manga artist. He does that at home."

"Glad things worked out. How about for your cousin?"

"I heard when Mary turned eighteen, she suddenly felt huge remorse for what she'd done to Randy. So she confronted my uncle about it, blamed him for brainwashing her as a child and demanded he do something to get Randy out of prison or she'd go to the newspapers. I'd love to have been a fly on the wall the day she confronted him. This is a man who thinks he's incapable of a mistake and responds to the slightest questioning of his authority like it's a personal threat. I don't know what happened, but I can tell you that within a month, Randy Street had been let out of prison. Ten years early."

"Could your uncle really arrange for him to be let out? Is that even possible?"

"You can do anything you want in this world if you have enough money."

"What happened to your cousin after that?"

"At first she cut off ties completely. She moved to California, did odds and ends trying to make a living without her daddy's money. I guess I can give her a little credit for trying. But in the end, the princess couldn't support herself like a normal, honest person. So she went back to my uncle and this time demanded money for her silence."

"And he paid her?"

Carol nodded. "With cash instead of a pony. And she bought a nice house off in the woods of northern California. I heard she lives by herself, off a fat bank account and sells her shitty nature paintings to the neighbors."

"Have you talked to her since?"

"We've had no communication since I was nine and I want to keep it that way."

"Does Randy know?"

"I don't think anyone told him."

"What happened to the racial harassment case against Magic Lumber? Randy wasn't the only one organizing, was he?"

"No, but he was the leader. When he was first arrested for the molestation, the lawyer who was preparing the lawsuit against my uncle's company was still in the process of putting it together. Then, out of the blue, that lawyer dropped it all. Gave up. When that happened, any will to pursue the lawsuit by the other activists dissolved. No one would come forward anymore. And I'll tell you something else. That lawyer, who was young and idealistic and genuinely full of passion for fighting for the rights of people like Randy, quit her legal career and disappeared. Obviously, Randy wasn't the only person my uncle got to."

"When did you start giving him food at the café?"

"He just walked in one morning and asked if we had any old bread we were throwing away. I nearly had a heart attack when I saw him. But he didn't recognize me. Not that he would. I only met him once at the mansion when I was a kid. I thought about telling him the truth, but I think it would've broken him even worse. The best I can do is just pass on food to him whenever I can and otherwise try to see to his well-being. Listen to his weather reports and show him a little human decency."

"And give him a ride to his mother's house if he asks."

She nodded.

"So, you think there's no chance Randy had anything to do with Jophia Williams?"

"None."

"How can you be so sure? You said yourself he's got mental problems. And time in prison tends to…criminalize people."

"I know him. The guy couldn't hurt a fly."

"I've heard that before. Randy said he knows where Jophia is. But when I tried to talk to him again, he just said a bunch of nonsense."

"Really?"

"I assume he's so psychotic he can't logically piece things together."

"He was messing with you. Or he was trying to tell you something and you just didn't catch it. He's a little paranoid, and he talks poetically sometimes, but trust me, he's not psychotic."

"Carol, any way you can visit him at the jail and ask him where Jophia is? He'd talk to you."

"I already tried to visit him, but he didn't put me on the visitor's list and he won't take my phone calls."

"Jesus, if you're not on his visitor list, who is?"

"No one is. I checked. Not even his mother."

"Hey!" Strait sat up with an inspiration. "Why don't you tell Kladspell what you told me? He'll listen to you."

"I can't."

"Why not?"

"Because the whole thing has legal implications that stretch into a lot of people's lives. Including my husband's. He's completely blameless, but he has protected my secret for years. He could go to prison. So could I."

"Maybe that's what you deserve."

"Chief Kladspell wouldn't believe me anyway."

"You're probably right."

"Do you believe me?"

"I think so. You and Randy's mother seem to be telling the same story. But my believing this doesn't help Randy, if Kladspell won't believe it. You know, the person who Kladspell might believe is your cousin. What she says about Randy's case has a lot more credibility to a judge than what either of us say. I know what I can do. I'll find her and convince her she needs to confess."

Alarm jumped on Carol's face. "She'd never do it. She won't tell you anything."

"How can you know that? You haven't spoken to her in years. And you heard she was remorseful."

"Being remorseful is one thing. Doing the right thing is another."

"We'll see."

"Please don't."

"Listen. If what you say is true, then I've got to do my best to fix it. It wouldn't just be for Randy. If I get him out of jail, maybe he'll finally be willing to tell me something coherent about Jophia's whereabouts. It's a slim chance, but I have nothing left to work with. Also, there's a good chance that he needs me as much as I need him."

"Why?"

"I was prepared to kill him. If you and Etta are right about his innocence, then I might instead have to protect him from someone else who wants to do the same thing."

***

Carol left his room not much less distraught than when she'd come.

Using the codes Graham had provided, Strait dialed into the FBI databases. With some trial and error, he was able to piece together details of the life of Mary German, alleged false accuser of Randy Street. What he found didn't speak directly to Carol and Etta's claims about her, but there were some peculiarities. Within a day of her eighteenth birthday, Mary German moved out of her family's massive Utah estate, where she'd spent her whole life, to a small apartment in southern California. For a year, she worked a string of odd jobs: a Denny's waitress, a landscaper, a clerk in a porn shop. She obtained a student loan and took a stab at getting a degree in fine arts at the University of Southern California, but dropped out after only one semester. Low-paying, dead-end jobs, a high-interest student loan. In May, about the same time Jophia disappeared, she went to court and changed her name from Mary German to Mary Commons.

Records showed that in September, only two months ago, in the town of Manton, in northern California, she had purchased a three-bedroom house marketed at over seven hundred thousand dollars. She made it hers free and clear with only one payment. Clearly, her financial problems had been solved.

The remote town looked to be nothing more than a sprinkling of expensive mountain homes inserted into the rugged terrain of the northern Sierra Nevada range, close to Lassen National Forest. The driving directions Strait downloaded to get from Pine River to Manton had sixteen steps, with larger arteries giving way to smaller and smaller streets and roads. A fourteen-hour drive if he didn't get lost.

Mary Commons had no Facebook page or other social media footprint. However, a Google search turned up a website on which her artwork was displayed, with nominal prices. Trees, flowers, and alpine landscapes, but with a dark, impressionistic tinge to the colors, a slight warping of the contours that made them look vaguely diseased.

The local address pinned to the post office box listed on the website was the same one for the house Mary Commons had bought. There was an email address, but when Strait, in the guise of a potential customer, wrote her an email, it was returned with the message that the address was no longer valid. She didn't seem interested in actually selling the paintings.

Strait sat in his room thinking the matter through, his gaze upon the silly painting with the blue rabbits prancing in a field. Such foolishly happy rabbits. They just hopped around all day, not a care in the world. The painting was poorly, even comically rendered, but somehow it was better than any of Mary German's.

Strait found a website where he could make his own business cards. He created a couple and printed them out on his little portable printer. Then he went shopping and bought provisions for the trip and gassed up the car. Early the next morning, he set out for California.

***

Mary German had done a good job of hiding herself. After driving for nearly two days, the last third of which involved pushing the ailing station wagon along steep, snaking mountain highway in middle-of-nowhere forest, Strait finally passed a rustic wooden sign on log-posts that proclaimed, "Welcome to Manton!" The words were backgrounded by painted mountains draped with green-blue forest capped with snow.

Strait found a coffee shop and pulled into the parking lot. It looked like one of those upscale cafes you'd find in trendy towns like Sedona, the type that specialized in exotic herbal teas and dainty, overpriced cakes the size of a half-dollar. The building had a mauve awning in front with a wooden latticework overhead that had the dry, brown remains of grape plants that probably a couple months back had been heavy with fruit. The edges of the winding pathway that led to the front door were formed from pinkish oval stones, traces of snow from a recent storm still on them.

He ducked his head to enter without hitting himself on the doorframe. The thirty-something woman behind the counter had a freckled face and wavy blonde hair tied back. She was drying a dainty ceramic cup with a towel. She stared at Strait like he was something from another planet.

"Howdy. Sit anywhere," she answered after collecting herself.

"Got any decaf?" he asked.

"I'll bring it right out."

The four tables in the small room had silver metal-framed tops of thick glass, and the floors were stone tile with alternating patterns of red and green. Some kind of Mexican design. Paintings, all tasteful landscapes, hung along the walls. Strait was the only customer.

He chose the table nearest the window overlooking the parking lot and the mountains across. The woman approached. This time she was smiling.

"Here you go," she said, placing a small cup of steaming coffee in front of him. "Sorry I stared at you like that. We don't usually get truckers in here. Especially asking for decaf."

"I'm not a trucker."

"You look like one. A little young, maybe, but you're built for the part. What are you, then? Military?"

"I'm an art scout."

"A what?"

"An art scout. My museum—my consortium, actually—sends me out on the road searching for obscure, talented artists. Painters, mostly."

She smiled like he was joking. "Honestly?"

Strait held his right hand aloft. "I swear." He pulled out one of his fake business cards and handed it to her.

She read it, her lips moving. "Wow. Well, good to make your acquaintance, Mr. Reynolds. I've never met a painter talent scout before. Maybe that explains the decaf."

"Actually, I'd love to have it caffeinated, but doctor's orders. No caffeine, no salt."

"Blood pressure?"

"Something like that."

"I get you something else?"

Strait skimmed the menu dubiously. "Do you have anything besides these little cakes?"

"Sorry. It's that kind of place. Boutique café. My mom's dream come true. I could whip you up a sandwich, though. We have fixings in the back."

Strait considered. "Well, that's highly decent of you. *Highly*. But I think I can wait until I get a bit further down the road. You could do me a favor, though. I'm in town to meet a particular artist whose paintings my employer is very interested in."

"Who? We have a few of them living up here."

"She has a website?" Strait pulled up Mary German's website on his iPhone and showed it to her. "A most unique perspective, we believe."

"Sure. Mary. She's up near Moose Falls."

"Might I enquire where that is exactly?"

"I'll draw you a map. Hope you got four-wheel drive."

Strait topped the tank in the town's only gas station. For an hour he wended his way about the rough mountain roads, following the hand-drawn map, which seemed to match reality better than the map on his phone. He finally pulled up to a driveway blocked by a log gate that appeared to lead to the correct house. The gate was padlocked and there was no place to park his car, so he drove up through the heavily forested area until he found a space beside the road wide enough to park, then he walked back. He tried to make his way around the gate, which was taller than he was, by pushing through the thick trees to either side of it, but found himself face-to-face with an equally tall barbed-wire fence. So he went back to the gate, climbed up the five thick horizontal logs, and jumped over the top.

It took ten more minutes of walking to reach the house. It was a cozy-looking log cabin with a spacious porch and an overhanging roof supported by two pine poles on either side. The porch was hung heavily with red ceramic flowerpots cradled in thick macramé roping and at least a dozen wind-chimes of various sizes and shapes. As he walked up, a breeze tilted all the wind-chimes to one side, bending them in unison like a grove of seaweed in a wave, and sent them tinkling as he climbed the three steps to the porch.

From somewhere inside, he could hear mellow jazz playing. He knocked. After no answer came, he knocked again and the door was suddenly flung open.

The woman who opened it was one of the most attractive Strait had ever seen. She stood in blue jeans and a short-sleeved yellow t-shirt with a single red flower between her breasts. Her sleek, dark hair was parted in the middle and fell back loosely over her shoulders. She looked up to him with intelligent, tea-brown eyes.

"Can I help you?"

"Ms. Commons?"

"Yes?"

Strait pulled out his card and held it out. "My name is Arthur Reynolds? I'm a representative for the Metropolitan Museum of Art. In New York City?"

She read over the card with interest. She flashed a glance at Strait and then looked at the card again. "This is so cool," she said finally. "So my internship wasn't as bad as I thought."

"Your…?"

"Internship. That's what this is about, right? I did an internship three summers ago at the Met. Under Dr. Johnson?"

That wasn't in the databases.

"You know? Dr. Johnson. Eastman Johnson? You must know him. He's in charge of outreach?"

Strait looked at his shoes. "Sure I do. We work in different buildings, though. I guess the request for me to contact you came indirectly because of that. I never really know for sure about where the requests first come from."

Mary nodded.

"But I've been asked to come out here and take a look at your paintings in person. They're putting together a display of regional art that doesn't receive enough exposure. Kind of a promotion of potential greatness."

"That's a real honor. I don't know what to say."

"Sorry for dropping by unannounced, but there was no phone number on your website and when I sent an email to the address you listed, it bounced."

"I should take down that website. My customers are all local."

"Can I see your paintings?"

"I have a small gallery inside. I can show you the ones I have up in there now. Can you give me a second to straighten up first?"

"No problem."

"Be right back." She shut the door. Strait walked off the porch and took in the surrounding forest. The hills were covered with pines and spruces, all over forty feet tall. The air was pure and scented with pine. The quiet was so all-encompassing, so peaceful. Strait wondered if he should get himself a cabin in the woods too.

The door opened and Mary stepped onto the porch. Cradled under her right arm, business end pointed in his direction, was a double-barrel shotgun.

"Okay, asshole," she said. "Eastman Johnson was one of the co-founders of the Met, as anyone who really works there would know. His name is engraved on the entrance. He died in 1906. Who are you really?"

"You've got to be kidding," said Strait.

"Do I look like I'm kidding?"

"This is the third time this week someone's pointed a shotgun in my face."

"Then you must be a real prick. Are you here to rape me? I'll shoot your balls off."

"I'm here because of Randy Street."

Her mouth fell open. She lowered the shotgun.

"Shit," she said.

She brought the shotgun up again. "Did he send you here to get revenge?"

"He doesn't even know I'm here. You're right, I lied. I'm not from the museum. But I didn't think you'd even talk to me if I started off with the truth. Can you give me a minute to explain?"

After a moment's hesitation, she nodded.

Strait told her everything, how he was on leave from the FBI and had been asked to help find the missing girl, how it had led first to Marvin and then to Randy, who was now in jail and had a good chance of going back to prison for the murder of Jophia Williams, based solely on his having a prior conviction for molesting a nine-year-old girl.

"But I was told that this prior conviction was a set-up. Based on lies told by his accuser."

Mary was gripping the shotgun so tightly her hand was white and the finger on the trigger was twitching. A tear fell down her cheek. "Who told you?"

"Someone who would know."

"Fuck."

"Someone who knows Randy Street would never hurt a fly."

"Fuck."

"Is it true?"

"You're not some lawyer? Trying to get money?"

"Absolutely not. Understand that even if Randy is innocent, he still seems to know where the girl is. There's a chance the girl's still alive. If I help him get out of jail now, he'll probably help me find her."

Mary sagged and sat down on the porch, dropping the gun at her side. She wiped the tears from her face. "If I tell you the truth, how do I know you won't tell someone else?"

"You don't."

"Fuck."

"But for what it's worth, I give my word that I won't tell anyone what you tell me. I'm not here to get you in trouble. The start and end of my purpose is to help find that missing girl."

She sat with her face in her hands, her shoulders jerking up and down as she sobbed. After a while, she managed to get some words out. "He went to prison the first time because of me. My testimony was all bullshit. Oh, Jesus, I fucking sent an innocent man to prison! Because my fucking father pushed me to. It never goes away! It never will, will it? I'm fucked for life."

"You have a chance to fix what you did."

"What can I do? I confronted that *devil* on my eighteenth birthday. I told him that when I was a little girl I didn't understand what I was doing and I would've done *anything* for him."

"You did it to get a pony."

She glared up at Strait. "I didn't do it for that goddamned *pony*. I did it because I *worshipped* him. But when I grew up, I don't know when exactly, but it came to me in flashes and finally I realized I'd actually sent Randy, who was a nice guy, to a fucking *prison*. So I finally got up the nerve to tell my father I was disowning him. Plus, if he didn't get that man out of prison immediately, I was going to find as many journalists as I could, starting with CNN and the *New York Times*, and tell them all about what he'd had me do. Confess everything. And I would have done it too, but, poof! Like magic, he got Randy out. In less than four weeks. So I didn't tell anyone."

"He gave you a bunch of money too, didn't he?"

She nodded miserably. "I couldn't make enough money to support myself on my own. So I went back to him."

"You blackmailed him again?"

"I asked him for money and he gave it to me."

"Sounds like he bought you."

"Fuck you."

"It's the truth, isn't it?"

"Hello? I was a victim too. I was nine years old."

"You were a victim, I get it. But you still victimized someone else and you haven't done right by him."

She gazed off into the trees and didn't respond.

"Mary, I came to hear from you whether Randy was originally guilty, and now I know he wasn't. I promised I wouldn't tell anyone, and I'll keep that promise. But keep in mind the whole police department in Pine River is now working to put Randy Street on trial and send him back to prison, mostly on the basis that he's been convicted before. And none of those cops will listen to my opinion on Randy's innocence."

She put her face into her folded arms and started crying again.

"But you have the power to stop them by admitting that the original conviction was based on a lie."

"I can't."

"Why not?"

"They'll put *me* in prison."

"Get a good lawyer. Unlike Randy, you can afford one."

"I'm sorry. I just can't. I'm…I'm a coward."

"You told your father you'd go to the media."

"Maybe I was bluffing."

"You'd really let that poor guy go back to prison?"

Her only answer was to lower her head and sob.

"You make me sick."

By the time Mary German stopped crying and lifted her head, Strait was gone.

Chapter Twenty-nine

The building that housed the corporate headquarters of Magic Industries looked about how Strait imagined it would. It took up the entire twenty-third floor of Wells Fargo Center. The gleaming steel and concrete edifice was the tallest building in Salt Lake City. On his return trip to Pine River from Manton, Strait took a long detour to reach this office building. Although he'd had ample time to consider the possibilities, he still wasn't sure what he would do when he finally came face to face with Bruno German.

All he knew for sure at this point was he was filled with disgust for most of the human race. At least the segment of it that was occupied by creatures like Bruno and Mary German. By Kladspell and Gelder and Greyson. By people with lots of power they didn't deserve. Power they abused.

He knew he wanted to confront the CEO of Magic Industries about what he'd done to Randy Street and to motivate him—perhaps with a boot in his ass—to help solve Randy's new plight. Bruno German had gotten him out of prison before, so he could do it again. Another reason Strait had for visiting was a kind of perverse curiosity. What would a man who sold the soul of his own child be like in the flesh? Would he have horns?

Strait had spent the night at a motel working up his cover story to get into the man's presence. In the morning he went to a department store and bought a business suit. Then he went to the local print shop and made copies of another business card he'd created on his computer. This version of himself was a representative of a furniture manufacturer from an east coast company interested in a new source for raw lumber for its factories.

He entered and took the elevator to the twenty-third floor.

The doors opened directly into the front office, where a receptionist sat behind a huge desk of polished wood. The carpet was ornate with gold curlicues and in each corner of the room was a fake Grecian column painted gold. A gold-colored chandelier hung from the ceiling. The receptionist was a woman in her thirties with blonde hair pulled into pigtails. She wore a nametag: Mary Anne Bunting.

Her lips parted in surprise to see him emerge from the elevator. Something about the woman, maybe the pigtails or the way she openly gaped at him, made her seem out of place in the gawdy front office. On the wall behind was a metal rendering of the company logo, an abstract representation of a couple of pine trees that looked somewhat like twin bolts of lightning. It was backlit all around with an orange aura. Underneath the logo was a line of neatly arranged framed photographs.

When Strait approached, Mary Anne grinned.

"Gosh! You're a big one. Can I help you?"

"Yes, I'm here to see Bruno German."

She frowned. "Did you have an appointment?"

Strait tried to look sheepish. "Actually, no. The truth is, our supervisor rushed us through a training over the past couple of days and sent us out to prospective companies without time to prepare. In the rush, I have to admit, I didn't get around to actually making an appointment. Any way I could see Mr. German anyway?"

"I hate to tell you, but he's out the whole week at a conference in Germany. And right after that, he'll be going on vacation for another week." She giggled. "That's actually kind of why I'm here. This is the time of year when the company gives a lot of its home office workers two weeks off. The regular receptionist is off too, so I'm, like, fill-in? This is the third year I've done this, and trust me, this place is dead this time of year. I can just sit here and play Candy Crush all day and get paid for it."

"Sweet."

"I'm real sorry. You want to make an appointment for when he gets back? I think he has slots open in about three weeks."

"Hmm. My schedule is still up in the air for a few weeks from now. Probably I should call when I'm sure. I have his number somewhere, but do you happen to have one of his cards I could take with me?"

"Sure." She rummaged about her desk but found nothing. "Give me a sec." And she got up and went through the door near the side of the reception desk.

Strait looked over the photographs behind the desk. A hodgepodge of industry-related history. A black-and-white picture of a ribbon-cutting ceremony, a smiling young man in front, tall and broad-shouldered and blonde-haired, who Strait assumed was Bruno German. Three or four photos of buildings with the Magic Industries logo and one showing a Sawdust beer factory in Colorado. Strait scanned the wall further and saw a section full of children. Groups of kids amidst goats, pigs, and horses. A laughing boy chasing a chicken. Three small girls grinning before a big rectangle of poster paper showing the growth cycle of a grain seed to shoot to plant to harvest. A posed group, about fifty kids aged about five to ten years old, standing and sitting in rows, the back one comprised of tweens flanking on both sides a man with a big belly. The man was quite short, even shorter than the pre-adolescents near him. A banner was suspended on trees behind them with the words LITTLE SHOOTS GETAWAY 2015 painted in red. Strait leaned forward and squinted and his breath stopped in his throat.

Holy shit.

In the bottom row, slightly to the left side, was Peter Letoche.

The dead boy from Gallup who was found at the New Mexico border. Seated next to him was Sarah Taylor, one of the other missing Gallup children.

Sitting between Peter and Sarah was Jophia Williams.

The three kids were among the very few African Americans in the photo, all bunched together, maybe drawn by their visible difference. Strait found only two other black kids in the picture.

"Interesting picture?" said Mary Anne. She was standing behind him. She had her hand outstretched with a business card.

"Yes, interesting," said Strait. "What is this?"

"That's Little Shoots summer camp."

"Little Shoots?"

"It's a group for kids. Kind of like 4-H, only more local. It promotes agricultural skills and stuff. Mr. German's, like, their biggest financial supporter?"

"Wow."

"Is that surprising?"

"No. It's just…a coincidence. I've been considering setting up something just like this in our area, because I grew up in farmland. Up in Nebraska? And where I live now, kids don't get enough exposure to this kind of thing. Maybe I'll talk to Mr. German about this too when I see him. Is this guy in the back Mr. German?"

She laughed. "Mr. German's way taller. He donates lots of money, but he doesn't do anything himself with the kids. He wouldn't want to get his expensive suit dirty. That's his cousin Gunnar."

"Cousin Gunnar doesn't worry about getting his suit dirty?"

"Gunnar and Bruno are like, opposites? If you want to start something up like this, he's really the one to talk to. I don't think Mr. German knows the first thing about it. Mr. German's got the money, and Mr. Wilson's—Gunnar Wilson—got the hands. He was some kind of big farmer before he came to the states. And he loves kids."

"He's from Germany?"

"You'd think so, but no. The family got kind of broken up after World War II, and some of them immigrated to other countries. Some of them came to America. Like Mr. German's grandfather did. So his sister, Mr. German's grandfather's…um… sister, that is…

"His great aunt."

"Right. His great aunt was separated from her brother and travelled around with another family member through, like, three or four countries."

"For a fill-in staff, you sure know a lot about the boss's family."

"Well, yeah, but like I've been a fill-in for, like, seven years? And everyone in town kind of knows about the family anyway, because they're so rich. Plus," she said, tossing back a pigtail in a show of pride, "I make it a point to keep informed."

"I respect that," said Strait. "Some people just sort of sleepwalk through life."

"You can say *that* again."

"Any way I could contact Mr. Wilson directly? I mean, before I meet with Mr. German? It'd be good to have something to take back to my boss, even if it's only to say I made a contact about starting an agricultural charity our company can sponsor. Do you have Mr. Wilson's phone number?"

"I don't think I have Gunnar's contact information. But he has a personal website. Just Google his name."

"I'll do it. Does he live in Salt Lake City?"

"Oh, no. He's travelled here a few times to visit Bruno, but he lives in Arizona."

Strait stared at her.

"Do you know where in Arizona he lives?"

"Um, I forget the name. Someplace rural."

"Flagstaff? Prescott?"

"No, smaller. Pine something."

"Pine River?"

"That's it. You know it?"

"A bit."

"It's funny that Gunnar moved to a small town like that. He's so cosmopolitan. He lived all over the world when he was growing up. France, Italy, I think Greece for awhile. Then they left Europe altogether to finally settle down."

"Where?"

"New Zealand."

Chapter Thirty

From the parking lot, Strait tried to call Graham. No answer and no voice mail. Strait went to a café with wifi and on the search site typed in the security code Graham had given him. The words ACCESS DENIED flashed at him. He tried again and got the same message. Strange.

He wrote an email to Graham explaining all he'd learned about Gunnar Wilson, cousin of Bruno German, and his connection to Small Shoots, which Jophia and the other disappeared kids had been members of. He asked him to call back as soon as possible and told him the code he'd given him was not working. And told him he needed intel on Gunnar Wilson immediately.

Strait then typed "Gunnar Wilson" into the Google search engine. A surprisingly large number of parents with the surname Wilson had chosen to name their sons Gunnar. Strait browsed through the selection of hits but couldn't find any candidates that made sense. He added Small Shoots to the search. This time, at the top of the search list, he found the website he was looking for.

The name of Gunnar Wilson's website was BEYOND THE PALE, which was executed in red capital letters on a field of black. Beside the title was a posed photo of Gunnar grinning in front of a boulder on the snowy summit of a mountain. The photo shunted to the left and was replaced with another, this of him bent in a sleeveless down jacket and sawing a log, big biceps flexing. A powerfully built man with tousled blonde hair. More photos followed on the rotating loop, all showing Gunnar Wilson in a very favorable light. The pictures were set up carefully to hide his short stature. Gunnar Wilson was probably not more than five and a half feet tall. He also noticed that every photo depicted Gunnar alone. No other human subjects.

A row of icons below the banner represented categories on the site, such as “Gunnar’s Story,” “Gunnar’s Business,” “Gunnar’s Thoughts,” and “Gunnar’s Hobbies.” On the sidebar, a separate button was labelled *Small Shoots*. Strait clicked on it and found a lot of photos with no text. There were similar to the ones he’d seen at Magic Industries. Pictures of kids in farm settings, riding horses, petting sheep and goats. A sub-link was labelled “Regional Getaways.” These also contained only group shots from summer camps, taken for each of the past five years. Strait clicked on each photo and enlarged it so he could see each face clearly. There they were. Jophia, Peter Letoche and Sarah Taylor. The three missing kids. He saved the photo on his laptop and used a photo app to clip and enlarge the three children in the group shot and make a separate JPEG of them. He also clipped out and did the same with the other two black children whose faces he didn’t recognize. He emailed the pictures to Graham and wrote another note asking him to scan the faces and do an image search in the FBI missing children databases.

He tried to call Graham again. Still no answer.

Strait clicked on “Gunnar’s Story.” After he read the first few sentences, he wished he hadn’t. *Gunnar Wilson, a man of exceptionally high I.Q. and far-ranging talents, spent much of his life on a sheep farm north of the New Zealand capital of Auckland. Most boys exposed to the hardships of farm life would have learned little else than the low-intelligence skills of mucking up and tending to livestock, but in the chest of little Gunnar beat the fiercely aspirational heart of twenty generations of solid Bavarian stock.”*

Strait winced. Solid Bavarian stock?

He scanned through the rest, which was peppered with more selectively attractive photos of Gunnar in various manly activities and a lot of evidence that Gunnar Wilson had a bloated sense of himself tied to his "Germanic stock." But he found nothing useful.

He sat back and considered. He knew in his gut he'd made a major discovery here, one that might well solve the mystery of Jophia Williams. But how could Gunnar Wilson be connected to the disappearance of Jophia? How did it all fit together? Strait considered trying to flesh out all the connections, but he realized that the bottom line was he needed to find Gunnar Wilson and have a heart to heart talk, perhaps with key points emphasized by Strait's Glock.

Where exactly did Gunnar live? Mary Anne the receptionist had said Pine River, but where specifically? Maybe it was someplace on the website. Strait clicked on "Gunnar's Business," which opened to three more links, "Imports," "Gear," and "The Farm." He clicked on Imports, which showed a grid of thumbnails of Maori dolls, Manuka honey, and jars of Vegemite for sale. It looked like he imported the stuff from New Zealand and sold it through the website at a substantial markup. Strait scanned with more interest the survivalist gear Wilson was also selling. A lot of old military supplies, all apparently bought from army surplus stores and sold at a profit. He had a range of camouflage clothing for sale. Seeing the thumbnails made Strait think about the shooter at Marvin's cabin. Like Gunnar, the gunman had been a short person, with broad shoulders. Strait clicked back through some of the selfies that Gunnar had posted. Yes, there it was. He was pictured in two photos on a big black motorcycle. It looked like the same bike that had followed Strait and Jessie to the river that day. And the shooter at the cabin had escaped on a motorcycle. With a chill, he realized Gunnar Wilson had been following him almost from the moment he'd come to town.

The shooter at the cabin must have been Gunnar Wilson. And he hadn't been trying to kill Marvin. He had been trying to kill Strait.

The phone hummed. The caller display said it was Footer.

"About time, Graham."

"James! Sorry I didn't get your calls. Busy day."

"You're still in Phoenix?"

"Yes. I was planning on flying out tomorrow, but after getting your email…"

"I found this guy's website and I think…"

"Hold your horses. The second I got your message and learned you couldn't get into the system, I started hunting. You'll be thrilled to learn that your New Zealand friend Mr. Gunnar is a very naughty boy."

"What do you mean?"

"After perusing all the sections on his site, which I of course found too, I checked out the email address."

"How could you finish all those sections so fast? There must be hundreds of pages."

"In the UK, they teach us an advanced reading strategy called 'skimming.' As I was saying, I did searches of his email address, the chipperly named happysmallshoots@gmail.com. I did an identity search and got several hits, most benign, but one in, of all places, Estonia, which listed a secondary email address for Gunnar Wilson, that is, gwbloodofsaints@gmail.com. You follow me so far?"

"I'm still waiting to be thrilled."

"I found an intriguing match for his blood of saints email address. Mr. Wilson is on the membership list of a group called New Confederation."

"Shit."

"Its membership lists were secret until Anonymous hacked

their computers and posted them on a website. Gunnar Wilson's name doesn't appear, just his email address. Anyway, pursuing this further down the rabbit hole, I found that Mr. Wilson is quite active on several neo-Nazi forums. On Stormfront, he goes by the username whitekiwi1488. And he's posted more than 5,000 comments. Thrilled yet?"

"What kind of comments?"

"Let's see. Here are some examples. "Negroes aren't capable of civilization. Every accomplishment of civilization is attributable to the white race." And "You wouldn't promote a monkey to a management position, so why would you promote a negro to one?" Let's see. Oh, here's an especially fetid one. "Any racially sane arrangement of society places the mud people below the whites, so the muds are laboring and the whites are enjoying the fruits of that labor."

"Jesus."

"I doubt Jesus has anything to do with this."

"I need to find him. I know he lives in Pine River, but I couldn't find an address."

"The farm he runs is so far off the beaten trail, it might not even have a street address."

"What farm?"

"Is that a serious question?"

"Yes."

"You really are slow, James. Look at the website, under 'Gunnar's Business.'"

"I did."

"Did you look at 'The Farm'?"

"No."

"Open it now."

Strait clicked on the icon. It looked like in addition to his selling New Zealand imports, Gunnar had continued his work as a livestock farmer. There were photos of a tract of land carved out of a heavily forested area, with several outbuildings, processing areas for the animals, large barrels of some kind of grain feed. Unconventional terrain for raising animals, but not unheard of.

His heart jumped. He quickly clicked back through the photos until he saw them again: the large, rectangular houses, the wide plastic rim filled with food affixed to the lines of dozens of cages filled with live animals. Gunnar Wilson had continued his business of breeding and harvesting farm animals, but he hadn't done so with sheep.

Chickens.

"Fuck me," said Strait.

"No time for fun, mate."

"He's running a poultry farm. But no address. Can we get a location from the geotagging on these photos?"

"Good idea. Why didn't I think of that? Oh, I already did."

"Of course you did."

"I'm texting you the GPS coordinates right now."

"Thank you. I don't know how you got through all this so fast. You're a genius."

"Stick to the superhero SWAT activities, mate. And I'll back you up with the genius lab rat act stuff. Brawn and brains. Together, we're an unstoppable crimefighting duo."

"Speaking of which, can I ask another favor? Can you fly in an army of SWAT agents by military helicopter and parachute them in to this chicken farm?

"Jurisdiction, James."

"Jurisdiction, my ass. At least two of those kids are from

New Mexico. It's federal."

"And logistics. You do recall the Arizona field office is a three-hour drive away. Not to mention there are procedures that must be followed. What I *can* do is write a memo to Gelder making a case for a move of jurisdiction based on the possibility of interstate kidnapping. It might work. If so, we can then request a warrant to conduct a search of Mr. Wilson's premises."

"That will take days."

"Months, actually."

"Do you want me to go up there all alone?"

"Of course I don't."

"If no one else is coming with me, that's what I'm going to do."

"I didn't hear a word you just said. And I suggest before you do anything rash, you give that bonehead chief of police another try. Show him the pictures you found."

"He'll arrest me before I can show him anything."

"Your British tourist friend provided you some leverage, didn't he?"

"Which certainly made him hate me even more. I tried giving him evidence before and he just threw it back at me. Even if by some miracle he decided to help, someone that incompetent would just get in my way."

Graham sighed. "If you're going up there by yourself, at least keep me informed. Carry your phone so I can track your movements."

"Sure you don't want to drive up here and go along with me?"

"I'm sorry, mate."

"I understand."

“Like it or not, James, this sort of thing appears to be your fate.”

“What the hell are you talking about?”

“You seemed destined to be the hero.”

Chapter Thirty-one

Strait kept the accelerator pedal pressed to the floor, straining the capacity of the station wagon's old motor to the highest speed it could produce. Only about 75 miles per hour. Not fast enough. It wasn't even over the highway speed limit, but the engine was grinding and clanking under the pressure. Strait had his phone open in the drink cup, the GPS targeted for the coordinates of Gunnar's farm that Graham had given him.

He'd done the eight-hour drive from Salt Lake City without stopping. As he rolled into the southernmost outlying region of Pine River, the afternoon sun was inching toward the ragged mountain horizon. All at once, Strait felt the steering wheel rattle violently in his hand and the engine gave out a *boom!* He pulled over to the emergency lane. His spirits plummeted at the sight of black smoke coming from the engine.

He got out and opened the hood and stared through the billowing smoke at the mess. No way he could fix it himself. He remembered the Bear brothers were not far from here. He took out their business card and called. Gus Bear answered.

"Bear Brothers. Talk to me."

"Gus? This is James Strait. Remember that car you sold me?"

Gus arrived in fifteen minutes with the tow truck. Strait threw his backpack into the space behind the passenger seat, relieved of the weight of, among other things, his Glock, his AR-15, and several boxes of ammunition. Gus hauled the car into the shop. James sat in the passenger seat of the tow truck, agitated.

"Listen, I'm in a real hurry to get somewhere. Any way I can get a loaner?"

"I think so. Let me check out what I got. Keith will write you up."

Keith Bear was at his usual spot in the office, behind the desk with its stacks of neatly arranged paperwork and its Holy Bible. Gus went out the back door. Keith said, "What's wrong with the car?"

"I don't know. Black smoke started pouring out the engine."

"Probably oil leaking somewhere in there. You're fortunate it didn't detonate."

"Really?"

Keith sniffed. "You need to maintain these vehicles. They're prone to failure if not cared for properly. This will take me a few minutes."

Strait stepped outside and crossed the lot in front of the shop. Gus had detached the tow truck harness from the station wagon but hadn't yet rolled it back onto the winch. He'd left the driver's door open and the keys in the ignition.

Disorganized prick. The car was still leaking acrid-smelling black smoke. He studied the road and the field across from it. A patch of flat, grassy land, about thirty feet across, that ended at a wall of trees.

Standing out against the thick growth of pine trees was something strange. A white spot. Looked like an old, dead branch. A vertical portion coming up from the ground gave way to two thinner branches of about the same length that spread at angles from either side. It clearly formed the shape of the letter Y. A white Y.

Randy Street's words came back to him. *Go to the why. The big white why. Just outside of town.*

Strait crossed the road and walked to the white formation. It was a dead branch, bleached by sunlight, about half his height. It looked like it had been carried over and propped up here as a marker. A marker for what?

What else had Randy said? Something about…bears.

The big white why is where the bears play. They play with chickens. And they skin rabbits.

Bears skinning rabbits. Strait shot a look back at the shop. No one was visible. What else did he say? Something about the grass. And a doll.

You want the doll? Look under the grass. You need a head, man!

Had Randy been here and witnessed something? Or found something? The grass in front of the white branch was thigh-high and thick. Strait brushed his hand over its surface. A huge green grasshopper leapt up and landed scrambling amidst the long grass. He yanked up the grass from the ground and tossed a handful to the side and pulled up some more. After a few more fistfuls, he'd cleared a patch of dirt. Nothing. He cleared some more immediately in front of the white branch. This time, the roots of the patch of grass he pulled out disrupted the soil underneath and left a concavity that had something lumpy pushing through the surface. Strait pressed his fingers into the wet soil and wrapped them around an object buried there and pulled it and held it up to the sun.

The head of a teddy bear.

He perceived movement behind him. He turned and found Gus Bear aiming a shotgun at him.

Chapter Thirty-two

For a long moment, Strait and Gus stood staring at each other. The small man looking up at the much bigger one, a smirk on his red, wrinkled face, his finger tight on the shotgun trigger.

"What'd you find there, Soldier?"

Strait held up the teddy bear head.

"Looks like it's missing something."

"Yep." Strait took a step toward the road. Gus moved smoothly in front of him and lifted the shotgun barrel to Strait's face.

"You ain't going nowheres."

Strait held his hands up, one still holding the bear head. "What's wrong?"

Keith Bear came running out of the shop. "What in God's creation are you doing, Gus?"

"War hero here was snooping around and found what we was looking for all that time. I think he knows something he shouldn't."

Keith looked at the teddy bear head. His eyes narrowed. "How did you know where it was?"

"I didn't."

"He's lying," said Gus. "He's been acting like he's got worms in his pants since he got here. Who sent you here? Kladspell?"

"No one. That shitty car you sold me broke down and I wanted to get it fixed. That's all."

Keith said blandly to Gus, "even if he happened to find this by accident, we can't let him leave."

"What bad thing did I discover? You smuggling teddy bears?" Strait tried to laugh, but now Keith pulled out a big handgun from under his coat and pointed it awkwardly at him. A .357

Magnum.

Strait took inventory of the situation. He could take out Gus Bear, who was stupidly standing way too close, which would prompt Keith Bear to safely blow his head off from his own position ten feet away. And if he went for Keith first, Gus would just blast him through the right side as he passed. Classic no-win, you're completely fucked situation. Only one thing to do.

Strait jumped to Gus and used his forearm to smack the shotgun barrel to the right. Gus was forced to turn with the shotgun and Strait stepped sideways behind him and wrapped his left arm tightly around Gus's neck and reached over his right shoulder, took control of the shotgun, and pointed it at Keith.

"Drop it," he said. Keith dropped his gun like it was on fire. He threw his hands up over his head. *Not fighters.*

"Get on the ground, face down. Stretch your arms out in front of you."

Both men did as Strait ordered. Gus was muttering curses. Keith seemed to be in shock.

A car appeared at the crest of the road and slowed down as it passed. A man was driving and a woman was in the passenger seat and they were both staring wide-eyed at him. Strait spied the woman pulling out a phone as the car disappeared down the hill.

"You move a muscle in the next ten minutes, I'll kill you," said Strait. He ran to the tow truck and threw their guns in next to the winch. The keys were still in the ignition. He started it, threw it into gear, revved the engine and took off, whipping up a cloud of grit that showered the two men on the ground. The harness had not been rolled up and its metal hook clanged against the highway pavement behind the truck. Strait looked in his rearview mirror to see Gus standing and pulling out another gun he had in one of his pockets.

Strait floored it. Through the roar of the engine he heard the *crack! crack!* of gunfire and a hole appeared in the rear window and he felt the sting of a bullet grazing his right ear. A spiderweb fracture appeared on the windshield.

More gunfire followed but Strait was too far away to hit.

PART II

Chapter Thirty-three

THE SCREAMS OF THE NEW GIRL tore Jophia Williams from her dream.

She'd been in a warm place, a happy place. A family picnic in Pine River park. Her father and mother laughing, a cornucopia of delicious food spread on the picnic table covered with a white and red checkered tablecloth. Her sister was chasing her around the picnic table, trying to tickle her.

Jophia opened her eyes to the night screams. She was in tar-black darkness. She was lying on a mattress, her head on a pile of straw. Like the howls of an injured forest creature, the girl's screams echoed up the mountainside, growing louder as she was brought closer to the building. This old barn. The smell of the animals lingered even now, long after there'd been any in here, a heavy, sour odor in the thin wooden walls and in the rotting floorboards under the mud.

The building used to stable horses. Now it stabled children.

The children had only straw to use for pillows, but they were given a mattress each and a thin blanket. The mattresses were ripe with mildew and the blankets hadn't been washed in a long time.

Jophia blinked her eyes to try to bring contours into the black but still could see nothing. The building was drafty, its slatboard walls barely subduing the winds that blew across the mountaintop. In the hayloft above them was a large window, but the men had boarded it up. In the daytime, sunlight could only filter through the space at the bottom of the sliding doors and through the seams and cracks in the walls. But it was now nighttime, which meant you needed to see with different senses than seeing. The feel of the air told her sunrise was another hour's coming.

Jophia lifted her head from the straw. The movement jostled the iron chain that connected her ankle to the wall. The screams had awakened the others too. She could hear their chains moving and in her mind's eye connect their sounds with their positions: in the stalls on her side of the barn were Luther, Beth, Linda, with little Jeffrey in the far corner, and John and Ellie on the other side.

With a bone-jarring squeak, the doors slid open. The moon flooded blue light into the black interior, backlighting a dark figure of a man. In front of him was a smaller form. The new girl. None of the children made a sound. They all knew what would happen if they spoke without permission.

Jophia could tell by the shape and height of the silhouette which of the two brothers it was. Master Gus. The mean one. Master Gus was the short, fat man with one eyebrow who held his shotgun with the stock gripped under the bend of his elbow and kept the pudgy fingers of his right hand wrapped around the upwards-pointing barrel. The wrong way to carry a gun. She prayed every day for Gus to stumble and shoot himself in the head.

Gus shoved the new girl toward the empty stall across from Jophia. The girl stumbled and screamed. Gus barked, "shut up and get in there with them other niggers."

The girl turned and shrieked at him, "I want to go home!"

Jophia prayed he wouldn't hit her. He'd done it to Jophia a few times before she learned to outsmart him. She'd come to understand that Master Gus was basically a big, dumb coward, but it was better not to make him mad. There was nothing more dangerous than a coward with power over people smaller than himself.

"You shut your mouth and sit down there. There! On that mattress. Get on it or I'll stick you in the oven."

Jophia wanted to explain to Master Gus that if he just treated the new ones more gently, there wouldn't be as many problems. But it was not in Gus's nature to listen to anyone, certainly not someone he thought was a "nigger." She could see the girl more clearly now. She was much younger than Jophia. Maybe five. Her hair was sticking out everywhere and her eyes were huge and her cheeks were wet.

The girl collapsed on the mattress. Gus, crooking his shotgun in his right arm, bent down toward her and noisily hoisted up the thick, iron chain bolted to the floor. It was the same chain that had once held Peter, the one he'd managed somehow to slip out of. Gus snapped the metal cuff shut around the girl's ankle and she started screaming wildly, pure panic. Gus raised his fist. "If you don't shut your fucking mouth now, I'll break it, you hear?"

"Y'all okay in here?" The other man was at the doorway. Gus's brother. Master Lennon. Much taller, much broader. The nice one. The gentle giant. He didn't carry a gun.

"Permission to speak, Master Lennon?" Jophia said.

Lennon turned to her. "Yes, child?"

"Can I lay next to her tonight? She doesn't know where she is and she's scared. I can calm her down and make her quiet. Luther did the same thing for Beth, and she's a good girl, isn't she?" Luther was eight years old, second oldest to Jophia, and he was perfectly obedient in every way, so he was one of the children they trusted most. But she knew he secretly hated them as much as she did.

Lennon considered a moment. He said to Gus, "Brother, that might be a good choice for tonight, all things considered."

"I ain't gonna unchain that one. She'll run off."

"She won't. She knows she won't get far."

Gus glared at Lennon, a haze of hate seething from him at having his authority questioned. Jophia could see it even in the dim room. Gus stomped out. Lennon came over to Jophia. He was smiling.

"You ain't going to bite me now, are you, girl?"

"No, Master."

Lennon chose a key from his keychain and opened the padlock that held Jophia's ankle restraint in place. She noted that he replaced the keychain in the right pocket of his overalls. As a matter of habit, she always kept track of that keychain, and the larger one Master Gus kept in his pocket, in case she could figure out a way to steal it. "Okay, you can go to her."

Jophia crept over. The girl was still sobbing. "There, now, honey. It's okay. You got nothing to be afraid of. You aren't alone here." At the sound of Jophia's voice, the girl stopped sobbing and stared out at the new face in the dark. "We don't need to cry now, honey. Let me explain what's going on here."

Lennon nodded to Jophia. "I'll be back at daylight. When I come, you best be right here where I left you."

"Yes, Master."

Lennon gently slid the doors shut and locked them. His footsteps trailed off into silence.

Jophia said, "What's your name, honey?"

The girl stuttered through her sobs. "Shantelle."

"Shantelle what?"

"Shantelle Collins."

"Shantelle, my name's Jophia. I'm ten years old. How old are you?"

"Five."

"Good girl. Now, listen. First off, there's five other kids in here with us." Jophia raised her voice slightly and spoke to the blackness: "Ain't that right?"

"That's right," said a boy's voice. "I'm Luther. I'm eight."

"And I'm Linda. I'm seven."

Two other voices piped in, higher, nervous voices of younger children, John, aged six and Ellie, aged five.

"Jeffrey?" called Jophia, but no answer came. Jophia said to Shantelle, "Jeffrey's only four and he's shy."

"I want to go home," Shantelle moaned.

"Shantelle, let me tell what's happening here. Those men out there? They took you to help with their farm chores."

"I don't want to help!"

"I know."

"I want my mama!"

"Shsh. I know, Shantelle. You'll go home to your mama, soon. I promise."

"I'm scared!"

Jophia wrapped her arms around the smaller girl and held her close. "I know how you feel. I felt the same way when I came here. But right now, we got to do what we got to do. The first thing is to keep our voices down real low, pretend we're mice and be just as quiet. Believe me, somebody's going to come rescue us soon. But until then, we got to do exactly what those men say. If you do exactly what they say, and be a real good girl, they won't hurt you."

As she spoke, Jophia could feel the girl's panic recede. Her gasping breath slowed and the racing heartbeat that hammered against Jophia's chest calmed. Jophia said, "There now, honey child. We're all going to be rescued soon. And we'll go back to our homes. And everything's going to be okay."

Words, words. Just empty words. The words Peter had told her when she first came. Jophia had drawn the will to live from those words Peter whispered to her at night and she'd repeated them every day in her head, from dusk to dawn. Like a prayer. *Don't you worry, Jophia,* He'd whispered, *Don't you lose hope. We're going to be rescued soon*. Then, after months and months of *We're going to be rescued soon*, one night, Peter whispered to her he was going to run away.

Master Gus came in the next morning and Peter was gone. He'd slipped out of the chains and broken the lock on the sliding doors. When Jophia told Gus she didn't know anything about Peter's escape, he took a shovel and hit her on the leg. Master Lennon stopped him before he could hit her again. The bruise lasted a week.

The day Peter escaped, the kids were not allowed to leave the barn. Instead of using the outhouse across the clearing like they always did, they needed to use a bucket for a toilet. They only got old bread to eat.

They could hear the dogs had been turned loose outside and were roaming the grounds, yelping each time Gus hit them. The next day, the kids were let out again to work again, like normal. Neither Gus nor Lennon spoke a word about Peter's disappearance. It was like Peter had never existed. The kids were dying to know where he'd gone, but they didn't dare ask. They worked the chicken houses during the day as though nothing had happened, and endured Mistress Jinny's strange school lesson at night.

On the following morning, Master Gunnar had come and demanded that Jophia tell him where Peter was and how he'd escaped. When she didn't tell him, he put her in the oven. That was her first time and her last time in the black iron box, and if she lived to be a hundred years old, she knew she'd still have nightmares about it.

Many days after that, Master Gunnar roared up again on his black motorcycle. He lined up the children in front of the horse barn.

Master Gunnar had eyes like small oysters, grey and moist. From a leather satchel he pulled out the yellow Pokemon shirt Peter always wore. It was ripped up and covered with blood. He told them Peter was dead. He told them that this is what happened to runaways. You run away, you die.

Jophia almost died that day even without running away. She understood to the core of her soul that all the prayerful words about getting rescued were lies. Master Gunnar was too strong, too smart, too evil, to let it happen.

She had fallen into a dull, grey time. As the days shortened and the temperature fell, she felt her spirit shrinking into dust. The hopelessness swallowed her up. For days at a time, she didn't even talk to the others. Sometime in there, her birthday had come and gone without notice and she had changed from nine to ten. She knew that on some future, unknown day, indistinct from all the other days of laboring in the chicken houses, she would turn from ten to eleven, and then from eleven to twelve, and on up until the day they decided she was of no use to them anymore.

All the other kids still believed they'd be rescued, though, and Jophia continued to comfort them by repeating the idea. The certainty of getting rescued was like the existence of Santa Claus. A fantasy story that made children happy and protected them from the cold reality of life. They were lies, but she just kept on telling them to the younger kids. And now she was telling this new girl Shantelle, who was drifting off under the gentle stroke of Jophia's hand over her hair: *you just relax now, girl, someone's going to rescue us all real soon.*

No one would rescue them and running away was impossible. But she knew there was a third choice.

Fight the men.

Each time she thought about it, Jophia melted with terror, because they were small children and their keepers were large adults with guns and attack dogs. But she knew they had to try it. They needed to find a way to fight them, to beat them, maybe even to *kill* them.

Because anything, even death, would be better than spending the rest of their lives as slaves.

Chapter Thirty-four

Jophia held Shantelle close and listened to her breathe. She saw the first dim morning light glowing under the door and the small rips in the black plastic over the windows. She lay and waited until she heard the approaching tromp of boots on the packed Earth in the clearing outside that told her it was time.

The lock was new because Peter had broken the old one, but the key still squeaked as it turned like the mechanism was rusty. The doors rolled open. Jophia squinted against the burst of sunlight. Shantelle jerked awake and sat up and Jophia held her and whispered, "be quiet, everything will be okay."

It was always Gus and Lennon who came to get them up. Gus was mean and threatening, and Lennon was quiet and gently prompting. Gus limped from stall to stall, his shotgun propped under his right arm, unlocking the kids and yelling at them to get up. Lennon, the giant, watched from his position at the doorway.

After Gus woke all the children up and unlocked them, he returned to the door and picked up a plastic bag. He went to the stalls again and at each one pulled out a bread roll and tossed it to the children and ordered, "eat!" He let Jophia stay with Shantelle and tossed two rolls to them. When Gus finished throwing them bread, he came back around with another bag, this one with small plastic bottles with water in them that he tossed to the children, barking, "drink!" Finally, Gus ordered, "toilet!"

The youngest child, Jeffrey, emerged from one of the back stalls, rubbing his eyes. He was filthy and he had a stream of snot gummed up clear from his nose to his chin. As usual, he looked like he'd been crying half the night. He'd also wet his pants.

Gus shouted, "You fucking monkey, get to the pump and

clean yourself." Lennon stepped from the doorway and moved between Gus and Jeffrey, a subtle movement, thought Jophia, that didn't exactly challenge Gus but still prevented the boy from being harmed. Lennon took Jeffrey by the hand. "C'mon, boy, let's get you washed up."

One by one they took the children out of the building. Jophia was allowed to take Shantelle by the hand and accompany her. The sky was dabbed with grey-black clouds moving fast over the circle of trees surrounding the farm, propelled by a cold wind. Jophia immediately was shivering and she could see on the faces of the other kids how cold they were. Jabbing the shotgun in their direction, Gus commanded them to cross the clearing to the other side where, hunched into a broad stand of pine trees, was a decrepit outhouse. On the right side of the outhouse was an iron pump.

Gus spat and put his rifle on the ground. He pulled a pack of cigarettes from his overalls and a box of wooden matches. He pushed a cigarette between his fat lips and took out a wooden match and struck it on the black edge of the box. A blaze hissed up on the stick. Jophia wished she could put her fingers on that little fire to warm them up. Gus put it to the end of the cigarette, sucked some smoke in deep, and killed the fire with a shake of his wrist. He pointed with the cigarette at the outhouse. "Use the toilet and come out and wash up. And don't make a fucking mess in there. After that, Jophia, you tell the new nigger how things work around here."

After Jophia and Shantelle had used the toilet and come out again, they took turns pumping their heads and scrubbing their faces and tried to splash off as much of the dirt off them as they could without taking off their clothes. "We only get a change of clothes on Sunday morning," said Jophia, "so wash your clothes as best you can with the pump water." While they washed themselves, Gus looked the other way at the horse barn where they'd slept, watching his larger brother there at the doorway. Hate in his eyes.

Gus and Lennon gathered the seven children. Jophia explained things to Shantelle as they walked across the farm. Gus moved closely alongside them and listened in, his ferret's eyes gleaming. The farm was small. Along with the horse barn where the children slept, there was just a main house with a kennel behind it that housed the four killer dogs. There were also four white concrete buildings. Three of them contained the chicken cages and another was for slaughtering chickens for meat. "But they don't kill many of them yet. Mostly, this is an egg farm. And getting those eggs and taking care of the chickens is our job. That's why we're here."

Gus grinned. "Tell her about the oven."

"Yes, Master." Jophia turned back and pointed out another structure, this one about ten yards to the right of the outhouse behind them. It was a black box, mostly buried in the ground with only a few inches showing.

"That's the oven. They call it that, because it gets real hot in there in the summer on account it's iron and it's painted black. They put us in that box if we break rules or don't obey orders. It's not so hot in the winter like now, but even so you don't want to go in there. It's so small, you can hardly move, and it's totally black and scary, and they don't let you out for days. They'll put us in there if we don't call them 'Master', so don't ever forget to say it. And they'll put us in there if we talk without permission. Don't forget."

Shantelle opened her mouth to speak, then clapped it shut again.

Gus chuckled. "You know all about the oven, don't you, Jophia?"

"Yes, Master."

"You learned the hard way, didn't you?."

"Yes, Master."

"But you ain't been in there since, 'cause you now an obedient little nigger knows her place, ain't you?"

"Yes, Master."

"And you gonna make this new little nigger the same way, ain't you? Now you teach her the job."

"Yes, Master."

They approached the closest building. Shantelle's hand was cold and wet in Jophia's. The other kids trailed behind, watching the two. Everyone was silent. The building was about forty feet long and ten feet wide and had a row of solar panels attached to the roof. With one door on its short side and no windows, it looked like a small airplane hangar. Jophia said to Shantelle, "This is chicken house number one. First thing we do here is take out the eggs the chickens laid last night. When we finish, we need to feed all the chickens. Then we need to clean all the cages and sweep and mop the floor. Then we move to chicken house number two and do the same thing. Then chicken house number three. We get lunch around noon and we get water and toilet breaks, but only at the times they say. Don't ask to use the toilet. If you got to go, hold it in until they say it's time. When we're working, we can talk, but only about the chores. We aren't allowed to talk about our personal lives before we came here or anything else. Only the job. Understand?" Jophia said it sharply because Gus was listening.

Lennon opened the door of the chicken house and flicked on an overhead light. The children came inside, two by two. Gus didn't enter. The room was lined on both sides with rows of silver wire cages, stacked on three levels and suspended by metal rods that ran the length of the room. Two aluminum channels ran next to each row of cages, one above to hold chicken feed and one below to collect eggs. Each cage contained three or four chickens. The white-feathered birds were crowding the sides of the cages, gawping with their round, orange eyes and pecking at the bars.

"We take one of those carts and load it up with those big blue trays. You walk by every cage and pick up the eggs and put them in these holes here. And don't ever drop one. That's something you never, ever want to do." Shantelle's eyes widened at the thought of what would happen to her if she broke an egg.

"If you find an egg that's dirty, you need to clean it with one of these dry sponges. But you let me do that. I'll be with you the whole time today, so don't worry. You'll get through this. When we get done taking the eggs, we roll the carts over to Lennon, and he takes them from there to sell at the farmer's market."

Jophia pulled a cart out with about ten blue plastic egg trays on it.

"For lunch, the lady of the house, Mistress Jinny, that's Master Gus and Master Lennon's mother, fixes sandwiches and we get cold milk too. Sometimes we even get cookies. We sit outside under the trees and eat. You got to eat quick because we only get about fifteen minutes. When we're all done with the three chicken houses, it'll be time for school."

"School?"

Jophia glanced over at Lennon, who was positioned at the door, too far away to hear. She said in a low voice, "It's not real school. It's just Mistress Jinny's lessons where she tries to teach us how good slavery is."

"Slavery?"

Jophia stared at her. "You don't know slavery?"

The girl shook her head.

Jophia gestured around the room at the children working at the chicken cages.

"White people making black people work for free. This is slavery."

Shantelle stared at Jophia in horror.

Jophia whispered firmly. "I know. It's evil. But you just sit in those school lessons and listen and don't say nothing about how you really feel. If she asks you a question, you just give her the answer she wants to hear. You keep your true self hidden, girl. Do you as you're told, hide yourself inside, and wait for the day this is over. And it will be over. Someone's going to come soon and set us free."

Shantelle's eyes were shimmering. "You promise?"

Jophia looked down at the girl, held her terrified gaze. She hated to lie to the girl. Papa had always taught her it was a sin to lie.

"I promise," she said.

Chapter Thirty-five

After they'd finished cleaning the third chicken house, Lennon took them into the main house. Master Gus and Master Lennon called it the *big house*, but it wasn't big at all. It was smaller than the chicken houses and smaller than the horse barn where she slept. It was a mangy one-story building made with an uneven hodgepodge of logs and stone, a couple of solar panels dangling wires on the roof. But the big house did have a large fireplace and was very warm. It was the only reason Jophia liked to go in it.

The children were brought into the front room of the house. Gus wasn't there. Jophia explained to Shantelle that almost every day one of the brothers left the farm because they ran the car repair shop near town. There were times when both of them were gone, and only their mother watched over them. She knew Gus and Lennon from when she rode her bicycle past their shop on her way home from school. She was riding her bicycle by the shop that bad, bad day when Master Gunnar had jumped out of the parked pickup truck to grab her. She had tried to escape by riding across the clearing toward the forest, but she hit a bump and fell, and her backpack opened and her stuff went flying all over the grass. Her books, her pencil case, her teddy bear. Without thinking, she snatched up the teddy bear and tried to run, but Gunnar caught her by the hair and threw her down. She'd tried to fight him off and in the wrestling match, Gunnar had grabbed at her teddy bear and she held on tight and the head ripped off.

Lennon led the children into the front room of the big house and told them to sit on the seven chairs arranged in a semi-circle in front of a rocking chair. Jophia sat on the chair farthest to the right and closest to the front door and had Shantelle sit in the chair on her left. On the next chair down the line, the one on Shantelle's left, sat Luther, and to his left, the younger girl, Beth, five years old, whom he'd taken under his wing a few weeks before. Next to her was Linda, who was the same age as Beth, and the row continued on down descending by age. While Jophia was watching over the new girl especially, she knew that because she was the oldest she was also expected to watch over all the other kids too.

The left wall had a long dining table where they all would eat dinner after their lesson. On the table was a heavy ashtray made of thick, cut glass. A smaller ashtray was on top of the table next to the rocking chair. Both ashtrays were overflowing with cigarette butts. The room stank of smoke so bad it made Jophia's eyes water and her throat hurt.

Above the table was a window where you could see the clearing, the chicken houses, and, if you craned your neck, the horse barn. A door on the back wall opened to the kitchen and other rooms beyond that Jophia had never seen. Next to the door was a fireplace. A fire was lit and the room was very warm. A gunrack was mounted above the fireplace and three rifles and a shotgun were resting on its pegs.

Jophia had examined those guns from across the room many times. Her sister had taught her how to shoot. If she could manage to run over there and pull one down, she might be able to aim it and shoot any of them who tried to stop her. But the guns might not be loaded. She didn't want to think about what they would do to her if she tried and failed.

An old woman appeared at the kitchen door. Mrs. Jinny Wilson. Every day, Mistress Jinny wore the same dress. It was a garment constructed of many layers of extremely thin, fine, white material, maybe silk, that puffed up and down in slow-motion with her every movement because the fabric was as light as a cobweb. Her hair was also ghostly white and came out of her head in every direction as wild and tangled as the runners of some creeping weed. She was an extremely thin woman, so thin it seemed a strong breeze could lift and blow her kicking over the trees. The mistress's skin was as finely wrinkled as crepe paper and so white it looked bleached. Protruding between her milky, ice-blue eyes was a sharply pointed nose crawling with blue veins. When she spoke, it was with a genteel southern accent, produced by a voice so low it might have been a man's.

Jophia had pieced together from eavesdropping that Mistress Jinny was married to Master Gunnar. The monster. Jophia had first met Gunnar at the Small Shoots summer camp. As camp director, Master Gunnar was Mr. Wilson, and he'd seemed warm, kind, and funny. But that was all an act. Gunnar was the scariest person Jophia had ever met. Master Gunnar was far quicker to punish them and his punishments were worse than those of Lennon or even Gus.

"Welcome, children." Like a spider queen taking her throne, Mistress Jinny bent creakily into the rocking chair, layers of her diaphanous clothing and her wild white hair puffing up with the movement. She lit a cigarette. "Who would like a nice glass of lemonade?"

All the younger children on Jophia and Luther's left shot up their hands. Jophia and Luther glanced at each other and raised their hands too with damp enthusiasm. Jophia nudged Shantelle and she put her hand up too.

Shantelle said, "'Scuse me, ma'am, but I want to go home."

Mistress Jinny had horse teeth that protruded yellow from her mouth when she grinned. "What was that? Jophia, Lennon tells me that you have taken this new girl under your wing. Have you not taught her that we are never to speak at the lessons unless given permission to do so?"

Jophia snapped at Shantelle, "Keep your mouth shut and listen." For a split second, Shantelle looked like she was about to say something, but she shut her mouth, bit her lip hard, tears pooling up in her eyes.

Mrs. Wilson clapped her hands. "Lemonade! Lennon, darling, please bring the nigra children some lemonade!"

Lennon nodded and left the room. Mrs. Wilson retained her mad grin as she scanned the row of children, her eyes falling finally on Shantelle, whom she stared at the way a jungle cat studies prey.

Lennon returned with a serving tray with seven plastic tumblers and one glass. He handed the glass to his mother and the tumblers to each of the children. "What do you say to Master Lennon, children?"

The children said in unison, "Thank you, Master Lennon."

The lemonade was ice cold and very sweet. Mistress Jinny sipped from her glass, leaving a lipstick stain on the rim. She put the glass on the table at her side. She picked her cigarette from the ashtray, sucked it noisily, and blew out a sidelong cloud of smoke.

"Now then, children, listen to Mistress Jinny carefully. Who of you has heard the phrase, 'pecking order'? No one? I shall explain it to you. Some birds are bigger than other birds, aren't they? And the bigger birds get the food first, because they can push the smaller birds away. In nature, there's a natural order to things, isn't there?" She sucked on her cigarette, blew. "Things aren't all the same among the animals. There's no equality. Some animals are bigger, some animals are smaller, some animals are faster and some are slower. Linda, can you think of a fast animal?"

"A horse?"

"Very good. And a horse is faster than a mule, isn't it? It's the same way, everywhere you look. No equality between different kinds of animals. At first, this seems unfair, doesn't it? But if we understand that this is the world God created, then we know that everything is perfect, all part of His mysterious, glorious plan. And we see that while there isn't equality amongst the species of the world, there is a divine order to things. Birds are not as smart as people, but people don't have wings. Fish aren't as smart as people, but people can't live underwater, can they? Beth, dear, would you want to live underwater? I thought not. What a funny thought! If you think about it, you can see that this isn't true just between species, like birds, fish, and people, but also within species. For example, which kind of dog would you want as a guard dog? A wolfhound as big as Lennon over there, or a tiny Chihuahua? I'll bet you would want the wolfhound, wouldn't you? Of course you would. But they're both dogs."

She took a deep drag on her cigarette and blasted the smoke out. "But, they are different *breeds* of dog. And they are not equal. Are they?" Mrs. Wilson paused to let this sink in to the children. She took a sip of her lemonade, her heavy lipstick leaving another red smear on the edge of the glass. "Now, I have some surprising news for you all. Surprising and wonderful news! Something you probably never heard before because you were raised on ideas that were, sadly, not true. There are *different breeds of human beings too*. That's right! Isn't that interesting? Especially after you were raised to think that all people were the same. You were probably taught that idea at school and taught that idea at home and maybe even taught that idea at church, if you went to an anti-Christ church, which most of them are. Children, don't feel bad, because this isn't your fault! But think about it! All animals have breeds, don't they? There are all kinds of cats, from roaring lions to sweet little calicoes. You know why some horses are called quarter horses? Cause they can run the first quarter mile of a race faster than other breeds of horses. Can you think of even one animal on God's green Earth that doesn't have different breeds?"

Jophia knew, because she'd learned it in her life science class from Miss Kapfer, that the different kinds of animals this witch-woman was talking about were mostly not *breeds*, but *subspecies*, which humans did not have. But she kept her mouth locked shut.

Mistress Jinny sucked at her cigarette and blew out white smoke.

"Each breed has different kinds of sizes and skills. So of course people have breeds too. It's crazy, it's *unchristian*, to think we don't. Now this doesn't mean that one breed of people is better than another breed of people. It does mean, though, that some breeds of people are better suited to do some kinds of things, while other breeds of people are better suited to other kinds of things. You know, the yellow breed of people in China and Japan? They are very, very good at working together in big teams to make products cheap, so we can buy all sorts of things here for only a dollar. Those people, even the children, can work 16 hours in their factories without eating. Can you do that? Can I? Of course we can't. Because we aren't Orientals. But the little yellow people can!" She sucked out the last of her cigarette, tamped it out, and lit another. "They're a lot smaller than us, so their fingers are tiny. So it's good they're doing the kind of work they're doing. They like to make robots because they're a little bit like robots themselves. Communism is probably better for their robotic group brains."

Jophia clenched her teeth to force herself not to point out that her friend Lin, whose parents were from China, was nothing like what she was saying. And Dr. Watanabe, at the hospital where her best friend's Eliza's mom worked, was a doctor who'd written books and discovered new things by himself and wasn't anything like a human robot.

"Children, do you know why your skin is black?"

The older children looked at the floor. The youngest ones looked eagerly at Mistress Jinny, wanting to know the answer.

"Well, it's very interesting! You have a chemical in your skin called melanin, and that chemical is kind of magical because it protected your ancestors from the harsh sun in Africa and protects you now from getting skin cancer. My ancestors were not equal to you in this way, because they didn't have melanin and could catch skin cancer easier. And so can I. How I wish I had your black skin! Then I wouldn't have to worry about skin cancer. Isn't it wonderful for you? Of course it is."

It was at this time in the process of enduring Mistress Jinny's lessons that Jophia always found herself thinking the most about the guns on the rack above the fireplace. She thought about how far it was between the back door, where Lennon stood watching them, and the gunrack over the fireplace. He was only about ten feet from it, but if she suddenly ran very fast, she might be able to snatch one from the rack and aim it at Mistress Jinny's head and pull the trigger before Lennon stopped her.

"Children, even your African ancestors knew about the natural order between human breeds, because they happily sold people from Africa to white slavers to be carried to the new America, where they could be sold to farmers as workers. And these new black citizens, who some described with the very insulting and hurtful word "slaves," worked hard and happily for their masters, using the special skills God gave them. In return, they were provided a house, regular meals, good doctor's care, and of course got lots of exercise working in the fields. Under the hot sun, which we know now is much less dangerous to them than to someone like me, with my weak, white skin. I know you've probably heard about the mean masters who weren't nice to their slaves, but I'm telling you, children, most of those slaves were happy people. And why on Earth wouldn't they be? In Africa, they lived in a world of cannibals and tribes of naked warriors murdering each other with spears and poisoned arrows. After the ships brought them to the new land of America, they could live in civilization. A civilization they weren't naturally able to develop themselves—as we can still see in Africa today. They also were brought to the Lord Jesus!"

She smiled sweetly at the children. "Are you hungry?"

Jophia nearly sagged off the chair with relief when the horrible woman ended her "lesson" and Lennon began to bring in the dinner.

It was the same routine, every day except Sunday. They'd work the chicken houses all day, then come to the big house and get an ice-cold drink that, to the exhausted children who'd had little water all day, was like a glass of heaven. Then Mrs. Wilson would launch into one of her "lessons" intended to teach the children to think that everything they'd learned about slavery and racial equality was wrong. To prove that slaves of the past had been well-fed, Mistress Jinny fed the children well. She worked much of the day in her kitchen to create small banquets for them. The dinners they ate in the big house were usually better than what they had been fed at home. There was almost always some chicken dish, and piping hot dinner rolls and corn on the cob and mashed potatoes swimming in gravy and butter, and fresh okra. For dessert, they had ice cream or homemade pecan pie.

For the first couple of weeks of being a slave, Jophia grabbed on to these dinners like a drowning girl would a life preserver. It was the only thing she had to look forward to. But then she realized what was really happening. The dinners were part of a sneaky project to brainwash the children into thinking their "masters" were decent, to change their parents and teachers in the previous home into liars, and to get them to believe the insane things Mistress Jinny told them.

By the time they finished dinner, the sun had set. Jophia heard the noise of Gus's tow truck approaching. He pulled up to the big house, the headlights flaring through the glass of the front window. He returned as always with a scowl on his piggy face and a rifle in his arm. He and Lennon brought the children back to the outhouse where they took turns using the toilet and the pump to wash. The kids were then corralled into the horse barn and locked up for the night.

Gus forced Jophia to lay in her own horse stall and ordered Shantelle to sleep by herself in the stall across from her. Shantelle started to beg him to let Jophia sleep with her and Gus barked at her to shut up and she did. After they heard the men's bootsteps fade off into the distance, and the front door of the big house slam shut, the kids started whispering to each other.

From two stalls down, Jophia heard Linda say, "I heard a helicopter today."

"You did not," whispered John from another stall.

"I did!"

"I didn't hear nothing."

"Me neither," said Luther. "Maybe it was something else."

"I don't know. Maybe I was just wishing. I wish it so much. I want to go home."

Beth said, "But it's not that bad here, is it? We got no

homework, the food is good…"

"Stop talking like that," snapped Luther.

"I want my mama," cried Jeffrey suddenly.

"Jeffrey, don't shout," scolded Jophia. "Use your mouse voice or the man with the whip will come."

"But I want to go home!" cried Jeffrey.

"Listen," whispered Jophia sharply. "We're going to get out of here. Just hold tight. Listen, Jeffrey, how about a bedtime story?"

"Yes, please," he sniffled.

The room went still and Jophia launched into a story. On many nights she'd told them stories her father had told her that made her feel safe. But on this night, she made up one on her own.

"Once upon a time," she started, "on the other side of the world, there was a rabbit in a village who had no fur. His name was Mite. His parents called him Mite because Mites ate off all his fur when he was a baby so bad he couldn't grow any new fur."

"Jophia, what's mite mean?" asked Beth.

"It means a little bug."

"No, it doesn't. It means power," said Luther.

"It means both," said Jophia. "Because Mite had no fur, he looked funny and all the other rabbits made fun of him. Mite's life was real bad because all around him at school he saw nothing but rabbits with wonderful fur in beautiful colors. Velvety brown and glowing orange and sky blue."

"A blue rabbit?" demanded Luther. All the children laughed.

"The rabbits on the other side of the world come in every color of the rainbow on account of it's a magic place. Now, Mite the rabbit felt ugly without the beautiful fur the other rabbits had, so he begged God to give him fur. But no matter how hard he begged, God didn't answer his prayers. To make things worse, the other rabbits teased him all the time. They teased him in class, they teased him in the cafeteria, and they teased him on the playground. One rabbit, a girl named Snowball, had fur that was pure milk-white and all the rabbits thought she looked the best. But she was the meanest rabbit of all. One day she tricked Mite by acting like she was his friend. She had him come under the big willow tree in the corner of the playground, where her friends were waiting up in the branches. When she was sure Mite was standing right under them, Snowball gave them a sign and they dropped a bunch of glue and a big bucket of crow feathers on him. This made Mite look like a big, black crow-rabbit. All the other kids ran up from across the playground to see what was happening, and when they were all there, Snowball laughed at Mite and said, "How do you like your new fur?" And all the kids laughed.

"Now, Mite had a strange reaction to what they did to him. He used to cry when the other kids teased him, but this time he didn't cry. He didn't show any feelings at all. He didn't say a word back and not a single tear fell from his eyes. From that day on, he never showed them how much they hurt him. He kept all his hurt locked up in his heart, like a little yellow-red ball of fire. That ball of fire kept him moving, kept him from just giving up. Years went by and that little ball of fire got hotter and hotter.

"A night came when the ball of fire got so hot inside him that it exploded like a bomb. While all the rabbits in the village were asleep, he snuck into all their houses and shaved all the fur off every rabbit. Now all those rabbits with velvety brown and glowing orange and sky blue fur now only had bald, silly-looking pink-white skin. The next morning, the rabbits all poured out of the houses in a rage. They wanted to kill Mite the rabbit, but they couldn't find him, because when rabbits don't have fur, they all look exactly the same.

Not only that, they all look completely silly. So the rabbits with the best fur in the village were especially ashamed because now, not only did they look just like all the other rabbits, but they looked very foolish too. Suddenly, the anger of one of the rabbits melted away when she saw how ridiculous it all was. She started laughing. She was followed by another rabbit, then another, until all of the rabbits were howling with laughter at each other and at themselves. Only one rabbit was too ashamed to laugh and that was Snowball. She fled the village to live by herself in the forest. She never came back.

"That day they lost their fur, the rabbits learned a lesson: without their beautiful fur, which made some rabbits look more beautiful than others, they were all the same underneath. They apologized to Mite and they never teased him again. And the rabbits lived happily ever after."

When Jophia had finished, peace had fallen over the room. At least one of the children had already fallen asleep and the others followed soon after. Jophia lay in bed awake by herself, listening to the deep breathing of the other kids.

A long time passed. At least an hour, maybe two, and she still was awake. Suddenly there were voices coming across the clearing. Gus and Lennon. And the sounds of sniffing and trotting and the jingle of dog collars. They'd let the dogs out for exercise. Jophia could hear the clink of a bottle being passed between the two men.

In a low voice that Jophia could just make out, Lennon said, "Got something to tell you. I talked to Gunnar on the phone today. He says we're going to need to clean things up here soon. He's worried we can't hide the project much longer."

"No shit."

"Since the cops found the boy, he thinks they might put all the parts together and find us."

"What does Gunnar want us to do about the kids?"

"Dispose of them."

Long silence.

"How?" asked Gus.

"A lot more carefully than we did Peter. In a way that doesn't leave bodies for the cops to find. I figure the best way is to dig a ditch out back behind the dog cage and line them up and shoot them in the head. Less messy that way. Then wrap them in that leftover plastic sheeting we got and haul them down to animal processing. Gunnar and Keith can handle the rest from there."

When Gus spoke again, his voice was strained. "When's he want us to do this?"

"He's got some prep to do on his end. Says to wait for him to give the word. Probably next week."

"Um, does this bother you any?"

Lennon yawned. "Why would it? My whole life's been in animal control. It bother you?"

"No…no, 'Course not."

Lennon laughed. "You ain't scared of a little blood, are you?"

"Just too bad we have to stop the experiment's all. We worked so hard to set it up."

"We'll have other experiments. We better get to bed. Tomorrow's a long day."

Lennon emitted a short whistle and Jophia could hear the sounds of several dogs trotting up.

The men's bootsteps faded away.

Jophia was paralyzed. The hammering of her heart was making her whole body shake. She lay desperately trying to tamp down her terror. She started crying and bit her arm to make herself stop. She had to work out a way to get her and the others out of this hell. *There's got to be a way*, she told herself and she somehow got a grip on the terror and wrestled it into a hole. She needed to think of a plan. *Now.*

How did Peter escape? Knowing how he'd done it would be a start. Jophia didn't know. All she knew was that Peter had said good night to her from the gloom of his stall across the way just before she fell asleep and when she woke up the next morning, he was gone.

When Gunnar Wilson had come later, he had ordered Gus and Lennon to take the children outside. It was late summer, murderously hot and humid, and the sky was threatening a thunderstorm. Sweat dribbled down Gunnar Wilson's bald head. Gunnar went right up to Jophia and said, "You helped him, didn't you?"

"No, I swear I didn't, Master Gunnar."

"You're the only one who could've seen. How did he get out?"

"I don't know, Master Gunnar."

"You lying nigger."

He slapped her. She fell in the mud, shrieking.

"You helped him!"

"No!" she screamed and he bent over and slapped her again.

"I'll ask you one more time, nigger. Where is he?"

"I don't know," she sobbed.

"Put her in the oven," Gunnar ordered Gus and Lennon. "Don't let her out until she tells us how the boy got away."

When Gus and Lennon went for her, Jophia lashed out, punching and scratching and biting, so Gus came out with a control pole for dogs with a band of leather sticking from the end and caught her around the neck and cinched the leather loop and dragged her screaming along the ground to the black box. He unleashed her and got her up by her arms and tossed her into the box. Lennon slammed the heavy black lid down and clacked the padlock shut.

It was an ancient iron box, rough with rust, not much bigger than a suitcase. It was pressed into the ground so the lid was a couple inches from the Earth. The pit was completely dark. She needed to lay on her side with her legs bent and had almost no room to move. For the first few minutes, the heat pushed into her the way it would if she was wrapped up in a thick blanket. The heavy heat seeping through her skin worsened by the second. It was cooking her skin and pushing into her bones. It made her think of the monster jellyfish she'd seen in a movie that wrapped itself around a submarine and sucked away at its walls until they collapsed and it ate the people inside. She could feel sweat drooling off her face and onto the rusty floor. She screamed for help. She beat her fist over and over against the lid. No one came.

The bottom of the box was grainy and viciously hot and was burning her cheek. She jerked her head back and forth and managed to get some of her hair pushed under her cheek, which reduced the frying heat to just painful heat.

The lock clattered and someone kicked open the lid. The light was so bright it burned her vision orange-white and she opened her mouth to scream and someone threw water on her. She screamed through the blast of water and another bucket of water hit her. The lid slammed shut.

Some of the water landed in her mouth. She realized through the shock that the cool water felt good, and the bit of water that got in her mouth had slightly relieved her thirst. The heat began to eat into her again. This time, she was soaking wet, and she felt herself being poached.

She cried. A gasping, sobbing cry. She tried to beat on the

door again, but she didn't have the strength to lift her hand.

A long time passed. The lid clanged open again. The light jabbed into her and she squeezed her eyes shut. She had been…not asleep…in a waking dream, in a forest, a hot pond, small fish chewing on her.

Master Gunnar's voice. "How'd that boy get out?"

Her throat was so dry and burning she could only make a gagging noise.

"Where did he go?"

Jophia opened her mouth. Praying for another bucket of water to be thrown at her. She gasped and tried to lift her hand to point at her mouth.

"Leave her in here another day to think about it. No water."

"Boss, you sure? I mean, look at her." Gus's voice.

"Shut it!"

The iron lid came down and the lock snapped shut. Jophia lay blinking up into the sudden black, her mouth still open.

It could have been hours or days or lifetimes before the men came back. At the first sound of the lock clattering, she shut her eyes against the blast of light but no light came because it was night.

"You can come out," said Lennon.

She couldn't walk, so Lennon reached down and took her in his big arms. No light came from the windows of the big house. Gus scooped water into a cup from a bucket and gave it to her. It eased the scorching in her throat. He soaked more water into a towel and patted her face. Gus and Lennon didn't ask her any questions about Peter. Neither said anything at all.

Jophia felt so broken she scarcely understood what was happening, but it seemed Lennon, and even Gus, took special care not to hurt her as they carried her into the horse barn and placed her gently in the hay.

But that was then.

Lennon's unperturbed voice tonight came into her head: *Figure the best way's to dig a ditch out back behind the dog cage and line them up and shoot them in the head.* The fear boiled up and overcame her and then she was sobbing into the hay. Sobbing as uncontrollably as a much younger and more innocent version of herself. Sobbing, *Papa! Help me!*

Chapter Thirty-six

"Hey, Jophie?"

She was startled by the voice in the dark.

"Luther?"

"Yeah. You okay?"

"Why?"

"You were crying."

"I had a bad dream. Luther, did you hear the men talking outside?"

"What men?"

"Gus and Lennon."

"No."

"Luther?"

"Yeah?"

"We got to make a plan. You and me, we're the oldest. It's up to us."

"Plan?"

"We need to escape out of here."

"Nah, Jophie, that's not the way. All we need to do is sit tight and wait for help. We obey them and everything will be okay until the people from town come to rescue us."

"No one's coming."

"Sure they are."

"How do you know?"

"I can feel it. The police are going find us real soon, you'll see."

"Luther?"

"What?"

"Nothing."

"No, what?"

"Nothing. I'm just tired. Let's go to sleep."

"Night, Jophia."

"Night."

Jophia listened to the boy's breaths deepening in the dark. She did not sleep.

Chapter Thirty-seven

The next day, the children got up as usual, went to the outhouse and washed up at the pump. Then, under the watchful eyes of Gus and Lennon, they trooped over to the first chicken house. The kids entered the room and took their egg trays to their assigned spots. The brothers stood at the door. Soon, Gus would go to work at the car shop, leaving them alone with Lennon. The children loved it when Gus left. In the presence of only Lennon, they became more relaxed, but in Jophia's mind, he was now a monster. She kept stealing glances at him. The sight of his friendly smile was horrifying.

Jophia stayed close to Shantelle. The girls put their egg trays side by side under the rows of chicken cages. They started gathering the eggs from the trough and placing them in the pockets on the tray. The chickens poked their heads through the bars and watched them.

Shantelle smiled at Jophia and said, "Thanks for telling us that rabbit story last night."

"No talking!" roared Gus.

From up the line, Jeffrey began crying.

Gus stomped over from the door, wielding his shotgun. "What the fuck is going on?"

"Jeffrey wet his pants, Master Gus," said Linda.

"Jophia!" Gus bellowed.

"Yes, Master?"

"Get over here and clean this kid up."

Jophia took a step down the line and heard a big crash behind her. She whipped around and saw Shantelle standing rigid with terror. When Jophia had gone to pass her, Shantelle stepped aside and jostled the egg tray on the cart and knocked it to the floor. About fifteen eggs now lay smashed all around her feet.

Gus charged up. “What did you do?”

Shantelle’s mouth was wide open, but no words came out. Her eyes were riveted on Gus.

Jophia jumped in. “Master Gus, she didn’t do anything. I did it. I knocked over the tray. When I was moving over to help out Jeffrey, like you told me to.”

Gus gazed at Jophia with pure hatred.

“Oven,” he said.

Lennon approached. “What happened?”

“This nigger needs to go in the oven.”

“Why?”

“She broke them eggs.”

“Did she break them on purpose?”

“She broke them because she’s a stupid nigger.”

Lennon said to Jophia, “Girl, why did you break these eggs?”

“I was going over there to see about Jeffrey.”

“What’s wrong with Jeffrey?”

“He wet his pants. Master Gus told me to go see about him.”

“And when you moved to see about Jeffrey, you bumped the egg tray?”

“Yes, sir.”

“Brother, maybe we ought to let this one go.”

“Lennon, Goddamnit, you know what Gunnar says. Break even one egg, for any reason, it’s the oven. We told these kids a hundred times. If we don’t put her in the oven, Gunnar’ll put *us* in the oven.”

Lennon seemed amused. “Not sure I’d fit in there,” he said. “Gus, how about we just have her clean up the mess and chock this up to an act of God?”

"We got to follow the rules."

"How's Gunnar going to know? He's not even here."

"Gunnar'll know because I'll tell him, that's how."

"Don't be stupid."

Gus gripped his shotgun with both hands. He tilted the barrel forward until it was pointed at Lennon.

"She's going in that oven."

Jophia saw the room dissolving into a shimmery gauze.

Lennon stepped back, his hands raised over his head. His smile was gone.

Gus prodded Jophia with his boot. "Go on," he said. She realized she too had her hands held above her head. She managed to take a step forward, then another.

Outside, they walked toward the oven. Gus kept prodding her with the gun, jabbing the barrel into her back. He poked her once especially hard and knocked the breath out of her and she was so scared, she couldn't pull another breath in. She forced her mouth open and tried to gasp in some air, but nothing would come and that made her fear even worse. The Earth started to act funny. It moved up on one side and down on the other, like that time Papa'd taken her in a rowboat to Pinetop Lake to go fishing in a storm.

"Get up!" It was Gus, shouting down at her. She lifted her head from where she'd fallen and even that small movement caused everything to move up and down like the world was attached to a bouncy spring. All at once, she vomited in the dirt. Gus shouted at her to get up and nudged her stomach with his boot, but she couldn't.

All at once she was moving fast, with a grinding sensation on her back and fire in her head. Gus had grabbed her by the hair and was dragging her across the clearing. She closed her eyes and moaned.

Gus kicked the oven lid open and rolled her into the pit. He got on his knees and bent down low, so his fat, round face was almost touching hers. Each of his cheeks was bulging with tiny red veins. Jophia could smell tobacco smoke on his breath. She was shocked to see tears welling up in his eyes and to hear his voice cracking, not with anger but with remorse, as he whispered, “I don’t want to do this. But I got no choice. He’ll kill me if I don’t.”

Gus slammed the lid shut.

Chapter Thirty-eight

The first time Jophia had been in the oven, she was too shocked by the heat to pay attention to the passing of days but this time it was winter and the oven wasn't hot. It also wasn't completely dark. She could see a jagged sliver of light, like a tiny lightning bolt, slanting in from a crack on the side of the iron wall closest to her. The sliver was so close to her face that she could almost tilt her head forward and see through the crack to the outside. Almost.

Even though it was cool in the pit, being forced into one position with no way to stand up or move around was a torment. Jophia needed to shift her position the small bit she could by crossing and uncrossing her legs and transferring the weight of her body from the front part of her side to the back part. With some worming around, she could point her arms downward, her right arm tucked under her side, or she could stretch both arms above her head, but she couldn't unbend them all the way.

As the day faded into night, the lightning bolt disappeared and she couldn't see anything. A long time passed and her mind wandered. She might have slept because suddenly she was aware that it was much colder. She put her arms above her, unbending them as far as possible. She rubbed her hands together, trying to get some warmth into her numb fingers. She unbent them and scratched at the box. The part she was touching was the place where two walls met at one side and both also joined the floor. Her fingers dragged through stuff that was coming off the walls. It felt like sand. She was pretty sure the sandy stuff was rust. She moved her fingers to the floor. More rust. No. This stuff felt different, finer, softer. Dust, not rust. With some small bits of rock in it. Jophia ran her fingers through it idly while trying yet again to think of a plan to escape from the farm.

Those guns in the big house. They were the key. If she could somehow get to that gun rack and pull one of those guns down, she could…what? Shoot the men? Shoot Mistress Jinny? The thought of shooting another person sent her heart bucking. Then she remembered they had killed Peter. And they were planning to line the kids up at a ditch and shoot them in the head. Then Jophia thought probably she could do it.

At the thought of Peter, she dug her fingers deeper into the dust and rust and grated her fingertips against the surface of the box harder. Where the walls met with the floor, she noticed a raised surface, a V-shaped piece of metal that was stuck there to hold the flat pieces of the box together. She picked at it. It moved.

Moved? She played with the metal piece some more. It was small and thin, about two inches on each side of the V shape. Her father had taught her what this part was called. A bracket. It was clear from the way it wobbled that both surfaces it was attached to were rusted badly and cracking apart. Attached how? Jophia felt carefully and found a round bump on the end of each part of the V. She tried to get her fingernail under one end but it was so firmly rusted over and stuck to the bracket that it seemed like part of it. She tried the other end. It moved. Just a slight wiggle, separate from the wobbling of the bracket. The whole thing was set in metal that was almost completely rusted through.

She groped around the floor and brushed aside the layer of accumulated stuff. "Ow," she said as her finger hit something sharp. She touched around the space again and found the sharp thing and touched it carefully. It was a piece of the floor that had rusted through. A jagged, pointed part formed from cracks. She pressured her finger under the sharp metal part. Clenching her teeth against the pain, she pushed it upwards. Her finger met slight resistance that stopped almost instantly as the piece of rust-worn metal snapped off. Between her fingers, she held an iron blade, about about two inches long and barely thicker than a piece of paper.

She probed around as far as her hands could reach and found the same condition everywhere. The bottom of the box was falling apart. What spots weren't rusted through to the ground were so thin they could be broken without much effort.

At the spot where she'd ripped off the piece of metal, she scraped her fingertips against the Earth. The soil felt like hard-packed clay, still wet from the last rain. She could dig her fingers in it a little and pull away some, but it was very hard and the work pulled back her fingernails painfully. She tried to dig with the sharp, rusted blade she'd torn off and it broke into smaller pieces.

All at once, she had an inspiration. She got her fingers around the V-shaped bracket at the base of the wall again. She wiggled the loose end to make it even looser. It wasn't hard, because the base was also rusted through and the metal was thin and damaged. It took only a little persistence to pull it free. Soon Jophia lay in the dark running her fingers over the bracket in her palm with its two long, thin bolts still sticking in it. She moved it to the opened space and scraped it against the clay. Soon she had dug a hole the size of her fist.

She lay there, breathless, thinking about what this meant. They always left her alone in the box from nightfall to sunrise, so she had at least eight hours of uninterrupted time. Could she dig her way out by then? Probably. But then what? Run away? Fight them? How?

Wait. Why could she see the bracket so clearly?

She'd left a big hole in the side of the box when she pulled out the bracket, and the sun was coming up. Light was slanting in through the hole.

The moment she realized this, she heard bootsteps approaching.

Chapter Thirty-nine

Jophia managed to push the bracket into place in the nick of time. Lennon lifted the lid and looked down at her.

"You can come out now, girl."

Lennon was alone. He held out his hand and after a moment's hesitation she took it and he pulled her to her feet. "Can you walk?" he asked. She nodded.

As they made their way back to the horse barn, she asked, "Where is Master Gus?"

"He had to do some business down the hill with Master Gunnar. He won't be back for a couple of days."

"I hope my mistake didn't make Master Lennon angry at Master Gus."

"Don't you worry yourself about that. Just be more careful about them eggs."

"Yes, Master. I'm sorry."

He smiled down on her. "If I let you go wash up now and use the privy while I get the others, you ain't going to run off, are you?"

"No, Master Lennon."

"Okay, then."

She went to the toilet and washed herself at the pump and continued to think about what she would do. By the time she finished, she'd made a decision. Gus would be gone tonight. That gave her the best chance she'd ever have. She would wait until later that day and do something to get herself thrown in the oven again. She could probably dig herself out from the box early enough to have a long head start, maybe five or six hours. Probably a lot longer than Peter had when he ran off. She hated to leave the other kids behind, but she needed to find help before they were all killed.

Lennon brought the other kids out as she finished at the pump. She stood to one side and waited for them to finish washing, then they all set out for the first chicken house. They worked through the day in silence and finished the third chicken house at close to dinner time. To get herself put in the oven again, Jophia planned to do something to disrupt Mistress Jinny's "lesson."

As the children started to walk to the big house, a silver pickup truck came roaring into the clearing so fast the kids had to jump out of its way to avoid getting hit. Gus was driving. Before he'd even stopped he was hollering out the window at Lennon, "we got trouble."

Gus jumped out and ran to his brother and said something Jophia couldn't hear. Lennon said to the kids sharply, "You all wait here. Don't you dare move a muscle." The men went in the house. Jophia could hear a lot of shouting back and forth between the two brothers and Mistress Jinny, but couldn't make out what they said.

Gus then came out and pointed his shotgun at the children.

Oh no oh no they're really going to do it.

Jophia glanced around desperately for a rock, a stick, anything to fight with, but there was nothing. Lennon came out behind Gus and stopped at the porch, where he paced back and forth while talking on his phone to someone. He hung up and said to Gus, "Gunnar said we need to lock all the kids in the barn right now."

"Now?"

"Yep. Forget dinner and school. Just lock them in there and get in the house."

"Okay, you heard what he said," shouted Gus. "You niggers get in the barn, now!"

The kids started walking quickly back toward the barn. But one kid didn't move.

"Jophia, what the hell you doing?" demanded Gus.

"Why do we need to go in the barn?"

"You don't ask questions. You do what you're told."

"But why? What happened?"

"You go to that barn, or I swear…"

"You swear what, Master Gus? You going to shoot me?"

"Nigger, move!"

Jophia folded her arms across her chest and stared him straight in the eye. "I'm not a *nigger*. I'm a ten-year-old girl. *You're* the nigger."

Gus's mouth dropped open. "What did you say?"

"You heard me. You fat, bald, white nigger."

Gus, his features twisted and his face bright red, seemed to hover in mid-air for several seconds. Then he threw his gun to the ground and ran roaring at Jophia. No words, just raw bellowing rage, like a gorilla charging.

Jophia leapt to one side just as Gus tried to dive on top of her. He landed with a painful thud on the hard ground. He made an *oof* sound when the air got knocked out of him. He was such a comic sight, with his face to the ground and his jeans falling down, that she almost laughed. She drew up her foot and kicked him on the ass.

An iron hand gripped her arm. Lennon towered over her. "Oven."

Jophia didn't resist as he pulled her to the metal box. She even climbed in obediently and lay on her side, like she was going to bed.

Lennon looked down at her with a look more amazed than angry. "Are you crazy, girl? Gunnar might never let you come out of here again." He slammed the lid closed.

Her whole body was shaking. From outside the box, she

could hear shouted orders, Gus's voice croaking furiously at the others to get in the horse barn. Then she heard the barn doors slide shut and Lennon and Gus in a muffled, heated discussion as they walked quickly back to the big house. As soon as the sound of their footsteps disappeared, she tore off the bracket and started to dig frantically into the clay.

Suddenly she heard the door to the big house open. She quickly shoved the bracket back into its place and listened. The sound of a vehicle door opening and closing, then the engine of the SUV revving. The big black vehicle rumbled past and down the forest road. After waiting a while and hearing nothing more, she began to dig again.

Making a hole big enough to escape took longer than she thought. It was well past sundown before she could squeeze her head and shoulders outside. She lay still for a minute, enjoying the glorious night air against her face and listening for any sounds of the house's occupants, then pushed her way out of the hole. Lying flat on her stomach she peered up at the house. All the windows were dark. She gathered her courage, stood up and ran for the road. She was lightheaded with panic over the scraping sounds her feet made in the dirt. She hit the road and started running at full speed away from the farm.

All at once the sound of an engine broke the stillness of night. Jophia jumped into a stand of trees on the right side of the road just as the headlights of the black SUV exploded over the rise to the clearing. The SUV roared past, leaving a cloud of dust. Jophia stared out from the trees.

From behind her, a hand shot out and covered her mouth.

A man whispered into her ear, "don't scream."

Chapter Forty

Jophia stared up at the dim form of the man in the trees and thought for a second it was Lennon. This man was a giant too, but he had hair and Lennon didn't.

"I'm here to help you," the man said.

"Who are you?" she whispered.

I'm a…policeman. You're Jophia Williams, aren't you?"

She nodded.

"My name is James. I've been looking everywhere for you. Your friend Eliza asked me to find you." The giant man turned toward the house. "Where are the other kids?"

She pointed. "That barn. They're locked to the walls. With chains."

"Is anyone hurt?"

"No."

"How many other kids?"

"Six."

At this, the man went silent for a time.

"How many bad guys?"

"Two. And one bad woman."

"What can you tell me about them?"

"There's one big one, he's Lennon, and the other one…"

"Short and fat? Named Gus?"

"Yes. They got four killer dogs too."

The giant man frowned. "Where are the dogs?"

"In a cage around the other side of the house."

"Who's the woman?"

"She's Master Gus and Master Lennon's mother."

"Master?"

“That’s…” Jophia’s words were cut off by a swell of tears. “…That’s what they made us call them.”

The giant man looked down at her long and hard. He dropped to his knees. He placed his two big arms around her and she fell against his chest and he hugged her close and stroked her back.

“Soon, they’ll be calling us master,” he said.

Chapter Forty-one

After the bullet cracked through the rear window of the tow truck and buzzed past his ear, Strait slammed his foot on the accelerator and laid two black stripes of rubber on the asphalt until the truck was out of range. Without slowing, he fished his smartphone from his pack and called Graham. No answer.

The big hook dangling free from the back of the tow truck whipped around scraping and bouncing against the asphalt for half a minute before the chain snapped. Strait watched through the shattered rear window as the hook clattered against the asphalt with a burst of sparks and shot into the air and went clanging off the edge of the road and into the trees.

Gripping the steering wheel with one hand, he thumbed up the GPS map with driving directions to Gunnar's farm. Every few seconds he glanced at the rearview mirror, watching for cars in pursuit.

The directions from the GPS app told him to make a left at an off-ramp coming up. Strait swung into a one-lane road with unmaintained pavement and headed straight as an arrow to the west. In front of him rose the mountains, layers of pine-covered slopes as pristine as Eden. Within a couple of minutes the asphalt gave way to dirt and the road began to wind into the foothills.

A billboard on two upright wooden beams came up on the right. It showed a giant cartoon deer being sighted by a huge cartoon hunter and the words WILSON ANIMAL PROCESSING ONE MILE. FARMER'S MARKET EVERY SATURDAY AND SUNDAY. The sign triggered a childhood memory for Strait. It was the place hunters took the animals they'd killed to be cut down into pieces of meat. His father took him to this place a few times when he was a kid after their hunting trips. The weekend farmer's market held in the parking lot was popular amongst the locals.

For a small price, the butchers in the shop would process the carcasses of deer and antelope and wild pig and any other game you brought into a choice of minced meat, steaks, and even sausages. His father was chummy with Old Man Wilson, the owner. James remembered how much like a grown-up he felt among his father and other hunters gathered in front of Mr. Wilson, who always had some dirty joke to tell. He had been a jovial, boulder-headed man in his sixties with a huge belly and an infectious, roaring laugh and he made James laugh too even though he was scared of the man because he wore a rubber apron splashed with blood. Strait remembered watching fascinated behind his father and the other men beside a big metal tub with an industrial meat saw, huge blade like a circular saw with its safety guard removed, the body of a dead deer suspended partly into the air by a steel hook driven through its neck, draped into the tub with Mr. Wilson standing over it, his muscular fingers gripping the handle of the circular saw and pausing before running the saw through the animal to tell an obscene joke in his thick German accent about a nude woman on a banana boat.

Wilson.

Strait brought the truck to a screeching halt. He sat staring at his fists, the knuckles flexing, the skin nearly white from gripping the wheel so hard.

Wilson.

Must be a coincidence. It was a common name.

No time for this. He needed to get to the farm. No matter what, the chicken farm was the most likely place to find Jophia. He floored the accelerator again. A moment later, he sped past a sign, a smaller version of the billboard he'd seen a mile back, with an arrow pointing to a driveway that led to a one-story box-like building with cracked, grey walls with the name Wilson Animal Processing painted in huge red letters across one side. The facility's slogan, also in red paint: *You slay'em, we flay'em.*

Using the GPS to guide him, he followed the winding road as it climbed into the mountains and deeper into the forest. The sun flashed brightly through the boughs of the trees. *She's on the mountain. Under the sun.* Narrow roads that branched off the main one started to come fast and furious and he needed to slow down. Some were capillaries leading farther into the mountains and some were driveways to private cabins. All looked the same and none had signs. As he drove farther and approached his goal on the GPS map the roads branching off gradually disappeared until there were none at all.

He kept driving another fifteen minutes. All at once, the road came to an end. It was blocked by a waist-high metal fence with a sign on it: "DEAD END." On the side of the fence, someone had set up concrete blocks to prevent driving around. He got out of his car and stared incredulously at the sign. He looked at his smartphone to confirm that he was in the right place and the screen showed only a black space with a red, blinking battery symbol.

Fuck.

All at once the Earth seemed to sag below his feet. Then it heaved up, tilting to the right. Nausea swelled up inside him. He fell to his knees. He stayed very still but the ground around him was shifting liquidly back and forth. He took deep breaths through his nose. The tinnitus in his right ear had switched in an instant from a whine to a roar.

Not now. Please. Strait shut his eyes and forced himself to sit. He took ten very deep breaths through his nose and blew them slowly out his mouth. He groped at his front shirt pocket and pulled out the chewable Dramamine and took one. Then popped out four more and threw them in his mouth too. He chewed the whole lot and swallowed.

The ground gradually stopped moving. With extreme care he stood again and moved his head left and right. A little dizzy still, but the feeling of an imminent attack had passed.

When the road ended, he'd been no more than an eighth of a mile due north from Gunnar Wilson's farm. Exactly the same direction as the road he'd been following before it dead-ended. If the dead end weren't there, he could probably drive straight to it.

Weird. He'd passed the last human habitation miles back and certainly almost no one would bother coming out here. Was the GPS map wrong? Strait walked over to the sign and studied it. Beyond the sign, the road gave way to an area of patchy, ankle-high grass then onwards to what appeared to be untouched forest.

He knelt carefully, on guard for vertigo. He bent low and examined the grass on the other side of the sign. Most of it stood upright like it should, but, separated by several feet, two wide strips of the grass were pushed down. Tire tracks.

The tracks headed north for about twenty feet, then veered into the trees. Strait examined the sign some more. He found what he was looking for on the right side, below the lower bar. A small rectangular handle that, when turned, would open the gate and let a vehicle through. Strait tried turning it but it wouldn't budge. Locked. He found the keyhole at the base. No key.

He got back into the tow truck and started it and turned around and headed back the way he came. He drove for about five minutes until he found an opening in the trees. He wound into it. A path was here, about a car's width, heavily overgrown. An old logging trail, probably. He could just get the truck onto the path far enough to be concealed from the road, but could go no farther because the path was blocked by a fallen tree.

It was going on late afternoon. The dimming blue of the sky visible through the tree tops was blotted by clots of fast-moving black clouds. He could smell rain in the air that might turn to snow later tonight. He checked that the Glock in his jacket was fully loaded with the safety off. He retrieved the gun case from behind the seat of the tow truck and removed the components of the MP5 and assembled it. He strapped the machine gun over his shoulder. To his belt, he attached the magazine pouch. He snapped on the Yaqui holster and put the Glock in it.

He took a few steps into the forest, then stopped and put the MP5 in the grass. He took off his backpack and pulled out his medicine bag. From it he removed his spare box of Dramamine. He ripped it open and took out another three chewable tablets and swallowed them. He took out his water jug and drank down a packet of the Chinese medicine. Then, as a final measure, he took out a tube of the vicious diuretic liquid the doctor had given to him for emergencies. *It suck every drop of water from your body. Very powerful. Taste like shit.* He ripped off the end of the tube, held his breath, and drank it down in one gulp.

Chapter Forty-two

He moved through the forest in the direction the GPS had shown before the smartphone died. He kept the movement of his body fluid around the natural obstacles, the hanging branches, the loose rocks, the mounds of pine needles. As quiet as a mouse. He stopped every few seconds to survey the terrain for any sign of other people.

Darkness was settling over the forest. Strait wished he had his infrared goggles and a detailed optical terrain map beamed to him from a satellite-linked drone. But he then realized he knew this kind of terrain already. He'd grown up in this region, had hiked hundreds of forest miles with his father. He knew the meaning of every scent and sound as well as he knew anything.

The comprehension he had of the landscape was on a level of intuition that was far more useful than any conscious, logical analysis. He understood, better than any gadgetry could inform him, that from the shifting arrangement of moist Earth, rotting forest mass, and pine needles under his boots a rise was only a short distance off and that it led to a ridge that overlooked an open, flat area. He found the base of the rise, felt a downward flow of chill wind descending from the top. He climbed toward it. The moment he reached the top, the sound of an approaching vehicle made him drop to his stomach. He heard the slam of a door and distant voices of men. He raised his head slightly, just enough to see the setting below. A decrepit log house. To the left of it, a building that looked like a red barn. Windows boarded up. In front of the log house, a clearing and in front of the clearing, closest to Strait, three white concrete buildings in a row. In the clearing was a black SUV and a silver pick-up truck. Dust was still billowing up in front of the truck where it had just stopped.

Two men stood next to the truck, one short and fat, the other tall and brawny. Gus and Lennon Bear. Gus was agitated, gesturing wildly, and speaking excitedly to his brother.

Trailing the men was a group of children, all black.

Strait attached the telescopic sight on the assault rifle and aimed it at the head of the fat one. *Gus fucking Bear*. Strait put his finger on the trigger. He took a deep breath and relaxed the pressure on the trigger. Not yet.

Lennon was talking on a cellphone. Gus was now shouting something at the children and they were responding by moving toward the barn to the left. All except one. A girl. Strait looked through the scope at her. His heart jumped.

Jophia Williams.

She was shouting something at Gus, her hands on her hips in a posture of defiance.

Gus suddenly lunged at the girl and Strait sighted him again but the girl jumped out of the way and Gus fell to the ground.

Jophia got behind him and kicked him in the ass.

What the fuck?

Gus fell over on his face and Lennon ran up and grabbed Jophia by the arm. Strait aimed the rifle at Lennon and followed him as he pulled Jophia away. Gus scrambled up from the ground and started following them, shaking his fists and screaming. It seemed Lennon was putting himself between Gus and Jophia. Was he protecting her? He traced the tall man in the scope, ready to drop him at any sign of hurting her. The man placed her gently on the dirt next to what looked like a half-buried black box. He threw open a lid on the box. She climbed inside, apparently on her own. He said something to her and closed the lid.

The men corralled the other children into the barn and everyone disappeared from view. Then the two men emerged from the other end of the building.

It was almost too dark to see them. He could hear their agitated voices threading up the ridge through the trees. He couldn't make out the words, but he knew what they were talking about. Him.

Lennon climbed into the SUV and drove off. From inside the house, Strait could still make out voices, shouting, distraught. One voice sounded female. If only Gus and the woman were in the house, Strait could take them down easily. But where was Gunnar Wilson? Were others in there too? Strait knew from firsthand experience the danger of charging in prematurely.

He watched and waited. He wanted more than anything to get down to that black box and free Jophia and to that barn and rescue the other kids. But it would do none of them any good if he went down and got shot by someone hiding in wait for him. At the window of the house, maybe. Or behind the barn.

He waited several hours until the lights in the cabin went out. And then waited another thirty minutes. Almost certainly the inhabitants were asleep. He sidled down the ridge and moved silently around the strip of forest bordering the farm. Then he headed west until he was well beyond the barn and the black box, then shifted north. Here the ridge tapered off and the elevation lowered to a flat area with sparse vegetation and only a few stands of pine trees separated by spaces with no cover. He was pretty sure no one could see him from the house, but when moving across the land between the trees, Strait crawled on his belly to be sure he wouldn't be seen.

He could see by the yellow-blue moonlight a space in front of him where the grass had been smashed down in two broad lines. This was where Lennon sped away in the SUV. Somewhere up the rise and to the left was the dead-end sign that had stopped him. Lennon must have opened it and driven onto the road. Strait crossed and entered the forest, relieved to be concealed in the trees again.

He moved through the woods in the direction of the property. He froze when he heard the unmistakable sound of someone walking fast. On small legs. The footsteps were approaching on the overgrown road to his right. Very close to him now.

Suddenly the roar of an engine broke the silence and headlights appeared bouncing through the branches and the child broke into a run and Strait stepped toward her through the trees and the little girl jumped up in front of him, her back to him. The big black SUV roared past. Strait put his hand around the girl's mouth and whispered, "Don't scream."

Chapter Forty-three

"Where are we going?" said Jophia. They had waited in the trees for a long while in silence as Strait made sure no one in the house was watching for them. He had then led her down the overgrown road, past the detachable dead end sign. They'd walked for ten minutes down the road.

"I have a truck. I'm parked about five more minutes' walk this way."

From the direction of the farm, they heard the distant shouts of men. Then they went silent.

"We need to get out of here. If you hear a car coming, you jump into the trees so they don't see you."

"Why are we going to your truck?"

"To get you to safety."

"But my friends are still back there."

"I know that. I'll come back later for them."

"You can't! We have to…"

More shouts pierced the night. Pure rage. A terrified adult cry threaded into the shouts, like someone was in pain.

"Be quiet," hissed Strait. "We need to keep moving."

"But…"

"Shut up!"

They walked on for another five minutes, and Strait could feel the girl's anger radiating at him as she marched ahead furiously. Suddenly, she turned to him and said in a fierce, breathy whisper, "Master Lennon said they're going to dig a ditch and put all of us next to it and shoot us in the head."

Strait stopped. He thought it over. These men had enslaved a bunch of children and killed one of them. They knew they were all looking at the death penalty or life in prison already.

Nothing to lose.

He cupped Jophia's face in his hands and said, "Okay. Listen. I'm not going to let them hurt the others. But I need you to go down this dirt road by yourself. Follow it until you can find a light in the woods. Or a mailbox next to a driveway with someone's name on it. It might be a few miles, but if you can find a house with people at home, knock on their door and tell them you were kidnapped and you got away and you need the police. But don't try to stop any cars. You hear a car coming on this road, you jump into the woods and hide. You understand?"

"I'm not going down there."

"You don't need to be scared."

"I'm not scared. I'm coming with you."

"No, you aren't."

"Yes, I am."

"No, you're not," Strait said firmly. "I can't help your friends if I need to babysit you."

"I'm not leaving my friends behind."

She stared up at him with unnerving intensity.

"Jophia, go. Now. I'm the grown-up here and you're the kid."

She folded her arms. "You don't know shit about kids."

From the direction of the farm came more shouts. Then the sound of a car starting and an engine revving.

"Jophia, they're coming. They found out you're missing. I'm ordering you to do as I say. Start down that road or I'll…give you a spanking."

Jophia's gaze lingered on him a few more seconds. She seemed to come to a decision. She nodded curtly and turned and walked away down the hill.

She had just gone out of his view when Strait heard the SUV approaching. “Jophia! Trees!” he shouted and jumped into the trees himself just as the SUV crested the hill. It blasted past him. He stepped out onto the road and listened. The SUV hadn’t slowed and was now far away, still going full bore down the hill. Jophia must have done what he’d told her to do.

Strait started hiking back to the farm. He thought about the girl. For one so small, Jophia sure had guts. She didn’t act at all like Strait’s idea of how kids should act.

I don’t know shit about kids.

Chapter Forty-four

The house was still dark when Strait returned. He could make out the black metal box that Jophia had escaped from, a mound of Earth by the hole she'd dug out.

He figured that Lennon had noticed the black box was open and found Jophia had escaped, Gus or Lennon had driven out to capture her, while the other brother waited inside. If he was lucky, both of them had gone, which left him with only the woman to deal with. As it stood, he had two jobs to do, subdue two or maybe one suspect in the house and get the kids out of there.

He stifled a yawn. The dizziness had left him but the mountain of medicine he'd taken was making him sleepy. Maybe it would be better just to sneak the kids out at this point. But going directly to rescue the kids could get him trapped in the barn. Either Gus or Lennon could easily shoot him and the kids through the walls. Or they could catch them on the road. Better to erase any threat that was in the house first.

Okay, here we go. He ran from the trees and made a beeline for the house. He stomped up the porch, pounded his fist twice on the front door and crouched to the side and bellowed, "FBI! You're surrounded! Come out with your hands over your heads!"

No sound came from the house.

He called again. "FBI! Open the door and come out with your hands up!"

Nothing.

"This is your last warning. If we enter the house, we will shoot you on sight!"

The only noise he could hear in response was the whir of a pair of bats that arced in from over the roof and shot skywards toward the forest.

Strait jumped off the porch, scraped up a rock, and hurled it through the nearest window. Then he lifted his MP5 and fired at the other window, three rounds, *pop! pop! pop!*

He dropped to the ground. He took in as best he could in the moonlight the surrounding woods. He listened. Absolutely silence, from both the woods and the house. He moved onto the porch and turned the doorknob and threw the door open. He jumped inside and swept his hand against the interior wall for the light switch. Light filled the room.

The first thing he saw was the color red. It was splashed so thoroughly around, it seemed like some kids had had a free-for-all fight with a bathtub of red paint. But it wasn't paint. It was blood from the bodies of the two men on the floor.

The fatter one on top of the taller one. Although they were battered and hacked as basely as slaughterhouse animals and their facial features were decimated by the violence, Strait knew it was Gus and Lennon. Gus's head was mostly gone, smashed to pulp floating with pieces of bone. Strait circled around and could see that Lennon's head too was crushed. Whoever had done this had gone for Lennon first, which is why he was on the bottom. The bigger threat.

No search for a murder weapon was needed. A large sledgehammer, the head and handle well soaked with blood, had been tossed in a corner. Given the noise this must have raised, the attack must have happened after he had left with Jophia. And happened very fast.

The only other person in the house had been the old lady. No old lady had swung this sledge with the force it took to kill these men. That SUV. The big, black vehicle that had roared past when he first encountered Jophia in the woods. Jophia said it was Lennon returning, but Strait understood now that it wasn't only Lennon. Gunnar Wilson had been in the car.

Given the time frame, Gunnar Wilson must have gone straight into the house with Lennon and slaughtered both men in the space of only a minute or two. What kind of man would do something like that?

Strait quickly moved through the rest of the house. Two bedrooms and a kitchen. No sign of the woman. He ran out of the house to the barn. At the sliding doors, he pulled out his Glock and held it in his right hand while he put his left hand on the handle. The same ominous silence prevailed over the barn and it seemed for a moment that the fear of what he would find was so strong that he might not be able to enter. He took a deep breath and pulled the doors open.

The barn was divided into small stalls, each formed from partitions. Strait felt his spirit collapse when he saw the walls were deep red. Then he remembered that the barn itself was painted red. His eyes adjusted enough to the darkness that he could maneuver around the room. He moved from stall to stall with the Glock pointed ahead of him, bracing himself for finding a pile of bodies in one of them. He got all the way to the end, and then moved back to the door.

There wasn't a soul in the barn. The children were gone.

Chapter Forty-five

As Strait tried to steer the tow truck down the winding roads of the mountainside, tires squealing at each weave of the vehicle, he was going insane.

Fuck!

In the fifteen minutes he'd been getting Jophia out of that place, Gunnar Wilson had managed to murder Gus and Lennon and take the kids away.

They're still alive.

The time it had taken him after finding the bodies and checking the horse barn and then sprinting around the farm, with a long look especially at the cage where four vicious Dobermans, still locked inside, barked at him furiously, another fifteen minutes had passed. That means those kids had been taken no more than thirty minutes ago. *Where?*

He needed to get to a phone. Call the police. Kladspell couldn't ignore him now that he'd actually found Jophia. Maybe she was already inside someone's house and had called for help. Or she was still out here somewhere. He scanned the sides of the road as best he could in the dark but he didn't see her. If she'd obeyed him, she would have ducked into the trees at his approach and he wouldn't see her anyway. He kept his eye out for any residences where he could ask to use a phone, but he saw nothing. No lights between the trees, no cars on the road. Soon he found himself back on the wider dirt road heading toward the highway.

On his right, coming up fast, was the place he'd passed before. *Wilson's Animal Processing*. A light was on in the front. Two vehicles in the parking lot.

A motorcycle. And a black SUV.

Strait slammed on the brakes. He went into a spinning skid that turned the truck completely around. He smashed his foot into the pedal and shot forward. He blasted into the parking lot and stopped behind the SUV. He put his car in reverse, backed up, snapped it into drive and floored it again.

With a tremendous *bam!* the car hit the back of the SUV. Strait shouldered up the MP5 and pulled the Glock and leaped out of the car and jumped around to the opposite side just as the front door of the office burst open and a man came running out. Keith Bear. He had a yellow rubber apron tied over his suit and tie.

Keith came around the back of the SUV and stood gaping at the tow truck, which had rolled back a few feet, taking with it the SUV's rear fender and scattering shards of its taillights on the asphalt. Strait circled crouching around the front of the vehicle and came up on him from behind. Keith sensed his approach and turned and Strait gave him a ferocious sidekick to the knee. Keith squealed and dropped to the asphalt. Strait stomped on his face, then smacked him across the temple with his Glock. Keith moaned and lay still.

Strait crabwalked to the building and moved through the open door, glancing right, left, up, down, and moved to a second door behind a reception desk. He positioned himself to the side and reached over the doorframe. He turned the doorknob slowly, pushed the door open. Bright light poured out but no sounds.

"FBI!" he shouted. "Throw down your weapons, put your hands over your head, and come out."

No sound.

Unlike the deathly silence of the house at the farm, the quiet in the next room had the spoor of concealed life, of living animals holding their breath. Resonances of life suspended.

"Gunnar Wilson. I know you're in there. I'm not going to say it again. You can't get away. Come out."

A child cried out, a muffled, terrified sound, and Strait leapt into the room in a crouch, gun forward. What he saw stopped his breath.

Strait had been in this room before. In his childhood.

One side was taken up by a cooler with a glass case. Behind the glass were stacks of produce in boxes—eggs, tomatoes, and carrots and other stock for the farmer's market. In the other part of the room were four tables sheeted with polished aluminum that reflected the hanging lamps and the thick chains and meat hooks suspended above them. Each table had an aluminum sink at one end and a range of extendable tools affixed to a modular array atop an aluminum cabinet at each table's side: meat shears and shredders and drills, and bone saws with serrated circular plates half an inch thick and wider than a human stomach.

Behind the table farthest from him, at the back wall beside another door, stood Gunnar Wilson. He was considerably older and broader than the man depicted in the photograph Strait had seen at Bruno German's office. Unlike the Gunnar in the photo, this man was utterly hairless, revealing that the shape of his head was irregular, with random concavities and lumps and furrows, and that his skin was sow-belly pink. His eyes, which were riveted on Strait, were so tiny and lusterless they seemed to be the result of someone snipping the rubber erasers off two pencils and shoving them into his eye sockets. His thickly muscled right arm was held aloft, his fingers wrapped tightly around the black handle of a circular bone saw. His index finger was on the black trigger button that, if pressed, would activate the saw. With his left hand, he gripped the hair of a girl of about five and held her head in place over the sink. The configuration of the saw to the girl was such that if the saw were lowered, it would cut through her neck and drop her head into the sink.

The other children were arranged along the wall in a line starting next to Gunnar and ending at the cooler. An old woman with spidery white hair was standing about midway down the line. She held a shotgun pointed at a little boy next to her, who looked no more than four.

Gunnar observed Strait placidly. He pressed the trigger on the saw. The circular blade let off a loud whine as it started spinning.

"Let the girl go, now!" Strait had his Glock pointed at Gunnar, who was smiling back at him calmly.

"Mr. Strait," shouted Gunnar over the sound of the sound. "It's wonderful to finally meet you." New Zealand accent.

"Let her go!"

"Here is what you're thinking," responded Gunnar. "You're thinking you can get one shot off and drop me, then turn and shoot my beautiful wife fast enough that she can't shoot any of these other children. Right?"

Exactly what Strait was thinking.

"However, if you shoot me, I will collapse and let go of this saw. Notice that I've flipped the mechanism that locks the saw, so that even if my finger falls away, the saw will continue to turn on its own and drop on this girl's neck. And the instant you shoot me, my wife will shoot at those children there. She will not be able to kill them all, of course, before being shot herself, but she will get at least a couple of them, given a shotgun's wide spray. So to clarify for you what you have perhaps not yet clarified for yourself, you are faced with a choice of either shooting me and causing the deaths of at least three of these seven children or dropping your weapon on the ground now and saving them all."

Strait continued to point the gun at Gunnar. "You're planning to kill them anyway," he said.

"Oh, no, Mr. Strait. Nothing of the sort. We were discussing the best thing to do with them when you chose to drop by. Killing these unfortunate creatures was only one of many options. I'm open to negotiation. Negotiation is always possible between reasonable men, isn't that so?"

From the slippery way Gunnar spoke and the glint of humor in his unhuman eyes, Strait knew he was playing with him. He *had* already decided to kill the children. If Strait had shown up ten seconds later, the girl's head would already be in the sink.

"Why would you want to kill these kids? It doesn't make sense. You're already caught." Strait struggled mightily to keep Gunnar's face in his gunsight and not to look at the panic-stricken face of the girl under the saw. All that medicine he'd taken was impacting his ability to focus his eyes and the gun felt almost too heavy to continue holding up.

Gunnar laughed. "Caught? My lovely Jinny and I can be at the Mexican border in five hours. On a plane to South Africa, where I hold dual citizenship, by morning. Do you know how easy it is to disappear in Africa? As for why we would kill these *kids*, the truth is, they're not *kids*. They're not people at all. They're *mud* people. Only marginally more intelligent than a pack mule. And they've outlived their usefulness to us. You've been brainwashed by your multicultural, white-hating upbringing, Mr. Strait. So sad. Here you are, a perfect specimen of the Aryan man, and you're still a slave to the idea that everyone is equal. Even though it's never been that way for even a minute of the last 10,000 years of human civilization. *White* civilization. Our society every day kills stray dogs and cats, and far less humanely than I was pondering doing here with this splendid, machine-tooled rendering saw. Do you know that this saw is the same one my grandfather used decades ago when he built this place? A fine product, this saw. A white man's invention. Grandpa must have presided over the renderings of thousands and thousands of animals, large and small, brought to him by thousands of hunters who killed them. Do you shed a tear for *them*? Those poor deer and elk and foxes and rabbits? Of course you don't. Yet here you are, giving me a look that says, 'how could you do anything so monstrous?' Shame on you for your hypocrisy."

"Here's a reality check for you, Gunnar. This place is about to be swarming with cops. You're looking at a life sentence and maybe the death penalty."

"Death penalty?"

"For the murder of your wife's sons. Gus and Lennon Bear."

"Jinny told me of their tragic passing, but I personally know nothing about that."

"You lying sack of shit."

"They killed each other," called out Jinny. "Gus was reluctant to continue with our social experiment. Lennon wasn't. They fought with a sledgehammer."

"With only one sledgehammer? Did they take turns hitting each other?"

"Yes," responded Jinny, smirking. "It was quite…cinematic."

"You don't seem so broken up about the death of your sons."

"They weren't my sons. And they weren't brothers. We were members of an organization in Tennessee, the New Confederacy, with a similar vision to our own, a desire to reverse the mistakes of history after the great southern war, to bring back the natural order. But this group was not earnest in its beliefs. They only talked a big game. They were also very good at raising money, but when it came to using the money to actually take action, it was only we four, Lennon, Gus, Keith and myself, who had the courage to do what needed to be done. We took their money and resettled out here in Arizona to really do something to bring about the revolution. It was more convenient to pretend a family relationship."

"And Gunnar?"

"I met Jinny online," said Gunnar. "Two kindred souls, separated by whole oceans. I couldn't believe I'd actually found a woman whose vision of the world was as clear as mine."

"Maybe you can still write love letters to each other on death row."

"We are without guilt."

"You killed a child."

"You're referring to that dead picaninny? Peter whatshisname? I know nothing about that. I was not even in the country when that happened and I have the passport stamps to prove it. I believe it was Lennon. He was a bit of a psychopath."

"Okay, then. That's good, right? You're just facing kidnapping charges. That means some prison time, but with good behavior, you'll get out, maybe even in only a few years. But if you kill any of these kids, you're back to a life sentence or a death penalty."

The confident way Gunnar laughed was unsettling.

"Here's a reality check for *you*, Mr. Strait. I'm not going to face charges for anything. You really are a fool, do you know that? I knew it the day I watched you crawling around on your hands and knees at the riverside, digging up grubs. Because the girl was taken much too close to home—a miscalculation on my part, I must admit—I had intended, to deflect local intrusion, to make it look like she had been murdered, but your snooping around, as inept and bumbling though it was, disrupted what would have otherwise been a perfectly efficacious plan. I knew you were a fool too when you leaped out of Marvin Williams's house that day and ran straight into my line of fire. If that old Negro had died, no one would have cared. And every bit of police interest in the missing girl would have ended. But there you were, muddying the waters with your strange interest in affairs that don't concern you. And you, the only person in this hee-haw town who could have investigated, would have been gone too. It was only by pure, fool's luck that you managed to shoot me. The wound wasn't bad, nothing my wife couldn't bandage up. But you know the real reason you're a fool, James? Here's why. There are no police on their way here and you know it. The chief of police, that Kladspell moron, doesn't even know these children exist, except for one girl he thinks is dead."

"And where is that one girl Kladspell thinks is dead, Gunnar? Where is Marvin's daughter?"

"She's…" a shadow of doubt passed over his face. "Jinny," he said to the old lady, "which one is it?"

Jinny Wilson looked up and down the line of children. "She's…" she said and she trailed off, confused. She counted and a look of shock came over her face. "Gun, she's missing."

Gunnar's amused expression changed to anger. He glared at Strait. "Where is she?" he demanded.

"How the hell would I know?" asked Strait.

"I'm serious."

"So am I! It looks like one of your subhuman animals outsmarted you."

Gunnar tightened his grasp over the handle of the saw, swinging it a little. "We've come to a crossroads, James. Within five seconds, you'll drop that gun on the floor and tell me where the girl is. Or *this* girl…"

The window shattered. Something came flying into the room and hit Jinny in the face. It took Strait a split second to understand that she'd been struck by an egg. She tried to wipe off the egg yolk and egg white dripping from her face and two more eggs shot through the window and hit her again, both in the chest. Gunnar turned toward his wife and Strait shot the saw he was holding. He pumped six rounds at it in two seconds. The blade burst into pieces.

More eggs sailed in through the window, pelting Jinny's face. She dropped her shotgun and tried to protect herself with both hands just as Gunnar realized with befuddled horror that he was holding only the plastic handle of a broken saw and Strait shot him in the head.

He dropped lifeless to the floor and released the girl. She didn't move at all but maintained the exact position over the sink as though any movement on her part might still bring on death.

Strait turned his gun toward the old woman but the children nearest her had jumped on her and were attacking her with a fury you never expect to see in children. They assailed her with their feet and fists and mouths. The smallest ones leaped on top. Strait vaulted over the table and pulled the kids off her. He snatched Jinny Wilson up by one arm and threw her face-first against the wall.

She twisted around snarling and spat at him. He gripped her shoulder and knocked her legs apart with his foot to brace her better against the wall and she tried to bite his hand, clacking her teeth together as she snapped her jaws.

A tiny hand was slapping against his leg. He looked down and saw the smallest boy there holding up a roll of duct tape. He lifted Jinny and dropped her to the floor and taped her wrists to her ankles. She was as light as some calcified beast whose meat had been picked away by carrion birds and left to resolve to elements under the sun. But still alive. Still dangerous.

Strait took off his coat and threw it over the corpse of Gunnar Wilson. He went to the girl at the sink. The other kids followed him. She was still in the same position, eyes closed tightly, head suspended over the sink. Her arms were bent and crossed over one another rigidly, in the way of insects about to die.

He very gently lifted her in both arms. He whispered that it was all over and she was safe. Although she was breathing and outwardly uninjured, she did not open her eyes, did not respond, and her arms remained crossed.

He placed the girl on a sofa in the office. He went outside and found Keith where he'd left him, still laid out and unconscious on the asphalt. He restrained his hands and feet too with the duct tape.

Jophia was standing a little ways off. She approached him. She was still clutching an egg in each hand. "Outside, around back, they keep a stack of trays with these eggs, so I…"

"I *ordered* you to…" he said and she dropped the eggs and ran to him and put her arms around his waist and hugged him tightly. He stopped his scolding in mid-breath. He reached down and lifted her up and held her in his arms.

Strait used the office phone to dial Footer's number. Graham answered jovially.

"Might this finally be you, my dear James?"

"Finally be *me*? Don't you ever answer your phone? I tried to call you five times."

"I was tied up in a meeting."

"A meeting? I've got a dead body here, and two suspects in custody who probably both need medical treatment. I've also got seven rescued children, with at least one of them in shock. Children who come from at least one state other than Arizona. That puts their rescue in the jurisdiction of the Federal Bureau of Investigation. Would you mind, if you can pull away from your fucking meetings, orchestrating some agency assistance?"

At that moment, James heard the sound of approaching helicopters. And the wail of sirens. Many sirens.

"I imagine we can pop over momentarily," said Graham.

Chapter Forty-six

In dealing with criminals and enemy soldiers, James Strait had encountered his share of threatening looks. But never had he seen contempt quite so vicious as that erupting from the faces of Brian Gelder, Special Agent in Charge of the Richmond, Virginia field office and Bruce Greyson, Senior Special Agent of the FBI Science and Technology Branch.

Phoenix daytime temperature in late December averaged 70 degrees, but the heater for the room they sat in was still turned up high. He could feel sweat dripping from under his arms into his dress shirt. They were seated in a staid room full of dark colors: black leather chairs, brown wall paneling and dark blue carpet with the FBI logo ten feet in diameter emblazoned upon it. Gelder and Greyson sat behind a long desk that faced a row of chairs where Strait sat beside Special Agent Graham Footer. On the wall behind them was an immense portrait of the President of the United States, whose rubbery orange, purse-lipped countenance glared down fiercely upon them also, like some clown-like Big Brother.

The day after Strait had killed Gunnar Wilson, the FBI had swooped down on the hotel and snatched James and driven him to Phoenix. Graham had been placed under house arrest on the same day and was also confined to field office dormitory room. Several days later, Strait and Footer were visited by nameless agents who brought them suits approximately in their size and told them to come to this hearing at six o'clock. Gelder and Greyson had flown down from Virginia the previous day and would superintend. The purpose of the meeting was implicitly clear. Strait assumed Gelder would concentrate on ripping pieces of flesh out of him, and Greyson would take charge of flaying Footer alive, after which both Gelder and Greyson would round out the proceedings by gnawing casually on the balls of both men.

Gelder addressed the room in a booming voice. “Special Agents Strait and Footer, let me clarify why we’re meeting today.”

Greyson sat at his left, leaning inward, head stretched even farther forward on his long, stalky neck, as though to be closer to Strait and Footer to better enjoy their discomfort. Greyson wore his hair military style, shorn to the scalp. His powerful muscles pressed against his uniform and his lips were arranged in a sneer. He had a broad, flat nose and eyes so black the eyeballs seemed to be missing. Gelder was an austere, stiff-shouldered man in his fifties with short grey hair parted neatly on the side and a face so rigidly serious it seemed to be carved out of sandstone. His thin, slightly hooked nose, and his intense blue eyes gave him the appearance of a hawk on the hunt.

Gelder said, “the boys downstairs worked hard to piece together the story about you two and what went on up there in Pine River. They delivered me their report yesterday evening at the hotel. I spent a good deal of my night going over it. I can tell you it makes fascinating reading.”

An ominous-looking binder thick with pages rested in front of him. He opened it and flipped through the first few. “Let’s see, just for the sake of review, you two were roommates at the academy and later you partnered in FBI SWAT out of the Richmond field office? And you both gained a certain notoriety when things went south on that raid on the Barton Cult. Special Agent Strait, the story goes you took it on yourself to run into a burning building filled with armed combatants and somehow secured eight hundred gallons of nerve gas and stopped a potential catastrophe which could have made 9-11 look like a stubbed toe. For which you got your picture on the cover of *Newsweek* magazine." He sneered. "In short, a fucking American hero."

Gelder slammed the binder shut in a way that showed unambiguously he was not at all impressed by Strait's exploits. He shifted his furious look to Graham. "And you, Special Agent Footer? What were you doing while your friend was making himself famous? You didn't run into the burning building with him, did you?"

"Sorry, sir. I was shot. Perhaps you recall? You visited us in the hospital."

Gelder swiveled his look of contempt back to Strait. "A fucking American hero. That's what everyone *thinks*. Which makes it doubly shameful that you didn't carry this badge of heroism with anything approaching the professionalism that the honor suggests would be natural for you." He opened the binder to another page.

"I'm going to summarize what I have here. After a stay in the hospital, you travelled to your hometown, Pine River. On the government's dime, you were lodged in a fancy hotel to recuperate from a supposed disabling condition. You were required to rest and await the results of your disability claim. Instead, you conducted an unauthorized, extra-jurisdictional, illegal one-man missing person investigation. A triple-dick fuck-up."

"Sir, the police in Pine River wouldn't…"

"Don't interrupt me, Agent Strait. I've already spoken to Police Chief Kladspell. I know all about the things you did there."

"But..."

"You'll have a chance to speak after I'm finished."

"But…"

"Shut your mouth, agent."

James shut his mouth and ground his teeth together.

"…in the course of this triple-dick fuck-up, you, with the help of your friend Agent Footer here, made illicit use of a range of agency resources, including blood analyses, insect forensics equipment, and the VICAP and other confidential databases. You also entered the Navajo Nation and harassed individuals there."

"I didn't harass anybody."

"That's not what my report says. You also committed assaults on several individuals."

"No, I didn't."

"No? I have here a statement from a Mr. Jaybee Brown of Terrace Heights that says you assaulted him.

"Who?"

"This occurred in Meadows Park on the night of November thirteenth. The child says you attacked him."

"A child? Are you serious?"

"He's fifteen years old. Legally a minor."

"He's a gangbanger. He threatened me and I defended myself."

"He says different."

"He's lying."

"I also have a statement from a Mr. Conrad Shoemeal, an employee of the Window Christian Mission for homeless men. He says you attacked him with a stick because he wouldn't divulge confidential information about the clients in his care."

"His *care*?" said Strait. "The non-fiction version is that *he* was threatening the homeless residents with an illegal Peacekeeper RCB. I *defended* them by disarming him."

"He says different."

"He's lying too."

"Worst of all, you assaulted a police officer."

"Bullshit."

"Were you or were you not placed under arrest at a saloon called, um, the Horse's Mouth, after confronting officer Duane Dumphey of the Pine River police department in the parking lot?"

"I never laid a hand on him. He and his friends assaulted *me*. And when this was exposed, those charges were dropped."

"At each stage of committing these infractions of agency rules and violations of law, you had every reason to quit what you were doing. But you kept pressing on. Why?"

"Sir, I swear I never wanted to do any of it. But some good people asked me for help in finding this missing girl. And the local police bungled basic forensics that would have helped locate her. It became clear to me that the girl was probably still alive, but no one was looking for her."

"And all of this led ultimately to you single-handedly conducting an unauthorized raid on a farm inhabited by several armed suspects and another unauthorized raid on an animal skinning center where three other suspects were found. Do you have the faintest idea how insanely reckless that was?"

"I know exactly how insanely reckless it was. But it would've been far more reckless not to do it. Those lunatics were going to kill seven children."

"But you raided these places all by yourself! You could've gotten those kids killed!"

"As I already explained, the police wouldn't help me. I previously had tried to call Graham several times to tell him the situation and ask for emergency backup, but he didn't answer his phone."

"Agent Footer, why in the goddamned hell didn't you answer your phone?"

"Because I was meeting with you, sir. Remember? You ordered me in here to yell at me? After you found I was using agency resources to help Agent Strait. Don't you remember, sir? It was only a few days ago."

Gelder aimed his narrowed eyes on Graham like he was sighting a howitzer. "Are you mocking me?"

"No, sir. I'm answering your question. Agent Strait attempted to get reinforcements many times, and he would have gotten them, if not for your…"

"Agent Footer, it's time for you to shut your mouth. You're up on so many charges that you'll soon be bawling for the good old days when the only punishment you received was a piddly reprimand."

"Sir, in that case, it's time to come clean and make a full confession. The moment you were through with your piddly reprimand, I checked my messages and found Agent Strait was in immediate danger. In danger because he was, by any reasonable measure, behaving with incomparable heroism by risking his life to save those children. I tried to call him back but couldn't get through, so I signed in, without authorization, to our satellite tracking system whereby I traced his whereabouts using his phone's primary signal. So there's another unauthorized usage you can add to your fucking list."

"What did you just say to me?"

"And to justify the emergency deployment of Hostage Rescue I needed to make up a fanciful story about an international drug cartel holding local children captive. I lied in order to provide Agent Strait necessary backup. So please add that to your fucking list too."

"You're doomed, Agent Footer."

"I don't regret anything I've done."

"Shut your mouth."

"Furthermore, you must know that every time I followed leads that Agent Strait mentioned, it was completely my doing, not his. He never once accessed any of the systems or resources. I did it all. Of my own choice and free will."

"You're lying."

"I'll testify, under oath, to this in any hearing or trial where I'm questioned. And I'll state so aggressively to anyone in the news media I can talk to. It wasn't his fault and you can't blame him."

"Shut your stinking, insubordinate face!"

"That's all I have to say."

"Agent Strait! You and Agent Footer have put me in a very difficult position. Outside this building are hundreds of reporters wanting to get a glimpse of the American hero who has become an American hero *again* because of his daring rescue of these children. Yet here I sit, and I can't even count the number of felonies you committed."

Strait sighed. "Yes, sir." He slumped in his chair, resigned to whatever they were going to do to destroy him.

"I told you I spoke at length with the chief of police." Gelder picked up the phone receiver on the table and said, "Aileen, can you send in August Kladspell, please?"

The door opened and chief Kladspell entered. Strait felt a flush of anxiety when he realized that Kladspell had recently sat in another meeting, this one at the jail, where a certain fake British tourist had accused officer Duane Dumphey and his associates of beating up Strait. The fake British tourist was now seated on Strait's left.

"Chief Kladspell," said Gelder. "Thank you for travelling all the way down here."

"It was the least I could do, Mr. Gelder."

"You can sit in this chair next to me." Kladspell sat on a chair to Gelder's right, such that he was facing Graham directly.

Gelder said, "Chief Kladspell, the purpose of gathering here today is to bring this whole affair to a resolution that's best for everyone. Now, since this is informal, no records are being taken and you're not being sworn in or any of that stuff."

"I understand."

"Please tell us about your relationship with Agent Strait."

The chief showed no sign of recognizing Graham. He kept his gaze directed at the far wall.

"It's a little embarrassing," he said.

"Go on."

"Agent Strait visited my office one day. We talked cordially for a time, and he started in asking about the Jophia Williams case. A short time later, I heard through the grapevine that he was privately investigating the case. Checking out the crime scene and whatnot. Now, at this time, we were assuming the girl'd been murdered by her father. Agent Strait showed up again to talk to me, this time saying we were targeting the wrong man. Now, here's where I need to offer my sincere apologies to Agent Strait."

Strait looked up from the floor.

Kladspell looked sheepish. "He was right. It was obvious to me that his training had prepared him better than what we had on our force. We're just a small town department, you know. We don't usually have to deal with these kinds of cases. Now, I admit at first I thought he was intruding, but then I saw two things coming together. One, his involvement would take the investigation in the direction it needed to go. Two, to make his involvement legal, I'd need to deputize him."

Strait's mouth dropped open. *What the fuck was going on?*

"I need to say I'm sorry to *you* too, Agent Gelder," Kladspell continued. "Because I convinced Agent Strait to be deputized by promising I'd keep you fully informed. I figured it couldn't hurt for him to be a deputy even though he was on medical leave. It wouldn't encumber Mr. Strait with too much physical activity. He'd be more like a consulting expert than an on-duty cop. On top of that, he was a real good sport about it, even though he wasn't getting paid. He was just eager to help. But he insisted that your agency be kept in the loop, to keep everything on the up-and-up. And that's where I failed. The truth is, I wasn't sure it'd be approved by the FBI because of some bureaucratic bullhockey, and I was scared to lose such a skilled deputy. So I didn't inform the FBI. Completely my fault." Kladspell rubbed his forehead in a gesture of remorse.

Strait shook his head with amazement as it dawned on him what was really happening. He turned his gaze from Kladspell to his own intertwined fingers.

Gelder said gruffly, "Chief Kladspell. Do you have the paperwork that shows Agent Strait was deputized?"

"That ain't how we do things in Pine River. We're a small town. I just had him raise his right hand and say a few words, and it was a done deal."

Gelder sat back in his chair and made a show of silently contemplating matters. "This certainly puts a big wall in front of any prosecutor interested in filing charges against Agent Strait. In fact, I doubt any prosecutor would bother trying it, given Chief Kladspell and Agent Footer here are taking the blame for everything."

Gelder gazed at Strait long and hard, the silence pregnant with unstated meaning.

"Anything you want to add here, James?" he asked finally.

Strait shook his head.

Gelder sighed. "So all's well that ends well? It's looking like it'll be easy now to present this to those reporters outside in a positive light. Agent Strait, can I count on you?"

"Count on me?"

"To talk to those news people out there. I guess you haven't seen the TV the last few days. It's one goddamned video after another of those children, on all the stations. I don't know how they did it, but they got video of most everything. They've got footage of the kids coming out of that animal processing place and being put into ambulances, and of you too. There's one of that girl hugging you. It's a real tearjerker, I tell you. There's a lot more footage too, of the farmhouse, of the kids in their hospital beds. Reporters have gotten to the parents too and broadcast interviews with some of them. Of course, there's all sorts of rehashing of the Barton Raid and your role in that. My point is that everyone is obsessed with you, Special Agent Strait. They want to see their hero. And they *don't* want to hear about you doing things that any lawyer from the Justice Department watching, or anyone in the upper echelons of the agency, would understand were flagrantly illegal. That means they want to interview a hero who doesn't talk about things like that."

"I see. So I go along with this sanitized bullshit version of how it all went down, and everyone in this room comes out squeaky clean. Is that it?"

"Count yourself fucking lucky we're going that way, considering the alternative."

"You did this to me before, you fuck."

"You don't want to talk to me like that."

"You think I can't beat any charge you throw at me?"

"I know you can't."

Strait gestured at Kladspell. "None of this would have happened if this motherfucker had done his job correctly."

Gelder's eyes blazed. "Goddamnit, Strait, listen to reason. This isn't about you! The only important thing is that those kids are safe. And in the end, you are really a hero. Sort of. The rest is just…details."

"I don't want to talk to the reporters."

"That's right, I remember. You're shy. Even when *Newsweek* put you on their cover, you wouldn't give any interviews."

"What're are you going to do to Graham?"

"Me? I'm not going to do anything to him. He's Agent Greyson's responsibility. What do you say, Agent Greyson?"

Greyson stretched his head forward on his tendony neck, He had watched the whole proceedings like a vulture observing a dying animal.

"I go by the book," he said simply.

Strait said, "If you want me to go out there and face those cameras, Graham faces no charges."

"Footer isn't going to face *criminal* charges. That would conflict with your public image in this, Strait. But internally? His ass is mine. He'll face full disciplinary proceedings when he gets back to Virginia." said Greyson.

Strait ignored Greyson and said to Gelder, "If you want me to get out there and relate this bullshit with a straight face, Graham Footer faces no consequences. On top of that, Graham played a big part in saving those children, so he needs to get credit for his role. He's the real hero here."

"Can't be done," said Greyson.

"Tell you what, Greyson. I change my mind. I'm going to go

out there in front of all those microphones and cameras and tell the whole world how you set me up to get killed by the Barton cult."

"The fuck you talking about?"

"You disobeyed my direct orders in the raid and apprehended the Barton girl on her bicycle. You deliberately set off a meltdown in the compound that I had no choice but respond to. And you got Amelia Garcia killed, you evil prick." Strait looked Gelder in the eye. "And I'll tell them how you and Gelder pressured Graham and I to cover it all up."

Greyson was white as a sheet. "You son of a bitch."

"No one will believe you," said Gelder.

"You're wrong. *Everyone* will believe me. Especially after I play the recording of the conversation I kept."

"What?"

Strait grinned. "You didn't see that coming, did you? I secretly recorded the conversation in the hospital. Every word."

Gelder was halfway out of his chair. "You did not."

"I did. On my smartphone."

"You're lying."

"You wish."

"You're bluffing."

"Try me."

"But that's illegal."

Strait laughed.

"You're a piece of human shit, Strait," said Greyson.

Strait laughed harder. "Last chance, girlfriends. Forego any disciplinary action against Graham and give him public recognition for his heroic actions in helping rescue Jophia Williams, or I'll destroy your lives."

The two men were too furious to speak.

Strait smirked. "Oh, come on, guys. Listen to reason. This isn't about you! The only important thing is that those kids are safe. The rest is just…details. Right?"

"But how can we let him off the hook?" demanded Gelder.

"You'll think of something."

Chapter Forty-seven

Strait stood with Katherine in the kitchen while she made finishing touches on the Christmas cookies she was baking. She wore a red dress, rather fancy, and had a kitchen apron over it. She was smiling, but the struggles of recent days had left their mark. Her eyes were puffy and her face was thinner. Strait had arrived early for the Christmas party, planning to help out. But she wouldn't let him.

Francis was not there. He had left town to stay with his parents in Baltimore. His giving a false alibi to Marvin Williams was a scandal at the university, and he was battling to keep his teaching position. He had received death threats.

"Why did he do it?" asked Strait.

"His only reason was to protect Marvin Williams. Not even I knew he'd lied. He convinced Marvin to go along with it and keep it secret. I'm still angry at him about his keeping it a secret from me. But otherwise, I support him. He knew for a fact Marvin was being targeted unfairly by the police and that his giving an alibi could save him."

"It looks bad."

"His intentions were good, but yeah, it was a mistake. A lot of the scandal comes from the idea that he was protecting a guilty man, which everyone now knows he wasn't. Now that the real criminals have been exposed, this will all eventually blow over."

"I don't know."

"Francis is going to write a book about this eventually."

"Good luck to him."

"We better get you into the living room before all the guests arrive."

Katherine put James in a "special chair," a padded recliner

next to the beautifully decorated Christmas tree which, he had to admit, felt very good. His body was still sore all over. Jessie, who had come back from New York while James was in Phoenix, sat at his side. Guests started pouring in.

Another catered buffet had been set up. A table that extended across the room was brimming with delectables Strait couldn't eat. But Katherine had this time worked with the children to prepare special low-salt dishes for him that were also great.

Katherine had organized a procession to pass his chair, where each person would have a turn to greet him. The children's parents, many of them having driven over from Gallup, came up and communicated their gratitude. They cried and shook his hand and gave him hugs.

Randy Street, not long out of jail and wearing a fresh set of clothes and a brand-new eyepatch, approached with Carol. He shook Strait's hand warmly. "I told you, Chief. It was your destiny."

Marvin Williams shocked everyone by emerging from his cabin and coming. He limped up to Strait and grasped his right hand with both of his own. "Brother," was all he said.

Dr. Watanabe sauntered up drunk and cackling. Strait tried to thank him for his life-changing help, but the little man interrupted by patting Strait's belly with his bony hand and trying to tickle him. "Goddamn, you a giant!" he said over his shoulder as he walked away.

The last to approach him were the children. They gave him a wrapped present and a card. Jophia and Eliza, the two best friends holding hands, headed the group. Jophia said, "you can open the card now, but open the present later when you're alone."

The card was a folded piece of construction paper with a photo of all the kids in front of a painted sign that said, "Thank you,

James!"

One of the children was not there. Shantelle Miller, the five-year whose head Gunnar Wilson had threatened to cut off, was still in the hospital. She hadn't spoken a word since the day of her rescue.

To Strait, the party seemed like a wake. It felt like the ceremony held in honor of his father after he was killed. A slow-moving procession of half-drunk people gripping his hands and saying kind words that, although well-intentioned, seemed as substantial as writing on the surface of water.

Strait left the party as soon as he could, with the explanation that his medication was making him sleepy.

Jessie drove them to his hotel. They parked and walked to his room. He flicked on the light. On the floor was a large envelope. He picked it up and opened it.

Inside were several pages. The first sheet had the emblem of the Social Security Administration embossed at the top. It read:

Dear Mr. James Strait:

We are pleased to inform you that your claim for disability has been approved. Commencing February, 2018, and subject to a five-year review, you will receive *$1,889* *dollars per month for living expenses. See enclosed for details.*

Strait fell back on the bed. When he did, the roar in his right ear grew louder, and the room bobbed slightly.

"What is it?" asked Jessie.

"My disability claim has been approved."

"Congratulations?"

"All my worries are over."

"How do you feel?"

"I don't know."

"For real. Tell me."

He turned to her. "I've never felt more empty in my life."

"Why don't you open the present the kids gave you? It might cheer you up."

He sat up and tore off the wrapping. Inside was a copy of *Newsweek* magazine. His face was on the cover. It was an original issue, the one that came out after the raid on the Barton Cult. The photo was blown up to capture only his face and shoulders, with his hair tousled and sweaty, his flak jacket slightly askew, a soldier fresh from a courageous battle. The splash of blood on his face stretched across his right cheek as though blown back by strong wind, narrower and thinner in the front and thickening to discrete globules around his ear.

"Wow," he said.

Jessie smiled. "A real collector's item. But, look, the kids changed it." She pointed at the title, which had originally said AMERICAN HERO. They'd crossed out "AMERICAN" and wrote "OUR."

Jessie peered into his face. "Doesn't this make you happy?"

"I'm happy the kids are alive."

Jessie opened the magazine to the article. "You were a lot better looking back then."

"My hair was more tousled."

She read a portion aloud. "Doctors say that among the injuries Agent Strait suffered were multiple shots to the leg, which will require numerous surgeries to repair. They confided that there was only a small chance that Strait would ever walk again."

Strait frowned. "They actually wrote that?"

Jessie stared at him. "You never read this article?"

Strait shook his head.

"Jesus. Why not?"

Silence.

"The man I'm reading about here should be proud of what he did. 'With the almost certain chance that he would be killed by the many shooters guarding the nerve gas, it would have been natural for Agent Strait to wait for back-up to arrive. Instead, he single-handedly performed what counts as a modern-day miracle. He shot his way into the building, through two heavily guarded doors, where 800 gallons of deadly VX were on the verge of being dispersed through the heavily populated neighborhood. He got rid of the last piece of resistance and, although seriously injured, guarded the lethal gas until other law enforcement and national guard members arrived to secure the compound.'"

"What bullshit."

She sat next to him on the bed. She gently placed her hand on his shoulder. He flinched.

"What really happened, James?"

"What really happened?" He picked up the card from the children with the photograph of them in front of the sign they'd made. He ran his finger along the line of their happy faces.

"I couldn't think," he said.

He'd come out of the van and rushed forward to the Barton house because it was either that or die. At that moment, the thought that he needed to save everyone from the damage of that VX agent hadn't consciously occurred to him.

He couldn't think. He was a charging animal. Rabid with adrenaline. Scared to death. Attacking anything in his path and moving instinctually toward shelter inside the building. When the men came pouring out, through broken windows and doors, he'd shot first before they could hurt him.

"This guy appeared at a window. He was smashing his way out of the house. He was an old guy, couldn't hurt a fly. He had a hammer that he used to smash the window and he sort of held it up and I shot him in the face."

It wasn't until he had descended into the pit of the house that the idea of securing the VX began to rise into his consciousness again. It was only when he saw the girl, her finger poised on the activator to set the whole thing off, that his purpose for being there, his duty, came into focus.

Tears dripped down the girl's cheeks. "You killed my papa."

"No."

"Liar! I saw you! My papa was just hammering out the windows for us to get away and you *killed* him!"

Strait cleared his throat. "I didn't come here to hurt anyone. And I know that you don't want to hurt anyone."

"He couldn't hurt anyone and you killed him! Coward!"

"Please listen. You pull that switch and all that poison in those cans will kill thousands of people."

"Devils," she said miserably.

"Little girl, please…"

"James!" Graham had suddenly called out as he ran into the room.

The girl turned her head to look but Strait did not. He raised his gun precisely as he had been trained and pulled the trigger of his Glock. Two taps. One for the head, one of the heart. *Tap, tap.*

Jessie put her arm around him and touched the back of his bent head.

"Later, it came out in the wash. That guy I shot coming out the window? It really was that girl's father. She was right. I killed her dad." Strait sagged and put his face in his hands. "And then I killed her."

The air in the room pressed in.

"You know it wasn't your fault, right?"

Strait didn't answer.

"A lot of people wouldn't understand why you feel so bad about this."

"I know."

"A lot of people would say you had no choice, that you were under siege and were justified in every shot you took. You'd feel a lot worse if you hadn't shot her and the poison was blown into the air. If you hadn't shot her, she might still have let the poison go."

"I don't think so. She was just a kid. You could tell she was scared and didn't want to do what she was doing. It was my killing her father that put her finger on the button."

"I understand that you think you're not the hero people are making you out to be. But what I see is that you're feeling bad about being a human being, like the rest of us. Doesn't make you any less of a hero."

"Not so, Pastor. Listen to the rest of the story. I lied about what happened and got rewarded for it. Almost no one knows the way things really went down. Just a handful of upper-echelon guys who took me and Graham in a room and interviewed us. Or interrogated us is more like it. Gelder was one of them. It was crazy. We were both still in the hospital, me in the leg wing and Graham recovering upstairs from surgery to get the bullets out of his stomach and we actually met in a room there in the hospital. Armed guards outside. Me in shock still too because on top of everything else,

Amelia had been killed only a week before. They rolled us in there in wheelchairs. After we finished telling them everything, they convinced us that it was best for the country if, and I quote, 'the man who saved us from the next 9-11 didn't do it by shooting a defenseless child in the face.' It's lucky I was doped on pain meds or I would've really gone crazy. Those fuckers cleansed history. It wasn't even in the official report to Congress and the president."

"That's horrible."

"They told us we had a choice of two career paths. One, we could have a pleasant and rewarding life in the FBI, full of streamlined promotions within our favorite departments. Two, we could have one filled with constant, unexpected hurdles and difficulties that would probably make us decide that the FBI wasn't the best choice for us after all. Which of these paths we would ultimately follow was contingent, of course, upon if we decided to cooperate with their official bullshit version of what happened. They left us alone in the room to talk about it. I was ready to tell them all to go fuck themselves. But Graham was worried. Understandably. He has a wife and two kids. He practically begged me to go along with it."

"And you did."

"Finally. But I refused to do any interviews with the press, which pissed Gelder off. Especially for that fucking *Newsweek* article. I did accept the call from the president, though. I always liked that guy. I wish he was still our president. But my not saying anything in public that conflicted with their official story cooled things down and they left me alone. Graham *did* give interviews. And he was given a decent forensics position at Laboratory Services. His dream come true. And he's done great there. As for me, they had a lawyer and a doctor at the hospital constantly maneuvering me toward putting in for disability and getting me out of the agency completely. They wanted me out. And this—" Strait indicated the envelope from Social Security. "—is how they finally did it."

"No way to get around it?"

"Not that I can see. I have a real clinical condition."

"The man who rescued those kids is not disabled."

Strait nodded.

"So what are you doing to do?"

Strait picked up the envelope from Social Security. He held it between the thumb and forefinger of both hands.

He tore it in half. Then he tore the halves in half.

"Wow," said Jessie. "Maybe I should have said, what are you going to do for *money*?"

"Not this."

She touched his hand. "Can I stay here with you tonight?"

Strait looked away from her and studied the painting on the opposite wall. Blue rabbits prancing in a field. After his first attack in Pine River, that painting was one of the first things he'd seen clearly. A peaceful, ridiculous, fairy-tale image.

"I'd rather be alone," said Strait.

"Oh." She looked disappointed.

"Ah, Jessie," he said, his throat tight. "It's a seriously fucked up world, isn't it? It's full of monsters. Monsters who want to bring back slavery and monsters who kill kids. Monster racist cops. Monsters willing to frame an innocent man for child molestation and send him to prison. Monsters in power who lie and get rewarded for it. Pastor, how can you preach hope to your congregation in a world like this?"

"Because along with the monsters, we've got courageous people who fight against them. Like Randy Street. Like Katherine."

She held his hand. “We’ve got brave people like you who risk their lives to help those who can’t fight for themselves. There are monsters but there are heroes.”

“Isn’t that good-versus-evil stuff a little too simple?”

“Of course it is. We don’t live in a comic book. Which is why I don’t make that the focus of my sermons. But I use it to lead into the more inspiring idea that we can all overcome the worst parts of our nature, the monsters in ourselves. We can develop the courage and humility to recognize that the enemy is a lot more like us than we’re comfortable believing, and that we all have the same basic weaknesses, the same vulnerabilities to prejudice, jealousy, greed, and hatred, empowers us to overcome those weaknesses with forgiveness and love. It enables us to work together with anyone, even with those others we fear and hate so much, to make this fucked-up world a better place.”

She moved closer on the bed and leaned toward him. She grazed her lips on his right ear. She whispered, “we can heal.”

Strait was silent for a time. Then he folded his large hands over her small ones. He looked into her eyes and managed the start of a smile.

“Can you stay here with me tonight?”

Did you like this book? If so, please consider leaving a review on Amazon and Goodreads. It is by such reviews that Indie novels thrive or perish.

Made in the USA
Las Vegas, NV
10 May 2023